The Buffer Girls

Margaret Dickinson

The Buffer Girls

MACMILLAN

First published 2016 by Macmillan
an imprint of Pan Macmillan
20 New Wharf Road, London N1 9RR
Associated companies throughout the world
www.panmacmillan.com

ISBN 978-1-4472-9088-9

1 3 5 7 9 8 6 4 2

A CIP catalogue record for this book is available from the British Library.

Typeset by Palimpsest Book Production Limited, Falkirk, Stirlingshire
Printed and bound by CPI Group (UK) Ltd, Croydon, CR0 4YY

Visit www.panmacmillan.com to read more about all our books
and to buy them. You will also find features, author interviews and
news of any author events, and you can sign up for e-newsletters
so that you're always first to hear about our new releases.

For
Zoë, Scott, Zachary and Zara
With My Love Always

Acknowledgements

My grateful thanks to Dennis Trickett, who kindly talked to me about his life in the cutlery industry of Sheffield, and also to Alison Duce, the Collections Manager at the Kelham Island Museum in Sheffield, for her warm welcome and help on my visit to the museum. And to Kenneth and Kathryn Ibbotson of Ashford-in-the-Water for the loan of some wonderful photographs of the village. As always, my sincere thanks to the staff of Skegness Library for their continuing help and encouragement.

A great many sources have been used in the research for this novel, most notably *Diamonds in Brown Paper* by Gill Booth (Sheffield City Libraries, 1988) and *Back to the Grindstone* by Herbert Housley (The Hallamshire Press 1998).

Although in this novel I have used real place names, streets and even actual buildings, the characters and events in the story are entirely fictitious.

My love and thanks to my family and friends for their constant encouragement, especially those who read the script in the early stages: David Dickinson, Fred Hill and Pauline Griggs. And never forgetting my wonderful agent, Darley Anderson, and his team, and my editor, Trisha Jackson, and all the team at Pan Macmillan.

Margaret Dickinson Q&A

1. Have you always wanted to be a writer?
I started writing at the age of fourteen always with the hope of one day being published. My first novel was published in 1968 when I was twenty-five.

2. How long did it take you to write *The Buffer Girls*?
I write a novel a year, but that doesn't mean I'm writing all that time. I undertake about six weeks' promotion when a new book is published and I give talks throughout the year.

3. Do you have a routine as a writer?
When I am writing, I like to be at my desk by 9 a.m. and work for the morning. Often I work in the afternoon for a couple of hours, but it's more a target of words per week (10,000) rather than the number of hours spent writing.

4. Which books have inspired you?
As a child, Enid Blyton's books – also *The Wind in the Willows*. As an adult, the novels of Victoria Holt and Mary Stewart. The one book that has influenced me the most is *Pride and Prejudice*.

5. How did you come up with the title of the book?
It seemed to be the most appropriate title as the story is about the buffer girls of Sheffield.

6. How much of the book is fact and how much is fiction?
All the characters and events are entirely fictitious, but the background details have been thoroughly researched.

7. What would you like readers to take away from _The Buffer Girls_?
A sense of how hard-working the women of that time were.

8. Are you writing a new novel at the moment?
I have begun work on a sequel to _The Buffer Girls_.

9. Do you have any tips for people researching historical events?
A great deal of information is now available on the internet, but it is wise to double-check it if possible. Visit the place being written about; its libraries, museums and archives, and talk to people who have been involved with the subject.

10. What advice would you give to aspiring authors?
Learn as much as possible about the craft of writing, study similar books that have been published and NEVER give up!

One

'You're not serious, Mam.'

Emily Ryan stood with her hands on her hips, her curly blond hair flying free, wild and untamed, and her blue eyes icy with temper. She was tall and slim, with a figure that had all the young men eyeing her longingly as she strode through her young life. Her lovely face, with its perfectly shaped nose and strong chin, was the epitome of determination. Nothing and no one would stop Emily Ryan doing exactly what she wanted with her life, except maybe one person: her mother, Martha.

'I'm deadly serious,' Martha said firmly, folding her arms across her ample bosom. She knew she had a battle royal on her hands as she faced her daughter. Emily resembled her mother, but the older woman's hair was now grey and drawn back into a bun and her once lithe figure had thickened with age and child bearing. Her face was lined with the anxieties life had brought her; her eyes were still bright but they turned cold when she was angry. And she was ready now. Battle lines were being drawn but Martha knew she would win in the end. She always did.

'But this is our home. You can't take us away from

all this.' Emily swept her arm in a wide arc to encompass the small, friendly Derbyshire village where they lived, and the surrounding fields and hills. 'It's Dad's life. He was born here in this cottage. His parents and grandparents are buried in the churchyard. You can't drag him to live in a *city*.' She spat out the word. 'He'd hate it. 'Specially now.' Her voice dropped as she thought about her beloved father, sitting huddled by the kitchen range where he now sat every day, so cruelly maimed by the Great War that he could no longer work. He'd been the village candle maker, working in the front room of their cottage and supplying the local village shop and several others in the district. And he'd always served those who came knocking on the front door. It had earned him a modest income and the family had been content, until the war had come and taken away the tall, strong man with a ready smile and a gentle manner. Now he was unbearably thin, his shoulders hunched. His hands shook uncontrollably and any exertion left him gasping for breath. His two children – Emily and Josh – had taken on the work and were trying to keep his small cottage industry going, but it wasn't the same without their talented father at the helm.

'He'd no need to volunteer,' Martha said quietly, her thoughts still on the carnage that had robbed her of the man Walter had been. 'He could at least have waited until he was called up.' Her mouth curled. 'He'd no need to be a hero.'

'Oh really,' Emily said, her tone laced with sarcasm, 'and have everyone around here brand him a coward? Handing him a white feather every time he set foot in Bakewell Market?'

'He could have found work in a reserved occupation and appealed against his call-up whenever it came,'

Martha snapped. 'But he didn't even wait to find out if he was to be conscripted. Off he went to answer the country's call as if Kitchener had been pointing his finger directly at him.'

'The ones who stayed were lads too young to go or old men,' Emily argued. 'The ones like Dad – fit and strong and healthy –' tears smarted at the back of her eyes as she thought about the proud, upright man her father had been before he'd marched away to fight for his country. But she kept her voice steady, silently vowing not to cry in front of her mother. Later, alone, perhaps she would allow the tears to fall. But not now. This was one battle she had to win, for her father, for her younger brother and for herself too – 'they all went and such a lot of them never came home. At least, Dad came back.'

For a long moment, Martha stared at her. Then she glanced away and murmured flatly, 'Aye, he did.' The unspoken words lay heavily between them. Perhaps it would have been better for all of them – including Walter himself – if he had not survived to be the broken wreck he now was.

Walter Ryan had been injured on 1 July 1916, the first day of the battle of the Somme, when thousands of his comrades had been mown down by enemy gunfire and blown to smithereens by their shells. It was a miracle he had not been killed and even more amazing that he had survived his terrible injuries to make it home to Blighty. The shrapnel in his leg had been removed and the wound had healed, but an earlier exposure to a gas attack and the constant pounding of the guns had left him gasping for breath, shell shocked and unable to speak.

Martha and Emily were standing in their small back

garden, which Josh and Emily had planted with rows of vegetables. They were well out of Walter's hearing and Josh was at work in the front room. There was no one to overhear the quarrel.

'What I don't understand, Mam, is why? We're happy here, aren't we? Josh and I are doing our best with the candle making. I make the wicks –' the braiding of the fine cotton threads required nimble fingers – 'and Josh makes the candles. He's got some exciting ideas. He wants to try making coloured candles and scented ones too. He's already carving some of the bigger ones and he showed them to Mrs Trippet at the big house. She said they were wonderful and she placed an order there and then. Oh, I know we're not as good at it as Dad, but we're getting better. And everyone around here helps us with Dad, if we need it. Mr Clark and Mrs Partridge have been wonderful. They come and sit with him and talk to him, even though he never answers them. Who's going to be on hand in the city?'

Martha bit her lip; this was where it would get really difficult. 'It's for Josh's sake. I've got to think of his future. There's nothing for him here.'

'What do you mean? Not many lads of seventeen have their own little business ready made for them.'

'Josh will be eighteen next month,' Martha said, 'and besides, he won't have much of a business soon. The demand for candles is decreasing with every day. You know yourself it is.'

'Ah,' Emily said slowly. 'Now I understand. It's always about Josh, isn't it? You want to uproot the whole family and take us to Sheffield – all for Josh.'

'Of course it's all for Josh,' Martha snapped, not even attempting to be apologetic. 'He's a man and he's got to make his way in the world.'

4

'And what about me?' Emily asked softly. 'Do I really count so little with you, Mam?'

'Don't be silly, Emily. Of course you *count*. But you'll get married. You don't need a career. Not like a man does. Not like Josh does. And you tell me –' Martha prodded her finger towards her daughter – 'what else there is around here for him that would make him a good living – that would make him someone – because if you know of something, then I'd like to hear it.'

Emily couldn't answer her. There was nothing locally that could offer Josh the opportunities he would find in the city. But she was not about to be beaten yet.

'What about Amy?' she said, trying a different tack. 'She and Josh are walking out together now.'

Martha's eyes narrowed. 'Are they indeed? And when did that start?'

Emily shrugged, wishing she hadn't said anything. It was not her secret to tell, but it was done now. 'They've always been friends, but just lately – well, they've got closer. Or are you thinking that she'll come with us?'

Martha shook her head. 'No, she wouldn't leave her dad.'

The village blacksmith, Robert Clark, who lived next door, had been a widower since his wife had died shortly after giving birth to Amy. In the early years, Robert had paid a kindly woman, Mrs Grace Partridge, who lived in one of the cottages further up the lane, to care for the infant whilst he worked. But at all other times, father and daughter had been – and still were – inseparable and so it had brought Robert peace of mind when Josh Ryan had begun courting Amy. Whatever happened, he would still have his daughter close by. Perhaps they could even live with him, he had daydreamed, and, in time, maybe another little one would bring joy to his life.

Emily stared at Martha. 'So, you don't care about tearing them apart? I thought you liked Amy.'

'I do. She's a sweet girl, but Josh can do better for himself. If he marries, he needs someone who'll help him achieve his ambitions.'

'*Your* ambitions, Mam. Let's be honest about this. Josh is quite content to stay here, make candles, marry Amy and raise a family. But that's not good enough for you, is it? What do you want him to be? The owner of a steel works and live in a mansion?'

Martha shrugged. 'Maybe one day. If he would only apply himself, work hard and—'

'Mam, have you taken leave of your senses?'

'Don't you talk to me like that, Emily Ryan, else you'll feel the back of my hand.' Martha raised her arm as if to carry out her threat.

Emily faced her unflinchingly and smiled grimly. 'I've felt it often enough. One more time won't make any difference.' But Martha dropped her hand and turned away, saying over her shoulder, 'And don't you go telling Josh. I'll be the one to tell him tonight.'

Through narrowed eyes, Emily watched her mother go into the cottage by the back door, but even though she knew her father would need attention, the girl made no move to help. Her mind was working feverishly. Not for the first time in her young life, she was about to disobey her mother.

Two

The Ryans lived in the picturesque village of Ashford-in-the-Water in Greaves Lane. Stone cottages and houses lay beside the River Wye as it meandered towards Bake-well, just over a mile away. The village had, in its time, boasted several small industries; the quarrying, cutting and polishing of black marble; lead mining; and cottage industries of stocking making and candle making. A member of the Ryan family had been the village's chand-ler for at least four generations. No one was quite sure when the small business had begun, but the Ryans knew that Walter's grandfather, Luke, had certainly been the first in their family to take it on in the mid-1800s. Since then, each successive generation had continued with the profession. Now it had fallen to a very young Josh to carry it on. And it was what he wanted to do. He loved the work; he even gloried in the strong-smelling tallow, rendered from animal fat, though now he experimented with a refined form called stearin, which gave off a more pleasant odour. Special candles for the church or for the wealthy houses in the district were made from beeswax and Josh still made these too. But the young man was full of other ideas to move the business into the twentieth century. Next door to The Candle House was the village smithy, with its wide door open to the street whenever Bob Clark was working at his anvil with the glowing coals of the forge behind him. And next to that, on the corner of the lane, was the building that had once been a beer house.

After the confrontation with her mother, Emily walked through the cottage, passing her father still sitting in his rocking chair by the kitchen range. She didn't even glance at him, so afraid was she that he might see the anger in her eyes. She entered the front room, which their great-grandfather had made into a workshop for the candle making, on the right-hand side of the cottage's front door. In that way, customers could visit the small workshop without disturbing the rest of the family. Emily sat down beside Josh. He glanced up at her with a swift grin before carrying on with the intricate carving of a large, thick candle with a thin-bladed tool.

'I'm still working on it, Em, but I'll get it right one day. I'm getting better at it.' It was something new that Josh was trying and one of several ordered by Mrs Trippet, the lady in the big house near the Sheep Wash Bridge over the River Wye that flowed beside Ashford.

Emily glanced at her brother, resisting the impulse to ruffle his tousled hair. She loved him dearly, even though she'd always been aware that he was their mother's favourite – a fact Martha had never even tried to hide. He was a good-looking boy, who was swiftly growing into manhood. He was thin, but deceptively strong and would grow taller and broaden out. Soon, he would look very like their father had once done, with light brown hair, hazel eyes and a merry face that always seemed to be smiling. But Emily knew that the news he would receive this day would wipe the smile from his face. The thought brought a lump to her throat and her voice was a little husky as she said softly, 'Josh,

Mam is going to tell you something tonight so you must promise to act all surprised when she does.'

With a sigh, Josh laid aside the tiny knife, stretched his shoulders, yawned and then turned towards her with a wide grin. 'What is it, Em? Out with it.'

Emily licked her dry lips. 'She's planning to move us, lock, stock and barrel, to Sheffield.'

'Eh?' Josh dropped his arms, the smile disappearing from his face. 'What did you say?'

'She's planning to move us to Sheffield.'

For a stunned moment, he stared at her. 'Whatever for?'

'She doesn't think there are enough opportunities here for you to go up in the world.'

'But I don't want to go up in the world. I'm perfectly happy here. I like making candles and I like the villagers dropping in to buy them and have a natter. And I've a regular order for plain candles and tapers from Mr Osborne at the corner shop.' He nodded his head towards the window to the shop across the road. 'And besides, there's Amy. I'm not leaving Amy and she wouldn't come because she won't leave her dad. So that's it.' He picked up his knife again. 'We're not going.'

Emily sighed. There were going to be ructions in this house tonight and no mistake.

'I've made your favourite for tea, Josh,' Martha smiled at him as she placed a plate of steaming food in front of him, 'stew and dumplings.'

Josh breathed in deeply. 'Smells wonderful, Mam.' He picked up his knife and fork and began to eat hungrily whilst, by the range, Emily gently spooned stew into her father's mouth. There was nothing she could do to prevent Walter hearing Martha's plans and,

9

whilst he could not speak, she knew he would understand. Just occasionally, she could see a look of comprehension in his eyes or a faint smile on his lips. She smiled at him tenderly, knowing that in a few moments his whole world, such as it was now, was going to be shattered.

Martha sat down at the table, but she was not eating. She faced her son across the snowy tablecloth and took a deep breath.

'I've been talking to Mr Trippet.' Martha cleaned at the Trippets' home, Riversdale House, two days a week. It was unusual – but not unknown – for her to talk to the master.

Josh looked up and Emily, glancing briefly towards him, marvelled at his acting prowess. 'Oh, he's home at the moment, is he? Is Trip here too?'

Thomas Trippet – 'Trip' to his friends – was the son of Arthur Trippet, who owned a cutlery-manufacturing business in Sheffield but lived the life of a country gentleman in Ashford. At nineteen, nearly twenty, Trip was only a few months older than Emily and almost two years older than Josh. The four children, for they'd always included Amy Clark, had been friends since childhood, running wild and free through the village and roaming the hills and dales close to their home. They loved to stand on Sheep Wash Bridge, near to Trip's home, watching the farmers, who still used the river to wash the sheep before shearing.

'Oh, look at the poor lambs,' tender-hearted, six-year-old Amy had cried the first time the children had seen the old custom. 'They're crying for their mothers. Why are they being penned on the opposite bank?'

'To make the ewes swim across to them,' Josh, two months older and so much wiser, had laughed. 'That way they'll be all nice and clean when they scramble out the other side. Come on, I'll race you home. Your dad will be watching out for you.' And then he'd taken her hand and they'd run down the road towards their two homes that stood side by side. Two years older, Trip and Emily had lingered by the bridge until dusk forced them home too.

At other times, the four of them would fish from the bridge with home-made rods and lines or throw sticks into the flowing water and then run to the other side to see whose stick emerged from beneath the bridge first, to be declared the winner. Often, they would beg chopped vegetable scraps from the cook at Riversdale House or birdseed from Mrs Partridge, who kept a bird table in her garden, to feed the ducks that always gathered around the bridge. One of their favourite spots was Monsal Head, where they looked down on the viaduct and watched the trains passing between Rowsley and Buxton. A rare treat for the children had been to catch the train at the little station halfway up the hillside of Monsal Dale and ride to Buxton, the two girls clutching each other as they travelled through the dark tunnels on the journey. One of their favourite times of the year – and one in which the children would all be involved – was the thanksgiving for water celebrated on Trinity Sunday and accompanied by the dressing of five wells dotted about the village.

Grace Partridge would always be the one to dress the well in Greaves Lane and each year she would say to Amy, 'I need you to help me. Your dad and Uncle Dan –' Grace referred to her husband, Dan Partridge – 'have got the bed of clay ready for me and now we must pick the flowers and press the petals into the clay to make a picture. What shall we do this year? A picture of the church, d'you think? We could use seeds to make the walls and cones for the trees. We can use anything we like, Amy, as long as it grows naturally.'

Sadly, since the Great War, the custom had ceased.

'I reckon folks don't feel like merrymaking just now,' Grace had said wisely. 'But I expect they'll revive the tradition one day. I do hope so.'

And with the end of the dreadful war that had left so many grieving, those idyllic childhood days were gone and now, since leaving boarding school, Trip had left the village to work in his father's factory in Sheffield. Arthur Trippet was a strict disciplinarian and had made his son start at the very bottom and work his way up in the business. There were no privileges of position for young Thomas Trippet. He even had to stay in lodgings in the city rather than travel home each night in his father's grand car.

Trippets' made penknives and pocketknives. Trip was first put to work as a grinder. It was a dirty job, sitting astride a seat as if he were riding a horse, with the wheel rotating away from him in a trough of water. The cutlery industry had originally developed in Sheffield because of the waterpower available from the city's fast-flowing rivers for the forges and grinding wheels. The tradition of the 'little mester', often working alone with treadle-operated machines, but sometimes employing one or two men and apprentices, has always been an important part of the city's famous trade. With the coming of steam power, which could operate a line-shaft system to drive several machines at once, large factories were built, although these were still made up of individual workshops rented out. Trippets' factory, built for one owner by Arthur's grandfather in the nineteenth century, was a rare phenomenon at that time.

'I'll not have you treated any differently from my other employees,' Arthur had told his son. 'You'll work your way up in the firm just like anyone else and, if you prove yourself, one day you'll take over, but only if you've earned it, mind.'

Now, hearing his name mentioned, Emily's heart skipped a beat. She'd been in love with Trip from the age of twelve. It had been then that she'd realized he meant more to her than the other village lads. As she'd grown up, they'd become even closer. Emily believed they were soulmates and would never be separated. But they had been, for Trip had been sent away, first to boarding school and then to Sheffield. Hearing her mother's plans now, Emily felt torn. She didn't want to leave Ashford and she dreaded the thought of what such a move would do to her poor father – and to Josh. But if there was a chance of being nearer to Trip . . .

Her wandering thoughts were brought back to what her mother was saying. 'Never mind about Thomas just now. This is about you. About your future.'

With a supreme effort, Josh kept a puzzled look on his face. 'My future, Mam? What has Mr Trippet got to do with my future?' Then his face brightened and Emily stifled her laughter. Oh, this was better than going to the theatre in Buxton. What a star performer Josh was!

'You mean,' her brother was saying with feigned innocence, 'he's placed a huge order for candles for Riversdale House?'

'No, I do *not* mean that, Josh,' Martha snapped, her patience wearing thin. 'Will you just listen to me? I've been asking Mr Trippet's advice and he says that although he has no vacancies in his factory at the moment, he has business colleagues in the city and he's willing to put in a good word for you.' As Josh opened his mouth to speak, Martha rushed on. 'He was the Master Cutler of The Company of Cutlers in Hallamshire for a year, you know, a while back. I expect his name is listed on a brass plaque somewhere in Cutlers' Hall in the city. Now, wouldn't that be something if one day your name was up there too?'

Josh blinked. Now, there was no more need to pretend ignorance. 'You mean you want me to go and work in Sheffield?'

'We'll all go. We'll move there. Emily will soon find a job of some sort.' Emily was amused to hear how she was brushed aside as if she were of little or no importance. 'And your dad will be nearer a hospital, so it'd be better for him.' This was something Emily had not heard before; her mother must have come up with that persuasive argument since they'd spoken in the garden. But it was all designed to bend Josh to her bidding. 'And I'm sure I could find cleaning work to keep us going until you earn a proper wage. I expect there'll be some sort of apprenticeship you'll have to do.'

'Aye, about seven years, I shouldn't wonder, and an apprentice lad's wage would be paltry, Mam. It would be years before I could hope to earn decent money.'

'But it'd be worth it.' Martha leaned across the table, pressing home her point. 'In the end. Don't you see?'

Josh shook his head. 'No, I don't. We're doing all right here. I'd rather be a big fish in a little pond than a sprat in a river. I'm a country bumpkin, Mam, not a streetwise city lad. I'd be eaten alive.'

Martha sighed and shook her head in exasperation. 'No ambition, that's your trouble, Josh.'

'It's hard work, Trip was telling me the last time he was home for a weekend.'

Emily wiped her father's dribbling mouth as she remembered that glorious June Sunday when the four of them had walked from Ashford following the river's twists and turns until they had come to Monsal Dale and, this time, had walked beneath the viaduct to watch the fast-flowing water tumbling over the weir. They'd laughed and joked and had such fun. That had been a few weeks ago and she hadn't seen Trip since. But he would come back, she consoled herself. This was his home. He'd always come back to Ashford. But would it be to see her?

Thomas Trippet was a handsome young man in anyone's eyes, not only in Emily's. He was tall with black hair and warm brown eyes. His skin was lightly tanned from roaming the hills and dales near his home – he loved the outdoor life – and the lines around his eyes crinkled when he laughed. And he laughed often, for he was forever teasing and joking. Emily knew the friendship between the four of them was strong, but did Trip feel as much for her as she now knew she did for him? It was a question she often asked herself, but one she could not answer. When he'd left that weekend, he'd hugged her and kissed her cheek but there'd been no promise to meet again, not a hint that he wanted her to be 'his girl'.

Her thoughts were brought back to the present with a jolt. Suddenly, Josh jumped up from the table, sending his chair crashing to the floor behind him, making them all jump and agitating Walter. His shaking was suddenly worse and he clasped Emily's hand, his eyes wide and pleading. 'It's all right, Dad,' she whispered, trying to reassure him, but she couldn't make her voice sound convincing.

'I'm not going, Mam.' Josh was shouting now. 'You

do what you like, but I'm staying here, making my candles and marrying Amy – if she'll have me.'

'She'll have you right enough,' his mother snorted. 'She knows a good catch when she sees it. And I expect her father's pushing for the two of you to get wed, just so's he can keep her close by and looking after him. He'll want you moving in there with them, I shouldn't wonder.'

Josh bit his lip. The matter had already been talked about between them when Josh had asked Amy to marry him on the day when the four of them had walked to the viaduct. Falling behind Emily and Trip, he and Amy had paused beneath the shadow of the arches. He'd kissed her and asked her to be his wife.

'Oh Josh, yes.'

'Let's keep it our secret for a while, shall we?' he'd whispered. 'I've got to get my mother used to the idea first.'

Amy, a pretty girl with delicate china-doll looks that belied an inner strength, had giggled and shaken back her fair hair. 'Well, there's no need to worry about my dad. He can't wait to walk me down the aisle and he's already said we can live with him.'

'That's settled, then.' Josh had hugged her again. 'And how do you feel about a spring wedding in the village church?'

'It's what I've always dreamed of.'

'Marrying me, I hope,' he'd teased her, but Amy had been solemn as she'd said, 'Of course. There's never been anyone else for me, Josh.'

He'd kissed her again, his kisses becoming urgent with desire now that they were promised to each other. Since that day, they'd met often, just the two of them.

16

With Trip gone, Emily didn't seem to want to go with them.

'I'm not playing gooseberry,' she'd laughed.

Though nothing had been said, Emily could see the love between her brother and Amy blossoming and she wasn't going to stand in their way. But now it seemed as if all Josh's plans lay in ruins as he stood glaring at his mother across the table.

'I'm not going,' he declared again. 'I'm not leaving Ashford – or Amy – and that's final.'

Three

Martha lay in her single bed, her eyes wide open and staring towards the ceiling in the darkness. She and Walter had separate beds now for his constant restlessness disturbed her sleep. But tonight it was not Walter who was keeping her awake far into the night; it was her guilty conscience. Martha couldn't remember ever having told lies in her life, except perhaps a little white one when Mrs Partridge had bought a new hat and asked Martha's opinion. Of course, she'd said it was lovely and most appropriate for the woman with a surname like hers. The hat had been swathed in flowers with a tiny bird nestling in the crown. But it had been like a creation a music hall star might have worn! But tonight, even the memory of that moment could not bring a smile to Martha's lips as it normally did. Her lie to her family had been a whopper. She had, indeed, spoken to Mr Trippet as she had told them but his reaction had not been one of kindness and a promise to help Josh find work in the cutlery manufacturing trade for which Sheffield was justifiably famous. His answer had been the opposite. Arthur Trippet was a large man, overweight through years of good living and self-indulgence. Although his sleek hair was thinning, he sported a well-trimmed moustache. His heavy jowls were speckled with tiny red veins and his blue eyes were cold and calculating, yet he always dressed like a smart

Edwardian gentleman in morning coat and striped trousers, a waistcoat and white, wing-collared shirt and bow tie. The motorcar he drove to and from the city each day was more up to date than his mode of dress; it was a black and yellow 1919 Silver Ghost Rolls-Royce, complete with the flying lady emblem on the bonnet. It was the object of admiration or envy when it passed through the village.

Leaning back in the swivel chair in the room set aside in Riversdale House as his study and puffing on a huge cigar, Arthur Trippet had pursed his thick lips and shaken his head. 'Oh no, Mrs Ryan. I don't think it's the kind of thing your son would take to. Besides, he's doing very nicely with his own little cottage industry.' The words – and his tone – were condescending. 'And what about your poor husband? Here, he has friends and neighbours to help you should you need it.'

This was true and Emily had touched upon the same thing. Walter was well known and respected in the village. He had been born here, in the very house they still lived in, for whilst it was rented accommodation, the tenancy had passed down the generations to him and would one day likely pass to Josh. But Martha was not willing to see Josh as the next generation of chandlers. She had visions of his name being on one of the panels in the Cutlers' Hall in Sheffield and of him living in a big house like the Trippets.

Martha had no intention of taking Arthur Trippet's advice. He's jealous, that's what it is, she told herself. Just because his lad has had to start at the bottom in the business – not bright enough to be given a decent position from the off, I expect – he doesn't want my Josh outshining his own son.

Thomas Trippet was a nice boy, a good boy, and Martha had been pleased enough that he was a friend of both Josh and Emily. She had seen it as a way for Josh to go up in the world. For her son to be friends with the offspring of the wealthiest man in the village had been a feather in her cap.

'Master Thomas is coming to tea with us tonight,' she would say loftily to Mr Osborne, who ran the corner shop just opposite the Ryans' home. 'A nice piece of your best cooked ham, if you please. Yours is so much nicer than I can cook myself,' she would add with a smile that was almost coquettish, hoping her flattery would earn her a few coppers' discount.

But they saw little of Trip now and it was not only Josh and Emily who lamented his absence; their mother, too, was frustrated at the severing of ties between the two families. She took it as a personal affront, believing that Arthur Trippet thought the Ryans were not good enough company for his son. Martha's ambitious nature had been thwarted when she was young. She had been brought up in a large family, one of nine children, none of whom, in her words, 'had amounted to much'. Being the eldest girl, she had often been obliged to stay home from school to help her mother with the younger children. As soon as she was old enough, she'd been sent from Over Haddon where she lived to Ashford to work in a small stocking mill there and that was how she'd met Walter Ryan, son and heir to the village candle maker. To Martha's young mind, Walter, with his own business, would hold a respected position in the village. Pretty and vivacious, she had set her cap at Walter, sweeping aside any competition from the village girls and ensnaring him almost before he had realized what was happening. She had been a good wife and mother

– no one could deny that – but from the day that her son had been born, she had become a boastful mother and soon the locals grew tired of hearing about how Josh had walked and talked earlier than any other child, how he could read even before he started school and knew his times tables by the time he was seven. Even then, she had firmly believed that her boy was going up in the world.

We'll show Arthur Trippet, she told herself softly in the darkness. Josh will prove he's ten times the man Thomas is. One day Josh will be 'someone' and where will young Trip be then? Nowhere, that's where. But how am I ever to persuade Josh to move?

She lay there for a long time, twisting and turning as she thought over the problem. Sleep was impossible until she— and then she thought of something; something with which Josh could not possibly argue.

Her determination strengthened as she turned over onto her side, closed her eyes and pushed away her guilty thoughts. It would all be worthwhile in the end. What was the saying she'd heard? 'The end justified the means.' Yes, that was it. Well, the end of all this would be that her Josh would rise in the world. He would rise so high that he'd leave all the Thomas Trippets on this earth wallowing in the mud at his feet. But first, they were all moving to Sheffield and now she knew how she was going to bring it about.

Her decision made, Martha slept.

The argument raged on for days and into weeks. Emily watched as Martha launched a tirade of reasons why the whole family should move to Sheffield. She hardly dared to look at her father, whose ravaged body seemed to shrink even more. He hadn't spoken since the day

21

he had come home from France, but Emily was sure he understood every word that was spoken in his hearing.

'Just think of the opportunities you'd have in the city,' Martha persisted, trying to wear Josh down. 'You'd have a skill and a job for life.'

'I've got a skill now,' Josh muttered, his normal happy-go-lucky smile wiped from his face.

'Pah! Makin' candles! And how long d'you think folks are going to want them? We're moving into a new age of inventions that folk like us have never dreamed of. Candles will be a thing of the past, but cutlery and the like will always be wanted.'

'You sure, Mam? Maybe some clever feller will invent something that feeds us without us having to use knives and forks.'

'None of your sarcastic lip, my lad,' Martha snapped. 'I'm only thinking of you and your future.'

'Candle making is the family business, Mam, a business that our Great-granddad Ryan took on and Granddad and then Dad continued. Doesn't that mean anything to you?'

'Not much, no. Not when it's your future at stake.'

And then, Josh blurted out the news that he had been trying to keep secret, but now found impossible. 'I've asked Amy to marry me and she's said yes. We're going to be married in the spring.'

Emily's head jerked up. For a moment she gaped at Josh and then her attention focused on her mother. What would she do now? To her surprise, Martha was smiling smugly.

'Has she now?' Martha said slowly. 'Josh, you're seventeen and so is she. What do you think her father's going to say to that?'

Josh shrugged. 'I'm eighteen in three weeks' time.

Besides, her father's all for it. He's even said we can live with him.'

Martha nodded slowly. 'Of course he's for it. It'll keep her at home, won't it? Looking after him. Oh, you're the perfect match for her as far as he's concerned.'

'I'm the perfect match for Amy, an' all.'

'Of course you are,' Martha said again. 'Nice little business already going—'

'Exactly. Now you've said it yourself.'

'And how d'you think that *little* business is going to support two families?'

Josh stared at her for a moment and then was forced to look away. The income from candle making wasn't vast by any means and some weeks the Ryan family only just managed to scrape by. If he married Amy, he would obviously be expected to contribute to their household expenses too.

Emily rose from her chair beside her father where she'd been sitting holding his hand and patting it absently as she listened to the quarrel. She'd kept silent until now. Pushing aside her own secretly held reasons for wanting to move to the city to be nearer Trip, she said, 'We can increase output. I could have a stall in Bakewell Market on a Monday. We used to do that years ago. You ran it yourself, Mam, before – before the war.'

'You keep out of this, miss. It's none of your business.'

'Yes, it is,' Emily said hotly, 'if I'm to go to Sheffield too. And what sort of job can I get? I only know candle making, like Josh.'

Martha rounded on her. 'You can pick up a job anywhere.'

'Doing what?'

'*I* don't know,' Martha snapped impatiently. 'But

23

there'll be plenty of jobs in the city.' She turned her attention back to Josh and Emily knew that she was forgotten.

'Listen to me, Josh.' Martha's tone took on a gentle, almost pleading tone. 'Don't you think I have your best interests at heart?'

At the expense of everyone else, Emily thought, but now she said nothing.

'I know that, Mam, but I don't want to go "up in the world". I just want to be happy. And I will be – with Amy.'

'She's not the right wife for you. She's no drive, no ambition. You could do far better for yourself.'

'I love Amy and she loves me.'

'And when did all this happen, might I ask?'

There was a moment's pause before Josh muttered, 'We've been walking out together for over two months.'

'And you never thought to say anything? You left it to your sister to tell me and that was only yesterday.'

Slowly, Josh raised his head. 'I – we wanted to keep it to ourselves.'

'Because –' Martha nodded knowingly – 'you knew that I wouldn't agree to it.'

'No – that wasn't the reason. I didn't know you wouldn't be happy for us. I thought you liked Amy.'

'I do like her. She's a nice girl, but she's not good enough for you.'

Josh gaped at Martha and gasped. 'That's a horrid thing to say. Who on earth do you think *we* are to be so high and mighty?'

'Nobody – yet,' Martha said, 'but you're going to change all that.'

Josh shook his head. 'No – no, I'm not. I am staying here and—'

'You are *not*. You are moving to Sheffield and one day you're going to make even the likes of Arthur Trippet sit up and take notice.'

'You can't make me.' Josh was showing stubbornness that none of them had ever seen in him before and whilst it frustrated Martha, it filled Emily with pride and admiration. She'd thought she was the only one who ever stood head to head and argued with their mother. Now she was a mere bystander as Josh remained adamant.

But Martha had a trump card up her sleeve and now she played it.

'You're not of age yet, Josh. You're not even eighteen. You need my consent to get married before you're twenty-one.'

Josh stared at her, dumbstruck now in the face of her declaration, which he knew to be no idle threat.

'You – you wouldn't?'

Martha smiled as she said softly, 'Oh yes, I would, Josh. It's for your own good. I'm not letting you throw yourself away on the likes of Amy Clark when you can do so much better for yourself. Do you think Arthur Trippet would let his son marry Emily? Of course he wouldn't and I'm not going to let you marry beneath you either.'

At her mother's words, Emily's heart constricted. It was like a physical pain in her chest. She'd never stopped to think for one moment that Trip's family would be against their friendship, but now her mother was voicing it.

'I shouldn't wonder if that's not why he's sent young Thomas away to work – and live – in the city. To get him away from the village and prepare him for his rightful place in the world.'

Emily felt her legs weak beneath her and she sank back down into the chair beside her father. To her surprise, Walter reached out a shaking hand and put it over hers. She turned to face him with tears in her eyes and though he did not speak she could see his features working with emotion and the anguish in his eyes broke her heart. She knew that he understood every word that was being said, but was helpless to do anything about it. Though his hand trembled against hers, his touch and his obvious understanding comforted Emily, even though, in that moment, hope died within her. Emily loved and respected her mother, but she had always idolized Walter. He had always been a kind and loving father, never too busy to mend a broken toy, to join in a childish game or to bathe a scraped knee. Martha had been the one to discipline their children, to teach them right from wrong and instil in them the right values and morals – a good code of life – but it had been Walter who had brought fun into their lives. Sadly, now he could only sit and listen to the raging argument, unable to voice his point of view, at the mercy of Martha's sharp tongue.

Josh was still not ready to capitulate. 'Dad would sign for me. I know he would.'

'No doubt,' Martha said tartly. 'But, even if he could still sign his name properly, which I doubt, who is going to take the word of a broken man against mine?'

Now Josh had no answers left – and neither, sadly, had Emily.

Four

'Now, is everything on the van?' Martha said, bustling around the empty house, leaving it neat and tidy for the next tenants. 'Emily, take your father out. He can sit by the driver. We can climb in the back.'

The candle shavings – the greaves – had been swept up and all Josh's tools had been carefully packed into crates and stored in Mr Clark's garden shed.

'I've got to do what Mam says, Mr Clark,' Josh had told Amy's father. 'But I promise you – and Amy – I'll be back when I'm twenty-one and we'll be married. You'll keep all my tools safe for me, won't you? I'll be wanting them when I come back.'

'I will, lad, but your business might have gone in three years' time. How will you ever pick it up again?'

'I don't know, but if I can't, then I'll find something else to do. But it'll be here, not Sheffield, I promise.'

'If your mother had said Amy could go with you, I'd've let her go, lad. I want you to know that.'

Josh shook his head. 'Even if I could persuade her to let Amy come with us, Amy herself wouldn't leave you. You know that.'

'I do, but I don't want to stand in the way of her happiness.'

'She wouldn't be happy leaving you or living in the city. I doubt I'm going to be, but we'll just have to be patient and wait three years and then I'll be back.'

'I'd like to wish you happy birthday, Josh, but it isn't, is it?'

With cruel irony, their moving date had fallen on the day of Josh's eighteenth birthday.

'No, it isn't,' Josh said shortly. The two men shook hands solemnly and as Bob Clark and his daughter stood watching their neighbours depart, Amy with tears streaming down her face, the older man doubted they would ever see Josh again. Oh, he believed the young man was sincere in his promise, but he recognized ruthless ambition when he saw it. And he saw it in Martha Ryan. Robert Clark – Bob to his friends and neighbours – had not fought in the Great War, for which he was thankful. As he was the village blacksmith, he had fully expected to be conscripted for his skill with horses, of which a great many had been taken to the Front, but it seemed he was of more value at home looking after the local farmers' horses. He'd still had to run the gauntlet of the jibes of cowardice, but, a widower, he had been desperate that his young daughter, as she had been in 1914, should not be left an orphan. Amy's welfare had been paramount to him, and it still was. If Martha Ryan had given the slightest hint that Amy could go with the family, then Bob would have given his consent. But the hard, selfish woman had only one thing on her mind: Josh's advancement, and Amy did not figure in her plans.

Emily came to them and held Amy's hands tightly for a few moments. 'I'll see he comes back to you, I promise,' she whispered so that her mother would not overhear.

Amy could not speak but shook her head. She was small and slight, with fair hair and delicate features, and though she truly believed Josh loved her – the

28

desperation was plainly written on his face this morning for all to see – she had the same misgivings as her father. Three years was a long time in their young lives. He might take to the city life. He might like the job his mother was determined to find for him and, worse still, he might meet another girl who would capture his heart.

Josh hugged Amy one last time and turned away before she could see the tears in his eyes. His mother had always taught him that it wasn't manly to cry and he wouldn't let Amy or anyone else see his weakness. Emily was dry eyed. She was distraught at leaving the village, her friends, especially Amy, but she clung to the hope that maybe, just maybe, she would see Trip more often. It was one of the first things she intended to do when they arrived in the city; seek out young Mr Trippet.

'Where exactly are we going, Mam?' Emily asked as the removal van bumped and bounced over the uneven roads, chugged up the steep hills and then down again into the city, which was covered by a pall of grimy fog from the tall chimneys that belched smoke day and night. Emily was appalled. This would kill her poor father. His breathing was difficult even in the clear, country air of Derbyshire. To bring him here to this was a death sentence.

'We're going to live in an area where all the little mesters are, though I want Josh to find work in one of the big cutlery businesses. Viners, perhaps, but I thought living amongst the folk who work in the industry we'd hear about any jobs going.'

Josh was silent. He asked no questions; he wasn't interested. His mind and his heart were still back in Ashford.

'Maybe I could find work there. At Viners, I mean.'

Emily said, but her mother only murmured absently, 'Perhaps.'

The van pulled up in a narrow street of terraced houses with courtyards behind them. A series of passageways ran between the houses, every so often opening up into courts. A warren of alleyways, dark and dangerous, ran amongst the courts.

'This is it, missus,' the van driver, Mr Rivers, said. 'This is t'address you gave me. Court Eight, Garden Street. What number's t'house?'

'Number four,' Martha said.

Emily jumped out the back of the van and stood looking about her. The air was thick and heavy with smoke and smuts. There were no children playing in the street and only a handful of women scrubbing their front step or cleaning their windows and eyeing the new arrivals.

Mr Rivers climbed out of his cab. ''As tha got 'key?'

'No. Someone called Mrs Dugdale has got it for us. Emily, go and see if you can find her.'

'Go through t'eight-foot, lass –' Mr Rivers jerked his thumb towards one of the passageways – 'an' tha'll see 'court.' He glanced around him. 'Nice little street, this. Tha's got a few shops and one or two little mesters, I can see. Tha'll be orreight here, missus.'

'What's a "little mester"?' Emily asked, intrigued, before she turned away to do her mother's bidding. It was the same phrase her mother had used and now Emily wanted to know what it meant.

Mr Rivers wrinkled his forehead, lifted his cap and scratched his head. A Sheffielder himself, he knew exactly what they were, but he found it difficult to explain to outsiders. 'They're self-employed men, who work from their own little workshops. Outworkers, I suppose you'd call 'em. And a lot of them are in this part of the city. Rather than having a huge workforce, firms will farm out part of their work to these self-employed cutlers. Usually, the little mesters will carry out one step of production for a bigger factory. Mebbe grinding or finishing and then pass the work on to another self-employed craftsmen for the next stage. Then you'll get the ones who assemble things.' He gave a low chuckle. 'I allus have to laugh when I hear talk of a "scissors putter-togetherer". Comical, in't it? Sometimes little mesters work on their own account, an' all – mebbe even employing a few men themselves – mekin' small items like knives or edge tools or pocket knives. Summat like that.'

'I see,' Emily murmured, but she didn't really. Not yet, but in the coming weeks she was sure she would find out.

'Little businesses. Just like making candles,' Josh muttered beside her. 'We'll be no better off here, Em.'

Emily didn't answer – she had the horrible feeling he was right – but instead she went down the passageway that opened into a cobbled courtyard with buildings all around. Some, she could see, were homes and one or two three-storey ones looked as if they could be the workshops Mr Rivers had spoken about. But the court-yard was dingy and cold; it looked as if the sun never had a chance to warm the cobbles. And the brickwork on some of the buildings was crumbling, the windows rotten, the glass dirty.

As Emily glanced about her, trying to guess which might be their new home, a large, round-faced woman in a grubby apron appeared out of one of the houses, beaming a welcome.

'You must be the Ryans? I've got 'key for you, though

there's no need for doors to be locked around here. Come on in, luv.' The woman turned towards the corner house, leading the way. 'You're younger than I imagined, but we're all neighbourly in this court. My name's Bess Dugdale, by the way.'

'I'm Emily. My mother'll be here in a moment. She's just helping my father out of the van.'

The woman looked back at her with startled eyes. 'Oh, I see. I thought . . . Ah, well, ne'er mind what I thought. You come on in and have a look round. Me and my daughter, Lizzie, have cleaned it through for you coming. Rough lot, they were, that's just moved out. They'd left it in a right state, I don't mind telling you.'

'That's very kind of you, Mrs Dugdale. Thank you.'

She saw the woman's glance go beyond her to the entrance to the alleyway and turned to see her mother and Josh coming towards them supporting Walter between them. He walked with a shambling gait, his head nodding, his hands shaking. Emily heard the woman's sharp intake of breath. 'Aw, poor feller,' she murmured. 'The war, was it?'

'Yes,' Emily said quietly.

'Aye, well, all of us around here know what that's caused. You'll not be on your own, lass. Mrs Nicholson in t'house over there –' Bess Dugdale nodded to the house in the opposite corner to the one where the Ryans were to make their home – 'lost her husband and two sons to the war. There's only her youngest left now. Billy. He works at Waterfall's cutlery works. So does she, as a matter of fact. She's the buffer missus in charge of about twenty girls and my Lizzie's one of 'em. And then there's poor Rosa Jacklin next door to her. She lost her hubby and she's been left with two little kiddies.

So, you don't need to tell us about 'war, an' if you want a bit of help –' she nodded towards the threesome making their way carefully across the cobbled yard – 'you only have to holler.'

From one of the taller buildings opposite came a rhythmic tapping sound.

'What's the noise?' Emily asked.

Bess smiled. 'You'll get used to it. These courts and the streets all around here are a mixture of houses and little workshops. The noise you can hear is Mr Farrell. He's a file maker. I work alongside him.' Now she laughed and shook her dirty apron. 'I don't allus look like this, luv. You wait till you see me in my best bib and tucker on a Sunday.'

Emily turned to Martha as her mother joined them. 'Mam, this is Mrs Dugdale. She lives next door and has the key for us, though,' Emily added with a grin, 'she says there's no need for locked doors around here.'

'Well, we'll see about that. Let's get your father inside. Josh, go and help Mr Rivers unload the van. Bring your father's rocking chair off first. Emily, see if you can light a fire and get the kettle going.'

'No need, luv,' Bess said. 'I've already lit one. I knew you was coming today and I've the kettle on the hob. There'll be a cuppa ready for you in two shakes.'

Martha blinked and stared at the woman for a moment. Then, seeming to think quickly – and Emily knew exactly what she was thinking – Martha smiled at her new neighbour. 'Now, that's really kind of you, thank you. Sorry, if I was a bit sharp, but . . .' She gestured towards her husband, who was leaning heavily against her and gasping for breath.

'I can see, luv. Come on, let's get him inside and settled near the fire.' As the woman led the way, Emily

33

whispered in her mother's ear. 'Mrs Dugdale and her daughter have cleaned the house for us, Mam. Evidently, it was left in a right state by the previous tenants.'

Martha raised her eyebrows but said nothing.

'Better a friend than an enemy, eh, Mam?' Without waiting for an answer, Emily marched across the yard to help unload their belongings, knowing she was only voicing what had been in her mother's mind.

Five

For the next half-hour, Mr Rivers, Josh and Emily carried everything from the van into the house, which had only three rooms. A young woman on the far side of the yard stood watching the proceedings in silence. Two little girls with runny noses, dirty pinafores and scuffed boots clung to her skirts.

'Afternoon,' Emily called out cheerfully, but the woman merely nodded, and, as one of the children began to whimper, she disappeared into her home.

The communal lavatory was in the yard, though it seemed that each house had its own tin bath, which hung on a hook outside the door. Emily shuddered as she thought of her poor father trying to totter across the icy cobbles in the depths of winter. Thank goodness they had brought a commode with them. At least the poor man would have some privacy in his own bedroom.

Shutters on the windows were open now as it was only September, but Emily guessed they could be used in winter to keep the house warmer. The door from the yard opened directly into the kitchen, where a fire burned welcomingly in the grate of the shining, black leaded range. On one side of the range were some built-in cupboards from floor to ceiling. On the other side was a cast-iron copper, set in brickwork over a fire grate. Next to that was a stone sink with cupboards beneath it.

'There's gas lighting in here and in the main bedroom,' Bess told them, pointing upwards with her thumb. Then she smiled at Emily and Josh. 'But there's no gas lighting in the attic, where you'll likely sleep. You'll need candles.'

So much for Mam's belief that candles are a thing of the past, Emily thought, but she said nothing.

'There's a coal cellar down here, luv.' Bess was still showing them round. 'Yer can use the area at the top of the steps as a larder. It's nice and cool. Cellar's a good storage place, an' all.' Bess nodded towards Martha. 'You'll find Mrs Eyre's left her washing tub, dolly peg and washboard and a clothes horse too. Though that's seen better days, I 'ave to say.'

Now she glanced around the kitchen. 'She's not left you much else, though. A rickety table and chairs and there's some iron bedsteads upstairs and a couple of battered washstands. No mattresses though.'

'No matter, Mrs Dugdale. I've brought our feather beds and bedding. And Walter's rocking chair. We'll do nicely, thank you.'

It was not Emily's idea of 'doing nicely'. She thought longingly of the fresh, clean air at home as she helped her father to his chair, which Mr Rivers had set to one side of the range.

'You and Josh will have to share the attic,' Martha declared in a tone that brooked no argument from either of them. Emily pulled a face. Much as she loved her brother, she didn't want to share a bedroom with him. A nineteen-year-old girl needed some privacy. And no doubt Josh would feel that he did too. But with only the one proper bedroom, there was nothing else for it; they'd have to share. Anyway, Emily reminded herself with an inward smile, it was only for three years.

'I can sleep down here – over there in the corner,' Josh offered.

'Oh no, you won't, m'lad.'

'It's not right that Emily has to share with a feller.' Josh was not going to let it go. 'And I'd tidy up after myself every morning. You'll never know anyone's sleeping here.' Suddenly, with an impish smile that had been missing from his merry face ever since his mother had first suggested them moving to Sheffield, Josh put his arm around Martha's shoulders. He was at least three inches taller than her and she had to crane her neck to look up at him.

'No, you'd be better off in the attic with no one to disturb you. You can hang a curtain down the middle of the room. It'll be quite private for each of you.'

Even over such a simple matter, Emily thought ruefully, still they could not win an argument with their mother.

Late in the afternoon, Emily waved Mr Rivers off when the last of their belongings had been unloaded. They hadn't brought very much with them; the house their mother had rented for four shillings a week was supposed to be fully furnished, but they'd brought their own bedding, household pots, pans, crockery and cutlery. It wasn't so bad, Emily supposed. At least the place was clean, thanks to Bess and her daughter. Once the beds had been made up and her hairbrush and comb had been set out on an upturned box, her few clothes hung on a rail at one end of the attic and her underwear stowed in a trunk they had brought with them, at least the bedroom they had to share felt a bit more like home.

'Just you mind you keep to your side of the curtain, Josh Ryan, 'specially when I'm getting washed.' The battered old washstand with a black marble top and blue and white willow-patterned ewer and bowl stood in one corner of Emily's side of the room beneath the sloping ceiling.

'Where shall I wash, then?'

'Downstairs in the kitchen, unless we can pick up another washstand cheap.'

'There's hardly any room to put one,' Josh said morosely. 'Oh Emily, what are we doing here?' He sat down suddenly on his bed, his shoulders hunched, his face a picture of abject misery.

'Doing as we're told – for the moment.'

He sighed heavily. 'Three years is an awful long time. Maybe Amy won't wait for me.'

'Of course she will. And you can write to each other every week.' She grinned, teasing him. 'That should keep the flame of true love burning brightly. And you can go back and see her at a weekend sometimes.'

But Josh was not to be cheered. 'Whatever job I get, I won't earn much to start with, will I? And Mam will need every penny both of us can earn.' He glanced up at her. 'What are you going to do? For a job, I mean.'

'I'm not sure yet, but something Mrs Dugdale said has given me an idea where I can start.'

Downstairs, Martha had stowed all her kitchen equipment in the cupboards and scrubbed the surface of the table just one more time. Martha was fussy about cleanliness and no one but herself could clean her kitchen table well enough.

As dusk came early into the enclosed yard, there was a knock on the door. 'It's only me, luv,' Bess called and opened the door at the same time.

Martha sniffed. She wasn't sure she welcomed such

familiarity so early in their acquaintance, but she held her tongue when she saw that Bess was carrying a large tureen.

'It's only stew and dumplings. I made extra knowing you'd be tired and hungry. There's only me, my son, Mick, and my lass, Lizzie. She'll be home from work soon. I'll send her round to say hello. But as for my boy,' she smiled indulgently, 'I hardly ever see him. But I'll get him to come and see you sometime.'

Was this how it was to be? Martha thought. Folks running in and out of each other's houses without so much as a 'by-your-leave'? For a brief moment, she felt a pang of uncertainty but then her resolve hardened. This was all for Josh. As long as Josh got a good job with the prospects she hoped for, then it would all be worthwhile. Martha forced a smile onto her face and said ingratiatingly, 'How *very* kind of you, Mrs Dugdale.'

'Bess, please. And you're . . . ?'

Martha hesitated. She wasn't used to such informality. Even with Bob Clark it had always been 'Mr Clark' and 'Mrs Ryan'. And Mr Osborne at the corner shop wouldn't dream of calling any of his customers by anything other than their surname. The menfolk, who'd known each other for years, called each other by their Christian names, but this had never extended to the women. Now Martha swallowed hard and with a thin smile, said, 'Martha.'

'Well, then, Martha luv, here you are. Pop it in the oven for a few minutes while you set the table. See you later, then.'

'Mm,' Martha said, very much afraid that she would. But ten minutes later, she was obliged to be thankful to her new neighbour as her family sat down to the unexpected hot meal.

'This is good, Mam,' Josh said, eating with surprising relish after being so recently heartbroken.

Emily, helping Walter to eat, exchanged a look with her father. There was a surprising twinkle in his eyes and she knew he was thinking the same as she was; the fickleness of a young man where his belly was concerned! Despite this, Emily was encouraged; her father under-stood what was going on and whilst he had not been able to voice any opinion – had not even been asked – perhaps, after all, he would be all right here. As long as he was kept warm and fed, maybe . . . ? But even as the thoughts entered her head, he choked a little on the food and began to wheeze and she realized that before long the sooty, smoky atmosphere of the city would be a serious threat to him.

Whatever had her mother been thinking of, she thought yet again, to drag them all from everything they loved to this strange, disturbing environment?

But of course she knew the answer only too well: Josh!

Six

A little before nine o'clock, there was another tap at the door.

'That'll be the girl, I expect,' Martha muttered sourly. 'Come to say hello. Don't we ever get any peace here? It's high time we were getting your father to bed.'

'Shush, Mam, she'll hear you.'

Martha sniffed but said no more as Emily went to open the door. In the light from the lamp, Emily could see a tall, slim girl standing there, a shawl pulled closely around her shoulders.

'You must be Lizzie,' Emily said, holding the door open and moving to one side. 'Come in, do.'

As the girl stepped into the kitchen, Emily could see that her long black hair fell in glossy waves to her shoulders. Her dark blue eyes were bold and she glanced around the room, swiftly assessing everyone. Her skin was smooth but pale, her mouth and nose well-shaped and her chin firm and determined. When she met Emily's gaze the two girls recognized the strength of character in each other. Without a word being spoken, they both realized that they would become either the best of friends or the worst of enemies. But Lizzie's glance was flitting around the room once more. She nodded to Martha and then her stare rested briefly, and with sympathy, on the huddled figure near the fire. But it was on Josh's face that her gaze finally came to rest. She smiled at

41

him, her cheeks dimpling prettily, her head tilting coquettishly to one side. 'My, my,' she said in a low, husky voice. 'Mam didn't say that a handsome young man had come to live next door.'

Josh's face reddened and he stuttered a little as he said, 'P-please, sit down, Miss Dugdale.'

'Oh, Lizzie, please. And, ta, I will, though I won't stay long.'

'Thank goodness for small mercies,' Martha muttered and Emily glared at her, hoping the girl hadn't heard.

'You must all be so tired.'

Emily sat down on the opposite side of the table. 'We are,' she said, 'but not so tired that we can't make a neighbour welcome. Your mother has been wonderfully kind.'

The girl laughed. 'Oh, that's Mam. Never too busy to lend a helping hand despite the fact that she does all the cooking and washing and cleaning for the three of us and works across the yard part-time as well.'

'Oh really?' Martha asked, her ears pricking up. 'What does she do?'

'She works alongside Mr Farrell and they make files for Waterfall's in Division Street. That's where I work. I'm a buffer girl there under Mrs Nicholson. Her that lives in the corner house opposite.' Lizzie gestured with her head. 'She's the missus over us buffer girls. Poor missus.' Lizzie lowered her voice in sympathy with the heart-breaking losses the woman had suffered. She glanced across at Walter, then added, 'There's only Billy, her youngest son, left at home now. He was too young to go to the war. He's only nineteen now – same age as me. He works at Waterfall's too, though not with his mam, of course.'

After a moment's pause, Emily asked, 'What exactly is a buffer girl?'

'We polish the cutlery – well, some of it. Fellers do the difficult stuff.' She pulled a face. 'They reckon women can't do it, but we've proved in the war that we could when there was a shortage of men, so we're fighting now to be treated equally. In the war, some of the firms turned to war production, you know, shells and such, but Waterfall's kept on with the cutlery.' She laughed. 'There was plenty of cheap cutlery required by the army. At least, that's what we made. But now we're back to making the better stuff and we want equality with the men if we're doing the same jobs.'

Emily heard her mother's derisory sniff. In Martha's eyes no girl would ever be able to do the same work as a man and especially not a man like her Josh.

'Would there be work for me, d'you think?' Emily asked swiftly, cutting off any remark her mother might have been about to make.

'More than likely. I'll ask tomorrow, if you like.'

'Would you? That'd be very –'

'Kind,' the two girls finished in unison and then burst into fits of laughter.

'Are there any jobs going for young men?' Martha asked. 'Josh is looking for work, but he wants to serve some sort of apprenticeship with the view to advancement in time.'

Lizzie's eyes sparkled as her intense gaze rested once more on him. 'I'm sure they'd be happy to take on someone like Josh.' Huskily, she added, 'I'll see what I can do for you.'

The words were innocent enough, but Emily had the uncomfortable feeling that there was a wealth of meaning behind them.

As the door closed behind their visitor, Martha said, 'We must be friendly to all our neighbours. They could be useful.'

Emily hid her smile. She had no intention of being anything else and not because of what they could do for her.

'Now, both of you, help me get your dad up them stairs. It's not going to be easy. They're narrower than the ones we had at home.'

It was a slip of the tongue, of course. Martha didn't mean to refer to Ashford as home, but Emily and Josh exchanged a glance. It was most certainly what they still felt.

The following morning, Martha tried to catch Mrs Nicholson before she left for work, but by the time she'd seen to Walter's early morning needs, both the woman and her son had gone and Bess and her daughter were nowhere to be seen either, though there was a steady tap-tapping and the noise of a grinding wheel coming from the tall building on the other side of the court. They had yet to meet Bess's son, Mick Dugdale.

'I expect she's at her work already,' Martha muttered, put out because she couldn't make a start on finding Josh a suitable job. 'They're early starters here but I'd best not interrupt her, especially if she's on piece work.'

'I'll go shopping, Mam. What do you need?' Emily was eager to get out into the city streets to find her bearings and, if she could, to learn where Trippets' factory was. She meant to find Trip as soon as possible. It was weeks since he'd last been home to Ashford.

'Go careful with the money, Emily. We've got to make it last. Even if Josh finds a job straightaway, he won't get any pay for a week or two. And you'd better start looking, an' all,' Martha added, almost as an afterthought.

Armed with a shopping basket, Emily left the court and stepped into the street beyond. The September sun struggled to penetrate the blanket of smoke that hung over the city but at least it was fine. Emily straightened her shoulders and set off down the street, swinging her basket and humming a tune beneath her breath.

'Good morning,' she greeted one or two women, who were donkey-stoning their steps or washing their windowsills. One or two spoke and others merely smiled and nodded. They seem friendly enough, Emily thought. Garden Street was a mixture of houses and small businesses. There were several shops; a tripe dealer, a grocer and a coal merchant – even a second-hand clothes shop. That might be useful, Emily thought wryly, if times get really tough. There was probably everything the family needed here in their own street and the neighbouring roads, but Emily was keen to see more of the city. She walked on, intrigued by the premises that she guessed were little mesters' workshops. The men were sitting at their workbenches in front of the windows – to make the most of the natural light, Emily supposed. She paused now and again to watch one man making a penknife and another producing a delicate medical instrument.

The largest building in the street was called Croft Settlement Hall, some sort of men's club, Emily guessed, and she thought how sad it was that her father was not now well enough to join. He would miss the camaraderie of male company that he'd had in Ashford. There had always been someone calling in to see him when he'd been the village chandler and even more so after he'd returned from the war. No one had shied away from seeing him in his pitiful state and they all showed their true friendship by continuing to visit. Bob Clark had been a faithful visitor almost very night after he'd finished his work. He'd sit and chat to Walter, just as if they were having a proper conversation. It didn't bother Bob – though it saddened him – that the poor man could no longer answer him. He'd come with all the village news and tell Walter funny little anecdotes he'd heard or that had happened to him.

At the end of the street, Emily paused at a junction with a wider road, not sure now which way to go. An elderly woman was coming towards her, carrying two heavy shopping bags.

'Excuse me,' Emily ventured. 'I'm new here. Please, can you tell me the way to the centre of town?'

The woman stopped, set her bags down on the pavement with obvious relief and straightened her back, sighing a little as she did so. 'Go that way,' she said, pointing to the right, 'and then take the second left into Rockingham Street and just keep going to the end. Turn left there and you'll see where you want to be, but if you're still not sure, duck, then ask again.'

'Thank you.' Emily paused a moment and on impulse said, 'Do you live far from here? I can help you home with your bags, if you like.'

The woman looked at her for a long moment and then smiled weakly. But her smile did not reach her eyes, which were dull and lifeless. 'That's very thoughtful of you, lass. I live just along here, but I'm on my way to my daughter's in Court Eight.'

Emily laughed. 'Why, that's where we've come to live. Come on, I'll go back with you. You carry my empty basket and I'll take both your bags. My,' she added as she picked them up, 'they are heavy. You shouldn't be carrying these.'

46

'I've got to help our Rosa as best I can. She's been left with two little kiddies.'

'Oh, I think I saw her yesterday when we moved in.' Emily hesitated before asking tentatively, 'The war, was it?'

'Aye.' There was a wealth of sadness in the woman's tone. 'Rosa's me daughter-in-law really. It was – it was my son we lost. My only child. Ronald.'

'I'm so sorry,' Emily said. She bit her lip to stop herself from blurting out about her father. At least he had come back to them even though he was a broken shell of a man. But no doubt this poor woman would think the Ryans were lucky in comparison.

'He went in 'sixteen just after Violet – that's the eldest – was born. He was on the Somme and lucky not to have been killed then. He was wounded and sent home and we all thought that was it – he was home for good. But no, he got better and back he went. And then –' she paused and drew in a shuddering breath – 'he didn't come back.' Surprisingly, her tone was a little bitter as she added, 'But he was home long enough to leave his wife pregnant again.' Then she smiled and her voice lightened. 'Mind you, our Becky's a little darlin'. We wouldn't be without her now, but having an extra mouth to feed doesn't make life any easier.'

They reached the court again and went straight to the house where Emily had seen the young woman with two children. The woman paused with her hand on the doorknob. 'I'd better introduce myself, since you're going to be Rosa's neighbours. I'm Clara Jacklin.'

'I'm pleased to meet you, Mrs Jacklin, and I'm Emily Ryan. We've moved here for my brother to find work.'

Clara Jacklin nodded and opened the door, not, at

the moment, curious to know any more about the Ryan family. 'Rosa,' she called, 'you there, luv?'

Rosa turned from the sink, drying her hands on a ragged piece of towelling. 'Aw, Mam, you shouldn't have struggled with all that. I could have gone later, if you'd've minded the kids. Oh . . .' She looked startled as Emily stepped through the door and set the two heavy bags on the table. Rosa was only young. She doesn't look much older than me, Emily thought, yet already she was a widow with two youngsters, who were playing on the floor around her feet.

'This is Emily. Her family have come to live across the yard.'

'Yes, I saw you arrive yesterday. Thank you for helping Mam. It's good of you.'

Emily shrugged off her thanks. 'We've come from a small village where neighbours helped each other. I thought it might be different in the city –' her smile widened – 'but I see it isn't. Mrs Dugdale made us so welcome yesterday. This –' she gestured towards the bags of shopping – 'was the least I could do. Anyway, I'd best be going. Bye for now.'

She reached the door but then turned back. 'Oh, do you know where the Trippets' factory is?'

Rosa gave a little cry. Her hand flew to cover her mouth and tears sprang into her eyes.

Startled by the young woman's reactions, Emily said, 'Oh, my goodness. I'm so sorry.' She turned towards the older woman. 'What have I said?'

Clara Jacklin smiled sorrowfully. 'It was where my son – her husband – worked. That's all. His loss is still so raw with us. Any sudden reminder . . .'

'Of course. I'm so sorry. I'll ask someone else.'

'No, no, it's all right,' Rosa said recovering quickly.

'It's a big square building in Creswick Street. It's a fair way from here, though. Ron used to cycle to work. Sometimes he went up to Solly Street and through all the little side streets, but your best way would be to go down 'street, turn left into Broad Lane and then . . .' Rosa reeled off a number of street names that Emily couldn't remember. She didn't like to press the young woman any more, so she thanked them and left, glad to escape from the gloom of the small house. She'd felt suffocated in there. Obviously, Rosa wasn't coping very well, but then she was young and only had the help of her elderly mother-in-law. Emily sighed. The war had an awful lot to answer for.

Seven

The city centre was buzzing with people and Emily felt excitement rising within her. It was dinner time now and workers of all sorts had spilled into the streets for a quick half-hour's break. Three girls were walking arm in arm down the pavement. They were wearing calico aprons, once white but now covered with black smuts. Even their faces were smudged with black, but they were laughing and singing together and calling out to people they knew. As Emily stepped to the side to let them pass, she heard her name called.

'Emily!' One of the girls stopped, pulling the two others with her to a halt too. 'It's Emily from near me.'

'Oh Lizzie,' Emily smiled, 'hello.' She hadn't recognized the girl dressed in her working clothes, with her hair covered with a scarf and her face blackened.

'She's just moved into our court,' Lizzie explained to her workmates. 'She only arrived yesterday.' She turned back to Emily. 'I asked Mrs Nicholson about work for you and she said to come and see her tomorrow morning. One girl's just left to have a babby, so she's short-handed.'

'Phyllis'll likely come back once she's over her confinement,' one of the other girls said, but the third girl added, 'No, she won't, Nell. Her husband's said she's to stay at home and look after the kiddie and have his tea on the table every night when he gets home.'

'Lucky her!'

The three girls fell into gales of laughter and the one called Nell pulled a comical face. 'Well, I wouldn't let any man tell me what to do and that's a fact.'

'Mebbe that's why you can't find a feller, our Nell. Still –' Lizzie turned back to Emily. 'You want to give it a go, Emily?'

'Of course, and thanks for asking.'

'Don't mention it. And I'm going to see the foreman about a job for that handsome brother of yours. I'll let you know tonight.'

'Ooo, has she got a brother?'

'Trust you to get in there first, Lizzie Dugdale,' the third girl said. 'Why don't you give the rest of us a chance?'

It was on the tip of Emily's tongue to say that Josh already had a girlfriend waiting for him back in Ashford, but she bit back the remark. She needed Lizzie to help them find work and if she were to let slip that Josh was already courting, the girl might lose interest and not be so helpful.

'Come on, Ida,' Nell said. 'Time we were getting back.'

As the girls hurried away with cheery shouts of 'Ta-ra, luv' and 'See you tomorrow', Emily turned away, thinking, I'll have to watch myself; I'm getting as devious as my mother! It was not a feeling she liked.

She delivered the shopping back home, helped Martha with household chores for a couple of hours and then said, 'I'm going out for a walk. You coming, Josh?'

Her brother nodded eagerly. Once outside and walking side by side up the street, he confided, 'She's been going on at me all morning to get out and find

51

work, but I don't know where to start. And when you came in and said you'd got some sort of interview tomorrow with Mrs Nicholson, well, I thought she was going to burst a blood vessel that you'd found summat before me.'

Emily grinned. 'I'm not the important one, Josh. That's all it is. Come on,' she added, linking her arm through his. 'Let's go and see if we can find Trip.'

'Trip? Do you know where to start?'

'Oh yes,' Emily said firmly, her eyes sparkling. 'Creswick Street. That's where his dad's factory is, so that's where Trip will be. Right, I know we set off down our street and turn left but then I got a bit lost. Rosa said all the street names so quickly, I couldn't remember them all.'

After asking for directions twice, they found the big, square building and stood looking up at it in awe. 'It's huge!' Josh said. 'I'd no idea Mr Trippet was so – so . . .' He was lost for words.

'Neither had I,' Emily said in a small voice. 'Makes you wonder why Trip was friendly with the likes of us when you see this, doesn't it?'

'Why he was *allowed* to be, you mean. Trip's got no side to him, no hoity-toity ways but . . .' He, too, fell silent for a moment before saying quietly, 'Maybe that's why his dad sent him away to the city. To live, I mean, not just to work.'

'Perhaps we ought not to—'

'Oh yes, we ought,' Josh said swiftly. 'Now we're here, we're going to see him.' He laughed wryly as the factory hooter sounded and the workers came flooding out, hurrying homewards. 'If we can find him in that lot!'

Trip was one of the last to leave, as befitted the

owner's son. Emily's heart lifted and she felt a flutter of excitement as she recognized the familiar figure wheeling a bicycle through the gates.

'Trip! Trip, over here.'

The young man in rough working clothes – dark trousers, worn jacket and cloth cap – looked up in surprise. 'Good Lord! Josh and – and oh, Emily.' He hurried across the road, leaned his bicycle against a lamp post and flung his arms wide as if to embrace them both. 'How good it is to see you.' He hugged Emily to him and then picked her up and swung her round. When he set her down, he glanced at each of them in turn. 'But whatever are you doing here?'

'My mother's brought the whole family to Sheffield. She wants Josh to find work in the cutlery business.'

'And,' Josh took up the story, 'she spoke to your dad, who said he hadn't any vacancies at the moment but that he'd put a good word in with some of the other owners.'

Trip frowned. 'Really? Father said that?'

'Yes.' There was a slight pause as Josh added hesitantly, 'Why, is something wrong?'

'No – no, nothing. It's just that we *do* have a vacancy that would be perfect for you. I've moved up the ladder as an apprentice a bit and the lad who took my place was useless. He was sacked two weeks ago.'

'That explains it, then,' Emily said. 'It's longer ago than that since my mother spoke to your father.'

Trip's face cleared. 'Oh I see, yes, that'll be it.'

Although, to Emily's sharp hearing, there was still a note of uncertainty in Trip's tone, but then he said, firmly, 'Right, no time like the present. We'll go and see Mr Bayes this minute. Come on.'

* * *

When Josh and Emily arrived home well after dusk had fallen, it was to find Lizzie, washed clean of all the grime of her job, her hair shining in the lamplight and dressed in a pretty floral dress, waiting with Martha. But their mother was in a fine old temper.

'Where on earth have you been? Out gallivanting when I could do with some help with your father.'

Josh put his strong arms round his mother's waist, lifted her off her feet and swung her round. 'Don't be cross, Ma.' It was his pet name for their mother, when he wanted to get round her.

'Put me down and stop your silliness.' Martha slapped him on the shoulder and he set her down on the floor again. 'And why shouldn't I be cross, pray?'

'Because, Ma, I've got a job and I start on Monday.'

Martha's anger evaporated in an instant and her mouth dropped open. 'How? Where?'

'At Trippets',' Josh said with a wide grin. Today was the first time Emily had seen her brother smile since their mother had dropped the bombshell of her intention to move the Ryan family to the city.

'Trippets'? But—' Martha bit her lip and for a moment she looked uncertain.

Quick to notice, Emily said, 'What is it, Mam?'

'Nothing, nothing,' Martha said, a little too hastily. 'Tell me how this has come about. Did you see Mr Trippet?'

'No – we saw Trip.'

'Thomas? Oh – oh, I see.'

Emily could see that her mother's mind was working furiously. 'But – surely,' Martha said at last, 'Thomas isn't in a position to hire folks. Is he?'

Josh shook his head. 'No, but he took us to see the foreman – a Mr Bayes. Of course, because it was Trip doing the asking, Mr Bayes said he was willing to give me a trial.'

But what would happen when Arthur Trippet found out? Martha was thinking, but aloud she said, 'Then that's wonderful, Josh.'

Lizzie pulled a face. 'It sounds as if you don't need *my* help now.'

Emily put her arm round Lizzie's trim waist. 'Of course, we do. You're going to take me to see Mrs Nicholson tomorrow, aren't you?'

Mollified a little, though with her impertinent glance still on Josh, Lizzie said, 'Tell you what, Emily, why don't we go across to see her right now? I know she's home.'

'Will she mind?' Emily was a little doubtful about troubling the woman after a long day at work.

'Not the missus, no. Come on and then you'll both be fitted up with a job on the same day.'

As they walked across the uneven cobbles, Lizzie confided, 'I'd so hoped we'd all be working together at Waterfall's. Ne'er mind, at least we're living close by.'

She knocked on the door and, after a brief pause, it was opened by a tall, fresh-faced young man with short, wiry red hair. He was still dressed in his working clothes but his smile was warm and welcoming. Though he glanced at the stranger briefly, it was to Lizzie he turned, his gaze never leaving her face.

'Hello, Billy. Is your mam in?'

'Come in, Lizzie luv.' As they stepped into the light of the kitchen, he added, 'And who's this?'

'My new friend, Emily Ryan. They've come to live next door to us and she's looking for work. I just wondered if your mam—'

'Of course.' He turned and shouted over his shoulder. 'Mam, visitors for you.'

The door from the inner room opened and a plump, middle-aged woman came in. She was round faced and smiling, yet the smile did not reach her eyes, which held a deep sorrow. But then Emily remembered. This poor woman had lost three of her family to the war. Billy was the only one she had left now. The Ryan family thought they had been hard hit, but it was nothing in comparison to Mrs Nicholson's loss or, for that matter, Rosa Jacklin's. She nodded to both girls as Lizzie said swiftly, 'Emily here is looking for work and we wondered – *I* wondered – if you'd give her a trial as a buffer girl, missus.' Even at home, outside working hours, Lizzie still called the woman the name she was known as by the buffer girls in her charge.

Ruth Nicholson looked the newcomer up and down. 'Well, you look presentable enough, but you won't by the time you've worked at a buffing wheel for a day. Are you sure it's what you want to do, lass?'

'I have to find work quickly, Mrs Nicholson. I'd be very grateful if you'd at least give me a chance.'

'You've not done any of this sort of work before, then?'

Emily shook her head. 'We've come from a small village in Derbyshire, but my mother wants my brother to have a chance to better himself.'

Lizzie grimaced. 'He's only gone and got himself a job at Trippets' today. I was hoping he'd come to Waterfall's too, but . . .' She shrugged in disappointment.

'Well, well, we can't have Trippets' getting all the promising ones, can we?' The woman was thoughtful for a moment and when Lizzie said softly, 'Her dad can't work any more. I expect you can guess why,' Mrs

Nicholson sighed and said, 'All right, lass. I'll give you a try. Come in with Lizzie in the morning and we'll get you kitted out and see how you shape up. We'll start you off as an errand girl. The last one left last week and I haven't had a chance to find a replacement yet. I'll give you a trial, at least.'

Eight

It was no hardship for Emily to be up early. At home – as she still called Ashford – she and Josh had always started their work at seven o'clock every weekday morning.

'That way,' Josh had said, 'we can allow ourselves an afternoon off on a Saturday and we can still see Trip then and on Sundays, when he's home.'

The four youngsters had been friends from childhood. They had attended school together, but when he was nine years old, Trip had been sent away to boarding school.

'He'll not want to know us when he comes home,' Josh had said dolefully. 'He'll have made some posh friends.'

But Josh had been wrong. Trip was only too pleased to see them and when they asked him about his new school, he'd pulled a face. 'I hate it,' he'd said. 'I wish I could come back to school here, but Father won't hear of it. So it looks as if I've got to grin and bear it until I'm old enough to leave.'

To the nine-year-old boy and his friends that seemed an awful long way off. All they could do was spend as much time together as they could in the holidays. Trip didn't even come home at weekends in term time. Emily left school at thirteen and started working for her father, often going to Bakewell Market to sell the candles on a stall with her mother. When Josh reached the same age seventeen months later, they expected that he, too, would leave school at the end of term and begin work with Walter. But even then, Martha had had grandiose ideas for her son.

'He'll stop on at school,' she'd declared. 'Learning's important for a boy.'

And so Josh had stayed on, working with his father and learning the trade of a chandler at weekends and in the school holidays. But early in 1916, the House of Commons voted for the conscription of all single men between eighteen and forty-one and two months later this was extended to include married men. Walter, at thirty-seven, would be obliged to go.

'I'm not waiting to be called up,' he'd told his startled family one sunny May morning. 'I've stood the jibes for long enough. I've volunteered and I leave on Monday.'

And so – much to Martha's chagrin – there was no choice; Josh left school. But by then, both he and Emily were skilled enough between them to carry on the business together.

The four young friends had still met up whenever Trip was at home, but since he'd left to live and work in the city, there'd only been the three of them. Soon, it became just Josh and Amy, once Emily became aware of the growing affection between her brother and her best friend.

But now, their working life was to be very different. Emily helped her mother get their father down the stairs for the day and seated him in the chair by the fire, then, when Lizzie came to collect her, the two of them left with Josh to walk to work.

'I do wish you were coming to Waterfall's with us,

Josh,' Lizzie said, linking her arm through his as they walked to the bottom of their street. 'You can't even walk to work and back with us. Trippets' is in the opposite direction when we get to the end of our street to the way me an' Emily will go. But it'd be nice to meet up at dinner time with you. Us buffer girls usually have a quick walk into town. Emily saw us yesterday, didn't you?' Lizzie glanced briefly towards Emily, but her gaze soon went back to looking up sideways at Josh.

She was definitely making a play for him, Emily thought uncomfortably. One of them would soon have to tell her that he'd got a girlfriend back home. But first, Emily decided – though the guilt swept through her at her deception – she needed to settle into the job Lizzie had found her.

They parted on a corner where Josh set off towards Trippets' and Emily and Lizzie headed to Waterfall's in Division Street.

The other girls greeted her with friendly laughter. 'Right, lass,' Mrs Nicholson said as the other girls began to dress themselves in their calico aprons and wrap brown paper or newspaper around their legs. 'Let's get you kitted out. You'll be doing the job of errand girl to start with but we'll dress you up like a proper buffer girl and later on I'll give you a try at a wheel.'

Mrs Nicholson – or 'missus', as the girls all called her – tied a clean, white smock-like garment around Emily, tying it at the back. 'This is called a buff-brat, though don't ask me where the name comes from, 'cos I don't know. It won't stop this colour for long and it's up to you to take it home and wash it. Once a week's enough, though it'll be caked with the flying sand by the end of a week. I'll lend you this one to start with, but when you start as a buffer girl, you'll have to provide your own.'

'We have a washday on a Saturday afternoon in the court,' Lizzie, who was still hovering nearby, put in. 'She can join us, can't she, missus?'

Emily felt a stab of disappointment. Working hours, she'd been told, were weekdays plus Saturday morning and she'd hoped she would have been free on a Saturday afternoon to meet up with Trip. Never mind, she told herself. There was always Sunday afternoon.

Over the buff-brat was a coarse, grey apron and then Mrs Nicholson held out two pieces of red material. 'Now, this is a head rag to protect your hair and there's a neck rag too to stop all the muck getting into your clothes, lass,' she explained. She stood back to look Emily up and down. 'Course if you were starting the buffing, you'd have a brown paper or newspaper apron over all this to catch the worse of the dirt, but you needn't put that on today.' She paused and frowned. 'You're a bit old to be starting as an errand lass, but since you've had no experience, I've no choice. And I can only pay you half a crown a week to start with, but I reckon you'll soon pick the buffing up. Watch how the other girls work whenever you can. Now, you're a bit late this morning. Not your fault, lass,' she added hastily. 'I knew Lizzie would have to bring you the first morning, so I came in early and got everything ready for them. You see, they're paid piece rates. You know what that means, don't you?' When Emily nodded, Ruth Nicholson went on, 'So, they mustn't be kept waiting for what they need. Usually, the errand lass must get here well before eight o'clock to get everything ready for the buffer girls coming in. So, from tomorrow, that's the time you must start. Now, first of all, you must light the fire in the stove and sweep up the work-shop. I like everything nice and tidy. I'm a bit of a tartar for the place being kept as clean as possible. Orreight?' For the first time since Emily had met her, there was a twinkle in the woman's eyes. It was good to see that she was sometimes able to forget the dreadful sadness in her heart, even if it was for only a brief moment. 'After that, I shall give you instructions as to how to fetch the work and share it out amongst the buffers. You'll also have to run errands for me and for the girls so that they can keep working. They'll ask you to do their shopping for them, but they'll give you a list, so always mind you've got a piece of paper and a pencil handy to write it down, 'cos if you come back without something, they'll only send you again.' She leaned forward and whispered, 'And I'll ask you to get me a bit of snuff now and again.'

Emily managed not to look surprised or shocked; she would ask Lizzie about it later. Instead, keeping her face straight, she merely nodded.

'Now, about dinner time,' the missus was not finished with her list of jobs the errand girl had to do. 'A lot of the girls bring their dinners in a basin – a stew, perhaps, or meat and potato pie – and it's up to you to make sure it's piping hot by the time they stop. Sometimes, they'll send you out for fish and chips as a treat, but mostly they bring their food from home. It's cheaper. And then,' on and on it went, 'you need to mash tea for them and wash out the mugs afterwards. On a Monday morning, your very first job – and this is important, Emily – is to mix up a new bag of Trent sand and oil. The girls use it in the buffing process. Share it out to each girl's place on t'side – that's the bench – near them. There, I think that's about it for now. I know it sounds a lot to remember, but you'll learn as you go along. And there's other little jobs you can do when you get a spare minute but I'll tell you about them when you've had time to settle in.'

A spare minute, Emily thought, what's one of those? But, of course, she said nothing.

Emily was thankful she had a good memory and was quick and neat in her work, whatever that work was. She felt Ruth's eyes on her, but she never slackened for a moment. She was at everyone's beck and call all day.

'Emily luv, I need more sand.'

'Can you go t'shop and get me some bread an' milk, else my ol' man won't have owt for his snap tin tomorrow.'

'Emily, fetch us another pan of work, luv.'

'Emily, you haven't dished the work out yet. We don't want the wheels stoppin'. Look sharp.' This was from the missus, whose orders Emily had the sense to obey first.

'Have you got the dinners on, lass? Me belly thinks me throat's been cut.'

'I'm 'aving fish an' chips today. Emily, can you fetch them for us?'

'I can't afford them this week. Bread an' dripping'll have to do me.'

'Emily, see what's on at the Empire this weekend while you're out, luv. I fancy a night out at the theatre. You up for that, Nell?'

But Nell would always shake her head and carry on working. It soon became clear to Emily that Nell was the hardest-working buffer girl of them all and the best at the job too. She loved to watch her working and see the shining spoons and forks emerging under her skilful hands; hands that bore the scars of cuts and burns from hot resin, an everyday danger for a buffer girl. Apart from walking into town at dinner time and meeting the other girls on a Sunday afternoon, Nell didn't go out very much. But still she sang every day at her wheel along with the other buffer girls. They sang all the latest music-hall songs: 'Burlington Bertie from Bow', 'Down at the Old Bull and Bush', 'My Old Man Said Follow the Van'. Nell's favourite was always 'Hello, Hello, Who's Your Lady Friend?'. Emily noticed that they avoided singing any of the songs like 'Oh! It's a Lovely War' and 'It's a Long Way to Tipperary' – anything that might remind them of the recent war that was still so painful for all of them. Nearly everyone in the buffing shop had a relative or friend who had joined the Sheffield City Battalion – the local pals' battalion – and many, mown down in the battle for the village of Serre on the Somme, had not come back.

Emily couldn't remember ever having felt so weary in the whole of her young life. Working beside Josh at the candle making was nothing compared to this. By the time the hooter sounded for the end of the day, every bone in her body seemed to ache and her eyes stung with the gritty sand flying about the workshop and with tiredness too.

By the fourth day, Emily had all her chores under control and it earned her a smile and a nod from Ruth Nicholson.

'You're doing ever so well,' Lizzie told her as they walked home. 'The missus doesn't give praise very often.'

As if to prove Lizzie's point, the next morning Ruth said, 'I'll show you how to cut out the paper aprons for the girls. We use the brown paper that's used for wrapping the finished cutlery in, but, failing that, we use newspaper. The girls bring in whatever they can at the beginning of the week.'

Emily nodded but said nothing. The Ryans could no longer afford the luxury of buying a daily newspaper to read although Emily promised herself that the very day she started to earn a decent wage, she would take one home for her father on payday. She knew he missed sitting at the table and reading the latest news. Sometimes, it was the only thing that seemed to stop his constant shaking. For the next two hours Ruth showed her how to lay out the paper on a table and cut out the shape of an apron. These were then stacked neatly for the girls to help themselves to whenever they needed one.

'I'll never remember it all, Lizzie,' Emily confided to her new-found friend one day as they walked home after work. 'There's so much to do.'

'The main thing is to keep the girls supplied with what they need. If you slow down their work, they'll get cross. It's money lost to them. Anything else can wait, though they do like their dinner ready on time.'

Emily groaned. 'Oh don't.'

'We'll all help you. Nell's sort of head buffer girl; she'll keep you on your toes. It's not an official title – she doesn't get extra pay – but she's the best worker of all of us, though it pains me to admit it.' Lizzie laughed. 'Oh, and by the way, I saw your face when the missus said you'd got to buy your own work clothes. Don't worry. I've got some old ones you can start off with.'

As they entered the courtyard, the door of Lizzie's home opened and a young man stepped out. He was wearing a grey suit and a striped waistcoat with a white shirt and tie, black boots and a cloth cap. Dark haired like his sister, he was thin faced, with a bony, hooked nose and steely blue eyes that were set a little too close together for Emily's liking. He grinned at her cheekily. 'So you're our pretty new neighbour Lizzie can't stop talking about. But to be honest –' and that was something Emily instinctively doubted happened very often in his world – 'it's your brother she talks about the most.' His piercing eyes raked her up and down, making her feel distinctly uncomfortable. Dressed in her workaday, drab and now dirty clothes, Emily felt at a distinct disadvantage. The young man was certainly not dressed for work and she guessed he was heading out for a night on the town. Unnecessarily, for Emily had guessed exactly who the young man was, Lizzie said, 'This is my brother, Mick. I told you about him.'

Emily smiled thinly and nodded in greeting.

'If you're off into town,' Lizzie said, 'just watch yourself, our Mick. Don't go getting kaylied.'

'Now, why would I get drunk? I've got to keep my wits about me in my business.'

'Well, don't go getting into any fights. You'll upset Mam.'

As he passed close to them, he tweaked Lizzie's nose playfully. 'You worry too much, Sis. I can take care of missen. Night, night, sleep tight, watch the bugs don't bite.' And he pushed his hands into his pockets and walked jauntily out of the yard, whistling loudly and, surprisingly, quite tunefully.

'He's a one,' Lizzie said, watching him go and shaking her head. 'He's a right worry to Mam and me. Always in some scrape or other right from when he was little. But he's a good lad, really. He looks out for me and

Mam. We don't go short of anything if Mick can help it. I just hope he doesn't get himself into real trouble. It'd be the death of me mam.'

As Emily walked in through the door of their house, longing to have a quick wash and lie down on her bed, even if only for a few minutes, Martha greeted her with the words, 'I need help with your dad. He's had a nasty turn today and his breathing's worse.'

'What did you expect, Mam?' Tired and irritable and thinking longingly of the little cottage back in Ashford, Emily snapped, 'Bringing him here . . . the air's thick with smoke. You can hardly see the sun sometimes.'

Martha's eyes flashed. 'I'll have less of your cheek, miss. And where's Josh? How's he got on today?'

Not a word of enquiry about her day, the girl noted wryly. 'I don't know. I haven't seen him since first thing this morning.'

'No doubt he's doing so well they want him to work late,' Martha said. Her faith in her son's abilities knew no bounds.

'Whatever it is you want me to do, Mam, I must have a wash first.'

For the first time Martha seemed to become aware of her daughter's blackened face and dirty hands. 'Go on, then,' she said impatiently, 'but be quick. I need to get your dad upstairs to his bed, else he'll likely fall out of the chair.'

It was a struggle to get Walter up the steep, narrow stairs.

'Couldn't we have waited until Josh gets home?'

'No, we'll have to manage. Josh has got his career to think of. We can't expect him always to be on hand. Right, you go downstairs and peel the potatoes whilst

I get him sorted. Come on, Walter, do try to help yourself a bit.'

Emily glanced at the pathetic figure of her dad. He was nothing like the man she remembered, who had marched away to war so proudly.

Downstairs, Emily began to prepare the meal, swaying with tiredness as she stood at the sink. She heard a slight noise behind her, a scuffle, and turned to see a huge rat looking up at her with bright eyes. She screamed and the animal scuttled away, squeezing through a hole at the bottom of the door. Her heart was beating fast as she leaned against the sink. It wasn't that she was afraid of rats – she'd seen plenty in the countryside – but she'd never seen one intruding into their home.

'Oh Mam,' she whispered, as tears ran down her face. 'Whatever sort of a place have you brought us to?'

Nine

When Josh arrived home each evening during his first week at work, Martha fussed around him. 'What sort of day did you have? What job are you doing now?'

On the Friday, Josh glanced around the kitchen. 'Where's Dad?'

Before her mother could answer, Emily said, 'He's in bed. He's had a bad day. His breathing's terrible.'

'Never mind about that now,' Martha snapped. 'He'll be all right. Tell me about how you're getting on. Did – did you see Mr Trippet?' Her mother seemed strangely agitated, Emily thought, but maybe it was just her eagerness to see Josh settled in a job with prospects.

But Josh was not to be diverted from his concern for his father. 'You should have waited for me to come home. You must have had a struggle to get him up those stairs.'

'We did,' Emily said tartly, ignoring Martha's angry glance.

'Well, wait for me to get home in future. I'll make sure I'm home on time every night.'

'We'll do no such thing. If you're needed to work, you'll stay there. How can you hope to advance if you don't show willing? We can manage.'

The brother and sister exchanged a glance but said no more.

'Did you see Trip today?' Emily asked.

'Yes, he came to see how I was getting on now that I've been there a few days. They've started me at the bottom, as you might expect.'

'Yeah, me too. I'm what they call an errand girl and—' Emily began, but her mother brushed her aside.

'At the bottom?' Martha said, ignoring Emily and disgruntled at the very thought that her precious boy had not been started at least halfway up the ladder. 'With all your talents, you should start a bit higher up than the bottom.'

'I know nothing about the cutlery industry, Mam. I'm a candle maker.'

'Not any more, Josh. You're going to be someone in this city and before very long, if I have anything to do with it. So, have they started you on an apprenticeship yet?'

'Sort of.'

'"Sort of"? What kind of an answer is that?'

'They've set me on as an apprentice table-knife grinder,' Josh replied shortly. 'But an apprenticeship at Trippets' can take seven years *and* you have to agree not to get married during that time. So, I'm not happy about that.'

He returned his mother's glare steadfastly and it was Martha who was the first to look away. 'Besides,' Josh added, trying to drive home his point, 'apprentices' wages are a pittance. I'd be better doing a proper job where I can earn a bit more.'

'It still won't be much if you take an unskilled job. You're better to get trained properly, though I don't like the sound of you being just a grinder.' She turned to Emily, almost as an afterthought. 'And what about you, miss? What will you be earning?' Still she showed no concern about the job Emily was doing or how she'd been getting on – just what money she would bring home at the end of each week.

'At the moment, half a crown a week.'

'Two and sixpence?' Martha shrieked. 'How do you think that's going to feed four of us, to say nothing of rent and coal?'

She gave a derogatory sniff and turned away, disappointed in both her children.

A little later, when Josh and Emily sat down to a late tea and Martha was upstairs helping Walter to eat, Josh said quietly, 'Trip sent a message.'

Emily looked up sharply, holding her breath until Josh said, 'He wants you to meet him near the Town Hall on Sunday afternoon at about two o'clock.'

As they heard their mother's footsteps coming down the stairs, Emily whispered, 'Thanks, Josh.'

Her brother grinned. 'I can see by the sparkle in your eyes that you'll be going, then?'

'Just try and stop me.'

'I wouldn't dare,' Josh said with a chuckle and then his smile faded as he murmured, 'I just wish Amy was here and we could all go out – the four of us – like we used to do.'

Emily shot him an understanding glance, but could say no more as Martha came back into the room.

'You doin' anything after?' Lizzie asked Emily as they walked home at dinner time on Saturday after that first long week at work.

'Only helping Mam – if she needs it.'

'When we've washed our work clothes and if yer mam doesn't need you, get yer hat on and I'll take you shopping in the best shops in town.'

Emily laughed, not too embarrassed to admit, 'I've no money to spare.'

But her new-found friend was not to be put off. 'Doesn't cost owt to look. I'll tek you to Walsh's.'

Excitement churned Emily's insides. She loved the hustle and bustle of the city and couldn't wait to see the shops she'd only heard about.

'All right. I'll meet you about two.'

Lizzie took her to the city centre. As they reached the busy streets, Emily gazed around her in awe at the magnificent buildings. People were hurrying to and fro or sauntering along the street, pausing now and again to look in the brightly coloured shop windows. Trams rattled past, a man in a top hat was driving a horse and cart delivering barrels, and there were several cyclists weaving in and out of the traffic. She felt a thrill of excitement at the vibrancy of the city after the placid lanes of the countryside.

'Oh, look over there, Lizzie,' Emily said, as a display of the latest fashions across the street caught her eye. In her eagerness, she stepped out into the road.

'Look out!' Lizzie yelled and grabbed her arm, hauling her out of the pathway of an oncoming tram.

Emily felt her heart race as the vehicle passed them.

'By heck,' Lizzie laughed shakily, 'don't go getting yourself run over. You're not in the country now, y'know. You'd better hang on to me.'

Gratefully, Emily linked her arm through Lizzie's and stayed close to her side.

They wandered through Walsh's department store, admiring the latest fashions in women's clothes, trying on hats when the eagle-eyed assistants weren't watching. On through perfumery, breathing in the expensive scents they'd never be able to afford. In the household department, the furniture only merited a cursory glance from the two young women, who were not even thinking of their 'bottom drawer' yet, but they did admire the delicate china tea sets and dinner services, the sparkling glassware and then Lizzie pointed to the display of cutlery. 'Look, they even sell some of ours. Don't they look grand set out in boxes?' She bent closer. 'They've got a lovely finish on them. I bet Nell did those. She's the best buffer we've got, you know.'

As they walked home arm in arm, Lizzie said, 'We'll go out again tomorrow afternoon and meet up with the other girls from work. We go most weeks – only window shopping, mind, when the shops are shut.' She laughed. 'It's the only way we can be sure we don't spend money. And, of course, we get dressed up in our Sunday best and show the lads what they're missing. Come with us, do,' she urged. 'It'll help you get to know the others. There's not much chance when there's noisy machinery going all the time at work. You haven't mastered the art of lip-reading yet, have you?'

Emily had been amused to see how the girls still talked to one another even though proper conversation was impossible; they were all expert lip-readers.

'Oh, I'd love to,' she said, trying to be sure her tone sounded regretful. 'Maybe another time.'

'Is it your dad? Will you have to stay home tomorrow and help your mam?'

'Well, yes and no.' Emily hesitated, unsure whether to confide in Lizzie. Their friendship was very new and she wasn't yet sure how trustworthy the girl was. She decided to be straightforward. 'Are you good at keeping secrets?'

'Ooh, Emily, do tell.'

'Only if you promise.'

'Cross my heart,' Lizzie said, her eyes dancing.

'I'm meeting someone on Sunday afternoon.'

Lizzie's mouth rounded. 'Who?'

'Trip. I mean, Thomas Trippet.'

Now Lizzie gasped and her mouth dropped open. 'Not him from Trippets'? The son?'

Emily nodded. 'I knew him back home. In Ashford. That's where his family have a big country house.'

'Oh.' There was disappointment in Lizzie's tone. 'So you're just old friends, are you? No big romance? Because I've heard he's ever so handsome. Half the girls in Sheffield are after him.'

Emily laughed aloud, visualizing the many hundreds of girls who must live in the city, queuing up to meet Trip. Mind you, she thought, I don't blame them.

'He is lovely and yes, we're just very good friends.'

There was a pause before Lizzie added softly, 'But you'd like it to be more, wouldn't you?'

Emily sighed. 'Oh yes, I would like it to be a lot more.'

Lizzie hugged Emily's arm to her side. 'Then you go to meet him on Sunday, but you must tell me *all* about it afterwards.'

'Josh knows, but not a word in front of my mother, please.'

'Of course not. I love secrets.' Trying to sound casual, Lizzie added, 'Is Josh the sort to go for a walk on a Sunday afternoon?'

Emily sighed and decided it had to be done. 'I really don't know about here in the city. Back home—'

Lizzie shook Emily's arm a little impatiently. 'You keep on about "back home". This is your home now. Yours and Josh's too.'

'Yes, I know, but . . .'

'But what?'

Emily took a deep breath. 'There were four of us who spent a lot of time together when we were younger. Josh, me, Trip and –' she bit her lip before blurting out – 'Amy.'

Lizzie's tone was tight as she asked, 'And who, might I ask, is Amy?'

'She lived next door with her father. He was – is – the village blacksmith.'

'And?'

'Well, she and Josh – she and Josh –' Emily ran her tongue around her dry lips – 'started courting properly about three months ago.'

Lizzie was silent for a moment before saying quietly, 'And are they still courting?'

'He's promised to go back when he's twenty-one and Mam can't rule him any more.'

Lizzie laughed wryly. 'If I really loved someone, I wouldn't let my mam stop me, I can tell you.'

'No, I can believe that. But Josh is a little different.'

'He's weak, you mean?'

'No, I don't,' Emily flashed back. 'Far from it. He wanted to marry Amy and stay in Ashford. He didn't want to come here any more than I did, but Mam said she wouldn't give her consent to his marriage and he needs that. He's only eighteen.'

Lizzie was thoughtful. 'So, is he still seeing this Amy? Does he plan to go back to visit her?'

Emily shrugged. 'I know he'd like to, but it's costly to travel back there. It must be all of twenty miles. He's written to her, though. I know that.'

At that moment, they arrived at the court and went into their own homes, but not before Emily had noticed the smug expression on Lizzie's face.

Ten

Amy sat at the kitchen table in the living quarters behind her father's blacksmith's shop with Josh's letter in her hand. He was a good writer; the letter was full of a description of their journey, their arrival in the city and his good fortune in finding a job so quickly.

. . . though it was all thanks to Trip, I have to admit. So, I'm working at Trippets' and Emily has a job too. A lot of folk who work in the cutlery industry live in this area of the city and in the court where we're living – it's a courtyard behind a street, with houses and small work-shops on all four sides – there's a nice girl living next door who's got friendly with Emily. She took her to meet the missus she works for – that's the woman in charge of the buffer girls – and she gave our Em a job. So, we're all fixed up, Amy, and the sooner I can get some money saved up, the sooner I can come back and marry you . . .

'What's he got to say for himself, then?' Bob Clark asked a little brusquely. He was more disappointed than he cared to admit that Josh had left the village. He had liked the lad – still did. He couldn't just switch off his fondness for Josh, even though the young man hadn't been strong enough to defy his mother. He couldn't do it any more than Amy could. But he couldn't bear to see the sadness on her face and the anxiety in her eyes.

'Not much really,' Amy said softly, her gaze still on Josh's scrawling writing. 'The place where they're living sounds a bit cramped but he says the folk there seem friendly enough.' She paused briefly, wondering just how friendly this pretty girl-next-door already was with Josh. She took a deep breath and went on, 'He's got a job at Mr Trippet's works. He says he met up with Trip and he got him the job.'

Bob looked up sharply. 'Did he now? Mm. I wonder what old man Trippet will say about that when he finds out?'

'Why? What d'you mean, Dad?'

'Oh nothing, love. What else does he say?'

'Nothing much – really. Except that he still intends to come back here when—' Suddenly Amy gulped and tears flooded down her cheeks.

'Oh Amy, me lass, don't take on so.' Bob pushed back his chair and came around the table to kneel at her side. He put his arms about her and she buried her face in his neck.

'It's all right, me little lass. Don't fret. I'll look after you – and the bairn.'

Amy gasped and pulled back a little from him to stare into his face with wide, frightened eyes. 'You – you know?'

'Aye, love, I do. I recognize the signs. I've seen you rushing out to the privy every morning and hardly able to stand at the stove to cook bacon and eggs for my breakfast.' He smiled sorrowfully. 'Just like your poor mam was when she was carrying you.'

'Oh Dad. I'm so sorry. I wouldn't have – but he said he loved me – said we were to be married in the spring.'

'I know, I know. And you loved him.'

'What would Mam have said? She'd have been so ashamed of me.'

Bob's arms tightened round her as he gave a soft chuckle. 'No, she wouldn't, because we had what they call a shotgun wedding. Your mam was three months gone with you by the time we got married.'

'And then – and then you lost her when she had me.'

'Aye, I did, but she gave me you and she'd've wanted me to stand by you and take care of you just as she would have done if she'd still been here.'

'Oh Dad!' Amy hugged her father and they clung together, gaining strength from each other.

'It'll be all right, Amy love, I promise. We'll tell Josh and—'

Amy pulled back a little and looked up into her father's face. Her tears tore at his heart. 'Please, Dad, I don't want Josh to know.'

'Why ever not? He's a good lad. I'm sure he'd come back at once if he knew, ne'er mind what his mother said.'

'But that's just what I *don't* want. If he comes back, it's got to be because he wants to and not out of a sense of duty.'

For a moment, Bob struggled to agree but then he understood. For Amy, a 'shotgun wedding' was not the best way to start married life. She would never know, deep down, if Josh had really wanted to marry her or whether it had been because he'd felt obliged to do so.

Bob's voice was unsteady as he said, 'I think you're wrong, love, but I do see why you're saying it.' He kissed her forehead and murmured, 'You're a brave lass and, if Josh doesn't come back, we'll look after the little one together.'

Touched by her gentle father's understanding, Amy's tears flowed even faster.

Sunday afternoon was cold, but fine and bright. After attending the nearest church that morning with her mother and brother and then helping Martha with the household chores, Emily slipped out of the house and found her way to the Town Hall where she stood on the corner beneath the clock to wait for Trip. Back in the court, from her bedroom window, Lizzie had watched her go. She was supposed to be meeting her workmates, but she'd hung back, hoping to catch sight of Josh. After half an hour of watching for him, Lizzie put on her best coat and hat and left her home, walking the few paces to their neighbour's door. She knocked quietly, just in case the old man was asleep. Josh's father wasn't really that old, she supposed – no older than her own mother – but because of his dreadful injuries, he certainly looked it.

After a few moments, the door opened slowly and Josh stood there. 'Oh hello, Lizzie. Emily's not here – she's gone out for . . . for a walk.'

'I know.' Lizzie winked conspiratorially. 'And I know where she's gone.'

Josh glanced nervously over his shoulder, then turned back towards her, grinned and put his finger to his lips.

Lizzie giggled. 'I know that, an' all. Not a word, I promise.' Lizzie paused and then, with her head on one side, she said, 'I've been thinking. It's a long walk to Trippets' and you won't want to waste money on tram fares, so I think you'll need a bicycle to get to Creswick Street. I'll ask our Mick, if you like.'

79

'It's good of you Lizzie, but I don't think I could afford—'

Lizzie waved her hand. 'Don't worry about that. You can pay Mick over several weeks. He won't mind – if *I* ask him.'

'What's he do, then?'

'Oh, this and that,' Lizzie said airily. 'Me and Mam don't rightly know. Some sort of wheeling and dealing, we reckon. Mick'll never tell us, but he's a good bloke to know if you want owt. He seems to know a lot of people and they all must like him, 'cos he can get them to do anything he wants. That's settled, then, I'll ask him. Now, I just wondered, if you've nothing to do, whether you'd like a walk out. I could show you a bit of the city.'

For a brief moment, Josh hesitated and Lizzie guessed he was thinking about this girl he had back in Ashford, but then, as if making up his mind, he smiled and said, 'Aye, why not? Dad's lying on his bed and Mam's having a nap in front of the fire, so I've nowt to do.'

Lizzie threw back her head as she laughed, an infectious, tinkling sound. Then in a broad Sheffield accent she said, 'Eeh, tha's even beginnin' to talk like us.'

Josh stepped back a little and pulled his cap from the hook on the back of the door. 'Right, I'm ready.'

As they crossed the courtyard they saw Billy Nicholson coming towards them.

'Oh no,' Lizzie breathed. 'I hope he's not going to tag along with us. He's forever chasing after me.'

But Josh smiled and held out his hand. 'Hello. I'm Josh. We haven't met before, but you know my sister, Emily.'

Billy nodded curtly, but did not take the proffered hand. Instead, his gaze went to Lizzie's face and then

80

his glance dropped to where she had tucked her hand, with a possessive gesture, through Josh's arm. 'You going out, Lizzie?'

'I'm just going to show Josh the sights. He's new here. He doesn't know the city.' She giggled. 'I don't want him to get lost.'

For a brief moment, a bleak look crossed Billy's face, but then he forced a laugh and said, 'I'd've thought your Mick would have been the best person to show him the city. He certainly knows it.'

Lizzie frowned. 'I wouldn't cross our Mick, if I was you, Billy –' she paused and added softly – 'or me.'

'Ooo, I'm quaking in me boots.' He nodded towards Josh. 'Well, good luck, mate. You're gonner need it, getting yourself involved with that family.'

Then he turned away back towards his own home, but Josh noticed the stoop of his shoulders and knew instinctively that he wished him anything but 'good luck' where Lizzie was concerned.

As they walked out into the street, Josh said, 'Is there anything between you and Billy?'

'Heavens, no! The very idea. Now, come on, let me show you this wonderful city of ours. Where would you like to go?'

Josh shrugged. 'I haven't the faintest idea. I don't know Sheffield at all – except the way to get to work – so you decide.'

'Right, then, we'll head for the Town Hall and I'll show you places on the way. All right?'

'Whatever you say.'

As they walked along – and she was gratified that Josh hadn't pulled his arm away from hers – Lizzie said, 'Your Mam's got big plans for you, hasn't she?'

Josh sighed. 'Yes, she has, but I don't think it'll ever

happen. She just had this bee in her bonnet about us coming to the city, where she's convinced I'll make my fortune. But I was happy back in Ashford.'

'What did you do there? Work, I mean?'

'I had my own little business – well, I took it over from Dad when he . . . when he . . .' Lizzie squeezed his arm comfortingly and Josh took a steadying breath and went on, 'I was the village candle maker.'

There was no mistaking the wistful note in his tone and Lizzie wondered if it was longing for his old way of life or the girl he'd left behind. Perhaps both.

'It sounds nice,' she said carefully, 'but I think your mother's right, you know. There are far more opportunities in the city for a clever young man like you.'

Josh chuckled and glanced down at her. She really was a very pretty girl but not, he thought loyally, half as pretty as his Amy. 'How do you know if I'm clever or not? You don't know me.'

'Ah, but I will,' Lizzie said and there was no mistaking the determination in her voice. 'And besides, Emily says you are.' Mentally, Lizzie crossed her fingers at the little white lie. 'Did she think you should come here?'

Josh shook his head.

'Not even to be nearer Trip – is that his name?'

Josh was quiet for a moment, mulling over what Lizzie was suggesting, then he said firmly, 'No, she didn't think we should move. She was worried for our dad. And she was right. He's been worse since we got here. He's spending more time than ever in bed.'

They had been walking for some time when Lizzie stopped and said, 'This is our Town Hall. Isn't it a lovely building?'

'Indeed it is,' Josh said, gazing up at the huge building and at the ornate clock tower.

'They say it's made of Derbyshire stone and it was opened by Queen Victoria about twenty-four years ago. My dad was there that day. He remembered seeing her sitting in her carriage dressed in black. She never got out, he said, but somehow a signal was sent and three men opened the doors, just as if she'd actually done it herself.'

Josh glanced down at her as he asked gently, 'What happened to your dad?'

For a moment, Lizzie's face was bleak. 'He died when I was ten. Consumption, they said, so you see, that's why me mam and me can sympathize with you. He was so ill and he had to go into Winter Street. It's a hospital for infectious diseases and – and tuberculosis.'

Josh squeezed her arm against him. 'I'm sorry I asked, Lizzie.'

'Oh, don't be. I'm quite glad to talk about him. I never like to speak about him to Mam, and as for our Mick, well, I daren't mention his name in front of him.'

'He took his death badly, did he?'

To Josh's surprise, Lizzie shook her head. 'No, he didn't. They didn't get on, you see. Mick's four years older than me and he was wild as a youngster. Me dad used to leather him summat rotten.' She paused and then asked, 'Your dad ever whip you?'

Josh wrinkled his forehead. 'Not that I can remember. He was a gentle soul, poor devil.' Then he laughed wryly. 'It was me mam who used to chase me with the copper stick. And Em – I reckon she got it more often than I did.'

They walked on in silence for a few moments, until Lizzie said more cheerfully, 'Come on, let's go and look at the parish church. It's even more magnificent than the Town Hall. We're very proud of it and actually it's a cathedral now.'

'Right you are, lead on and keep your eye out for Emily and Trip. She was meeting him outside the Town Hall. Maybe we'll see them.'

'I hope so. I'd like to meet this Trip.'

Eleven

When she saw Trip coming towards her, Emily felt a fluttering of excitement. Coal-black hair and a smile so wide and expansive that his eyes almost seemed to close.

'Hey,' he greeted her and, taking her shoulders in his hands, he kissed her forehead. 'You look very smart. A real "townie" already.'

Emily pulled a face. 'I'd sooner be back in Ashford, racing you up to Monsal Head – and beating you.'

Trip threw back his head and laughed aloud. Dressed in his Sunday best too, he didn't look so weary as he had done on the night they'd met him outside his father's works. He was every inch the handsome young man she remembered; the image of him she carried in her mind's eye – and in her heart. He took her hand and put it through his arm. 'Come,' he said, 'I want to show you Weston Park. It'll remind you of the countryside back home and it's not too far from where you're living. I thought it would be easier for us to meet there.'

Emily was heartened to hear him referring to Ashford as 'home'. But then she realized that, as his parents still lived there, Trip no doubt still considered it to be home. They began to walk back the way Emily had come. 'What about you? I don't even know where you're living.'

'I've got lodgings in Carr Road, just round the corner from the factory, but I've got my bicycle, so it doesn't matter to me where we meet. I was thinking of you having to walk.'

Emily's heart felt as if it had turned over. So, not only was he being most considerate to her, but he was also implying that they would be meeting frequently.

Trip pointed out places of interest as they headed towards the park, then suddenly he said, 'Oh look, over there. There's Josh.'

Emily followed the line of Trip's pointing finger and saw her brother and, to her dismay, Lizzie with her arm possessively through Josh's.

'Who's that with him?' Trip asked, squinting against the autumn sunlight. 'It's not Amy, is it?'

'No, it isn't,' Emily said, flatly. 'It's the girl who lives next door to us in the court. Lizzie Dugdale.'

'Oh.' For a moment, Trip looked uncertain. 'But I thought . . . I mean, he and Amy – aren't they . . . ?'

'Yes, they are. They're engaged and they wanted to get married next spring, but Mam had other ideas.'

'Ah, yes.' Trip sighed and added with a note of bitterness, 'I understand, if anyone does. I know all about parental control.'

'Come on, we'll have to go across, I suppose. Josh has seen us.'

As the two couples headed towards each other, Emily asked softly, 'Didn't you want to come to the city either?'

Trip wrinkled his forehead. 'It's difficult. If I'm to take over my father's business one day – and there's no one else to do it – I realize I have to learn it from the bottom up. He's right about that, I know, but . . .'

'But what?' Emily prompted gently.

He sighed. 'I get a lot of stick from the other men because I'm the boss's son. They're either jealous and make snide remarks about why I'm working where I am, or they take advantage and give me all the worst jobs they can find for me to do.'

'That sounds a bit stupid of them. Don't they realize that one day you will be in charge and you could so easily take revenge on them?'

'I *could*, but they probably know I wouldn't.' He grinned. 'I'm far too soft, Emily, and I'm pretty sure they all think I'm weak-willed because I didn't stand up to my father.'

'About starting at the bottom? Why would you – stand up to him, I mean – when you agree with him?'

'No – no, it wasn't about that. It – it was something else. Nothing to do with work or the business.'

Emily was about to ask what that was, but now Josh and Lizzie were within earshot and as the distance between them closed, Emily could see the self-satisfied expression on Lizzie's face. She looked just like the proverbial cat that had got the cream!

After introductions had been made, Lizzie said, 'Where are you two off to?'

'Weston Park,' Trip said. 'Want to come?'

Emily's heart sank. Not only did she want to spend the afternoon with Trip on their own, but she also didn't want to encourage Lizzie to be with Josh. The girl didn't need any more encouragement! But Emily was forced to admit that it was a merry foursome who arrived at the park. The only trouble for Emily was that it was Lizzie with them and not Amy.

They entered through the ornate wrought-iron gates and sauntered along the pathways, crossing the wooden bridge over the duck pond.

'The grounds are lovely. It's vibrant with colour in spring and summer when all the flowers are out, although the autumn golds and browns are lovely too,' Trip told them.

'What's that?' Josh pointed to a hexagonal-shaped structure with an almost pagoda type roof.

'It's the bandstand. They're not here today, but in summer there's often a band playing. People bring picnics and sit on the grass to listen.'

'Maybe we could do that,' Lizzie murmured. 'The four of us.'

Emily sighed inwardly. It sounded as if Lizzie had long-term plans for her friendship with Josh if she was already talking about outings next summer!

Although the last thing she wanted to do was to leave Trip, Emily said, 'Josh, it's time we were getting back home. I'm sorry, Trip.'

Wordlessly, but understanding completely, Trip squeezed her hand. 'Same time next week,' he whispered. 'Only next time, we'll meet here – near the bandstand. All right?'

Her heart thudded, 'Oh yes, Trip. That'd be lovely.'

He leaned a little closer. 'And we'll try and drop the other two, eh?'

Emily's expression was grim. 'If I have my way, there'll be no "other two" next week. I'll be having words with Josh.'

'Oh dear.' Trip grinned. 'Poor Josh.'

At times, Emily could be almost as formidable as her mother, Martha. '"Poor Josh" nothing. He's got a lovely girl back home.'

Trip sighed. 'I see you still refer to Ashford as "back home", just like I do.'

'Well, it is, isn't it? None of us – except Mam – wanted to come here, though I must admit,' she added, smiling up at him, 'it has its compensations.'

The three of them – Emily, Josh and Lizzie – walked home whilst Trip mounted his bicycle and set off in the opposite direction. Emily was determined to give the other two no more time alone together. As they paused briefly in the yard outside their homes, Emily said briskly, 'Come on, Josh, Mam will be needing our help.'

And indeed she was, for the moment Emily opened the door, Martha launched a tirade of reproach at her for having gone out at all.

'I know you have to work in the week, but I could do with a bit of help on a Sunday. Where've you been until this time?' On and on her grumbling went, almost until they went upstairs to bed. But not a word of rebuke, Emily noticed bitterly, was aimed at Josh.

When they'd retired to the attic room they were obliged to share, Emily tackled her brother about Lizzie. A curtain had been tacked to the ceiling down the centre of the room affording each of them a little privacy, but before Josh could disappear into his half of the bedroom, Emily grasped his arm and said bluntly, 'You know she's after you, don't you? Please, Josh, don't let her get her claws into you. Think of Amy.'

Josh turned to face her solemnly. 'I think of Amy all the time and, yes, I do realize what Lizzie is up to, but I won't let it go too far, I promise.'

'But don't lead her on. That's not fair either. I've told her you've got a girl back in Ashford, but I think she needs to hear it from you.'

'I don't want to upset her, though. She's been helpful to us – finding you a job, for one thing. And so's her mam. We don't want to make enemies of them. Mrs Dugdale is on hand if Mam needs help when we're not here.'

Emily sighed. 'I know and I agree with you. We've

got to be careful, but it would be good if you could somehow just let Lizzie know – tactfully – that there's going to be no romance between you.'

'I'll try,' was all Josh could promise her.

As she'd been instructed, Emily arrived at work the following morning at half past seven, before all the other girls, who were due to start at eight. She mixed new sand and oil and shared it out with a shovelful to each buffer's place on the bench – or side, as she learned the girls called it. Then she lit the stove, got the kettle boiling and set out the mugs for their first tea break of their day and then swept up the workshop. She glanced round, wondering if she'd forgotten anything. She wanted to make a good impression on the missus. She hoped Mrs Nicholson would let her train as a buffer girl very soon.

When the girls arrived, she counted only six. 'Where are the others?' she asked Lizzie.

'Taking a "Saint Monday".'

'Whatever's that?'

'It's an old tradition that most of the firms turn a blind eye to. Some of the girls and a *lot* of the men don't come in on a Monday and end up in the nearest pub as soon as it opens, playing cards or just drinking and chatting. You'd think it was another Saturday night.'

'But what about their work – their pay?'

'Oh, they make it up. They'll work like billy-o the rest of the week.'

Emily glanced round at the other girls, who'd arrived for work. 'But not all of you take Mondays off, eh?'

'We're paid on the amount we do, so, some of us can't afford to miss a whole day's work. Besides, we now get Saturday afternoon off and all day Sunday, so who needs another day? Unless, of course,' Lizzie added archly, 'you've got a beau to meet.'

Emily laughed. 'I shouldn't think Trip'd be allowed Mondays off. Even if he is the boss's son, he's still being treated like an apprentice.'

'And where did you two get to yesterday, might I ask?' Nell Geddis, the ringleader of the buffer girls' Sunday afternoon window-shopping expeditions stood, hands on her hips, facing Lizzie and Emily. She'd taken off the better clothes she'd arrived in, put on an old dress under her buff-brat, and wrapped herself in brown paper. She'd fastened the short sleeves up to prevent them catching in the machinery, tied on a head rag and wound the neck rag round her throat. 'I thought you were coming around town with us.'

'Ah well, we had better things to do,' Lizzie smirked.

'Really? Thanks for that,' Nell said sarcastically and then added, as if curiosity had got the better of her, 'Do tell.'

'We went walking in Weston Park with a couple of handsome young men.'

So much for Lizzie being able to keep secrets, Emily thought wryly.

Nell's eyes widened and then she grinned. 'In that case, you're both forgiven, but we want to hear all about it, don't we, girls?'

There was a chorus of agreement as the girls hurried to dress themselves in their aprons and newspaper and brown-paper clothing.

'When we have a tea-break, I promise,' Lizzie said as the missus came in, her sharp glance raking the room to make sure everyone was ready for work.

'You'd better get cracking, Emily. Be sure you've dished out enough sand for each of us,' Lizzie reminded her, and Emily felt a stab of guilt at the fact that she felt obliged to warn her brother against this friendly and helpful girl. But there was no denying, she thought in her own defence, that Lizzie Dugdale was a veritable siren when it came to men. And the trouble was, Emily was forced to admit, Josh was a softie when it came to a pretty girl with provocative eyes. She'd just have to make sure that he kept his mind firmly fixed on Amy back home.

Twelve

'Thomas Trippet!' Nell exclaimed, thrilled and shocked in equal measure. 'You mean Emily actually *knows* Thomas Trippet?'

'I most certainly do,' Lizzie said, triumphant to have a juicy piece of gossip that was holding all her work-mates enthralled. But now they turned with one accord towards Emily.

'How do you know him?'

'How long have you known him?'

'Are you courting?'

'Oh, you lucky thing. He's *so* handsome!'

The questions came thick and fast.

'We've been friends since childhood. We live – lived – in the same village.'

'But you've found him again – here in the city. How romantic. Are you seeing him next Sunday?'

'I – I hope so.' Emily's tone was unsure; not because of Trip, but because of her mother.

'Well, if you don't meet him, I certainly will.' Nell grinned. She waved her hand towards the other girls. 'You lot can go window shopping on your own.'

They all laughed, Nell along with them. With their blackened faces and rough clothes, they all knew they had little chance of ensnaring the son of a factory owner. And yet, when they dressed up on a Sunday, they were as smart and pretty as any other city lass out for a bit of fun. Nell had a strong face that on a woman would be called handsome rather than beautiful, but, nevertheless, she was a striking-looking girl with auburn hair and green eyes. She was tall and carried herself well, but her trim figure, which she was not ashamed to parade on a Sunday afternoon, was always hidden by the buffer girls' 'uniform' whilst at work and her glorious hair was tucked firmly beneath the head rag. But she was also a kindly, honest girl – if at times a little blunt – and now she touched Emily's arm. 'Don't worry, luv, I'm not out to steal your boyfriend.'

'You'd have a job, our Nell,' Ida shouted as she made her way back to her machine after their break. 'You're a good-looking lass, Nell, but you're not a patch on her with her blond hair and blue eyes.'

Emily blushed and tried to protest but all the girls laughed and, good-naturedly, Nell laughed the loudest of them all.

As they all returned to their machines, Nell prodded Lizzie. 'And you, miss. We'll hear all about your beau at dinner time.'

Oh dear, Emily thought, they're going to encourage Lizzie to make a play for Josh. As if the girl needed any prodding.

Later, as they sat eating, Lizzie said, 'He's Emily's brother, Josh. He's ever so nice.'

'Is he handsome?'

'Of course,' Lizzie said indignantly. 'Would I look at any feller who *wasn't*?'

Laughter rippled amongst them.

I ought to say something here and now, Emily told herself sharply, but somehow she couldn't force the words from her lips. A vision of her poor father floated before her eyes; her family needed the help of their neighbours and if she, Emily, were to antagonize Lizzie, not only would Martha no longer have Mrs Dugdale's support but, also, Lizzie was quite capable of turning all the other buffer girls against her. Emily's life would be made intolerable both at home and at work and she might even be sacked, since the missus also lived in their court. She couldn't let that happen; her family needed her weekly wage.

It would have to come from Josh, she decided, as they all returned to their work, their dinner-time jaunt into the city foregone; what Lizzie had to tell them had been far more entertaining.

But as they walked home that evening, Emily dared to say once again to Lizzie, 'Look, I know you like Josh, but, as I told you, he's engaged to Amy. You're a good friend to our family, Lizzie. I like you a lot and I don't want you to get your hopes up where he's concerned and get hurt. That's all.'

Lizzie was silent for several moments and Emily held her breath, fearing the worst. But then a low, almost seductive chuckle came out of the dusk of the October evening. 'Don't you worry about me, luv. I know exactly what I'm doing and all I'll say is, "Absence makes the heart grow fonder" –' she paused and then added, pointedly – '"of another".'

Emily drew in a deep breath but before she could say anything, Lizzie squeezed her arm and said, 'And yes, I like you a lot, an' all. And whatever happens between me and Josh, we won't let it spoil our friend-ship. Agreed?'

'All right, then, agreed, but—'

'Look, Emily, I appreciate you being honest with me and I can see you're worried about your friend Amy, an' all, but look, luv, if Josh truly loves this girl, then he'll give me my marching orders, now, won't he?'

'Well, yes, I suppose so.'

Emily couldn't keep the doubtful note from her tone. Her brother was so nice; too nice, sometimes, for his own good, she thought. Would he really be strong enough to stand up to Lizzie's wiles? Emily was very much afraid that he wouldn't have the streak of ruthlessness needed to fend off the determined girl.

Whenever she had an odd moment in the day – and there weren't many for an errand girl – Emily watched Nell working. She was fascinated by the way the young woman picked up about half a dozen spoons in one hand, a fistful of the oily, damp sand in the other, and then leaned in to her wheel.

Early in Emily's second week of work, Ruth said, 'Nell is going to let you have a go on her wheel at dinner break. She's our best buffer girl, so you listen to what she tells you.'

'Orreight, luv,' Nell greeted her after Emily had set out all the dinners the girls had brought in and had mashed tea for them. 'We'd better get you dressed up properly now, else you'll get covered in muck. Missus is lending you 'buff-brat and head rag you're wearing, but if she starts you proper on the buffing, you'll need to buy your own.' Emily glanced at what the other girl was wearing. Nell wore an old dress beneath the buff-brat, the short-sleeved, white calico overall, which fastened with ties at the back so that it was easy to take off if it got caught in the spindle.

'Right, lass. Fasten your sleeves to your shoulders with safety pins and then fasten this red cloth round your head like the missus showed you last week. That's it. When you're buffing, you can either tie the two ends on top of your head or leave them down to wipe your face with. Gets right hot in 'ere. But you've got to wear one. It's to protect your hair. We don't want that lovely blond hair getting caught, do we?'

Nell was a bit older than the other girls and they seemed to turn to her for leadership. Even the missus deferred to her on occasions.

'When you buy your own buff-brats an' that, be sure to get a red head rag. A white cap'd be nicer – we tried 'em once – but they get mucky so much quicker.' Nell grinned, showing white, even teeth against her face, which was already covered with grime after only a morning's work. 'Orreight?'

Emily nodded, not knowing how, at this moment, she was ever going to afford to buy the clothes she would need to become a proper buffer girl. Her mother needed every penny of the half-a-crown a week she was being paid now. So she listened carefully to everything that Nell told her. The sooner she could become a buffer girl and earn a little more money each week, the better.

'Now,' Nell went on, 'put this coarse apron on over your buff-brat and then let's tie the paper apron on you.' For the first time, Emily put on one of the brown-paper aprons she'd been cutting out for the other girls and tied newspaper round her legs. 'Missus might start you off as what we call a "rougher" – that's just to get rid of all the dents and marks – so you'll need a piece of sacking tucked in your belt. And then we fasten the other end to 'side. You'll have to get used to all these funny names, Emily luv, else you won't know what we're talking about half the time.'

'What's it for?' Emily asked. 'The sacking?'

'It catches the sand and stops it going all over the

floor, and you can use it again to throw on the spoons and forks when you're working. Now, watch what I do,' she added, picking up a handful of spoons, 'and don't be frit. It'll not bite thee.'

'It might,' Lizzie, overhearing, laughed loudly. 'If she gets her fingers in the wrong place.'

'You'd be better doing one at once,' Nell mouthed to her above the noise of the machine. 'Just to start with.' Emily wondered if she'd ever be as proficient as Nell.

They didn't have long during the dinner breaks, but at the end of the week, Nell came up to Emily. 'The missus says she'd like you to train properly as a buffer girl. She's seen what you can do now, but it's such a short time in just the dinner breaks and before she gives you a buffing wheel of your own, there're a few more things you've got to learn. So, she's said we can stop late after work for a few nights.'

'You mean you as well?'

Nell nodded.

'Will she pay you for the overtime?'

Nell threw back her head and her raucous laughter echoed round the workshop. 'Not likely.'

'I couldn't expect you to work late just – just to help me.'

'Why ever not? We all help each other.' Suddenly, all jollity had gone from Nell's tone and she was very serious. 'Mebbe there'll come a time when I'll need some help. You never know what life's got in store for you, luv. I'll teach you all I know, Emily, and I can do most of the processes a buffer girl's ever likely to need. I learned a lot in the war when the fellers went away – things they wouldn't normally let girls do.' She grinned suddenly. 'It's a horrible thing to say, but the war did a lot of good for women. We've earned some respect. They're even saying that we're all going to get the vote one day.'

But Emily's thoughts were still on the training that Nell was offering. 'If you're sure, I'd be so grateful.'

'Right, then, you tell your folks that for the rest of this week, and probably a couple more after that, you'll be home a bit later. And I'll tell my mam.'

'You still live at home?' Emily ventured. She knew very little about the other girls, and had only picked up snippets of information about their lives outside work. There wasn't much chance for her for conversation when the noisy machines were going full pelt, for she was hopeless at the lip-reading everyone else managed to do.

'Yes,' Nell said shortly and turned away, deliberately, it felt, cutting off any further questions.

At the end of another week, Nell told her, 'You're coming on really well, Emily, though there's still quite a lot I need to teach you, but I'll tell missus that I think you'll soon be able to work a wheel on your own. She'll give you all the easy jobs to start with, and then you'll move on to roughing. Don't forget you have to melt 'resin in a pan and dribble it over the leather buff and then let it set hard before you start like I've shown you.' Nell grinned at her. 'I know there's a lot to remember, luv, and you're only learning one or two processes at the moment, but you look as if you're a quick learner, though don't expect to earn a lot to start with, will you? You'll be slower than the rest of us, but we all are when we start.'

'What about my work as an errand girl? Who's going to do that?'

Nell laughed. 'That's partly the reason we're training

you up. Someone your age shouldn't be on such low wages anyway, and Ida's just told us she's got a niece who's itching to leave school and start work here. Mrs Nicholson promised her that if you prove yourself at the buffing, she'll set Milly on as the new errand girl. And now, we'd best get ourselves home. Our families will be wondering where we've got to.'

And my mam will be in a right old temper because I've not been there all week to help with Dad, Emily thought, but she said nothing. Perhaps her mother would be mollified a little by the thought that, hopefully, Emily would be bringing home a little more in her wage packet from next week.

They left the workshop and parted outside to go in opposite directions. Emily set off, her eyes gradually becoming used to the darkness as she entered the warren of alleyways that led to the court where she lived. They were dark, dismal back alleys, with rats running over discarded rubbish. She didn't like walking this way home, but it was the quickest route. She turned a corner and almost ran into someone. Strong hands gripped her shoulders.

'Well, well, look what we have here, lads. A buffer girl still dressed in all her muck. But looks like she's game for a bit of sport, if you're not too fussy.'

Three other lads surrounded her and her heart pounded in fear. It had been very stupid of her to come this way, especially at night-time. Her anxiety to get home as quickly as possible had robbed her of her common sense.

She was still being held fast, her arms pinned to her sides, as the youth pulled her to him and searched for her mouth, planting a wet kiss on her lips. Then he began to fumble with the fastenings of her blouse.

Struggling, she tried to pull herself free, but he held her fast. She kicked his shins and he yelped in pain, released her with his right hand, but drew it back and smacked her on the left side of her face.

'Ya little bitch! I'll teach you to—'

'Let her go.' Another voice came out of the darkness behind her attacker, a firm authoritative voice.

'Huh?' The young man holding her turned slightly to look at whoever had spoken. 'What you on about? Oh, I see, fancy her yourself, do ya?'

'It's not that,' the voice came again, and then he came closer and in the dim light Emily could just make out his features. She recognized him even before he said, 'It's Emily from our court. She's a mate of my sister's. So you just let her go, Pete, else I just might get a bit cross. And you don't like me when I'm angry, do you?'

The youth released Emily as if he'd been stung – so suddenly that she almost lost her balance. 'Sorry, Mick. I didn't know. I just thought she was some slag out for—'

'Well, she isn't. She's a nice girl. Not that you'd know one if you met one, Pete. Nice girls don't go for the likes of you.' He stepped closer and took Emily's arm, but now it was in a friendly, concerned way. 'You orreight, luv?'

'Yes – yes. Thank you, Mick.'

'Think nothing of it, but you shouldn't be out in the alleyways on your own at this time of the night. Tell you what, I'll walk you home.'

'Oh really,' Emily began to protest – she didn't want to be any more in the Dugdales' debt than her family already was – 'there's no need.'

'There's every need, if you meet another thug like Pete here. Come on.' He tucked her hand through his arm and began to lead her out of the alley. He turned briefly to call over his shoulder, 'I'll see you later, lads.'

As they moved away, Emily was sure she heard her attacker mutter, 'He does want her for himself. I knew he did.'

'So,' Mick asked as they walked side by side, pressed close together in the narrow alley. 'How do you like the big, bad city?'

Emily, recovering from her fright a little, forced a laugh. 'Until just now, I really liked it. It's bustling and exciting and oh, there's so much to see and do. But yes, you're right. I shouldn't have been walking home this late on my own, but I've been so used to just going out whenever and wherever I wanted at home, I – I didn't stop to think.'

It wasn't far to the entrance to their court but Mick walked her right to the door of the Ryans' home. 'There you are, back home, almost safe and sound.' They paused and turned to face each other. Mick touched her cheek gently. 'I hope that ruffian didn't hurt you.'

'No, I've had worse slaps than that in my time,' she murmured and thought, From my mother, if the truth be told. 'But thanks, Mick. I – I don't know what might have happened if you hadn't been there.'

For a moment his face was grim. 'Something not very pleasant for a nice lass like you.' He stared at her through the darkness and then appeared to shake himself before adding, 'Night, then, I'll be off.'

'Night – and thanks.'

He was already halfway across the yard. He didn't turn but merely waved his hand in acknowledgement.

'What time do you call this?' was Martha's only greeting. 'Get yourself washed and come and help me.'

Emily sighed and decided to say nothing about what

had happened, but, later, she would tell Josh. They had better both be on their guard from now on.

Sheffield, though a vibrant and exciting place, was not quite the safe little backwater she had been used to.

Thirteen

As autumn turned into winter, the house in the court became colder and damper. Washday on a Monday morning and trying to get the clothes dry if they could not be hung out in the yard, was a nightmare for Martha.

'It'll be your job to light the fire in the grate under the set-pot,' she told Emily. 'You'll have to get up a bit earlier.'

'The what?'

Martha smiled. 'It's what Mrs Dugdale calls the copper.' She pointed to the corner. 'That monstrosity.'

So on a Monday morning, as well as on a Saturday afternoon when she washed her own dirty work clothes, Emily rose at dawn to light both fires in the kitchen. Then, whilst she waited to be sure that they were fully alight, she fetched the tub, dolly and washboard from the cellar and, if the weather was bad, the clothes horse too. She sighed, hoping her father would be allowed to stay in bed whilst the kitchen was full of steam, especially if sheets, towels and all their clothes had to be strung on lines across the whole room. Sometimes, the steam helped his breathing, but at others, he ended the day shivering from the door being left open all day. It was hard work for her mother, Emily acknowledged that, but Martha never complained. It was all for Josh and, in her mind, it would one day be worth the hardship they had all endured.

On a wet washday, the house seemed to smell constantly of wet clothes and Walter's cough grew worse.

'We should never have come here, Mam,' Emily said, watching her poor father struggling for breath and hugging a blanket round him even though he was sitting as close as he could get to the range. She glanced at the fire and bit her lip, feeling guilty because she and Josh could not provide more coal.

'He's all right,' Martha said impatiently.

'We should have a doctor look at him.'

'And where do you think I'm going to find the money to pay for a doctor when I can't even feed us all properly? Josh needs his food. He's doing a man's work now. The rest of us can manage.'

Emily had noticed that her portions were less than they had been and now she glanced at her mother. Despite the bulky winter clothes, she could see that Martha had lost weight. No doubt she was going short herself to feed Josh. Emily looked back at her father. He, too, looked thinner, if that was possible, she thought wryly. He looked even frailer every day and his hacking cough was painful even to listen to. Emily turned away and went out of the house, closing the door behind her. She had to do something. She had to bring more money into the house somehow.

She had been working with Nell for four weeks now and the older girl said she was doing well. Dare she, she wondered, ask Mrs Nicholson if she would put her on a wheel now? She leaned against the rough brickwork of the house and dropped her head, tears prickling the back of her eyes.

'You orreight, Emily?' She started at the sound of Mick's voice close to her. She hadn't seen him come across the yard.

'Yes – no, I mean . . .'

'Well, which is it, 'cos I don't like to see a girl crying, 'specially one as pretty as you.'

Emily smiled thinly. 'It's just my dad is so very poorly and – and he ought to have a doctor, only—' She bit her lip.

'Only you can't afford one. That it?'

She nodded miserably, ashamed at having to admit her family's difficulties. There were others far worse off than themselves. You only had to look at poor Rosa Jacklin, struggling to feed herself and her children with only her elderly mother-in-law to help. Impatient with her self-pity, Emily brushed away her tears and tried to smile. 'Sorry, Mick. You caught me in a weak moment. I shouldn't have said anything.'

Mick shrugged. 'It's orreight. That's what mates are for.' He paused and seemed to be thinking, a slight frown on his face. 'Look, there might be a way I can help. I'll have a talk to that brother of yours.'

'Oh no, please, don't. I – I don't want him worried. He's got enough to cope with.'

Mick gave a bark of laughter. 'With our Lizzie, you mean? Aye, well, I can almost feel sorry for the bloke, 'cos when she gets her claws into a feller, she don't let go easy. Anyway,' he reached out and pinched her cheek gently, 'don't you worry your pretty head any more. You leave it to Uncle Mick.'

As he turned and walked away jauntily, thrusting his hands into his pockets and whistling, it wasn't just the cold that made Emily shiver.

That evening, there was a knock on their door and Emily opened it to find Mick standing there, his right hand holding the handlebars of a bicycle.

106

'I've brought this for Josh. Lizzie said he needed one for getting to and from work.'

'Oh Mick.' Emily didn't know what to say. She was grateful that Josh would no longer have the long walk to work and yet . . .

'Is he in?'

'Shut that door, Emily,' Martha called crossly. 'Either come in or go out, do. Your father's in a terrible draught and you're letting all the heat out of the house.'

'Come in, Mick,' Emily said quickly. He leaned the bicycle against the wall and stepped inside.

Softly, Emily said, 'It's awfully good of you, but I don't think we can afford—'

'What's going on?' Martha demanded.

Emily bit her lip. 'Mick's brought a bicycle for Josh to get to work on.'

'Evenin', Mrs Ryan,' Mick said, grinning and taking off his cap. 'Our Lizzie said Josh has a long way to walk to work and I thought—'

Martha came towards him, smiling. 'Why, that's very kind of you, Mick, I'm sure. How much do we owe you?'

With a swift glance towards Emily, Mick shrugged and said, 'How about five bob? And you can pay me a shilling a week, if that'd help.'

Martha's face was grim for a moment and she cast a resentful glance at her daughter, but she forced a smile back on her face and nodded, 'That'd be very good of you. Thank you, Mick. Can I offer you a cup of tea?'

'No, I'd better be off, ta very much, though.' With his hand on the door handle, he winked at Emily and added, 'And tell your Josh I'll tek him out with me an' my mates on Saturday night. Show him the city's night life.'

'Thanks, Mick,' Emily said quietly, but she had no intention of doing any such thing. The moment the door closed, Martha rounded on Emily. 'What have you been saying to the neighbours, insinuating that we're poverty stricken, have you?'

'No, Mam, I—' Emily took a deep breath as she prepared to bend the truth – just a little. 'It was Lizzie who said she thought Josh ought to have a bicycle. She said she'd ask Mick.' This bit, at least, was the truth, but Martha was not about to let the matter drop. 'So what was all that about paying him a shilling a week?'

Mentally, Emily crossed her fingers as she shrugged and said, airily, 'I expect that's the way most folks round here pay for things.'

Martha glared at her for a moment, but as Walter began to cough, drawing her attention to him, she turned away. Emily glanced at her father and, though she could not have sworn it in a court of law, she was sure he winked at her.

Emily no longer walked to work with Lizzie for she had to be there earlier than all the buffer girls to have everything ready for them. As she walked along one morning, pulling her shawl closely around her, she determined to speak to the missus that very day. Despite Martha's blind faith in Josh, it seemed he could not expect a wage rise yet.

'I'm doing my best, Em,' he'd said when she'd tackled him the previous night, their conversation carried out in whispers so that their mother would not hear. 'And Mr Bayes says I'm a good worker, but I don't even like it. It's hard and mucky.' He sighed. 'I should have stood up to Mam. We should never have come here. And what Amy must be thinking, I don't know. She's never written.'

'Not at all?'

Josh shook his head. 'Not once.'

'Have you written to her?'

'Yes, twice a week. I sent one myself when we first got here but now I give the letters to Mam to post and I leave her the coppers for the stamps so she doesn't have to spend her housekeeping money.'

'I don't expect she minds,' Emily smiled and added cheekily, 'if it's for you.'

Josh smiled wryly and then added seriously, 'I'm so sorry, Em, that I can't help you more.'

'Don't worry,' she patted his shoulder, 'I'll see Mrs Nicholson tomorrow.'

But now the moment was near, Emily felt her knees trembling as she let herself into the workshop and began her morning's tasks. She worked swiftly and competently now, so that by the time the buffer girls began to arrive, everything was ready for them. Mrs Nicholson glanced around and nodded her approval. 'You've made a good errand lass, Emily, but I think you're worth more. Nell tells me you've done really well. So, at dinner time, I'll see what you can do and maybe we'll be able to set you on as a proper buffer girl.'

Emily turned pink with pleasure, and also with relief that now she didn't have to approach the delicate subject herself.

At dinner time, Emily was nervous. This was so important, but after she had worked in front of the missus for half an hour, Ruth Nicholson smiled and nodded. 'You'll do, lass. You can go on t'side next Monday morning and your pay'll go up to five shillings a week. When you get a bit quicker at it, then I'll put you on piece-rate and then you should be able to earn a bit more. I'll start you on heeling and pipping.' Emily knew that this was what most buffer girls started on; buffing the end of spoon and fork handles. 'In the meantime,' the missus went on, 'I'll get Ida's niece in and you can show her the ropes for the rest of this week. That way, she might be some use by next week, though –' Ruth lowered her voice – 'I doubt she'll be as good as you've been.' The woman sighed. 'Still, I can't let you go on as an errand lass any longer. You deserve better and, besides, you have the makings of an excellent buffer girl.'

Emily glowed with pride. She couldn't wait to tell Trip. They'd been able to meet most Sunday afternoons but, as the weather grew colder, Emily suggested that he should come to her home instead of meeting her in the park. Trip had shaken his head. 'Best not,' he'd said and then he'd turned his refusal into a compliment by squeezing her hand and adding, 'Besides, I want you all to myself, though I do wish it was sometimes the four of us, like it used to be.'

'So do I,' Emily murmured, recalling the happy times they had spent together as youngsters.

'Josh and me were good mates – still are, I hope.'

'Do you remember that snowy winter when Amy's dad made two toboggans for us?'

'Yes, I do. And he made Josh and me promise faithfully to look after you two girls.'

'And you did. But you didn't look after each other very well, did you?'

'Well, we liked slopes that were steeper than the ones we dared to take you two on.'

'And once you nearly ended up in the icy river because you couldn't stop at the bottom of a steep hill.'

'Fancy you remembering that.'

'I remember everything,' she said simply. Trip put his arm around her shoulders and hugged her to him.

'How I wish we were back there again,' he said softly.

'So do I. Oh, so do I.'

Fourteen

Amy stood by the window of their small front room. The room was small because the rest of the house frontage was taken up with the blacksmith's shop, it's huge door open every day on to the street so that passers-by could see the glowing forge and hear the rhythmic clanging of Bob Clark's hammer. She gazed unseeingly at the dull October day. Josh and his family had been gone over a month. Bob watched his daughter, his heart aching at the look of misery etched into her pretty, gentle face. He glanced down and noticed that the mound of her pregnancy was just beginning to show. He sighed inwardly. Soon, poor Amy would have to face the whispers in the village when her condition could no longer be hidden. No doubt too, the wagging tongues would blame him, saying that he hadn't been a good father to let his daughter get into trouble.

But they'd both trusted Josh and were sadly disappointed in him.

'He's not coming back, is he, Dad?' Amy said softly, without turning round.

Bob hesitated for a moment, but they'd always been truthful with one another. His voice breaking a little, he said, 'No, love, I don't think he is. He hasn't even written again after that one letter, has he?'

Amy shook her head, not trusting herself to speak now. Bob crossed the room and put his arm around her shoulders as she leaned against him. 'Oh Dad,' she whispered, tears welling in her eyes. 'I'm so sorry.'

Bob squeezed her. 'Don't worry, love.' His voice was strong and determined. 'We'll get through this, I promise. And if that young scallywag ever shows his face around here again, I'll—'

'No, Dad, please don't. Please don't say anything against Josh. I – I don't blame him. It's his mother. I know it is.'

'Aye, well, maybe you're right at that.'

They stood together in silence watching Mr Osborne from the corner shop opposite take in all the boxes of fruit, vegetables and greenery that stood outside all day if the weather was fine. Only yesterday he had bemoaned Josh's departure to Amy. 'I'm having to tell folks I can't get candles for 'em this year, Amy lass. I've haven't found another supplier yet. Eeh, I do wish young Josh hadn't left.' Amy had smiled weakly and thought, So do I, but she'd said nothing.

It was growing dusk and Mr Osborne would soon be closing up his shop.

'After all,' Amy went on now, 'Josh doesn't even know, does he? About – about the baby, I mean.'

'Not unless you've written and told him, lass.'

She shook her head firmly. 'I haven't and I'm not going to either. I don't want him marrying me because he feels he *has* to. I did reply to his letter and I've written a couple of times since –' it was more than just a couple, Bob knew – 'but when he didn't reply and I – I knew for sure that I was in the family way, I stopped.'

'I have to say I'd've thought better of him. I thought he'd at least have written to you again, even if he can't afford to travel home.'

113

Amy said nothing, but she couldn't help silently agreeing with her father.

Bob put his arm around his daughter's shoulders. 'I think it's time to face the music, love. Let's go and see your Aunty Grace together, shall we?'

'Oh Dad, I can't. I can't face the disapproval in her face, even if she doesn't say anything.'

He hugged her to him. 'It's got to be done sometime – and sooner rather than later, because you'll not be able to hide it for much longer. Come on, let's go now – this minute. Strike while the iron's hot.' It was one of Bob's favourite sayings and no doubt it had something to do with his life's work as a blacksmith.

'All right,' Amy agreed at last in a small voice. 'I'll get my cloak.'

The copious winter cloak hid her pregnancy well but the baby wasn't due until March or April, Amy reckoned, and by the spring, there would be no hiding her condition.

Grace Partridge had been her mother's friend from their school days. They had been bridesmaids at each other's wedding and their husbands had become friends too. Dan Partridge worked on the land and, like Bob Clark, had not been conscripted for the war. When Bob's wife Sarah had died at Amy's birth, it had been Grace who had stepped in and taken over the care of the young baby, whilst Bob toiled long hours in the smithy, not only to provide for his daughter, but also to work out his grief. He had never remarried – had never wanted to – and Amy had been everything to him. Now, as they walked the few paces along the road to the cottage where Grace lived, his emotions were very mixed. The villagers would view Amy's condition as a shameful sin, but Bob was relying on Grace's love for the girl and her generous and understanding nature. She was a strong-minded woman who belonged to the Ashford branch of the Female Friendly Society, which had been founded in the late eighteenth century. Members contributed money regularly to help their fellow villagers, who needed support either because of illness or bereavement. Constance Trippet was its leading member.

'She's a nice woman, that Mrs Trippet,' Grace would tell anyone who would listen. 'You wouldn't think it, not married to that stuck-up husband of hers, but when you get to know her, she's a real lady, though down to earth as well, if you know what I mean.'

The women of the village did know what Grace meant for they all liked Constance Trippet. And if the rest of the villagers took their lead from Grace over Amy as they had in taking the trouble to get to know Constance Trippet, then the girl had nothing to fear.

'Now, love,' Bob said as they neared Grace's door, 'do you want to tell her or shall I?'

'I'll tell her, Dad, but I want you with me.'

He squeezed her hand and then knocked on the door. Grace opened it only a moment later, but it was time enough for Amy's legs to feel as if they had turned to jelly.

'Bob – Amy – what a lovely surprise! Come in, come in, do.' She beamed a welcome but then, as she saw the look on both their faces, her smile faltered and she glanced anxiously from one to the other. 'What is it? Is something wrong?'

'Not exactly, Grace, love, but we need to talk to you. In private, like.'

'Well, Dan's still at work, so there's just us. Come in and I'll make some tea.'

'It's not a secret from Dan,' Bob said, as they followed her through to the kitchen. He sighed as he sat down. 'And it won't be much of a one for long, anyway.'

He reached across the table and took hold of Amy's hand. 'You tell her, love.'

'Just wait a minute whilst I mash the tea and then you can tell me what's worrying you, love, because I can see for myself that there's something.'

Grace was rotund, with a round, cheerful face that was usually pink from cooking, or washing or ironing, for she loved nothing better than to be busy. Although she and Dan had never had any children, Grace was nevertheless a motherly type and looked upon Amy as the daughter she had never had. Since Amy had grown up, Grace had occupied her spare time with helping out the villagers whenever and wherever support was needed. She had become friendly with Constance Trippet and was never afraid to call on her for assistance.

'Now, my dear, what is it? You know you can tell your Aunty Grace anything.'

'I . . .' Amy began and then faltered. Bob gripped her hand tighter and then said, 'She's pregnant, Grace.'

Grace blinked and stared at the girl, but it was the look of concern on the older woman's face that brought tears to Amy's eyes. She wasn't shocked or disgusted, only dreadfully anxious. Perhaps her censure might have been easier for Amy to bear.

'Oh my little love, come here.' Grace stood up and opened her arms wide. With a little sob, Amy rose too and laid her head against the woman's ample bosom and wept, whilst Grace patted her back comfortingly. 'There, there, it'll be all right. Your dad and me – and your Uncle Dan – will look after you.'

When Grace had found a clean white handkerchief

for Amy and they'd both sat down again, she said practically, 'Now, then, I don't doubt that the baby's young Josh Ryan's. So, what's he going to do about it?' Her voice was firm and both Amy and her father had no doubt that if Josh had still been around he might well have received a clip around the ear from Grace Partridge.

'He doesn't know,' Bob said quietly.

'Doesn't know! Then he ought to be told and pretty quick.'

But Amy was shaking her head firmly. 'Please, Aunty Grace. I don't want him to know – not unless he comes back to see me and then he will find out. But, you see, I don't want him to feel obliged to marry me. And besides, his mother—'

'Oh, don't talk to me about Martha Ryan. Her and me have never got on. Too high an opinion of herself, has that one.'

'. . . will never agree to it anyway. And he's under age. He can't get married without her consent.'

For a moment, Grace stared at her and then, on a heavy sigh, said, 'Ah, I see.'

'Before he went away, he asked me to marry him next spring, but his mother put a stop to it, saying she wouldn't give her consent and then – and then – she took him away.'

'But he's writing to you, isn't he?'

Amy bit her lip and shook her head sorrowfully. 'He wrote once, just after they left, but since then there's been nothing. Not a word.'

'I blame that mother of his,' Grace said tartly. 'Have you heard from Emily?'

Again, Amy shook her head.

'Well, that does surprise me. I'd have thought better

of both of them.' After a moment's thoughtful pause, she patted Amy's hand. 'But don't you worry, love, we'll look after you and I'll mind that the tongues don't wag. You leave the folks in this village to me.'

'But you do promise me you won't tell Josh or any of his family, don't you? Or anyone else who might tell them. If he does come back, I want to be sure that it's because he wants to and – and not because he's heard I'm expecting his baby. Please, Aunty Grace.'

The woman sighed and, with obvious reluctance, gave her promise. She and Bob exchanged a glance. It had been in both their minds to write to the Ryans, but since Amy was so adamant, there was nothing more they could do.

Fifteen

'I'm going back to Ashford on Sunday to see Amy,' Josh announced as he sat down at the tea table. 'I haven't heard from her, even though I've written several times since we got here. And no, it won't cost me anything. I'll get a lift most of the way and walk the rest if I have to.'

'Huh! I don't know why you want to waste your time on her,' Martha said tightly, ladling out thick vegetable soup into four bowls. Vegetables sold late on a Saturday night were cheap yet nourishing, though Emily noticed that Josh had pieces of meat floating in his bowl. 'If she hasn't written to you at all, then she can't be that bothered. I expect she's already got her sights set on another village lad.'

'Amy wouldn't do that,' Josh said quietly. 'We're promised to each other.'

Martha's head shot up as Emily picked up one of the bowls and a spoon and moved across to sit on a low stool in front of Walter, but she was still listening to the argument between mother and son.

'I've told you before, Josh; that was a foolish thing to do. You're far too young to be getting yourself tied to anyone, *especially* Amy Clark.'

Josh glared at his mother. 'What do you mean? I thought you liked Amy.'

Martha shrugged. 'She's all right as far as village

lasses go, but you can do a lot better for yourself.' She regarded her son thoughtfully. 'You're too soft, Josh. You've no drive, no ambition. You need a wife who will push you just like I'm having to do at the moment. But what will happen when I'm no longer around?'

'I don't want *pushing*. All I wanted – still want, if it comes to it – is to run the chandler's business and live in Ashford.' And marry Amy, he thought, but he didn't say the words aloud. Instead, he added, 'And I don't care what you say, I'm going to see Amy at the weekend.'

'So, you'll deliberately disobey me, will you?'

For once Josh returned Martha's gaze steadily. 'Yes, I will.'

Both Josh and Emily finished work at lunchtime on Saturdays and as they walked home together, Josh said, 'Where's Lizzie?'

Emily grinned. 'In a huff, I reckon.'

'Why?'

'Because I told her you were going to Ashford tomorrow to see Amy.'

Josh grimaced. 'You shouldn't have done that, Em. We need her and her mother's help.'

'Don't you worry about Lizzie,' Emily said. 'I'll handle her. You just go and see Amy tomorrow.'

'Emily! Josh! You'll have to help me.' Dressed in her long, flannelette nightdress, Martha was shouting from the small landing below.

Emily shot out of bed and pulled a shawl around her shoulders. She bumped into Josh as he came around the curtain from his side of the room.

'What is it? What's the matter? Is it Dad?' He was still half asleep, his hair tousled.

'I don't know.' Emily hurried down the steps to see her mother standing in the doorway of their bedroom, supporting herself against the door jamb, clutching her stomach and bending almost double. 'I've got the most dreadful stomach pains and I've been violently sick in the chamber pot.' She retched again as if to give credence to her words.

Emily put her arm around her mother and led her back into the bedroom Martha shared with her husband. Ever since Walter's return from the war, they had slept in single beds, though still side by side in the same room. Walter had pulled himself up in the bed, looking towards his wife with wide, frightened eyes. They had no coal to light a fire in the bedroom and his whole body was shaking with fear and the cold of the winter's early morning. There were thousands of victims still suffering like Walter – the things they'd seen and experienced were beyond human understanding.

'See to your dad,' Martha said weakly, lying back against the pillow, her hand clasped to her stomach.

'She does look bad, Em,' Josh, who had followed his sister down, said. 'We should get a doctor.'

'No – no,' Martha gasped, stretching out a trembling hand. 'I'll be all right. It must be something I ate. I just need to rest. You must see to your father. *Both* of you.'

'I'll go down and light the fire,' Emily said. 'Josh, you get dressed if you're going—'

'No!' Suddenly, Martha's voice was remarkably strong. 'No – he's to stay here and help you. I won't be able to do anything today.'

Josh glanced at Emily and shrugged. 'I'll go next week,' was all he said.

Martha closed her eyes and relaxed back against the pillows. She spent the whole day in bed.

'Has she been sick again?' Josh asked in the afternoon.

Emily pursed her lips and shook her head, saying curtly, 'No, not once.'

'Oh that's good, then. D'you think she'll be all right?'

Emily glanced at the clock on the mantelpiece. 'Oh yes,' she said sarcastically. 'She'll be all right *now*.'

'What d'you mean – *now*?'

Emily glanced at her father sitting in his chair by the range. His eyes were closed and the shaking had ceased for the moment. She fancied he was asleep after having his night disturbed, but then he slept a lot these days anyway. She still kept her voice low, however, as she said, 'Now that it's too late for you to set off to Ashford.'

Josh's eyes widened as he stared at her. 'Em – what are you saying? That Mam did it deliberately?'

Emily put her finger to her lips. 'I don't know, Josh, but it just seems strange to me.'

The young man was thoughtful, then he smiled. 'Ne'er mind, there's always another time.'

And she hadn't been able to meet Trip that day either, Emily thought bitterly, or even to get word to him. She hoped he hadn't hung about too long in the cold, waiting for her in the park. During the last few weeks, Emily had felt they were growing closer; she didn't want anything to jeopardize that. But Trip was so kind and thoughtful. He'd shown that even when they'd been children. She was sure he'd realize that there was a good reason why she'd not been there.

The following Friday night Josh whispered to Emily, 'I'm going to Ashford tomorrow afternoon straight from work. And don't you tell Mam until I've had time to get well on my way.'

'Of course not,' Emily said, indignantly. 'What d'you take me for?'

Playfully, Josh tweaked her nose. 'Me big sister who always looks out for me.'

When Josh didn't arrive home from work as usual at dinner time the next day, Martha said indulgently, 'I expect they've asked him to work this afternoon. They must have an important job they want finishing.'

Emily rolled her eyes towards the ceiling. Did her mother's conceit where Josh was concerned never end? She glanced at her father and was sure he was trying to hide a smile.

'Perhaps he's gone to Ashford,' Emily murmured.

'I hope not,' Martha snapped and added, 'and certainly not in this lot.' She nodded towards the window. It was raining heavily, the cobbled yard becoming a lake when the water couldn't drain away fast enough.

At about four o'clock the door opened with a crash and Josh staggered in, cold and drenched.

'Oh my, where have you been, Josh? Did they keep you late at work?'

Shivering, Josh didn't answer as he moved towards the fire.

'Come on, get those wet things off,' Martha fretted, as she began to pull at his sodden clothing, just as if he was still a naughty little boy. 'You'll catch your death. Emily, fetch the clothes horse up from the cellar. We must put his things to dry near the range. And find his clean underwear.'

'Mam . . .' Josh tried to protest, but he was too cold and wet to summon up any resistance. Stripped and wrapped in a blanket, he sat on the opposite side of the hearth to his father and sipped a hot drink.

As she bustled about the kitchen, Martha berated

him gently. 'Don't walk home in weather like that again. Either stay longer at work – I'm sure it would make you look good in your boss's eyes – or get the tram. We can surely afford the fare for you once in a while. Now, you'd be better in bed for a while. Emily, take the brick out of the oven that's warming for your dad and take it up to Josh's bed.'

'No,' Josh said. 'Leave it for Dad. I will go up to bed, but I don't need a brick.'

'You'll do as you're told, Josh. Emily, do as I ask, please.'

With an apologetic glance at his father, Josh stood up, pulled the blanket closer around him and followed Emily up the stairs. Once in the attic, he said. 'I tried, Em, honest I did. But I couldn't get a lift. No one would stop for me. I expect I looked like a tramp.'

'Don't worry.' She put the warm brick in his bed and tucked him in. 'Have a good sleep, Josh. You look exhausted.'

'You didn't tell Mam, then?'

'I said you might have gone to Ashford, but she didn't believe me or didn't *want* to believe me. So, let's leave it at that, shall we?'

But Josh had already closed his eyes.

'Are you going to the ball on Thursday night?' Lizzie asked as they walked down Garden Street one wintry Tuesday morning early in November. Now that Emily did not have to be at work before the others, she could once more walk there with Lizzie. Josh walked with them as far as the bottom of their street before he set off on his bicycle in the opposite direction. 'And what about you, Josh? I could do with a handsome escort.'

'Ball? What ball?' Emily asked.

Lizzie fished a newspaper cutting from her pocket and handed it to Emily. 'It's an Armistice Ball this Thursday, the eleventh, at Cutlers' Hall. There's to be an orchestra and everything. It'll be a grand affair. It's to be held in the large banqueting hall there. Oh, do say you'll come.' Archly, she added, 'I'm sure Trip will be there, Emily, and, besides, it's something to look forward to when we're working so hard up to the holidays.' She giggled. 'Do you know what the first three weeks in December are called in the cutlery trade – and probably in some other trades, too, where they do piece work?'

Emily shook her head. Lizzie counted the weeks off on her fingers. 'Three weeks before Christmas is "calf week", two weeks before is "cow week" and the most important is the week just before Christmas, known as "bull week". We all do extra overtime to get more money. I bet you'll be doing the same thing, Josh, and likely Trip too. So, it'll be nice to have a night off and dress up in our best bib and tucker and go dancing.'

Emily read the advertisement from the *Sheffield Evening Telegraph*.

'Programmes, two shillings and sixpence,' she murmured. 'We couldn't afford that, Lizzie. I'm sorry.'

Lizzie flapped her hand dismissively. 'Don't you worry about that. Mick knows so many people in the city. He'll get us the tickets for free.'

The thought of spending an evening with Trip, of dancing in his arms, was hard for Emily to resist and she hadn't seen him now for over two weeks because of Martha's supposed illness. But she was torn. She could see that Lizzie was determined to go to the ball on Josh's arm and, if that happened, they'd be seen as a couple. And that, she was sure, was exactly what

Lizzie wanted. Emily sighed, her conscience doing battle within her: should she go, so that she could see Trip, or say that they couldn't go, in order to save Josh from Lizzie's clutches? But the decision was taken out of her hands as Josh, the very person she was trying to protect, leapt straight in. 'Of course we'll go. You deserve the chance of a bit of fun, Em. For once, we'll stand up to Mam. We're going. I'll tell Trip. Ta-ra,' he said as he mounted his bicycle. 'I'll see you both tonight.'

Lizzie shot a look of triumph at Emily, whose heart sank. Her worst fear was coming true; Lizzie would parade Josh as her young man but would she, Emily, get the same chance with Trip?

On the evening before the ball, Emily left work feeling depressed. Lizzie could not hide her excitement, but Emily was almost on the point of deciding not to go. Trip hadn't sent any message with Josh. What if he wasn't even going to be there or, worse still, what if he was and he ignored her? She would be devastated.

'You must come round to mine tomorrow straight after work,' Lizzie said, as they walked home, 'to get ready. Oh Emily, we'll have such fun and you'll see Trip.'

Emily sighed. She wasn't sure she would, but the hope still burned brightly within her. And the truth was that even if she stayed away, Josh was still going to take Lizzie to the ball and maybe – just maybe – if she were there, she'd be able to keep an eye on them.

'All right,' Emily said, forcing a smile. 'I'll come round after I've helped Mam.'

Lizzie grimaced. 'Well, as soon as you can, Emily. The missus has been very generous. She says anyone who's going to the ball can leave work a little earlier tomorrow and we'll have to leave home no later than seven. We don't want to be late.'

'Is she going? The missus, I mean?'

Lizzie shook her head. 'No. She can't face it after losing her husband and her boys.'

'What about Nell and the others?'

'Nell won't go. She never goes out at night. Something about her mother not being well, but I think that's just an excuse. Ida said she might go and one or two of the others too.'

Pushing aside her concerns about Lizzie's designs on Josh, Emily actually enjoyed being with her in her bedroom the following evening. They helped each other bathe and wash their hair.

'You're so lucky having curly hair,' Lizzie moaned. 'Mine's so straight I have to curl it up in rags every night just to get it to wave.'

'It's a lovely rich dark brown colour, though, and it shines so. When you have it pinned up on top of your head, you look very elegant,' Emily tried to console her.

'Do you think Josh will think so?'

Emily sighed but didn't answer. Was she never to be allowed to forget about the problem, not even for a moment?

'Yours looks lovely put up too,' Lizzie went on, their reflections in the mirror reclaiming her attention, 'with all those curls hanging down around your face. What are you wearing, Emily?'

Lizzie's mind was quicksilver, darting from one thing to the next in her excitement.

Emily pulled a face. 'I couldn't afford to buy a new dress. If I can't afford to buy my own clothes for work –' she was still using Lizzie's old ones – 'I certainly can't be buying fancy gowns. So, I've only my Sunday best. It's not really suitable for a ball, but it's all I've got.'

Lizzie stood back and eyed her critically. 'You're a bit taller than me, but we're about the same shape. Mam's made me a new dress, but I've got the one I wore when I was a bridesmaid for one of the girls at work last year. Let's try it on you.'

'Oh, I couldn't really . . .'

But Lizzie waved aside her protests and, moments later, Emily was standing in Lizzie's bedroom dressed in a dark pink satin dress.

'It's a bit short, but you have got some pretty shoes. That's a blessing. Other than that, it fits you quite well.'

'It's a bit tight when I breathe.'

Lizzie laughed. 'Then you mustn't breathe. Come on, it's time we were going. The others are meeting us there.'

'Is Nell going?'

'No. She made the usual excuse.'

'What's that?'

'She doesn't like leaving her mother alone at night.' Lizzie shrugged. 'Goodness knows why. I don't think there's anything wrong with her. Now, where's your handsome brother to escort us?'

They travelled on the tram and alighted at the nearest stop to the grand building in Church Street. Lights from its front windows and music filtered onto the street and they heard the excited chatter of those attending the ball as they neared the entrance and mingled with the crowd.

Lizzie gripped Emily's arm. 'Look who's waiting for you near the door.'

Emily glanced up and her heart felt as if it jumped in her chest.

'Trip,' she breathed. He looked so handsome in his

evening suit. She stopped and swallowed her nervous-
ness. 'But what if – if he's not waiting for me?'

'Of *course* he's waiting for you.'

Still, Emily hesitated. Trip was standing near the
entrance, his glance raking the people arriving in vehicles
of all shapes and sizes.

'He's – he's looking for someone.'

'Oh, do come on,' Lizzie said impatiently, but she
was laughing at the same time. 'He's watching out for
you, you barm pot.'

But Emily could not be sure as Lizzie pulled on her
arm and urged her forwards. And then, Trip spotted
her. He smiled broadly and stepped forwards, dodging
the flood of guests arriving. 'Emily, there you are. I
was so hoping you'd come tonight. I was going to ask
you last Sunday, but you didn't come again. Was your
father ill?'

'No. I'm sorry I couldn't make it, but didn't Josh tell
you we'd be here tonight?'

Trip shook his head. 'I haven't been able to see Josh
all week. No matter. You're here now.'

Lizzie stepped aside as Trip held out his arm to Emily
to escort her inside the building and up the wide carpeted
staircase to the first floor. Behind them, Lizzie said,
'Come on, Josh, give me your arm, then.'

Josh grinned as he looked down at her. Lizzie looked
very pretty tonight. Her hair shone and her eyes glowed
with excitement.

For the next few hours, he forgot all about Amy.

As she entered the banqueting hall on Trip's arm,
Emily gasped as she gazed around her at the twinkling
chandeliers, the gleaming, black marble dado and the
pillars rising to the decorated ceiling. Huge portraits of
several worthy gentlemen connected with the city,

former mayors and master cutlers, decorated the walls alongside one of Queen Victoria.

As soon as the dancing began, Trip took Emily in his arms for every dance, not letting anyone else near enough to ask her to dance with them. He stayed by her side the whole evening and, mesmerized by his closeness, Emily forgot all about her vow to keep an eye on Josh and Lizzie.

From the shadows, Arthur Trippet watched the dancing. His wife was not present; Arthur had not invited her and he knew that Constance would not demean herself to ask him. He had to be seen supporting such a prestigious event, but as soon as he could excuse himself from the other dignitaries present, saying that he had a long way to drive home, he would slip away to have his own bit of fun. But he would be sure to be home in Ashford at an hour compliant with having stayed late at the ball. That way his wife would never suspect . . .

He was about to turn away to sneak out of the ballroom when he saw his son amongst the dancers with a pretty, blonde girl in his arms. For a moment, Arthur wondered who she might be. He hoped she was the daughter of one of his factory-owning colleagues in the city, whom Thomas had invited as his partner. It was Arthur's dearest wish that his only son – his only child – should marry well and procreate a dynasty of Trippets. He narrowed his eyes. The girl seemed vaguely familiar . . .

And then Arthur felt his face growing purple with rage as he realized who the girl was. Emily Ryan! That bitch, Martha Ryan, had brought her family to the city after all. He cursed himself for not having noticed that The Candle House was no longer occupied as he drove past it. He should have been more observant, but the thought had never crossed the conceited man's mind that the woman would go against his advice – and his wishes. Hadn't he done enough to separate his son from consorting with an unsuitable family? It hadn't mattered when they'd been young, but when Thomas had grown and he'd seen that the friendship continued, Arthur had engineered for his son to go away to boarding school, hoping that he would make friends within what Arthur considered to be his own class. Even that had not worked; the association with the Ryan youngsters had still persisted. Then he'd decided that Thomas must begin work in the factory and had persuaded his wife that it would be advisable for the boy to stay in the city.

'He must live and work with my employees. It's the best way for him to learn – just as I did. There'll be no favouritism.'

Reluctantly, Constance had agreed and Arthur had breathed a sigh of relief. Thomas would soon forget the girl once time and distance were between them. But the wretched mother had brought them to the city and now here was Emily, as bold as brass, dancing in his son's arms and smiling and laughing up at him. And was the Ryan boy here too? His glance scanned the throng and then he saw Josh. Arthur's eyes narrowed. He'd have to see what he could do about this. Somehow he would have to find out where they were both employed and pull more than a few strings. Arthur turned away with an angry movement. There was nothing he could do tonight, but tomorrow he would make enquiries.

Blissfully unaware of his father's gaze upon him, Trip led Emily into another waltz. His arm tightly about her waist and his mouth close to her hair, he whispered, 'You look lovely, Emily. I wish tonight could go on for ever . . .'

But of course it could not and when they reluctantly parted in the early hours of the morning, all Trip said was, 'Meet me in the park on Sunday afternoon, won't you?'

'Of course,' Emily said and then she was being dragged away by Lizzie and Josh to walk home through the darkened streets. But not one of them minded the long walk. The music, the laughter and the chatter still rang in their ears and Emily imagined she could even now feel the warmth of Trip's arm around her waist.

Sixteen

'Well, we can't expect much of a Christmas this year,' Martha said the following morning, casting a resentful glance at both Josh and Emily. She begrudged them the fun they'd had at the ball and seemed determined to bring them back down to earth with a bump. Although Emily had had an increase in her wage now that she had become a proper buffer girl, it was still not enough to help support the four of them. Josh, it seemed, could not expect any kind of a rise in his pay.

'I'll have to ask Bess Dugdale if she can get me on the file cutting,' Martha added, trying – and succeeding – to make her son and daughter feel guilty. Emily cast an anxious glance at her father. 'You couldn't do that sort of work in here, Mam. It'd make Dad even worse.'

'Mebbe Mrs Dugdale can find me work across the yard.'

'You couldn't leave Dad on his own for hours on end. You know you couldn't. He's all right for an hour or two while you go shopping or to church, but he can't be left for a whole day.'

Martha turned away, unwilling to grumble any more for she knew exactly what her daughter would say if she did – what she always did: they shouldn't have come here!

*　　*　　*

On Christmas Eve – an unusually mild evening for the time of year – a knock came at their door. Emily opened it to see Mick standing there. She gasped in surprise as she saw beyond him. Lighted candles dotted around the courtyard, casting a gentle glow that softened the harsh poverty of the yard. Rosa and her mother-in-law were standing outside their house, with the two little girls, gaping in wonder as Bess and Lizzie carried a trestle table into the centre of the courtyard and spread a white cloth on it. Ruth – the missus – and Billy emerged from the corner house carrying plates, glasses, cups and saucers.

'Hello, pretty Emily,' Mick said. 'Come and join us. We're having a party. And bring your mam and dad too. Tell 'em to wrap up warm. And where's that rogue of a brother of yours? I need his help.' Without waiting for an answer, Mick raised his voice. 'Josh, come out, wherever you are. I need your strong arms to help carry a crate of beer.'

'Oh Mick – we couldn't. We – we've nothing to bring. We—'

'Don't worry about that, lass.' Mick leaned closer and lowered his voice. 'Do you reckon poor Rosa has owt to contribute? You just bring yourselves. This is on me.'

'It's very kind of you, Mick. I don't know if my dad's up to it, though.'

'I'll bring a chair out for him and some blankets. Let him come, if he can. It'll do the poor old feller the world of good.'

Mick's thoughtfulness touched Emily and she pressed her lips together to stop the tears. Emily Ryan rarely cried. Hardship or quarrels only made her tougher or more determined, but a happy event or a generous act of kindness could leave her weeping. The only time she could remember being really heartbroken was when her father had returned from the carnage of the trenches, a broken and damaged man, a sharp contrast to the proud, upright man who had gone to war.

Now she smiled at Mick. 'I'll try,' she promised.

But her mother, when she heard what was happening, was adamant. 'He can't go. I don't want the whole court laughing at him.'

'They won't, Mam. Everyone in this court knows what the war's done to folks, if anyone does. The missus has lost her husband and two of her sons. Rosa's lost her husband, and her kiddies, their father. There'll be nobody laughing at anyone.'

'What's going on?' Josh asked, arriving downstairs. 'What's Mick shouting his head off about?'

'He's organizing a party in the yard and he wants you to give him a hand.'

'Right-o. Are we all invited?'

'Yes, but Mam doesn't think Dad ought to go out there.'

Josh glanced at Walter. 'Why ever not? You'd like that, wouldn't you, Dad?'

They all looked at Walter, who blinked and then appeared to nod, although it was difficult to tell what he was trying to indicate.

'We'll wrap him up well and take a chair out. Mick'll help me.' Josh was suddenly unusually decisive. Martha merely shrugged and waved her hand as if relinquishing any responsibility.

'I'll go and see what help Mick wants first,' Josh said. 'You get Dad dressed warmly, Em.'

When the Ryan family stepped out of their house, a merry scene met their eyes – one they had never thought to see in the dismal court amongst the city back streets. Flickering candles illuminated the long table set now with what seemed like a mountain of food: dishes of steaming potatoes, Brussel sprouts, roasted parsnips, stuffing and cranberry jelly. And in the centre of it all sat a plump, roasted turkey. There was enough food to feed all the inhabitants of their court for a week, Emily thought, her eyes widening in wonder.

Bess hurried up, her face flushed from the cooking she must have been doing all day to prepare such a feast. 'Come on, luv,' she said, taking Walter's arm and leading him to a chair at the head of the table. 'You must have the place of honour.'

'Oh, I don't think . . .' Martha began, but Mick had moved to Walter's other side and he and his mother helped Walter to the chair and settled him gently into it and then solicitously wrapped a blanket around his shoulders and another over his knees.

'Bring that paraffin stove nearer Walter, our Mick. Don't want him catching a chill.'

Mick placed the heater just behind Walter's chair. 'Be careful, mind,' he laughed. 'We don't want to have to call the fire brigade out on Christmas Eve.'

It was a wonderful evening – the best they'd had since they'd left Ashford. After the turkey and all its trimmings, there was plum pudding and brandy sauce.

'Has Mick done all this?' Josh asked Emily in a low voice.

'So he said, and besides, I can't think of anyone else in the court who could afford to do it,' she murmured.

'What's he do? For a job, I mean.'

Emily frowned. 'I don't know. That's what worries me.'

'Why?'

'Just a feeling I've got, that's all.'

'What sort of a feeling?'

They were standing together, apart from the others, on the edge of the shadows, each with a glass in their hand and watching Rosa's children playing with Billy, who was leading them in a noisy game of tag.

'Just that –' she took a deep breath – 'it's perhaps not all honestly come by.'

'Oh,' Josh murmured and then, as understanding filtered through his mind, 'ah.' But he made no further comment as if not wishing to question their benefactor.

But Emily was not so willing to let the matter go. 'He seems to be at home at all different times of the day. He's always dressed smartly. You never see him in working clothes.'

To her surprise, Josh muttered, 'Drop it, Em. We don't want to cause trouble.' And to stop her carrying on, he moved away and walked across to where Lizzie was standing. The girl's face lit up as he approached and Emily groaned inwardly. Then she glanced about her. She was feeling comfortably full. Her father had eaten quite well for him, for his appetite was now birdlike and Martha's face was wreathed in smiles as she sat chatting to Mrs Nicholson. Rosa sat watching her children with her mother-in-law beside her. They'd probably been fed this night the best they'd been for weeks – months, even. And this was all Mick's doing, Emily told herself. She sighed. Not only were the Ryans even more in debt to the Dugdale family, but also so too were all the inhabitants of the court.

For all of them, the glow of that Christmas Eve celebration lasted throughout the following days, even over New Year and into the beginning of 1921, and when the girls returned to work after the brief holiday, the memories of the glittering ball in November were still the topic of conversation.

'We all saw you with Thomas Trippet,' they teased Emily, who couldn't hide her blushes. '*And* you with Josh, Lizzie.'

'Are you walking out with him now?'

'He's a handsome lad, Lizzie, much better-looking than that Billy who's always making eyes at you.'

'Ssh,' Lizzie said swiftly, putting her fingers to her lips. 'Don't let the missus hear you. Billy's her son.'

But, Emily noticed, she made no effort to dispel the rumours that she was now courting Josh. Emily wondered if anything had happened between them on the night of the ball. It certainly had between her and Trip. At the end of the evening he had pulled her into the shadows, had kissed her tenderly and whispered, 'You're my girl now, Emily Ryan, and don't you forget it.'

But now Emily felt a pang of guilt. In all the excitement of the ball and then Christmas she had scarcely given a thought to poor Amy and, what worried her even more, was the thought that neither had Josh.

Seventeen

Christmas in Ashford had been different for Amy and her father too. Outwardly, nothing had changed. They attended all the usual Christmas services at church and Amy wore a heavy, voluminous cloak to hide her growing bulge. By early in January, however, Amy's condition could no longer be kept secret, but she had a stalwart champion in Grace Partridge, who, whilst ordinarily not above a bit of gossip, spoke loyally of the girl she had helped to raise from birth.

'It's that young rascal Josh Ryan who's to blame,' she told the other women in the village, 'but he's gone off to the city to seek his fortune.'

'By all accounts,' Mary Needham said, as the two women stood on the corner outside the village shop. 'His mother was behind all that. She's a pushy one, is Martha Ryan. Always thought she was too good for the rest of us.'

'It was poor Walter I felt sorry for. He was a lovely feller. I set my cap at him, y'know, when we was all youngsters in the village,' Grace confided. 'He was a fine figure of a young man then – but Martha got her claws into him and that was that. Mind you, I wouldn't change my Dan for the world now.'

'What's going to happen to Amy, poor girl? Is she going away?'

'Lord, no!' Grace was scandalized at the suggestion. 'Her dad's standing by her – and so am I.'

'So, it's likely that my services will be needed in a few months' time, then.' Mary Needham acted as the local midwife and had been present at many a home birth for those who could not afford to pay for professional help.

'I expect so, Mary, yes.' Grace's tone hardened as she added, 'Amy's like a daughter to me, Mary, and I won't let anyone say a word against her – not in my hearing anyway.'

Mary Needham took the hint, promising herself silently that she would pass the word amongst the other women in the village for she knew that Grace would likely have another formidable ally – Constance Trippet. Although there was a difference between their stations in life, the two women were firm friends and Grace was Constance's 'conduit' to village affairs. Constance was a generous benefactor to the locals. If anyone was ill, she would send a hamper and the children could always rely on a small gift at Christmas and a card on their birthdays. She never forgot anyone. She had her own little car – a royal-blue and black, open-topped Richardson Light Car manufactured in Sheffield – and she could often be seen driving herself around the village or into Bakewell or Buxton, dressed in a fitted coat with her hat kept in place by a silk scarf tied over it. Whilst she was regarded as the 'lady of the manor', Constance was approachable. And so when the news of Amy's predicament began to become common knowledge, Grace visited Riversdale House, the square, ivy-clad home of the Trippets, ostensibly to discuss society matters, but in truth to impart the latest news.

'You know Amy Clark, don't you, Mrs Trippet?'

'The blacksmith's daughter? Yes, I do.'

'She's in the family way,' Grace said now.

Constance's face was at once sympathetic. There was no censure, no disgust, just as there had been none in Grace's when she had first been told.

'The poor girl,' Constance murmured. 'Is it Josh Ryan's child?' She knew all about the departure of the Ryan family from the village and the reason behind it, for it had necessitated her having to find a new cleaner to come into Riversdale House two days a week.

Grace nodded.

Constance raised her eyebrows. 'I'm surprised at him. I haven't a lot of time for Martha Ryan, even though she cleaned for us . . .' The woman's mouth twitched briefly with amusement. 'I always felt she thought she was doing us a favour, but I always liked Emily and Josh.' Her face sobered as she added, 'And as for poor Walter . . .'

There was a sympathetic silence between the two women as they thought of Walter Ryan.

'In all fairness, Mrs Trippet, Josh doesn't know about the baby.'

Now, Constance's neat eyebrows seemed to shoot up almost to her hairline. 'Doesn't know!' She was incredulous. 'Why ever not?'

Grace sighed. 'Amy – and her father, for that matter – well, they're both proud. It seems Amy had one letter from Josh shortly after they left. He'd found a job, he told her, at your husband's works, and he promised he would come back and marry her once he came of age.' Grace pulled a face. 'Martha refused to give her consent and, as we both know, poor Walter . . .' She lapsed into silence, but Constance understood.

Now there was a longer pause whilst Constance

remembered something that had occurred a few months earlier.

On the day that Martha had talked to Arthur Trippet about her son's future, Constance had been sitting on the window seat in the morning room, which faced towards the front of the house. From time to time she looked up from the tapestry on which she was working to glance down the driveway and through the gates to the village street beyond. And then she'd seen Martha striding away from the house, anger in every marching step, rage in the set of her head and the stiffness of her shoulders. Constance could remember frowning. The woman hadn't even come to see her to collect her weekly wage. What on earth had upset Martha Ryan so much that she had forgotten to collect her money? What have I missed?

Constance missed very little about the goings on within the household or, for that matter, what went on outside its perimeters.

Her marriage was not a happy one; but she had expected no less. An only child, she had been a moderately wealthy heiress and so had attracted in her youth a bevy of suitors, if not admirers. She was a slim, handsome woman with even, well-shaped features and dark hair, but she was not pretty – and certainly not beautiful – in the conventional sense. But Constance wanted to be married and bear children. She had no ambition to fight for the vote or to run the small estate in Derbyshire, which her father owned. At the age of twenty-one, she had sought her father's advice on whom she should pick from amongst the six or seven young men who came calling. In Arthur Trippet, her father, Robert Vincent, had seen an entrepreneurial streak and believed that the money and lands that he would one day leave to his daughter would be used wisely. The young man was already learning to take over his own family's cutlery manufacturing business in Sheffield and Robert surmised that Arthur would wish for his son to carry on after him. He was not mistaken; Arthur Trippet had grand visions of founding a dynasty, with sons – more than one, of course – to carry on the name of Trippet. Arthur worked hard – very hard – and, in time, became a Master Cutler, holding the position for a year.

When, after several serious discussions with her father, Arthur's proposal to Constance had been accepted, they both realized that neither of them was experiencing a grand passion. Although Arthur had been attentive during his courtship, showering her with gifts, Constance had not been deceived. They were not in love with each other, although there was a mutual respect.

'But, Mama,' Constance had said worriedly a few weeks before her marriage, 'what happens if I fall in love with someone else? I mean, after I am married?'

Elizabeth Vincent had sighed softly and taken her daughter's hand and said, 'A good woman never does, Constance.'

And so she had been 'a good woman' and as constant to her husband as her name implied. Unfortunately, the same could not be said of Arthur. And yet, her mother had warned her of this too.

'Your marriage is one of convenience, my dear, as are many of the marriages in middle-class society, and should your husband stray, you must turn a blind eye.'

Constance had stared at her mother's serene face and wondered if her own father's frequent absences to London, ostensibly on business, were, in fact, to visit another woman. Elizabeth was not about to confide in her daughter and she never would, but down the years Constance was to remember the conversation and draw strength from it when her own fidelity was not matched by her husband.

'I hope, though,' Elizabeth had said, 'that you will at least be fond of each other and that he will treat you kindly.'

As she'd watched Martha Ryan go through the gates at the end of the driveway and disappear from her view, Constance had sighed. She supposed Arthur had treated her well; materially, she had everything she needed and she had her son. She would have loved to have had more children, but after Thomas's birth she'd suffered two miscarriages and then there had been no more pregnancies. Gradually, Arthur had ceased to come to her bed and she guessed then that he had acquired a mistress and she had made it her business to find out. Often, over the fifteen or so years since then, Constance had tried to analyse her feelings, but strangely, she was unable to do so. Had she been in love with Arthur, then it would have been easy to define; she would have been distraught and humiliated. As it was, she had to admit that what she did feel was relief. No more would her body be wracked with the pain of childbirth or the agony of losing a baby. But she had Thomas and, whilst she idolized him, she was also a sensible woman who, although she wanted happiness for her son above all else – even above the success that her husband craved for his son and heir – she never spoiled him. And although it broke her heart when Thomas left home, first to attend boarding school and then to live and work in the city, she filled the empty hours with running the home for her husband. Embroidery, especially tapestry work, drawing and painting and playing the piano – all the accomplishments of a well-bred woman – helped to keep the loneliness at bay. And then, her involvement in village life made her feel respected and needed.

The recent Great War had frightened her and she could not quell the relief that her son was too young to be conscripted and that her husband was engaged in valuable war work. He would not be called up. Arthur had not turned his works over to the production of armaments, but he did manufacture bayonet blades, trench knives and cheaper cutlery for supply to the troops. Several of the young men from the village had been killed or maimed and her thoughts had returned to Martha Ryan as she thought of poor Walter.

Constance set aside her tapestry frame, left the room and went downstairs to the kitchens at the rear of the house.

'Mrs Froggatt,' she addressed the cook, 'I just saw Mrs Ryan leaving, but she didn't come upstairs for her money.'

'I think she saw the master, madam.' The cook paused in rolling out the pastry for a Derbyshire pie she was making for that evening's meal.

Constance blinked. The staff never approached Arthur for anything to do with household matters and certainly never for payment of their wages; that was Constance's domain.

Mrs Froggatt dusted the flour from her hands and stepped a little closer to her mistress. 'Polly –' she nodded towards the housemaid on the far side of the kitchen – 'said she heard raised voices in the master's study, but I don't know what it was all about, madam.'

Constance was annoyed with herself. She had missed that little piece of intrigue. If she'd known, she would have listened outside the door of Arthur's study. Constance was good at listening at doors; she learned a lot that way. But all she said now was, 'Thank you, Mrs Froggatt. I'll ask the master myself.'

She'd turned and left the kitchen. Of course, she had no intention of mentioning the matter to Arthur. She would wait. She would find out eventually. Constance could be very patient.

And now, maybe she would have to wait no longer. Grace Partridge had come with the answer to the question that had been puzzling her for months. Obviously, she had misread Martha's departure that day. Constance had thought the woman had been angry about something, but she realized now that she could have been wrong. She had not seen Martha's face and maybe her demeanour had been one of triumph. Martha Ryan had received the help she sought from Arthur, for now her son, Josh, was, according to Grace, employed at Trippets' works.

'What can I do to help the girl?' Constance asked now, breaking the silence at last.

Grace beamed at her. She'd known that she could rely on Mrs Trippet's kindness and understanding. 'Materially,' she said, 'there's nothing, Mrs Trippet. Her father will care for her and supply everything she needs, but you could be a wonderful help in the village.'

Constance smiled and put her head on one side. 'By stopping the whispering and the pointing fingers, you mean?'

'Exactly.'

'Oh, I'll do that with pleasure. And I'll see what I can find out about Josh Ryan too, because I think he should at least be told. Leave it with me, Mrs Partridge. We can't judge the young man for not standing by her if he doesn't even know about the child. And it rather explains something else that happened at Christmas. Thomas came home for two nights and I know he tried to see Amy, but he came back looking rather concerned. Her father had told him – quite brusquely, it seems – that Amy had a heavy cold, was in bed and wasn't well enough to see him. Now, I understand why she avoided him.'

That evening, over dinner, as she always did, Constance enquired about her husband's day at his works.

'Just the usual, my dear,' was always Arthur's reply and this evening was no different. 'We are slowly getting back to normal after the war, but we still miss those who volunteered and who did not come back.'

'But you've taken on new workers, I imagine? Men who were perhaps too young at the time to go to war.' This was leading nicely into what Constance wanted to ask him.

Arthur grimaced. 'Yes, but of course they take time to train up.'

'How's Josh Ryan shaping up? Is he a good worker?'

Arthur's head snapped up and he glared at her down the length of the table between them. 'What are you talking about, Constance?'

'Josh Ryan. He used to be the village chandler after his father came back so badly wounded from the war. But the whole family has moved to Sheffield and I understand that he's working at Trippets'.' She shrugged. 'I presumed you'd helped him.'

Arthur's eyes narrowed. 'I did no such thing.'

'Oh.' Constance pretended innocence. 'I thought you would have done. His mother was a very good worker for us and her poor husband—'

'"Her poor husband" be damned. I want nothing to do with that family.' He stopped short of telling his wife that he had seen their son and the Ryan girl at the Armistice Ball entwined in each other's arms, much too closely, for Arthur's liking. 'I'll put a stop to it all.'

He rose from his place, his pudding only half eaten. He threw down his napkin and marched out of the room.

Constance was left biting her lip, her appetite deserting her. She was very much afraid that instead of helping Josh as she had hoped, she had only made matters worse.

Eighteen

As the girls left their workplace on a cold and dark January evening, chattering and laughing, their breath misty in the freezing air, Josh stepped out of the gloom near the gate.

'Emily . . .'

She turned, startled by the sound of her name being called. Pushing her way through the hurrying throng, with Lizzie following her closely, she said, 'Josh – whatever are you doing here?' He was hunched into his thin winter coat and shivering. 'You shouldn't have come to meet me. There's no need. Lizzie and I walk home together so—'

'I daren't go home,' he blurted out suddenly. 'I've been sacked. I can't face Mam.'

'Sacked!' Emily was shocked and, beside her, she heard Lizzie give a startled gasp. 'Whatever for?'

There was no hiding the bitterness in his tone as he said flatly, 'Old man Trippet. He paid a visit today. I mean, he often does, but he hardly ever walks around the whole factory. Usually, he just arrives in his Rolls-Royce, spends the morning in his office with Mr Bayes and then leaves. He doesn't concern himself with the *workers*. But today, he decided to visit all the workshops.' He sighed heavily and added sarcastically, 'To wish all his workers a happy New Year, I suppose.'

He paused and Emily prompted, 'And?'

'He spotted me and then pointed his finger at me and said in his booming voice, "What's *he* doing here?" I couldn't hear Mr Bayes's answer but after only a moment, Mr Trippet strode across to me and shouted, "You're sacked" in front of everyone, Emily. I've never felt so embarrassed.'

'But why?'

Josh shrugged.

'Didn't Trip put in a word for you?' Lizzie put in. 'After all, he helped get you the job, didn't he?'

'He wasn't there. He works in another workshop, so I don't know if he even knows about it yet.'

'Didn't you go and find him? Get him to reason with his father?'

'Huh! There's no reasoning with a man like Arthur Trippet.'

'That's true, Lizzie,' Emily said quietly. 'His word is law, and, after all, it is his factory.' She slipped her arm through Josh's. 'Come on, let's go home.'

Still Josh was reluctant. 'What will Mam say?'

'Oh plenty, I've no doubt, but we'll have to face it sooner or later, so best get it over with.'

'Wait a minute,' Lizzie said. 'Let's go back in and have a word with the missus. She's not left yet and she might be able to help.'

Josh and Emily turned towards her.

'How?'

'What can she do?'

In the light from the street lamp, they saw Lizzie tap the side of her nose and smile smugly. 'There're things I know that not many others do. Oh, I can keep my mouth shut when it suits me.' She giggled. 'Though you wouldn't think so.' She leaned a little closer and lowered her voice. 'Bess Dugdale and Mr Crossland are – well, you know – friendly, shall we say.'

Mr Crossland was the foreman at Waterfall's.

'*Are* they?'

Lizzie nodded confidently. 'Oh yes. Haven't you noticed him visiting every Saturday night when Billy goes out with his friends?'

'You mean – Billy doesn't know?'

'Oh, I think he knows all right, but I expect his mam and Mr Crossland want a bit of time to themselves.' She winked and chuckled, then, all seriousness again, she linked her arms through both Josh's and Emily's and said determinedly, 'Come on. No time like the present.'

By the time the three of them walked home, Josh was feeling a little more hopeful. He hadn't exactly got himself another job – or rather, Lizzie hadn't quite managed to secure it for him yet – but they were all optimistic. Mrs Nicholson had promised to talk to Mr Crossland on their behalf. 'Though he'll want to know how you came to lose the job at Trippets',' Ruth had said. 'But he knows George Bayes. Maybe he'll have a word with him and then we'll see, eh?' She'd looked Josh up and down as if assessing him for herself. Then she'd smiled. 'I'll see what I can do. If you're anywhere as willing and able as your sister, then you'd do for me.' She'd leaned closer to Josh and in a loud whisper had said, 'But don't tell her I said so.' Then she'd patted the young man on the shoulder and said, 'You run along home and leave it with me.'

Outside their home, Josh had hesitated. 'Emily – you tell Mam. I – I just daren't.'

Emily took his hand and Lizzie gave him a gentle

push. 'I'll come in as well. Maybe she won't fly off the handle if I'm there too.'

But Martha Ryan's anger was not tempered by their neighbour's presence. When the three of them entered, closed the door quickly against the cold night air but still stood ranged in front of it, Martha looked up sharply from the hearth, sensing at once that something was amiss. She straightened up slowly and glanced from one to the other, her gaze coming at last to rest on Josh. 'What is it? What's happened?'

Behind her, in his chair, Emily noticed that Walter began to shake as if fearing trouble. Still, Josh made no move to enlighten his mother. With a slight sigh, Emily said, 'Mam, Josh has – has been sacked. It was—'

'*What?*' Martha shrieked. She moved with a suddenness that startled them all and slapped Josh soundly across the face. At once Emily grasped her mother's arm and pulled her away and Lizzie stepped protectively in front of Josh.

'You stupid fool! What have you done? Haven't we uprooted ourselves, dragged your poor father here, all for your sake, just so that you can better yourself? And now you've thrown it back in our faces! Oh, I see it all,' Martha sneered. 'You thought if you got yourself sacked, we'd go back to Ashford – back to that little trollop, Amy Clark. Well, you can think again, m'lad. We're here and we're staying here, so you'd best get yourself out first thing in the morning and find another job.'

Josh stood with his shoulders hunched, his eyes downcast, but still he said nothing.

'It wasn't his fault, Mam,' Emily began. 'Mr Trippet visited the factory today and when he saw Josh, he went straight to him and told him he was sacked.'

For a brief moment, Martha was unable to hide the expression on her face, but it was a look that mystified Emily and it was gone in an instant. Had she imagined it or, with the mention of Arthur Trippet's name, did her mother now understand why Josh had been dismissed?

'We've already spoken to Mrs Nicholson, Mrs Ryan,' Lizzie said calmly, 'to see if there are any jobs going at our place. She's going to speak to Mr Crossland on Josh's behalf.'

'That's good of you, Lizzie,' Martha said stiffly. 'We'll have to wait and see, but – thank you.'

She turned away and went back to the hob where a stew bubbled. 'You'd better sit down and get your tea – the pair of you.'

Lizzie smiled up at Josh, patted his arm and whispered, 'Good luck.'

Little was said as they ate. Emily, as usual, sat with her father and tried to feed him but the stew trickled down his chin.

'Don't waste it. If he can't eat it, let him be.'

'But he ought to eat something, Mam. He's thin enough as it is.' Emily smiled encouragement at her father, but his whole body only shook even more.

Martha glanced at her husband and then looked away again. Little conversation passed between the family that evening and soon after they had eaten, Josh helped his father up the stairs to the bedroom.

'Emily,' he said, as he went back downstairs, 'that bedroom is freezing. Can't we light a fire up there for him?'

'I don't think there's much coal left. Mam says it must be kept for the range and the copper and I suppose

153

she's right. If we run out completely, there'll be nothing left to cook or wash with.'

Josh sighed heavily and made a futile gesture with his hand.

'You go to bed,' Emily said, trying to sound soothing and reassuring at the same time. 'You're best out of Mam's way tonight.'

'You're right. I'll go up whilst she's still busy with Dad.'

Emily shook her head sadly as Josh crept quietly up to the attic.

'Where is he?' was Martha's first question when she came down.

'Gone to bed. He's upset.'

'Upset? I should think he is. After all I've done . . .' She glared at Emily. 'This is all your fault, you know.'

Emily looked up swiftly. 'Mine? How come?'

'You've taken up with Thomas Trippet again, haven't you?'

'I – I don't understand. What's that got to do with Josh?'

Martha moved closer and almost spat in her face. 'Everything.'

'But – but it was Trip who got him the job in the first place. Sort of.'

'Exactly!'

Her mother was talking in riddles. Emily frowned. 'I don't understand.'

Martha took a deep breath. 'When I told you that Mr Arthur Trippet had promised to help find Josh a job – that he hadn't any positions in his own factory, but that he'd recommend Josh to his colleagues, well –' she hesitated briefly before saying in a rush – 'that wasn't the truth.'

Emily gasped and her eyes widened. She was shocked. She'd never known her mother to lie deliberately. They'd always been in such trouble as children if they'd told even the tiniest fib.

'When I asked him to help,' Martha went on, 'he sent me off with a flea in my ear. Said that we'd be better staying in the village. That it'd be better for your father and that Josh had a nice little cottage industry going.'

Boldly – perhaps rashly – Emily murmured, 'I'd agree with him there.'

Martha flashed a resentful look at her. 'Oh yes, you'd see him trapped in a *little* job, wouldn't you, and tied to that little trollop who lived next door to us?'

'He could do worse,' Emily muttered, her mind flitting to Lizzie. It seemed Martha was also thinking of Lizzie, but in a very different vein as she said, 'He'd do better to marry Lizzie. I can see she likes him. And she'd be a better helpmate to him than ever Amy Clark would be.'

For once, Emily found it impossible to disagree. Lizzie had already been so helpful and they were depending on her yet again to help Josh secure other employment. Now, Emily's thoughts turned back to her mother's accusation. 'I still don't understand why I'm to blame.'

'Because I have the shrewd suspicion that old man Trippet doesn't want his precious son consorting with the likes of you. The Ryans aren't good enough for the son of a wealthy cutlery manufacturer. But just you wait and see. This is just a little set-back, that's all. One day, Josh will be someone in this city and then the fellers will be queuing at the door to marry his sister.'

Emily's eyes blazed. 'Well, if you think I'm going to hang around *that* long, Mam, you've another think coming. I'll be an old maid by then. Besides, I'll choose my own husband, thank you very much.'

Martha raised her hand as if to strike her daughter, but Emily faced her squarely and said softly, 'Don't you dare, Mam, or I'm leaving.'

Martha's hand fell and she turned away. Emily was a different kettle of fish to deal with compared to Josh. Josh would always do what his mother told him even, she believed, after he was of age, but Martha knew that she could no longer control her daughter; if she ever had been able to, she reminded herself ruefully.

No more was said that night and the following morning there was a strained silence in the household. As usual, a light tap came at their door when it was time for Emily to set out for work; Lizzie was calling for her.

Once safely out of the court, Lizzie asked, 'How're things?'

'How d'you think?' Emily said bitterly and then added hastily, 'Oh sorry, that sounded so rude.'

Lizzie laughed. 'No matter. You're right – I can guess. Let's just hope the missus can work her magic.'

Ruth Nicholson said nothing as the girls hurried to start the day's work and although Emily longed to ask the woman, she bit her tongue. It wouldn't do to harry her.

At dinner time the machines stopped, the girls ate their food and then set off into town.

'I don't feel like coming today,' Emily said. 'I'll – I'll just wait here and . . .'

'Then I'll stay too,' Lizzie said promptly. She shuddered dramatically. 'I don't fancy a walk into town in this weather. It's too cold. Besides,' she added, leaning towards Emily to whisper, 'I'm as anxious as you are to hear what the missus has to say. I hope she's spoken to Mr Crossland. The suspense is killing me.'

It was almost the end of their dinner break and the other girls were due back at any moment when Ruth came into the workshop. Two pairs of eyes turned expectantly in her direction and the woman smiled. 'Tell your brother to come and see Mr Crossland in the morning. He has a job for him, but he wants to speak to George Bayes first to get the truth behind his dismissal. It's not that we don't believe you, mind,' she added hurriedly. Ruth Nicholson had taken a liking to the newcomers in the court and especially to Emily, who was a good worker. The girl never shied away from, or complained about, the lowliest of tasks and Ruth had been more than happy to start her on the buffing when she knew there was a little lass ready to take Emily's place as their errand girl.

'Oh missus, thank you – thank you.' Emily clasped her hands together and there were tears in her eyes. 'He won't disappoint you, I promise.'

Ruth flapped her hand, dismissing the effusive thanks, but she was smiling.

When they returned home that evening, the two girls had some better news to impart.

'I'll come in with you,' Lizzie said. 'Poor Josh. I bet he's had a rough day.'

Emily could hardly refuse, but she sighed inwardly. They were getting deeper and deeper into Lizzie's debt and it worried her. Even though they were miles apart now in another county, she still considered Amy her best friend. She knew the young girl would be yearning for news of the family and especially of Josh. She hoped her brother had written to her regularly and she promised herself she would write to their friend as soon as she could.

As they entered, they saw Walter sitting in his chair and Martha bending to take a meat pie out of the oven in the range. It looked, at first sight, like any close-knit family, but then Emily saw that Josh was sitting at the table, his head in his hands. He looked up and her heart twisted to see the defeated, hopeless look in his eyes.

'Good news,' Emily said at once. 'Well, hopeful, anyway.'

'The missus has spoken to Mr Crossland,' Lizzie said, unable to keep quiet and let Emily explain. She was anxious to look good in Josh's eyes. And in Martha's. She sensed she had an ally in the young man's mother. 'You're to go to see him in the morning.'

'But he's going to speak to Mr Bayes first. He wants to know what happened at Trippets'.'

'Oh, I see,' Martha said flatly and then added bitterly, 'then I don't hold out much hope. They're not going to say anything against their lord and master, now, are they?'

'Mr Bayes seems a good bloke. And Trip might put in a good word for me . . .' Josh began, but stopped, biting his lip.

Martha shot an accusing glance at Emily, but said nothing.

'I'll be going, then,' Lizzie said. 'See you tomorrow.'

The door opened once again. Beside the fire, Walter shivered.

'I wish folks'd stop running in and out,' Martha muttered. 'It's hard enough to keep this place warm as it is without someone opening the door every five minutes.'

Before she could hold back the words, Emily said,

'Then we shouldn't have come here.' And even though her heart ached at the thought of not being able to see Trip every Sunday, as she was able to do now, she added heatedly, 'We'd all have been far better off staying back home in Ashford.'

She felt torn; she wanted the best for her father and she was sure that Josh would be happier making his candles and planning his future with Amy, yet she counted the hours to the following Sunday when she could meet Trip. On fine days they walked in the park or around the city centre. If it rained, they found shelter in the city, reminiscing and tentatively planning what the future might hold. They held hands as they walked and he put his arm around her waist when they crossed a road, but still he did not tell her he loved her.

For now, Emily told herself, she had to be content with what he'd whispered at the ball: 'You're my girl now.'

Nineteen

The following morning, Josh accompanied the girls to their place of work. Only minutes after their arrival, he was facing Mr Crossland, a big, jovial man with a broad Sheffield accent.

'Nah then, lad, I've had a word wi' George Bayes and he says he's blessed if he can understand why 'mester fired you. You're a good worker, he said, and learning fast, considering you've had no experience afore. I'd be glad to take you on and you can work alongside Chris Marples. He'll take you under his wing. In fact, if you've nowt else to do, you can start right now.'

'Thank you, Mr Crossland. I'm very grateful.'

Eddie Crossland put his hand on Josh's shoulder as he steered him through the workshop towards a tall, middle-aged man working at a grinder. Chris Marples had pale hazel eyes and thinning grey hair, but his smile was warm and his handshake firm as Eddie Crossland introduced his new workmate, and when Josh walked home that evening with Emily on one side of him and Lizzie on the other, he was grinning.

'It's a lot better than Trippets',' he told them. 'The blokes are all so friendly. There –' he referred again to his previous place of work – 'they all seemed so miserable. Just did their day's work and went off home. Here, it's a laugh a minute and they meet up for a pint at the weekends, Chris told me. He's invited me to join them on a Saturday night.' Josh chuckled. 'He asked me if I was any good at darts. As if.'

'You could learn,' Lizzie said, loyally. 'I bet you'd be good at anything you put your hand to, Josh.'

He glanced down at her, smiling. In fact, today he couldn't wipe the smile from his mouth. 'Thanks for the faith in me and thanks again for helping me to get this job. I really don't know what we'd do without you.'

Emily's heart sank.

That night, by the flickering light of a candle in her side of the bedroom, Emily wrote a letter to Amy. She found it difficult to write with the flow of words that once would have been so easy. Now there was a constraint, a reserve that she was sure Amy would notice and wonder at. Perhaps it would be better if she saved up to take a trip back to Ashford to see her, but every penny of her wages was needed to keep the family fed and as warm as possible. And it was the same for Josh; as trainees, they were poorly paid. When she read the letter through again, she knew her words were stilted and unnatural. Deliberately, she had not mentioned Lizzie and in avoiding doing so she was giving validity to the fact that Lizzie was a threat where Amy was concerned.

And she is, Emily thought. She intends to get her claws into Josh and I can't see what more I can do to stop it. I've tried telling her that he is engaged to Amy back home but that doesn't seem to bother her. In the darkness Emily sighed heavily. And we need her, her and her mother – even her brother Mick. The whole family needs them all. Since Christmas Eve, Emily had noticed extra items in their home that she knew her mother could not possibly have afforded to buy: a sack of coal, a joint of meat, extra butter and milk and a warm blanket for Walter's bed. The Ryans needed the Dugdale family's help. What else could she do?

Emily was troubled by the tone of the letter she'd written, but she thought it would be even worse not to send it.

'I've written to Amy,' she said the following morning. 'Have you got a stamp, Mam?'

Without turning round from the sink, Martha said, 'No, but leave it on the table. I'll post it when I go out shopping.'

Amy could no longer hide her condition and now the whole village knew that she was to bear an illegitimate child and they all guessed that Josh Ryan was the father. To her surprise, the villagers were very understanding.

'Bob Clark's done his best to bring up the lass on his own,' they whispered to each other, 'but it's not the same for the poor lass as having a mother's hand to guide her. Mrs Trippet says we must do what we can to help.'

And so little gifts began to appear at the smithy; tiny clothes to fit a newborn and a magnificent crocheted shawl. And Mr Osborne from the corner shop appeared almost daily with something to tempt the young mother-to-be's appetite. And on the day that a magnificent cradle, trimmed with white lace and complete with coverlets, was delivered to their door by Kirkland, the Trippets' chauffeur and gardener, Amy wept at the kindness of the villagers.

'Oh Dad, I don't deserve this. And to think that even Mrs Trippet has sent such a wonderful gift.'

Bob put his arm around her shaking shoulders, but he was unable to speak for the lump in his throat. He

162

too was overwhelmed, but then he'd known the villagers' kindness before when he'd been left with a small child to care for. They'd rallied around him then and now they were doing it once more for his daughter. It was as if they regarded her as theirs too.

'You must write a nice little thank-you note to Mrs Trippet.' He paused and then asked tenderly, 'Still no word from Josh?'

Amy shook her head. 'Nothing,' she whispered hoarsely. 'Nor from Emily. I – I thought at least she'd have written.'

Bob sighed heavily. He was acutely disappointed in the Ryan family. Oh, not poor Walter, who, in his condition, was helpless against his fiercely ambitious wife, but he had thought better of Josh and Emily. Surely the friendship that had existed between them for years had meant something. He sighed heavily and squeezed Amy's shoulder. 'Ne'er mind, lass, we'll manage. I'm glad our secret's out and that folks are rallying round.'

'I never thought –' Amy bit her lip and tears spilled down her cheeks – 'they'd all be so kind about it. I – I thought I'd be shunned.'

Bob chuckled wryly. 'Oh there're a few secrets I could tell you, love, if I'd a mind, but I haven't,' he added swiftly. 'But let me just say this, for a few folks in this village it'd be a case of the pot calling the kettle black.'

For a moment, Amy stared up at him and then, through her tears, she began to laugh.

On the first Sunday after Josh's dismissal, Emily met Trip with the words, 'Josh has been sacked from Trippets'. Did you know?'

Frowning, Trip stared at her. 'No, I didn't. Why? What had he done?'

Emily shrugged. 'Nothing – as far as I can make out.' Emily told him what had happened.

'My father, you say? He sacked him?'

'Yes. In front of everyone.'

'Oh, Emily, I'm so sorry. I'll – see what I can do.'

'Don't bother. He's got a job at Waterfall's and—' She'd been about to say that Josh liked it much better, but she stopped herself. This wasn't Trip's fault. She could see by the worried look on his face he'd known nothing about it.

She tucked her arm through his and smiled up at him. 'It's all right now so let's forget about Josh and enjoy ourselves.'

Trip took her hand and said, 'Shall we go somewhere different today? It's a bit cold for the park.'

'Where?'

'You'll see. Come on.'

They walked for some distance until Trip stopped and waved his arm. 'Here you are. Fitzalan Square. I thought you'd like to see some of the buildings here. Look at that one. It's what they call the White Building.' He laughed. 'I think it's supposed to stand out against all the sooty buildings round it.'

'Well, it does,' Emily said.

'And over there is the Electra Palace. I'll take you there one day, when I'm earning a bit more than a lowly apprentice's wage.'

'Is that all your father pays you?'

Trip grimaced. 'Says I've got to learn to manage my money. He does pay my lodgings, though I think Mother had something to do with that. She wanted me to have somewhere decent to live.'

164

'I don't blame her,' Emily said wryly. 'You can't really call where we're living "decent". The folks are nice, friendly and helpful, but I don't relish rats sharing the kitchen. Would you?'

'Not really. Come on, let's go and meet King Edward.'

'Eh?'

'The bronze statue in the centre of the square.'

When they'd wandered around for a while, Trip said, 'Do you want to take a tram back home? I think it's starting to rain.'

'Are you sure? I haven't been on a tram yet.'

'Come on, then. Top deck, so you can see all the sights.'

They parted at the end of Garden Street, Trip kissed her cheek lightly. 'See you next week and please tell Josh I'm so sorry about what's happened.' And then he was gone, leaving her staring after him, her fingers touching the place on her cheek where he'd kissed her.

'Have you written to Amy?' Emily asked Josh a week after her own letter to the girl had been sent.

'Yes, I've written several times now,' Josh said, 'but I've not heard anything from her all the time we've been here.'

'No,' Emily said slowly, 'neither have I. I find that strange, don't you?'

'I wish I could go to see her, but I just can't spare the money. Mam needs every penny to care for Dad and to feed us. It'd be so selfish of me. I was going to try to get a lift when I planned to go last time, so it wouldn't cost me much, but it's a bit chancy. I daren't be late back for the start of the week.' He laughed ruefully. 'I can't risk being sacked again.'

'No, nor me. I'd love to go and see her, but I don't

see how we can. Just mind you keep writing to her and *plead* with her to write back, if you have to. And another thing, whilst we're on the subject of Amy. Back off a bit from Lizzie. Ever since the ball, she's making out to all the girls at work that you're her boyfriend and, now you're working at the same place, it's getting harder and harder to prove otherwise.'

'I'll try,' Josh said, but he didn't sound too confident or determined.

As they left work on the Friday night having collected their week's pay, Emily said, 'Oh look over there, Lizzie. Mick's come to meet you.'

Lizzie glanced across the road at Mick standing on the street corner with two other young men. All of them were dressed smartly. None of them, Emily guessed, had spent the day at any form of manual labour.

Lizzie laughed wryly. 'He's not here to see us, Emily. Come on, let's go.' She grasped Emily's arm in a firm grip and hustled her along the street. 'Mick's with his mates, Emily. Best leave him to it.'

Josh was about to follow the girls when Mick shouted, 'Hey, Josh, let me buy you a drink, mate.'

Josh hesitated as Lizzie pulled on his arm and said urgently, 'No, Josh, don't go. Come with us.'

'But it'll look churlish to refuse, Lizzie. I'll see you later.'

Lizzie sighed as she watched him cross the road towards her brother. 'I wish he wouldn't,' she murmured. 'Oh, I do wish he wouldn't.'

'Why? There's no harm in him having a drink with Mick, is there?' Emily glanced across the road at Mick and his cronies. 'Though I hope he doesn't have to spend all his pay on buying a round for all of them.'

'Yes, yes, that's what I'm afraid of,' Lizzie said quickly

as they saw Mick slap Josh on the back and introduce him to the others.

Lizzie sighed. 'Come on. There's nowt we can do now, Emily. Let's go home.'

Josh did not arrive home until the early hours of the morning, long after the rest of the family had gone to bed, although Emily lay awake listening for him. Just after midnight, she heard the door downstairs open and then close with a bang. She heard him stumbling through the kitchen and then mounting the stairs to the attic. The door opened with a crash and he staggered into the room, grasped hold of the curtain between their beds, and pulled it down from the ceiling, the fabric tearing from the nails.

Emily threw back her bedcovers and got out of bed, taking hold of him and leading him to his bed.

'What on earth were you thinking, Josh? You've work in the morning. Just look at the state you're in. Whatever will Mam say?'

'Don't care,' he mumbled. 'It's all her fault anyway.'

He fell onto his bed and almost at once, he was snoring, his mouth slack.

'You can just stay as you are,' Emily hissed at him, though he was beyond hearing her. She returned to her own bed, shivering as she pulled the covers up. She hardly slept for the rest of the night, kept awake worrying about her brother and disturbed by his loud snoring.

Twenty

Arthur Trippet sat in the study of his grand country house drumming his fingers on the leather-topped oak desk. His mouth was tight, his eyes flashing with anger; a look that told all the members of his household to keep out of his way. But for once, his bile was directed at himself. He had been too hasty, he knew that now, but the fury he had felt on seeing Josh Ryan employed in his factory had overwhelmed him. The red mist had enveloped him and before he had stopped to think, he had dismissed the young man and bellowed at his foreman for being foolish enough to take Josh on in the first place.

'But – sir – it was your own son who recommended him. And he's a good worker, he's already—' George Bayes had been allowed to say no more. Arthur had prodded his finger into the foreman's chest and spat, 'Get rid of him this instant, Bayes, or you will be the next to go.'

Now, as he sat in the quietness of his study, Arthur realized that he had been rash and had played his hand openly instead of working deviously. And usually, Arthur was very good at scheming. Whatever he had wanted in life he had got by wiliness. His marriage to Constance Vincent had been a calculated act. He had courted her – and the promise of inherited wealth from her father – with pretty words, lavish gifts and gestures of affection.

His own father, from whom Arthur had undoubtedly learned his conniving ways, had nodded his approval and remarked bluntly, 'She's a plain-looking wench but she has a good figure and it's all the same when the light's turned off. Child-bearing hips, she's got, and that's all you need to give you an heir and possibly a spare.' He'd laughed sarcastically and winked knowingly as he'd added, 'And there's nowt to stop you taking your pleasure in the city, lad.'

Of course, inheriting the cutlery business from his father had been a foregone conclusion. He was an only son – an only child, as it happened – and there had been no competition. He had learned the trade from the bottom up, just as now he was obliging young Thomas to do. His mouth stretched into a grim line, bringing his thoughts back to his son.

Despite his efforts to dissuade the wretched Martha Ryan from removing her whole family to the city to enable her son, as she thought, to progress in the world, they had gone anyway. Now, he was in no doubt that the girl – Emily – had sought out his son and in so doing had engineered employment for her brother. That had now been dealt with but Arthur was afraid his rashness had shown his hand too early. He had yet to find out if Thomas and the girl were meeting regularly and now that might prove more difficult to do, but from what he had seen on the night of the ball, it was probable that there was a growing affection between them. And that must be stopped. Bayes could have found out for him from Josh, but now that route was closed to Arthur through his own impetuosity.

But perhaps there was a way. His mouth now curved

in a small smile as he thought about Belle, the voluptuous and accommodating woman he kept in a small terraced house in a modest street not too far from his factory and whom he visited once or twice a week. Mornings were for work, afternoons were for pleasure. At the thought, he felt a stirring of longing and knew that tomorrow he would first visit the works and then . . .

'Arthur, my dear. What a lovely surprise. I wasn't expecting you today.' Belle came towards him as he entered the house with his own key, her arms outstretched to enfold him to her ample bosom. He buried his face against her sweet-smelling hair. For an hour or so, his problems ceased to exist.

Arthur had first seen Belle on the music-hall stage. Constance had just suffered her second miscarriage and the doctor had warned that there should be no more pregnancies. Although he had one healthy son – Thomas – who was at that time two years old, Arthur was resentful at being told that they should have no more children. He was agitated and restless and looking for an outlet for his frustration. And then, on an impromptu visit to the theatre as a diversion, he had watched the dancing girls and his gaze had alighted upon one in particular; the brunette at the end of the line with a shapely figure that set his pulses racing and a pretty, lively face with eyes that sparked mischief.

After the show, he had persuaded the stage doorman to let him in as far as the door of the girls' dressing room. There he'd waited – not exactly patiently – for the girl to emerge. At last, she had come out, dressed in the fashion of the day: a long maroon-coloured dress, slim fitting, but which flared out from the knee to the floor and a broad-brimmed hat decorated with pink roses.

Arthur had raised his top hat courteously.

'May I introduce myself? My name is Arthur Trippet.' He saw no reason to disguise his real identity. 'I would deem it a great honour if you would have supper with me.'

Before the girl could reply, two other dancers came out of the dressing room and squeezed past Arthur in the narrow passageway.

'By heck, Belle, you've landed yourself a toff there. Say "yes" to whatever he's offering.' The girl who'd spoken winked and fluttered her long eyelashes suggestively at Arthur. ''Cos if you don't, luv, I certainly will.' Though pretty enough on stage, she was not so desirable close to. Thick stage make-up caked her face and her clothes, once glamorous, were fraying at the seams and grubby around the neckline. But the girl called Belle was still as lovely as she'd first appeared. More so, he thought, as he caught the scent of her alluring perfume and saw that her face was discreetly made up, her dress clean and neat.

When she spoke at last, her voice was soft and husky. 'I don't want you to get the wrong idea. Crystal was only teasing.'

'Quite,' Arthur had said tightly, hiding his disappointment. 'So, you won't let me take you to supper?'

Belle had smiled at him impishly. 'I didn't say that. I just didn't want you thinking I was some kind of street girl, that's all. Men come to the stage door all the time, hoping . . .' She hesitated. 'Well, you know. Bert – the doorman – is supposed to sift them, but he must have thought you looked quite respectable.'

That or the handsome bribe he'd given him, Arthur

had thought, but he'd said nothing, only smiled and inclined his head as if agreeing with her. 'So,' Belle had said, linking her arm through his, 'I'd be delighted. Thank you.'

Arthur's heart lifted. Although there was perhaps no hope of anything more that night, perhaps a kind of courtship with flowers and chocolate and champagne would very soon get him what he wanted.

But Belle Beauman was wily and not about to give way until she, too, had exactly what she wanted. Belle's early life had been tough. Born in the workhouse to a woman of the streets and left there once her mother had recovered, she had never known either of her parents. At thirteen she'd left the workhouse and found work behind the scenes in a theatre, sleeping in one of the dressing rooms and fed only by the generosity of the dancing girls. But she was warm and dry and she loved the backstage life – the laughter, the tears, even the quarrels – and when she grew to womanhood she, too, had become a dancer. Over the years, she'd watched the older girls, whose costumes she cared for and for whom she fetched and carried, and she'd learned from their mistakes. She saw them fall in love with stage-door Johnnies, whose motives were anything but honourable. She was a shoulder to cry on when a love affair went wrong, or a girl was pregnant and deserted. But now and again, there were the girls who found a 'sugar daddy' who set them up in an apartment or a little house and looked after them. But only once, during the seven years she'd lived at the theatre, had there been a marriage between a dancer and a handsome young man from a middle-class family. The girl had been lucky; even the young man's family had accepted her.

Belle had no illusions as to exactly what Arthur

Trippet wanted from her and she knew there was not the remotest chance of marriage. Arthur was married and he had no intention of upsetting his very full apple cart.

'My wife is a cold woman. She shows me no affection,' Arthur told Belle. 'She has done her duty by me, I will admit, and given me a son and heir, but there are to be no more.'

And so Arthur had secured a small house for his mistress in a discreet neighbourhood. For a while, Belle had continued as a dancer but when Arthur demurred, she happily gave up the life and devoted herself solely to his needs. There was only one sadness for Belle; Arthur said there must be no children. 'If you fall pregnant,' he'd warned her, 'I shall walk away.'

Belle had no pretensions about who or what she was. She was a kept woman, a mistress who could, she knew, be discarded at any moment if she grew too old to be desirable to her lover or if his wife found out or . . . The list was probably endless, but Belle preferred not to dwell on the 'what ifs' of life. She lived – and loved – for the moment and, for the past seventeen years, she had kept herself only for Arthur. He had been generous and she lived well and amongst people who, strangely to her mind, asked no questions. They were pleasant enough towards her when she ventured out, although she did not cultivate friendships. Arthur, when he could visit, was enough for her. During all that time they had parted only once. About two years into their relationship, Belle had had the misfortune to fall pregnant and Arthur, true to his word, had thrown money at her and ordered her to 'get rid of it'.

And then, he had walked out.

It had been a difficult time for Belle. She had left the

house and turned to the only friends she had: the theatre people. They did not fail her. They took her in and nursed her back to health. Her dancing days were over, but she worked as a dresser for all the music-hall performers.

She had thought she would never see Arthur again, but, after a lapse of several months, uncomfortable thoughts of the lovely young woman had drawn him, almost against his will and certainly against his better judgement, back to her again. He had found her eventually. Through discreet enquiries, he heard that she was once again working back at the same theatre where he had first met her. It was a lowly paid job she was now obliged to do and the young woman he had once so desired looked thin and ill. But back in the house he had bought for her and still owned, he told himself, and with good food, she would soon regain her beauty and the voluptuous curves he found so irresistible. He had no wish to find himself another woman; Belle was discreet. To his knowledge, no rumours had ever reached the factory and certainly not his home. He could trust Belle and that meant a great deal to a man like Arthur Trippet, for he guarded his reputation jealously. Installing her once more in her own home, with a generous allowance to enable her to buy new clothes, Arthur began to visit her again twice, sometimes three times a week. This time, however, he was more careful to take on the responsibility himself and prevent any further 'accidents'. They had never spoken of that dreadful time since.

Now, as they sat together on the sofa, his arm around her and her head against his shoulder, he said, 'My dear, will you do something for me?'

She snuggled closer. 'Of course. You should know that.'

His arm tightened about her as he explained. 'I believe my son is meeting with an undesirable girl.'

As he spoke of his son, Belle was careful to keep her head nestled against his shoulder and not to allow him to look into her eyes, which, despite her forced laughter, held a look of sadness.

'What is it you want me to do? Lure him away? I think I'm rather too old to appeal to a young man of nineteen or so, don't you?'

Her magnetism for him had never lessened, but he was obliged now to look at her through the eyes of a much younger man. He saw a well-dressed woman in her mid-forties, with luxuriant brown hair piled high on her head. Not for her the modern chic look of short, straight hair, though she dressed fashionably in modern styles, which certainly did not suit her curvaceous figure. Her face, to him, was as lovely as ever with smooth, cared-for skin, gentle brown eyes, a small, neat nose and well-shaped lips. If she'd been born into a different world, she might well have graced the drawing rooms of the wealthy, but Fate had decreed that she be born in the poor city back streets. Her only chance in life had been to use her looks and her talents as a dancer. But Arthur could see that his son would think her old and, besides, he didn't want Thomas finding out anything about his father's paramour.

'No, no, nothing like that.' He smiled at the thought. 'But I believe he is meeting a girl called Emily Ryan and the most likely time and place they might meet is in one of the city's parks on a Sunday afternoon. It's where the youngsters meet, I understand.'

Arthur was never with her on a Sunday, so her time

was her own. 'And you want me to see if I can find them?'

He nodded. 'I need to know if he is meeting her. If he is, then I have to stop it.'

'Why?' she asked him bluntly.

'She is not suitable as a wife for the future owner of Trippets'.'

'Why?' she asked again, greatly daring. 'If they love each other—'

'Pah!' Suddenly, Arthur withdrew his arm from around her shoulders and stood up abruptly. His hands behind his back, he strode up and down in front of the hearth, whilst she remained seated, staring up at him with wide, shocked eyes.

'He must marry a suitable girl, preferably someone who will bring money into the family, who will bear him sons – heirs to our business. Don't you realize,' he rounded on her suddenly and leaned over her, almost threateningly, 'he will be the fourth generation of Trippets? My grandfather arrived in this city from the wilds of the Yorkshire moors and worked his way up in the trade to begin his own small factory. My father enlarged it and it has been my life's work to continue that progress. Thomas will inherit a vast fortune but with it will come huge responsibilities too. He must be worthy of them. And a girl like Emily Ryan –' he almost spat out her name – 'would not help him. She would be a hindrance, not a helpmate.'

'And your wife is a helpmate?' Belle asked in a small voice. She rarely asked questions about his wife; she would rather not think about her.

'Constance has her own life,' he snapped. 'She is happy with her needlework and her good works in the village.' He resumed his restless pacing. 'I need to know.

I need to know,' he muttered more to himself than to Belle.

Belle hesitated for a moment. He couldn't – mustn't – know just what her Sunday afternoons meant to her. It would be a great sacrifice for her to give up the only time of the week that she could truly call her own. Arthur never, ever, visited her on Sundays. Occasionally, he arrived unexpectedly on a Saturday afternoon, but Sunday was the only day of the week that she could be sure he would never call. With an inward sigh, she rose and went to stand in front of him, placing her hands on his shoulders and looking up into his face. 'I'll do my best to find out for you, I promise, but it might not be so easy this time of the year. It's a little cold for walking in the park, but I suppose, perhaps, they've nowhere else to go.'

Arthur had the sudden vision of Thomas taking his paramour back to his lodgings and he resolved to speak to his son's landlady. After all, he paid for Thomas's board. The woman would do as he instructed her.

'So, what do your son and this girl look like?'

'He's tall and thin, good-looking and, on a Sunday, he will be smartly dressed. Whilst she,' his mouth curled, 'is just a country slut. They won't be hard to pick out, even in a crowd.'

Twenty-One

The morning following Josh's night out with Mick and his friends, he would have been late for work if Emily hadn't physically dragged him out of bed. As it was, he had to skip his breakfast and walk to work beside his sister and Lizzie as if he were in a dream.

'I told you not to go with our Mick and his mates, Josh,' Lizzie said, putting her arm through his. 'They're trouble. You'd do best to keep away from him – and them.'

But Josh wasn't listening to Lizzie. 'I've lost all me money, Em. I've nothing to give Mam this week. She'll go berserk.'

'Spent it, more like. Playing the big man in the pub, were you? Buying drinks all round?'

Josh shook his head, like a dog emerging from a river. 'I – I can't remember what happened, Em. I'm so sorry.'

'I'll talk to our Mick. He'll leave you alone, if I ask him.'

'Oh, don't do that, Lizzie. I wouldn't want him to think I'm stuck up. He's got a grand bunch of mates.'

Lizzie glanced at him sideways. 'You think so,' she murmured. 'Oh well, if that's what you want.'

Somehow, Josh got through his Saturday-morning's work, but when one o'clock came, he was only too pleased to lay down his tools.

'Don't come into work like that again, lad,' Mr Crossland said as Josh clocked out, 'else I'll have to sack you. Unemployment's rocketing in this city – all over the country, if truth be known – so there're plenty willing to step into your shoes and some of 'em, I might add, are a lot more skilled than you. So think on.'

'I'm sorry, Mr Crossland, it won't happen again, I promise.'

'Keep your drinking till Saturday night, lad, and if you'll take a tip from me, you'll steer clear of 'Dugdale gang. They're trouble.'

Josh stared at him. 'What – what do you mean? A gang?'

'Haven't you heard about the gangs we've got in Sheffield?'

Bemused, Josh shook his head.

'While the war were on,' Eddie Crossland explained, 'things were OK. A lot of the menfolk were in the services, of course, and, for those that were left, there was plenty of work in munitions and suchlike. But because they had plenty of money to throw around, gambling became rife in the city. So gangs formed to run all sorts of scams. Bare-knuckle boxing, betting on anything and everything – which is illegal anywhere but on a racecourse. You name it, someone would start a book on it. And they'd operate outside factory gates with runners inside collecting bets for them. But their favourite was pitch and toss, where they have three or five coins, toss 'em in the air and bet on what number of heads or tails comes down. They'd go up to Sky Edge – a patch of wasteland high above the city – where they could post lookouts. You'd get hundreds of fellers up there some nights. But after the war ended, the men came home and – those that did –' he paused a moment, as if paying silent tribute to all those who had not returned – 'couldn't find work. We were promised a land fit for heroes. Pah!' He made an explosive noise of bitterness. 'And, of course, with production for the war effort gone, there wasn't so much money around to spend on gambling, and so the gangs' income was drastically reduced, an' all. So, now they've turned to other forms of crime. They wait outside the factories on payday and just rob folks of their wages. They go into pubs and threaten the landlords. There's many a pub landlord lost all his profits in one night just because Mick Dugdale or Steve Henderson – they're the main two gang leaders in the city – paid them a visit and demanded free drinks and cigarettes. An' woe betides anyone if they flashed their money about in a pub. They'd find themselves beaten up in a dark alley and their wallet gone. And then there's the extortion racket—'

'Oh stop, stop.' Josh put his head in his hands. The previous night he'd got involved in a game of cards in the pub with Mick and his mates. He hadn't known how to play the game and that was how he'd lost his money. Emily had been right about one thing – he had been over-generous buying drinks – but the rest of his pay had been lost in gambling. Something that, according to Eddie Crossland, was illegal.

As he walked home, there was only one thing on his mind. However was he going to extricate himself from a growing friendship – if you could call it that – with Mick Dugdale? Oh, Mick'd seen him coming all right. I've been a fool. And this is one thing I daren't even confide in Emily about; she mustn't find out, Josh thought, she'd half kill me. Sometimes, his sister could be as fearsome as their mother. If only Mam had never brought us here, he moaned inwardly, I'd be safely back with Amy now and planning our wedding. At the thought of the pretty girl back in Ashford, his heart turned over.

Oh Amy, Amy why haven't you written? If only you'd answered my letters, none of this would have happened.

'That's it, lass, push. Now pant, now push again, just a little one. That's it. Good lass. You're doing so well,' Grace Partridge encouraged Amy. The girl lay in the front bedroom of the smithy, her face red and sweating from the efforts of giving birth. Her father had insisted she should have his bedroom. 'You were born in that room. Your mam would have wanted our grandchild to be born there too, God rest her soul.'

And now the time was here and Grace was at Amy's side, helping and encouraging her, and Mary Needham was there too, whilst Bob paced the room downstairs, like any expectant father, even though he was only the grandfather.

'It's coming too early,' Bob fretted. 'It's only the beginning of March and Amy thought it wasn't due until April.' He couldn't settle to his work; he needed to be close to Amy. 'He should be here. Josh should be here.' But there was nothing he could do about it; Amy had made her father promise faithfully that he would not contact Josh and, whilst he believed that she was wrong, he would not break his solemn promise to her.

From time to time, he glanced up at the ceiling, wondering what was happening up there. It was quiet; too quiet, he thought, as he remembered shuddering at the sound of Sarah's cries as she had brought Amy into the world. There were footsteps on the stairs and Bob braced himself and held his breath. Grace opened the door and appeared around it, beaming from ear to ear and carrying a white bundle in her arms.

'It's a boy, Bob. A strong, healthy boy and he'll do well, being a spring baby.'

'Amy,' Bob dared not look inside the shawl until he knew. 'Is she – all right?'

'As ninepence, Bob. Tired, of course, but very happy. Mary's just seeing to her.'

'But – but I didn't hear anything.'

Grace chuckled. 'It was a surprisingly easy birth, considering that Amy is such a little thing, and she was so brave; determined not to cry out and alarm you. Come on, now, Bob. Amy's fine and this is your grandson. You nurse him whilst I go back and help Mary.'

'Is he . . . all right, Grace? I mean, he's premature, isn't he?'

Grace shook her head. 'No, he's full-term and a good weight, seven pounds two ounces. Amy must have got her dates wrong, love.'

With the baby, still needing to be washed, in his arms, Bob sat in his rocking chair and allowed a few tears to fall. How his beloved Sarah would have cherished this moment, even though the boy had been born on the wrong side of the blanket, as one said; Sarah would have welcomed the infant and loved him. And Bob vowed to do the same.

'You're a fool, Josh Ryan. "A fool and his money are soon parted." Haven't you heard that saying? And you've been parted from yours even before you got home.' Martha was in full flow. 'Now what are we supposed to do? Live on fresh air for a week?'

She was still ranting at him, whilst Josh stood meekly

before her, his head bent, his shoulders slumped. There was no use in trying to make excuses; there were none. He should have stayed well clear of Mick and his friends. They were trouble. Emily had tried to warn him and, in all fairness, so had Mick's own sister. Now he had let his family down and come close to losing yet another job. He shuddered as he thought what else he might get dragged into if he spent too much time in Mick's company.

'Mam, he only had a night out. He—' Emily began. Though she was angry with Josh herself, she could see that Martha's tirade was upsetting Walter.

Martha whirled round. 'And you can keep out of this, miss, if you know what's good for you.'

The sound of knocking on their door was the only thing to interrupt Martha's ravings. 'See who that is, and if it's the rent man, I've no money this week.' She glared at her son as he turned away to open the door to Mick Ryan.

'Look, mate, I'm right sorry about what happened last night. Me mam's sent an apple pie and –' Mick fished in his pocket and pulled out a pound note – 'we're neighbours and I don't take from neighbours.'

But Josh put up his hand, palm outwards. 'No, no, Mick. It was my fault. I got carried away with the excitement of it all. I should never—'

Martha stepped forward and, in one swift movement, pushed Josh aside and tweaked the money out of Mick's fingers. 'Thank you, Mick. I'll not say no, seeing as you're the one who led my fool of a son into the wrong company. But he won't be coming out with you again, that's for sure.'

'I'm sorry, Mrs Ryan.' Mick sounded contrite but Emily, watching from the background, saw the look in his eyes and the smirk on his mouth. Mick Dugdale was enjoying this, she thought, even when he added, 'You let me know if you need anything else, Mrs Ryan.'

Mollified by what she took to be the young man's genuine apology, Martha said, 'We'll be all right now. Thank you for your generosity and your honesty.'

As the door closed on their visitor, Emily sighed. If there was anyone in this courtyard who was honest, then it wasn't Mick Dugdale, but she said nothing. She was thankful that the matter had been settled – for the moment.

But Martha had one last parting shot at her son that disturbed Emily even more. 'You'd do better to keep company with his sister.'

Twenty-Two

As 1921 wore on, it became apparent that the aftermath of the war was having a serious effect on the economic state of the country. The post-war boom didn't last long and the women who'd undertaken men's jobs during the conflict had – reluctantly, in many cases – returned to being housewives. Their jobs were now needed by those who had come back from the trenches still able to work; sadly, the streets were full of wounded men. But there were still not enough jobs and the unemployment figure throughout the nation rose sharply, causing hardship and real destitution. And for the wounded, there were even fewer prospects.

'Emily, stay behind, will you?' Ruth Nicholson said one hot August day as the girls stopped their machines when the hooter sounded. The missus turned away but not before Emily had seen the anxious look on the woman's face.

When the other girls had left, Ruth said, 'I've either got to reduce the piece-work rates or lay girls off. It's not fair to reduce wages, so, I'm right sorry, Emily, but I've to lay off three of you and you'll have to be one of them. We work on a "last in, first out" policy here.'

There was nothing Emily could say. She understood the fairness of the system and she was the most recent buffer girl. And there were to be two others too. 'Who else is going?'

185

'Lizzie and – and Nell.'

Emily's eyes widened. 'Nell? But she's your best worker.'

'I know, but she's only been here two years and only you and Lizzie have been set on since her.' Ruth sighed heavily. 'There's nothing I can do. She's got to go an' all. It's the rule we have to abide by, though I'm loath to let any of you go.'

Emily turned away, sick at heart.

'Mam, I've got some bad news,' she said as soon as she arrived home. There was no point in prolonging the moment. 'I'm to be laid off. Mrs Nicholson's laying three of us off. Lizzie's got to go, too.'

Martha straightened up from where she was bending over a pan of stew. 'Why?'

'They haven't got enough work to keep us all on.'

Martha was thoughtful for a moment. 'What about Josh? Is his job safe?'

Emily stared at her. Not a word of sympathy or comfort for her, just Martha's concern about her precious son. Emily swallowed the retort that sprang to her lips and said tightly, 'As far as I know, it's just the buffer girls they're laying off at the moment.'

'Aye, well, they'll want to keep men on, I expect. Men who've got a family to keep.'

I've got to help keep a family too, Emily wanted to shout, but she bit her lip and said nothing. Her glance went beyond her mother to where Walter was sitting in his chair. He was looking straight at her, his mouth moving, but no words were coming out. But his eyes told her what he wanted to say: Don't worry, love. It's not your fault. She smiled and nodded at him, her love for him overflowing. Silently she promised him that she would tramp the streets looking for work if it meant he would be kept warm and fed.

Martha dished out the inevitable stew and potatoes. 'Here, sit down and get your tea and then you'd best get out there looking for another job,' was all she said.

The following morning, Lizzie drew both Nell and Emily to one side. 'You've heard, then? The three of us are to go.'

Nell nodded, her eyes dark with anxiety. 'What are we going to do? I've me mam and— I've me widowed mother to keep. I can't afford to be without a job.'

'I've had a word with our Mick,' Lizzie said. She seemed to be the only one of them who didn't seem half out of her mind with worry. 'And he reckons we should set ourselves up as little missuses.'

Emily blinked and glanced from one to the other. 'I don't understand.'

'Our own buffing workshop taking in work from the little mesters or from the bigger factories,' Nell explained. 'But I couldn't run a business, Lizzie. I can work and work hard, but I was never much good at school, at the book learning, you know.' She lowered her voice as she turned to Emily. 'To tell you the truth – Lizzie knows, but please don't tell the others – I can't read or write very well.'

Emily smiled gently, trying to think what to say, but Lizzie saved her the embarrassment.

'Emily and her brother ran a little business together before they came to Sheffield. Making candles.'

Nell stared at Emily, wide-eyed. 'You did?'

Emily blushed, but nodded.

'Then why on earth did you leave that to come here?

187

To this?' She waved her arm to encompass the drab surroundings, the filthy working conditions.

'It was my mother who—' Emily had been about to say, 'who dragged us here', but it would have sounded insulting to the girls who had lived and worked in this city their whole lives, so instead she said, 'brought us here. She thought my brother could better himself.'

'I can't think of anything nicer than to live in the countryside with all that fresh air and to have a little business of your own too,' Nell said and her voice took on a dreamy tone. 'It'd be so good for children.' Then she shook herself out of her reverie and became the practical Nell again. 'Tell me more about the business you had. Candle making, did Lizzie say?'

'It was Dad's, really, handed down through the family for several generations, but when he went to war – and then came back too badly injured ever to work again – we took it on. Josh and me. But it wasn't what Mam wanted for Josh, so she insisted we come to the big city for him to make his fortune.'

'And has he?'

Emily laughed wryly. 'Hardly! I expect his job will be on the line next. He'll be one of the last in, too.' Then her thoughts turned back to their own predicament. 'What about premises and the machinery we'd need? And could we be sure to get enough work?' It sounded like a good idea, but the difficulties were endless, Emily thought.

Nell had worries of her own. 'We'd need to be sure that between us we could cover all the processes. I can do most things, even knives. I learned a lot in the war when the menfolk were away and women had to step in and do the work they normally did. You're pretty experienced, Lizzie, but, though Emily's coming along nicely, she's not learned everything yet. Spoons and forks are all she's done so far.'

'We'll manage. Mick'll help us,' Lizzie said confidently. 'He knows a lot of the little mesters. He'll talk to them. The work'll just flood in, you'll see.'

Emily saw Nell glance at Lizzie and then look away. She didn't look too happy about that arrangement and yet it promised work for all of them. Emily tucked her arm through Nell's. 'Don't worry, Nell. I can do all the bookkeeping, I promise, and you're the best buffer girl Mrs Nicholson's got. She's foolish to let you go.'

'All the better for us,' Lizzie said promptly. 'When word gets around that we've got Nell Geddis with us, the little mesters'll be falling over themselves to send work to us. Mebbe some of the big firms, too, can put a bit of work our way. Mrs Nicholson has promised to do that if she can. We'll start with just the three of us and see how it goes, eh?'

Nell gave a huge sigh, but then she nodded. 'All right, then,' she said flatly. 'We'll give it a go.'

When they'd parted from Nell at the end of the street, Emily and Lizzie walked the rest of the way to Garden Street. Emily was thoughtful, still concerned as to why Nell didn't seem enthusiastic about the proposition, but Lizzie's excited chatter made up for Nell's lack of eagerness.

'Our Mick'll see to it all. I'll ask him tonight and by the time we have to leave at the end of next week, I bet he'll have found us a workshop, machines and even our first customers. You'll see.'

But why, Emily worried, was Nell so reluctant?

'Why do you think Nell doesn't want Mick to be involved?' Emily asked Trip the following Sunday.

Trip wrinkled his forehead. 'I don't know. I haven't met him yet, but, from what you say, he sounds a generous sort of a bloke. He's being helpful, isn't he?'

'Very, though I expect it's mostly to help his sister.'

'That's understandable,' Trip murmured.

'I just wondered if . . .' She stopped, unsure how to continue.

'What?'

Emily sighed. 'If everything he gets for us is come by quite honestly. He won't let us pay for anything.'

'Do you want me to ask around? See if I can find anything out about Master Dugdale?'

Emily shook her head and said swiftly, 'No, word might get back to him and I wouldn't want to offend either him or Lizzie. Besides,' she added impishly, 'your workmates won't tell you anything. You're the boss's son.'

Trip laughed wryly. 'That's true. I'm never included in their conversations. I expect they think I'd go running to Daddy to tell tales. Little do they know,' he added softly.

'Anyway,' Emily slipped her arm through his, 'let's not worry about Nell or Mick or anyone else today. This is our day.'

Trip put his hand over hers and smiled down at her. 'So it is. Now, where do you want to go?'

'Not the park today. Let's go to the cathedral.'

Belle's mission was not as easy to accomplish as Arthur had thought. For several months, since he had first asked her, she had gone to one of the city's parks on alternate Sundays. She was determined not to give up every Sunday afternoon to what she now viewed as a wild goose chase. And as the cold weather had given way to spring and then to summer, there were a great many courting couples walking in the park and most were dressed in their finery. Today she recognized a group of girls walking arm in arm as buffer girls. They laughed and joked and called out boldly to the young men who hung about the park. One or two paired off and walked away arm in arm.

Belle sat on a bench to watch the youths and girls. A wave of longing for what might have been swept over her. But, as she always admonished herself when these moments of desolation engulfed her, Belle told herself that she was a fortunate woman. She had a wealthy man as her lover, who provided for her and, to her surprise, showed no sign of moving on from her to a younger woman now that the bloom of her own youth was gone. And, in a strange way, she was proud of herself that she had never resorted to standing on street corners touting for 'business'. Oh, she was a prostitute of sorts, she knew that, but she could live with being the mistress of a man of standing, even if it had to be kept secret. She wondered, sometimes, just what her neighbours did think when the Rolls-Royce was parked outside her little house, but since they always greeted her agreeably, she had ceased to bother about it.

There was only one deep-rooted unhappiness in her life and it was something which she could never tell Arthur.

And so she sat in the August sunshine, watching the young people, the ones who were already a couple and 'walking out', and the others who were flirting and coyly getting to know each other. Some tentative romances would progress further, others would not. She sighed, narrowing her eyes as she looked about her.

Arthur was getting very irritated with her that she had not made any progress after so long, but in all that time she had not seen anyone who seemed to fit Arthur's description of his son. She'd tried all the parks in the city, but because she had no idea which one Thomas and his girlfriend visited – if indeed they did at all – she could always have been in the wrong one. Belle sighed and lifted her face to the sun, enjoying the warmth. And then, just as she was about to give up yet again, she heard a girlish laugh and turned her head slightly to see a girl and a young man. He was tall with light brown hair and he had a merry face. He was quite smartly dressed, though perhaps not in quite the clothes that the son of a factory owner might wear, but Belle remembered that Arthur had told her he was making young Thomas start at the bottom and that he was working and living in the city. The girl was laughing up at him, her head tilted back. She was a pretty girl, but because she was wearing a hat, Belle could not see the colour of her hair. They were walking towards her on the path that ran in front of the bench where she was sitting. As they neared her, she saw the young man looking down into the girl's upturned face, smiling gently at something she was saying to him. As they drew even closer, Belle heard him say, 'We haven't seen Em and Trip in the park lately. I wonder where they get to?'

The girl laughed up at him. 'They want to be on their own, of course.'

The young man pulled a face. 'But I like old Trip. We're still good friends and I haven't seen him for ages.'

'That's because Emily wants him to herself.'

Oh my goodness! Belle was thinking as she overheard their conversation. This isn't the couple I'm looking for, but it sounds as if they know them. Thinking quickly, she put her hand to her head and gave a little moan. Then she began to sway as if she might fall from the seat. At once, the young couple were beside her.

'Oh madam, are you ill?' the young man said. 'May we help you?'

The girl sat down beside her and put her arm around her as if to support Belle should she faint.

'Is there no one with you?' The girl glanced around her as if trying to conjure up someone who might be with the woman. 'Are you alone?'

'Yes, yes, I . . .' Belle said, making her voice sound weak and shaky. 'I like to come for a walk in the park on a Sunday, but it's warmer than I thought, sitting here in the sun and . . .' She slumped against the girl, who held her firmly from slipping to the ground.

'I should fetch someone to help us,' the young man muttered.

'No, no,' Belle said, raising herself as if coming round slowly. 'I will be all right in a moment, I promise. Maybe if I just rest a few moments longer . . .'

He sat down on the other side of her. 'Then you must let us escort you to your home at least. Is it far?'

'Yes – it's – it's a fair way.' Today was only the second time she had come to Weston Park. She reached out a trembling hand and clasped his. 'You've been so kind. Won't you tell me your names?'

'I'm Josh and this is Lizzie.'

Belle's heart sank. She still hadn't found the right couple and now it was too late to try again today. This kindly pair would insist on seeing her all the way to her home, she was sure, but there would be no harm in that. Even if she felt obliged to ask them in, there was nothing to see there, nothing that could link her to Arthur Trippet. There were no photographs displayed –

indeed she didn't own a likeness of him – and none of Arthur's belongings were ever left there.

Steadily, they began to walk back to where Belle lived, one on either side of her, solicitously asking every few moments if she was all right. Gradually, as they walked, Belle pretended to regain her strength. 'I'll be all right now, truly. I mustn't keep you.' She smiled at them in turn. 'I'm sure you don't get much chance to be together. Sunday afternoons must be very precious.'

'We're just friends,' the young man said swiftly.

Lizzie giggled and bent her head towards Belle, saying in a loud whisper that she intended Josh to hear, 'That's what he thinks.'

Belle smiled. Oh, the wiles of young women, she thought, remembering how she had ensnared Arthur.

'We'll see you safely to your door and then we'll go,' Josh said firmly, ignoring Lizzie's remark. 'It's time we were getting home ourselves.'

At this, Belle saw Lizzie pull a face, but the girl said nothing more until they reached the street where Belle lived. Having reassured themselves that Belle was indeed all right now, the two young people turned away and, as she watched them walk away from her, Belle felt strangely bereft. But she was left with only one thought uppermost in her mind: What will Arthur say? He'd been quite angry last week when, yet again, she'd had nothing to report. The thought was swiftly followed by the realization that not only would he not be pleased, but she would also have to sacrifice yet more of her precious Sunday afternoons.

Twenty-Three

'Mick says we're to go and see a Mr Nathan Hawke. He's a little mester in Broad Lane,' Lizzie announced two days later. 'But he's also got a first-floor workshop in Rockingham Street suitable for us that's up for rent. We'll go after we finish at six.'

'You two go,' Nell said. 'I – I've got to get home. Me mam's not well and . . .' She broke off and then, as she turned away, added, 'I'll go along with whatever you decide.' As she walked away, Emily's sharp ears heard her mutter, 'I've no choice.'

'Come on, then,' Lizzie said, her excitement bubbling when they stopped work for the day. 'Let's go and find Mr Hawke.'

'Oughtn't we to go home first and change out of these mucky clothes?' Emily said, looking down at her blackened buff-brat. 'We must look a sight.'

Lizzie laughed. 'I think he's too old to set your cap at, Emily. Besides, in our working clothes, he'll see we mean business.'

As they walked along Rockingham Street, Emily wondered where these premises were. There didn't seem to be anywhere empty.

'Maybe it's in one of the courts.'

At the end of the street, they turned into Broad Lane and soon found Nathan Hawke's little mesters' workshop.

Nathan Hawke had been born into the world of cutlery making. His father and his uncle had been 'little mesters' and he had carried on their business with his brother, Clifford. When Clifford had died of consumption, Nathan had continued alone. He had been married in his twenties, but his wife had died at the birth of their first child and the baby, a little boy, had only lived a few days. Nathan had never remarried. His work had become his life. He was a kindly man who made friends easily and whose pleasures were simple: a pint in his local on a Saturday night, church on a Sunday morning and, after a long day at work, a meal, an hour reading his favourite books and then bed, to rise the following morning eager to get to his workbench. In the summer, on two nights a week, he would play bowls with his friends. Despite the tragedies in his life, Nathan Hawke was a contented man, though now, as he looked up to see the two young women entering his workshop, he wondered if 'trouble' was about to enter his life. He stood up to greet them, but he did not smile and that was quite unusual for Nathan; he was known for his affability and his gentle smile.

'So, which one of you is Mick Dugdale's sister?' he asked, as they stepped inside.

'I'm Mick's sister, Lizzie, and this is my friend, Emily. He's been to see you on our behalf, I understand.'

'Indeed, he has.' There was an edge to the man's tone that Emily couldn't fail to notice, but even if Lizzie detected it, she said nothing but carried on blithely. 'So, you have a workshop you're willing to rent to us?'

'I have.' His words were short, clipped almost. His welcome was not exactly warm or encouraging. 'I'll show you. I have two to rent.' He jerked his thumb up towards the ceiling. 'A small one above here and one

196

a bit larger in Rockingham Street. That one's above a grinders' workshop. Phil Latham rents that off me and I've no intention of turning him out. He's a good tenant and has been there years. The property belonged to my brother, but he died two years ago and, as he'd no other family, it came to me.'

'We'll look at the larger one,' Lizzie said promptly, but Emily put a warning hand on her arm. 'Shouldn't we know what the rents will be first? We might not be able to afford the bigger one, Lizzie.'

Nathan glanced from one to the other, but his scrutiny rested on Emily. 'I've – er – agreed to let you have a month's rent free. Just until you get on your feet.'

Emily gave him a dazzling smile. 'That's very generous of you, Mr Hawke.'

He nodded, his eyes still holding her gaze. 'Her brother was very – persuasive.'

Emily frowned and glanced at Lizzie, as if seeking an explanation, but the other girl refused to meet her eyes. Lizzie cleared her throat and said, 'Then if we may see the premises, Mr Hawke?'

He gave a brief nod and turned back to his workbench. 'Now, where did I put my glasses?'

The two girls were obliged to wait whilst he hunted around for his spectacles. When he was about to give up his search, he reached for his jacket from behind the door, put it on and then discovered his glasses in one of the pockets.

'Right. I'll just lock the door and we'll be off.'

They walked the short distance along the street and round the corner where Nathan ushered them through a door into a grinders' workshop. Three men were still working, their machines filling the air with noise and dust. Nathan pointed to a wooden staircase set at the side. 'Up there,' he mouthed.

The three of them climbed the rickety stairs and stepped into a large, first-floor room. There were some bits of old machinery, cobwebs of neglect strung between them, littering the room, though there were no buffing machines that would be useful. The walls were blackened with the dust of years but Emily's sharp eyes could see possibilities.

'When my brother was still alive,' Nathan said, 'we ran both places and the small workshop above my place was occupied by a little missus with a couple of workers, but she retired three months ago and it's been empty since then.' He glanced at them. 'You're very courageous to be setting up your own business in these hard times.'

'Needs must,' Lizzie said. 'Three of us have been given notice at Waterfall's. We can but give it a try and Emily here has run a little business in Ashford before she and her family moved here at the end of last year.'

Nathan's eyebrows rose a fraction as he turned to Emily. 'Oh, so you haven't been in Sheffield long, then?'

Emily shook her head.

'Ah, I see,' he said softly. Then, after a pause, asked, almost tentatively, Emily thought, 'And how do you like the big, bad city?'

Emily blinked and met his gaze. She'd thought he was joking, but his eyes were serious. 'It's – very different,' she said carefully and then she answered honestly: 'In some ways, it's very exciting, but in others it can be rather – frightening.'

Nathan nodded slowly and then, for the first time, he smiled, but his smile was directed only at Emily.

'We'll take it,' Lizzie said.

'Hey, wait a minute, Lizzie,' Emily laughed, 'I know

you're keen, but we need to know what the overheads are likely to be.'

Lizzie blinked and stared at her. 'What on earth are those?'

Emily heard Nathan stifle a chuckle, which he quickly changed into a cough as she said, 'All the running costs of the business. Rent and things like that, before you even start paying wages.' She turned back to Nathan. 'What rent will you charge eventually?'

With a quick, sideways glance at Lizzie, he said, 'Not much. I'll be pleased to have the building fully occupied and used.'

'And other outgoings?'

'I can't remember off the top of my head, but I'll write you a list before you give me a final answer.'

'There's no need for that, we'll take it,' Lizzie said adamantly.

'What about the smaller one, Lizzie? Perhaps it would be better to start with that.' Emily tried to be the voice of reason, of common sense, but Lizzie was carried away on a tide of enthusiasm.

'No, this one will do very well. Don't be such a worrier, Emily. Mick will help us sort everything out.'

In a low voice that only Emily heard, Nathan murmured, 'I'm sure he will.'

The three girls spent the following weekend cleaning the dusty workshop that had been unused for at least two years and Mick commandeered two of his mates and Josh to deliver three newish buffing machine and one of each of five different types of wheel needed for different processes. 'Let me know if you want any more of anything, Lizzie.'

'How much do we owe you, Mick?' Emily asked.

Mick shrugged. 'Call them a little present from me to set you on your way.'

'Oh, we couldn't do that,' Emily began and Nell agreed. 'Let us pay you for them, Mick.'

But the young man was adamant. 'Not this time, but if I bring you any more, then, yes, all right, I'll charge you. Right, lads, we're done here. You coming, Josh?'

It was an order rather than an invitation and Josh glanced at Emily sheepishly before meekly following Mick.

'Our Mick's a good friend to your Josh,' Lizzie remarked, as the door banged behind the four young men.

'Just so long as he doesn't get him drunk again and let him lose all his money.'

'I've told him not to let that happen again, and if there's anyone Mick listens to, then it's me. Now, come on, let's see if these machines work.'

'Where are we going to get work from?' Nell asked.

Lizzie waved her hand dismissively. 'Just wait and see. Mick's got it all in hand.'

Emily and Nell exchanged a glance and Emily was sure Nell looked decidedly uncomfortable, but she shrugged and they turned their attention to the machines.

'They're wonderful,' Nell declared after a few moments. 'I just wish . . .'

'What?' Emily asked.

'Oh nothing.'

'Right,' Lizzie said firmly as they stopped the buffing machines, which had been connected up to a line shaft with pulleys and belts to run from the engine that operated the grinders' machines on the ground floor. 'Now, we'll go and see Mr Hawke again. Maybe he'll have some news for us.'

'What sort of news?' Nell's tone was sharp.

'He's going to give us some work to start us off and then he's going to put the word around for us. Oh you'll see, we'll soon be in business. Mr Hawke promised Mick.'

'Did he now?' Nell murmured.

As they walked along the street, Emily touched Nell's arm and they fell a little way behind Lizzie, who was striding ahead, eager to visit Nathan Hawke.

'What is it, Nell, because I know there's something troubling you? You can tell me. I won't say anything.'

Nell sighed deeply. 'It's nothing – I'm just being silly, I suppose. But – but I don't want to get too deeply in Mick Dugdale's debt.'

Emily frowned. 'You mean he's suddenly going to demand payment for the machines?'

'No – no, not that.'

'Then what?'

'Oh, I can't explain and I suppose it'll be all right. After all, he's probably doing it more for his sister than for us.'

Emily laughed softly. 'I'm sure you're right about that. Let's just be thankful she's our friend and we're benefiting too.'

Nell smiled weakly. 'Yes, all right.'

'Now, come on. Let's go and see if Mr Hawke has some work for us.'

Moments later the three girls were standing in Nathan Hawke's small workshop.

'Actually, since Ruby retired –' Nathan jerked his head to indicate the empty workshop upstairs – 'I've been farming my buffing work out all over the place and, I have to say, it's not been satisfactory. It'll be good to have it done in the same place.' He sounded surprised at himself for saying it. He gave a short laugh and then added, 'I like consistency and I'd like the same person always to do my work. Not too much to ask, is it – considering?'

'Of course not,' the three girls chorused.

He glanced at each of them in turn. 'Now, no false modesty, if you please, ladies. Who's the best buffer?'

The girls laughed and both Lizzie and Emily pointed to Nell. 'She is.'

'Right, then.' He nodded towards a wooden box on the bench. 'There's your first order. Can you do knives?'

Nell nodded. 'I learned at my last place – before Waterfall's.'

Lizzie beamed. 'There's nowt that Nell can't do, Mr Hawke.'

For the first week, the three girls were busy with Nathan's backlog of work. 'These are a rather special order,' he explained, 'and I want them to look like a set.'

When Emily carried the box of shining knives, forks and spoons back to him at the end of the week, Nathan exclaimed in delight, holding up each item and examining it carefully. 'These are perfect. Who did them? Was it Nell?'

'Yes,' Emily said.

'Then I want Nell always to do my work. No disrespect to you and Lizzie, but—'

Emily laughed. 'None taken. We told you ourselves that she was the best.'

'And you were right,' he murmured. 'I shan't mind recommending you to my friends and colleagues in the trade now.' His voice dropped as he muttered, 'Even without Mick Dugdale's – er – encouragement.'

Delighted by the man's obvious pleasure in their work, Emily failed to pick up on his words or the resentment in his tone. It wasn't until a long time afterwards that she remembered what he had said – and she understood.

Twenty-Four

'So,' Martha said, 'you're a businesswoman now, are you?'

'Not exactly, Mam,' Emily said, trying to ignore the sarcasm in her mother's tone. 'It's just that three of us have set up a workshop to do buffing work. It's what a lot of women do in the city.'

'Huh! And where's the work coming from when they're already laying folks off in the big firms?'

'Mr Hawke gives us all his and one or two other little mesters he knows are now sending their work to us. We've got more than enough to keep us going at the moment. And he says we might pick up some work from the bigger firms too, if they get a time when the girls they employ can't cope.'

'Then why lay some off, might I ask?'

'Because,' Emily tried to explain patiently, 'they haven't got enough to keep them going full-time, all the time, but there might be occasions when they could do with extra help on a casual basis. A lot of the firms employ outworkers.'

Martha sniffed and turned away, but not before Emily had heard her say, 'Just so long as Josh doesn't get finished.'

The three girls had fallen into a routine of working. All three worked at the machines during the week, but on Saturday mornings, whilst Nell and Lizzie delivered the finished cutlery and collected new orders, Emily tackled the paperwork. It wasn't so very different from what she'd done for their little chandler's business in Ashford and soon she had everything entered into a ledger and all the purchases and sales invoices neatly filed.

Nell was awestruck. 'I don't know how you do it, Emily,' she said one Friday evening, as they were about to finish work.

'We all have different skills, Nell. You're brilliant at your work. I'll never be as good as you at buffing, if I live to be a hundred.'

Nell glanced over her shoulder, but Lizzie was still busy at her whirring machine and out of earshot. 'You're better than Lizzie and she's been doing it a lot longer than you.'

'Nice of you to say so.'

Nell was still hovering instead of hurrying off home as she usually did. Emily glanced up at her. 'What's up, Nell?'

'I ran into Ida last night on my way home. She – she's being laid off at the end of the week.' Nell bit her lip. 'I was just wondering . . .'

'If we could take her on?' Emily finished her sentence for her.

Nell nodded.

Emily was thoughtful for a moment. 'I think there's enough work for another pair of hands, but we might need another buffing machine. She's an "insider", isn't she?' An insider polished the insides of the bowls of spoons. 'But I don't like to keep taking advantage of Mick's goodness.'

Nell laughed wryly. 'His goodness, you say?'

'Well, he has helped us, hasn't he? I know he's probably only done it for Lizzie but – even so . . .'

Nell stared at her for a minute before glancing away. 'Maybe Mr Hawke would let us have one of his old machines done up. That'd be cheaper than buying another. Then we wouldn't have to ask any more – er – favours of Mick.'

'Why don't you go and see Mr Hawke?' Emily murmured, bending her head over her ledger as she totted up a column of figures.

'Ah, Lizzie's stopping,' Nell said, as they heard the other girl's machine slowing down. 'I'll go and ask her what she thinks.'

Emily looked up. 'I wouldn't; perhaps you might ask Mr Hawke about a machine first, 'cos you know what she'll say.'

Nell nodded, grimly. 'Yes, I do. "Our Mick'll get you one".'

'Exactly. Let's make some discreet enquiries first and then, if we draw a blank, then – well, maybe we'll have to go cap in hand to Mick again.'

Nell stared at her for a moment before turning away and muttering something under her breath, but Emily, adding up the column for the second time, wasn't listening. 'You don't understand, do you?' Nell murmured as she moved away. 'You really don't know what's going on.'

Nell walked along the road and round the end of the street towards Mr Hawke's workshop. Her head was held high, her shoulders straight, but her trim figure was hidden beneath the buff-brats she hadn't bothered to take off. She carried a box of polished spoons she'd finished that morning. As she opened the door into his place of work, her heart sank as she saw Mick Dugdale standing over Nathan as he sat at his work. At the sound of the door opening, they both looked up.

Nell paused a moment, disturbed by the look on Nathan Hawke's face, but when he saw who it was, his expression lightened and he smiled. 'Come in, Nell.'

''Lo, Nell,' Mick said. 'Everything all right?'

'Fine,' Nell said and forced herself to smile at him. 'Plenty of work?'

'Yes, we're very lucky.'

Mick smirked. 'Oh, I don't know about "luck", Nell, but Mr Hawke here is very pleased with your work and he's recommending you to all his cronies, aren't you, Mr Hawke?'

Nathan nodded, but his stare was still fixed on Nell's face. She thought he was trying to communicate something, but she couldn't guess what. Nell knew how to keep her counsel when necessary, so she smiled brightly at the older man and carefully placed the box on his workbench. 'That's the first half, but I'll start your next batch first thing on Monday morning.'

'No rush, luv, and I should have some more work for you the end of next week.'

'Nothing from anyone else, yet?' Mick asked, a sharp edge to his tone.

With a swift glance at Nell, Nathan shrugged, 'No more than the two I've already got for them, but I'm asking around. More work will come along very soon, I'm sure.'

'It'd better,' Mick muttered. There was an uncomfortable pause before Mick said, 'I'll be off, then. Duty calls, and all that. See ya, Nell.'

'Mick,' she murmured and waited until the door had

closed behind him and the sound of his footsteps receded into the distance.

Nathan heaved a sigh that sounded suspiciously like one of relief. 'I really don't like that young man,' he muttered.

'Is he – bothering you?'

'Not really. No more than usual, and I'm glad to help you girls anyway.' He glanced up at her. 'You know what's going on, don't you?'

Solemnly, Nell nodded. 'But Emily doesn't. She's not been here long and she's from the country. She's a lovely girl, and clever, but rather – naïve.'

'What about his sister?'

Nell frowned. 'D'you know, Mr Hawke, I really don't know about her. Sometimes I think she knows exactly what's going on and then, at other times, I think she just believes she's got a very clever brother who knows a lot of people who'll do favours for him.' She sighed. 'I honestly don't know about Lizzie, but I do know that Emily is as innocent as the day is long.'

Nathan Hawke nodded. 'I rather thought as much myself when we first met.' He paused and then asked gently, 'And what about you, Nell?'

He'd taken a liking to the girl and not just because she was good at her work. He would be rather disappointed if he found out she was in cahoots with Mick Dugdale.

Nell returned Nathan's steady gaze, her own open and honest too. 'I don't like it, Mr Hawke. I don't like it at all, but I have to work. I have to look after my – mother, and there's only me who can go out to work. So . . .' She bit her lip, hoping he understood.

'I see.' He sighed and then said, 'There's one thing I didn't say in front of him. The less he knows the better, though I expect he'll find out. I've got a couple of contacts for you who'll be pleased to give you some work.' He stood up and went to his jacket hanging on the back of the door and fished in a pocket. 'I've written their names and addresses down. They're not far from here. Here we are. Can you read it, Nell? I've lost my glasses again. I don't know where I've put them. I had them before Mick came in . . .' He looked around helplessly.

Nell chuckled. 'They're on your head, Mr Hawke.'

He put his hand up and found the spectacles he had pushed upwards. 'Oh, yes, so they are. Thank you, Nell.'

Nell took the piece of paper. 'I'll get Emily to go,' she said, without even glancing at the paper. 'She's got a way with people that I haven't and Lizzie certainly hasn't.'

'Oh, I'm sure you—'

'Now, now, Mr Hawke, no flattery. I'm good at me work, I know that, and, fortunately, I know how to do a lot of the different processes, but I'm no good with the business side of things. Emily is. She's done it before.'

'Oh yes, I remember Lizzie saying something about Emily having run a small business before. What was it? D'you know?'

So Nell explained what she knew of Emily's background, finishing, 'It seems her mother's no time for her. All her ambitions are for Emily's brother, Josh. He's a nice enough lad and Emily thinks the world of him, but he's a bit weak, to my mind. He didn't stand up to his mother when he should have done.'

'Ah well, maybe the lass will be the one to make the family's fortune.' He chuckled. 'That'd be one in the eye for the mother, wouldn't it?'

Nell laughed with him, then said, 'Oh, before I go, I nearly forgot what I came for, apart from bringing your work back.' Swiftly, she explained about their plans to take another girl on.

'I'll see what I can do for you,' he promised, and on that happy note she returned to their workshop waving the piece of paper with two more addresses on it.

The work flowed in steadily. Ida joined them when Nathan discovered an old buffing machine in the small workshop above his own.

'Ruby must've left it,' he told Nell. 'I'll get it running again for you, so you can set your friend on if you've got enough work coming in now.'

'We have, thanks to those two names you've given us and they, in turn, have already recommended another "little mester", who can put work our way. And, in case you're worried, I don't think Mick knows anything about them. Emily sees to all the paperwork and Ida now collects and delivers the work at the end of each week.'

'So you don't think Lizzie has told her brother?'

'I can't be sure, of course, but I don't think so. Not yet, anyway.'

'Let's hope she doesn't. I don't want him paying them a visit. They're good friends of mine. We play bowls together.'

Twenty-Five

Emily continued to meet Trip every Sunday. He was interested and excited to hear all about her venture, but he was apologetic about Josh having been sacked from Trippets'.

'D'you know why?' Emily asked him bluntly. 'Was it because his work wasn't up to standard?'

Trip shook his head and seemed, to Emily, to be avoiding meeting her gaze. 'I don't think so. George Bayes said he was getting on nicely.'

Emily thought she might know the reason after what her mother had admitted, but she didn't want to tell Trip. She didn't want to cause any trouble between him and his father, so instead she said brightly, 'Anyway, Josh now has a good job at Waterfall's and he really likes it.' She forbore to say that he was happier there than he had been at Trippets'. 'And our little business is doing very well.'

'That's my girl,' he said, seeming relieved that she had adroitly changed the subject. He put his arm around her shoulders as they walked through Weston Park one late September afternoon. Already, there was an autumnal chill in the air. 'I'm so proud of you. I hope the work keeps coming in for you, though, because times are hard. Mr Bayes had to lay off three women in our buffing shop only last week.' Trip sighed. 'I know it's unfair, but he lays off the women first and gives their buffing jobs to men. He feels the men have families to support, whereas—' He stopped and bit his lip.

'Whereas,' Emily went on, 'you don't think women have the same responsibilities as men.'

Trip sighed. 'Some of them do, I know, but unfortunately there's nothing I can do to influence Mr Bayes.' He laughed ruefully as he added, 'And certainly not my father.'

'I know.' Emily squeezed his arm. Trip was a kindly young man with none of his father's ruthlessness in his nature.

'Oh look,' Trip said suddenly, 'there are Josh and Lizzie. They're talking to some woman sitting on that bench over there. Let's go and say hello. I haven't seen Josh for weeks.'

Emily sighed but before she could argue, Trip was leading her towards her brother and Lizzie. She was disappointed to see that Josh and Lizzie were still walking out together on a Sunday. The more they appeared together in public, the more people would think that they really were a couple. And this was something she could do nothing about either. She was beginning to think, after all this time with no word from Amy, that perhaps the girl had met someone else back in Ashford and if that was the case, then she really couldn't blame Josh for keeping company with Lizzie.

As Emily and Trip approached, Josh looked up and waved. 'Hey there, you two, come and meet our new friend, Mrs Beauman.'

Beside her, Emily felt Trip give a little start and she glanced at him to see that he was staring at the well-dressed, pretty woman sitting on the park bench. But he recovered quickly and together they went forward to greet her. Emily smiled and shook her hand whilst

Trip bent gallantly over Belle's hand and kissed her gloved fingers. 'I'm delighted to make your acquaintance,' he murmured.

Josh explained swiftly. 'Some weeks ago, Mrs Beauman felt unwell here in the park and Lizzie and I took her home.' He glanced down at her again. 'We haven't seen you since. Are you quite well now?'

'Quite, thank you.' She smiled as she glanced up at Emily and Trip. 'Aren't you going to introduce me?'

'Oh, sorry. This is my sister, Emily, and this is Mr Thomas Trippet. You may have heard of his father. He owns Trippets' cutlery works in Creswick Street.'

Calmly, Belle smiled at them but inwardly her heart skipped a beat. At last, she was thinking, I've found them. As the young couple had approached, she'd had the feeling that this might be the young man she'd been trying to encounter for months. He fitted Arthur's description perfectly, though, to her mind, the girl did not. She showed no surprise on hearing his name and now her acting skills came to the fore as she pretended to frown. 'I've heard of the firm, of course, but I don't think I know Mr Trippet. Tell me,' she added, patting the bench beside her and inviting them to sit down, 'do you work with your father?'

'"For" rather than "with",' Trip laughed. 'Father believes that I should start at the very bottom and work my way up to deserve the honour of one day owning the factory. I'm an only son – an only child, actually – so I suppose I'm destined to take over one day.'

'Really?' Belle murmured. 'An only child, are you?'

'Yes.' His face sobered. 'I should have had brothers or sisters, maybe, but poor Mother suffered two miscarriages after she had me.'

This, Belle had not known; Arthur had not thought

fit to tell her details of his life with his wife. 'So,' she said, smiling wistfully, 'you must be doubly precious to your parents.'

Trip smiled, but did not answer.

'He's precious to all of us,' Josh laughed, thumping Trip gently on his shoulder. 'We've been friends since childhood and despite living in a grand house in the village and us being the children of a lowly village candle maker, Trip's never made us feel inferior to him.' Now Josh gripped his friend's shoulder and said huskily, 'He's one of the best, is Trip.'

'I'm sure he is,' Belle said softly and looked at the handsome young man with his black hair and his warm, honest brown eyes. She noticed how he glanced at the pretty girl beside him with love in his eyes and there was no mistaking the devotion in hers when she looked at him.

Belle felt a stab of guilt as she realized what she had to do.

The following afternoon, Arthur called to see Belle.

She had spent a sleepless night trying to decide if she dared to deceive Arthur, but in the cold light of morning she had resolved to tell him the truth. If he were to find out that she had not been completely honest with him, he would cast her off and, at her age, there would be no more wealthy lovers coming forward to take his place. It was very mercenary of her, she knew, but she had no choice.

As he entered the apartment, he headed straight for the bedroom and began to remove his clothing, so great and urgent was his need of her. Belle waited until he was ready, for he liked to undress her himself; it heightened his desire. But today, she took little pleasure in his lovemaking, if it could be called that, for he took her quickly and selfishly. Later, as he settled beside the fire in the living room and watched her whilst she poured him whisky and soda, he said, 'So, have you any news for me? Surely you must have found out something by now, or are you –' his eyes narrowed and Belle knew she had been right to believe his retribution for deceit would be harsh – 'playing with me.'

'I wouldn't do that, Arthur,' she was able to say truthfully as she handed him his drink. 'It's not been easy, for I never know which park to go to. I told you some time ago that I had met a couple, didn't I?'

'You did. The Ryan boy and his girlfriend, I believe.'

'I didn't get to know their surnames, but yes, the boy's name was Josh. Well, I met them again yesterday.'

Arthur grunted. 'Well, I hope this time you had the sense to find out a bit more. It'll soon be a whole year since I saw them together at the ball. God knows what might have happened in that time. You wouldn't make a very good detective, Belle.'

She put her head coquettishly on one side, trying to restore his good humour. 'No, it's not what I'm good at.'

Arthur had the grace to smile and said, a little less impatiently, 'Go on, my dear.'

'Whilst I was talking to them, another couple joined them. It was your son – Trip, they called him – with a pretty girl they called Emily.'

'Ah!' Arthur slapped the arm of his chair. 'I knew it. He is still seeing the little slut. Then I must put a stop to it, but this time I must tread carefully. It will need some planning.' Though he smiled up at her, there was a glint of triumph in his eyes that did not bode

215

well for the happy young couple she had met in the park.

After he had left, Belle sat late into the evening, thinking about Trip and Emily and feeling sorry for her part in what was likely to be the end of their romance.

But still, she reminded herself, at least she now had all her precious Sunday afternoons for herself once more.

The following Sunday afternoon, Trip came hurrying towards Emily when he saw her waiting for him in the park. Laying his bicycle on the ground, he put his hands on her waist, picked her up and swung her round. 'I've got something to show you.'

'What is it?'

Setting her on the ground again, he grasped her hand and said, 'Come on.'

He retrieved his bicycle and they walked to where Trip had his lodgings. Parked outside the house was a shiny new motorcycle.

Emily gasped. 'Is it yours?'

'Yes, my father bought it for my twenty-first birthday.'

'But that's not until November.'

'That's only next month. We're already in October.'

'I hadn't realized,' Emily murmured. 'We've been here over a year.'

He squeezed her hand. 'Any regrets?'

'For myself, obviously not, but for Josh – yes, plenty. He should be married to Amy by now, not mixing with Lizzie and her brother and his cronies.'

Josh still went out now and again with Mick, coming home the worse for drink and with some of their precious housekeeping money spent – wasted, in Emily's view. Surprisingly, Martha said very little and when

Emily dared to criticize him, all she said was, 'A young man's got to sow a few wild oats before he settles down.'

'And your dad?' Trip asked now.

'Not good, but he's better than I expected he would be when we first came here. I thought that first winter would be dreadful. The house was cold and damp and I thought we'd be forever fetching the doctor or that he'd be in hospital. He's been better through the summer, able to sit outside in the yard on really warm days, but now . . .' She stopped and needed to say no more. Now, they were facing yet another winter. How would poor Walter be this year?

They stood gazing at the motorcycle. 'It's a Wilkin, made here in Sheffield,' Trip told her.

'It's a magnificent gift. Your father must be very pleased with you.'

'It's the biggest present he's ever given me, but I think my mother's had something to do with it. She complains that I don't get home often enough.'

'You – you could go on a Sunday,' Emily said in a small voice.

'What? And miss meeting you? I wouldn't do that. I love my mother dearly, but . . .' There was a pause before he added in a rush, 'Emily, there's something I've wanted to say to you for ages, but it didn't seem right when I'm not earning very much.' Slowly, he turned to face her and put his hands on her shoulders. 'I love you, Emily Ryan. I think I always have. Dare I hope that – that—'

'Oh Trip, I've loved you for years. Ever since the four of us used to play together as children.'

'Oh Emily – Emily . . .'

He put his arms around her and kissed her, oblivious

217

to whoever might be watching. They drew back, breathless with the wonder of their declaration to each other. 'I can't ask you to marry me yet, you know that, don't you?'

'You'll be of age next month. You won't need parental consent then.'

'It's not that. I'm not earning enough . . .'

'But I'm earning. Our little business is doing very well – surprisingly well in these hard times.'

'But what if babies came along?'

Emily smiled and touched his cheek as she whispered, 'Now, wouldn't that be something.'

'Oh Emily,' he buried his face in her neck, 'don't tempt me.' At last, he raised his head and they stared again at the motorcycle.

'Can I ride on the back with you?' She pointed to the luggage carrier behind the rider's seat. 'I could put a cushion on that.'

'There's nowhere safe for you to rest your feet. I couldn't risk you getting your foot or even your dress caught in the wheel. Tell you what, I'll see if I can pick up a sidecar cheap and then I'll take you out. Would you like to go to Ashford?'

Emily hesitated and then said, 'Josh ought to go back, not me. Would you take him?'

'Of course,' Trip said at once.

That night, in their attic bedroom, Emily whispered, 'Trip's father's given him a motorbike for his twenty-first birthday. And he's going to see if he can find a second-hand sidecar to fit it and then he'll take me out, but he's also said he'll take you back to Ashford to see Amy.'

Josh stared at her for a moment and then shrugged.

'She can't want anything to do with me, Em. It's over a year now and she's not written – not once.'

'But you should at least go and find out for definite.'

Josh was silent for a long moment before muttering, 'I'll think about it.'

Twenty-Six

'Nearly Christmas already, Dad,' Amy said, a little wistfully. 'Harry's first Christmas.'

Bob smiled at his daughter. 'We'll make it a very special one, love.'

'It'd be special if—' She broke off and turned away so that he wouldn't see the tears filling her eyes. But Bob knew. He put his arms around her. 'I know, love, I know. But I think you'll have to come to terms with the knowledge that, after all this time, Josh isn't going to come back – or even write. Not now. It's been too long.' He paused and then asked gently, 'Are you still writing to him?'

Amy shook her head. 'I wrote a few times and then, when I didn't hear anything more from him, I – I stopped.'

'I think you've done the right thing. Now, I've got something to show you. Harry's asleep, isn't he? Just come with me. It'll only take a minute.'

Intrigued, Amy followed her father into the smithy. There, in the centre of the cluttered floor, was a baby walker fashioned in wood; a little box on four wheels and a handle at one side for the child to push it.

'Oh Dad, have you made that? It's wonderful.'

'I've seen him trying to pull himself up already and he tries to say his first words. He's a clever little chap.'

Amy laughed. 'Of course he is.' In her father's eyes,

220

little Harry could do no wrong and he was the brightest, cleverest child that had ever been born. Amy counted herself very fortunate in having Bob for her father; some parents might have disowned her and thrown her out of her home. Bob had not only stood by her, but he was also devoted to his grandson and couldn't do enough for him.

'Aunty Grace has knitted him a warm coat for winter and Mrs Trippet sent some lovely toys.'

Bob chuckled. 'I've a stack of little gifts hidden in my bedroom ready for Christmas Eve. We must hang a stocking up for him.'

'Oh Dad, you shouldn't have spent so much.'

'I haven't – at least, not yet.' He grinned. 'The presents I'm talking about are all from the villagers. Someone stops by most days and leaves a little something for him for Christmas.'

Amy's mouth dropped open and she stared at him. Her eyes filled with tears at the thought of such kindness from people who very well might have ignored her in the street. Instead, they were showing their understanding and support.

It was more than she could have dared to hope for.

Ever since Belle had told him that she had seen Thomas and Emily together in the park, Arthur had pondered the problem. Perhaps their meeting was innocent enough. After all, it had taken Belle long enough to find them. Almost a year – far too long for the impatient man. It crossed his mind that she had deliberately delayed telling him. No doubt, she had some ridiculous romantic notion about the young couple in her head. No matter, he told himself, but now, to be absolutely sure, he must see them together for himself. But how could he bring that about? He could hardly frequent the city's parks each weekend himself. Then the memory of them dancing together came into his mind and an idea began to form. It would cost him a lot of money, but if it separated his son from an unsuitable liaison, then it would be worth it. He would hire the banqueting hall at Cutlers' Hall and hold a Christmas ball for all his employees and, to be sure that the Ryans attended, he would ask Matthew Waterfall to join forces with him. That way, not only would it ensure that they were present, but it would also halve the cost for him. Matthew owed him a favour or two and now was the time to call in the debt. But would that ensure that the Ryan girl went? he pondered. He'd heard that she and one or two other girls had set themselves up in a small workshop, though the boy Josh was still working at Waterfall's. Still, Arthur smiled grimly as he reached for a pen and paper. There was always a way around every problem . . .

'You will never guess in a million years,' Lizzie announced one morning at the beginning of December. 'The missus stopped me in the court last night and told me that Mr Waterfall and Mr Trippet are joining together to hold a works' ball at Cutlers' Hall in a week's time. And best of all, we've all been invited because we were employees at Waterfall's until recently. Mrs Nicholson said Mr Waterfall himself had asked her 'specially to make sure that we were invited. Isn't that wonderful? And of course,' she smiled at Emily, 'Trip's bound to be there and you'll come this time, won't you, Nell?'

But Nell shook her head. 'I can't, Lizzie. Sorry, but

I really can't.' She turned away and started up her machine almost as if to prevent any more questions.

Lizzie shrugged and turned to her work. She was determined to go and that evening she waylaid Josh in the court as he arrived home from work.

'Have you heard about the ball?'

Josh nodded.

'We've been invited even though we don't work for Waterfall's any more. We're "Dugdale and Ryan" now. Doesn't that sound grand? Nell didn't want her name in the title and she doesn't want to come to the ball either.' Lizzie shrugged, mystified as to why any young woman would want to miss such a glittering occasion. 'So, I hope you're taking me.'

'Of course,' he smiled gallantly. 'Who else would I take, because I rather think my sister is already spoken for, don't you?'

'I'd've thought her an' Trip would have announced an engagement before now. They've been meeting almost every week for over a year.'

Josh stiffened. He and Lizzie had been seen together for all of that time as well. Was she hinting that they, too, should have a better understanding? Josh felt torn; in his own mind, he was still engaged to Amy. He glanced down at the girl beside him. She was pretty and lively and she was *here*. Amy wasn't and whilst, in his heart of hearts, he knew he still loved Amy, how could a man be expected to stay faithful if he never heard a word from her?

But for now, he pushed these uncomfortable thoughts aside; he didn't want to face them.

The two girls and Josh travelled to the ball at Cutlers' Hall together and once again, Trip was waiting impatiently for them. In full view of everyone, he kissed Emily, tucked her arm through his, and led her into the ballroom.

'Well, well, things have certainly progressed a little since last year,' Lizzie said, 'and be warned, my fine prince, I mean to have a kiss like that from you before this evening's over.'

Josh merely laughed. What harm was there in just one kiss?

It was a merry evening for all except for one person, who watched from the shadows with anger and resentment. After Belle had at last found out what he wanted to know, he'd laid his plans carefully and, now he could see the couple for himself, he was incensed. He would take no action until the New Year, he decided. Thomas was due home for the Christmas holiday and Constance would make her husband's life a misery if the occasion were spoiled by a quarrel between father and son. No, he would bide his time, but as he watched Thomas and Emily dancing so closely together, it took a great effort not to rush onto the dance floor and physically tear them apart.

Arthur turned away and left the hall to seek solace in Belle's comforting arms.

Trip and Emily couldn't remember ever feeling so happy. No longer were they hiding from the world, for tonight everyone could see the love they had for each other shining in their eyes.

Later, in a secluded corner, Trip whispered words of devotion. 'Oh Emily, I do so want to marry you. Please say you will.'

'Trip, darling,' she breathed. 'You know I will.'

He kissed her again and murmured. 'We'll announce

our engagement in the New Year. It might have to be a long one, my darling.'

'I'll wait,' Emily said simply.

As he walked her home through the darkness, Trip said, 'I won't see you until then, my love. I must go home to see my mother at Christmas and I really will try and see Amy this time. I tried last Christmas, but she was ill. I asked Mother when I went home at Easter, but she seemed very vague about what was going on in the village, even though I know she's involved with the Friendly Society. Father, of course, never takes any interest in anything that's happening in Ashford. He never has.'

'Of course you must go and see your mother. You don't get over very often as it is.'

'It'll be easier now I've got the motorbike, but I can't wait to get back to you. Will you meet me at the band-stand in Weston Park on New Year's Day? It's on a Sunday this year.'

'I'll be there,' Emily promised.

In the shadows of the court, Lizzie was doing her best to wheedle a declaration of love from Josh. 'Now, how about that kiss you promised me?' she murmured. She slipped her arms around his waist and offered up her face to him.

For a moment, Josh held back but then, with a deep sigh, he closed his eyes, bent his head and kissed her gently. As he felt desire surge through him, he held her tightly and his kiss deepened.

Triumphant in what she believed to be his capitula-tion at long last, Lizzie pressed herself against him.

She'd make him forget that he ever knew a girl called Amy.

225

Christmas Eve, 1921, was colder than it had been the previous year, with ground frosts at night, so, instead of arranging a party in the court, Mick prevailed upon his mother to hold 'open house' so that all the neighbours could visit the Dugdales' house and partake in a buffet-style meal. In addition, the young man took a hamper to each house in the court and toys for Rosa's children.

'Is there anything special your dad needs, Emily?' he asked. 'This cold weather can't be good for him.'

'You've done so much for our family, Mick.'

The young man grinned, his eyes glinting. 'It's my pleasure. What are friends for?'

'And we're so grateful for all you've done to help us with the buffing business too.'

'Is everything going well? Is old man Hawke still keeping to his side of the bargain?'

Emily frowned. 'I – I don't understand.'

'Keeping the rent low and finding you plenty of work?'

Some instinct – she didn't know why – stopped her from giving Mick any details. Instead she said airily, 'Oh yes, he still gives us plenty of work to keep us busy.'

'And the rent?' Suddenly, Mick's tone was abrupt.

'Yes, it's not much at all. He says he'd rather have the premises occupied than standing empty and deteriorating.' This was the truth for it was what Nathan had said.

Now Mick grinned, seeming satisfied by her answer. 'I'm pleased to hear it. I wouldn't like to have to pay him a visit. You know what I mean?'

He gave her nose a gentle tweak and walked away

leaving her staring after him, a puzzled frown on her forehead. No, she didn't understand what he meant.

As the celebrations in the court came to an end just before midnight, Mick put his arm around a slightly tipsy Martha. 'You'll let your Josh come out with me and the lads on Boxing Day, won't you? He deserves a bit of fun. I hear he's been working very hard at Waterfall's and is doing very well.'

'How d'you know that?'

'Oh, there's not much that goes on in this city that I don't know about, Mrs Ryan.'

Martha reached up and patted his cheek. 'You're a good boy, Mick. You've been so kind to our family. I don't know what we'd do without the extra coal you get us in the winter, but I do wish you'd let me pay you for it.'

'Nah, no need. Old Joe Ingall –' he referred to the coalman on Garden Street – 'is only too glad to help his regular customers out when times are tough.' He paused and then murmured, 'After I had a quiet word with him, of course.' He squeezed her shoulders as he added, 'So, it'll be all right if Josh comes out with us, then?'

'You'll look after him, won't you? Don't let him get into any trouble.'

Through the gloom, Mick grinned at her. 'Of course, I will. Lizzie's very fond of Josh and I'd do anything to keep my sister happy. Anything at all.'

Twenty-Seven

The next morning, both Emily and Josh were thinking about the Christmases they'd had back home. Church in the morning with all their friends in the village followed by a wonderful roast dinner and, in the afternoon, whilst Martha and Walter dozed by the fire, the youngsters would meet Trip and Amy and climb the hill out of the village to Monsal Head to stand looking out over the dale and the viaduct. But this Christmas Day was much quieter for the Ryan family, though they could hear merrymaking in the Dugdale household until the early hours.

There was a knock on the door, however, about mid-morning on Boxing Day; Mick had come to take Josh out with him.

'You ready, mate?'

'Where are we going?' Josh asked as he stepped outside and closed the door quickly behind him.

'You'll see.'

'Is Lizzie coming?'

'Not this time. Women aren't welcome.'

'Why? What's going on?'

But Mick only tapped the side of his nose and winked.

Outside in the street, two of Mick's pals were waiting and the four of them walked to Sky Edge where several other youths and young men were waiting. They nodded to Josh and then whispered to one another.

'Is he orreight, Mick?' Josh heard one of them ask.

'He's my mate, so of course he's all right. Besides, he's courting my sister. And I'm fussy who takes Lizzie out. And you should know that better than anyone, Pete.'

The other young man grunted and cast a resentful glance at Josh. 'What's he got that I haven't, eh?'

'She likes him, Pete, that's all it takes. Now, let's get this game started, eh? You posted the crows?'

'Course. We're all ready. Gary's on lookout duty over there,' he nodded towards the path that Josh and Mick had come along, 'and two of his mates are on t'other side.'

Mick turned to Josh. 'You ready, mate?'

But Josh was still standing gazing out over the magnificent view of the city. 'I never knew it was so big. What a wonderful view. I'll have to bring Em up here. She'd love this.'

'I wouldn't, if you know what's good for you,' Mick muttered. 'There's a lot goes on up here that nobody knows about, an' we don't want 'em to either, so you just keep pretty Emily away from here. Orreight, mate? Now, let me show you how we play pitch and toss.'

Suddenly, Josh realized what was happening. This was Sky Edge, which Eddie Crossland had warned him about. 'Oh, I don't think . . .' he began, but catching sight of the warning look on Mick's face, his courage failed. Seeing Josh's capitulation, Mick grinned and slapped him on the shoulder.

'I run these games so I'm what we call the "toller", 'cos I collect the bets and I take a toll of three bob in the pound on every bet placed for missen. And –' he fished in his pocket and brought out five shiny half-crowns – 'here's all we need. See, if we do get caught, the "evidence" is soon hidden amongst our own loose change. Now, you watch for a bit and I'll show you how it's done.'

Several men squatted down about the pitch and the game began with someone shouting, 'Heads a pound.' Then someone else responded with, 'Tail it.'

Josh watched in fascination; he couldn't help being caught up in the excitement. Money was quickly won and lost on how the coins would fall with each toss. They played for two hours, not bothering to keep their voices low; the 'crows' would warn of anyone approaching.

''Ere, don't we get a game or two, Mick?' One of the lookouts protested after a couple of hours. He jabbed his finger towards Josh. 'Can't he take his turn? He's got a fistful of notes already.'

After watching for a few games, Josh hadn't been unable to resist joining in. He had been winning steadily, much to the disgust of several of the other men. 'Is he cheating, Mick?' Pete asked at last.

'Course not. He's got the luck of the Devil, that's all.'

'But you're running the book . . .'

'Shut up, Pete.' Gary nudged Pete. 'Mick knows what he's doing.'

For a moment Pete blinked and then understanding seemed to penetrate his dull brain as he grinned and nodded. 'Oh, I see.' He raised his voice and said, 'Right, then, Josh. It's you against me.'

Josh stuffed the money in his pocket and shook his head. 'No, I'll quit while I'm ahead if you don't mind.'

'But I do mind,' Pete began and suddenly his face was menacing, until Mick put a warning hand on his arm.

'Leave it.' There was authority in his tone and the other young man, though he shot a look of disgust at Mick, did as he was asked. Pete held out his hand to Josh. 'As long as you give me a chance to win it back again next time, eh?'

'Course,' Josh agreed, taking the proffered hand, but he wasn't sure there would be a next time if he could help it. There was something vaguely uncomfortable about the whole set-up and his feeling of disquiet only intensified when Mick said, 'Right, Josh, your turn on lookout duty. You'll be paid for it, of course.'

Josh blinked. 'Lookout? What am I looking out for?'

Pete groaned as he muttered, 'What the hell have you brought us, Mick? He's a right barm pot.'

Nettled by the insult, Josh turned to Mick and said, 'Just tell me what you want me to do and I'll do it.'

'There you are, Pete. He can't say fairer than that, now, can he?'

But Pete's only reply was a grunt.

'Over here, mate.' Mick beckoned Josh to follow him as he led him to a high point overlooking the path they had taken to get here. 'Just keep a watch out for anyone coming and let me know. Don't shout, mind, just come and tell me right quick.'

Josh shrugged. He didn't understand what all the fuss was about. They were only playing what seemed to be a harmless game of pitch and toss – something he and Emily had played as children, only they'd called it 'heads or tails'. Even their dad had played it with them sometimes, though, he had to admit, their games had never been for money.

He stood there for half an hour, growing colder and colder. He stamped his feet and huddled further into his coat and glanced around him. There! Had he seen a movement? Maybe it was only a rabbit, but – the bitter wind was making his eyes water. He blinked furiously to clear his vision and then, through the gloom of the winter's day, he saw two figures coming up the path. Perhaps they were only a couple taking an afternoon walk with their dog, but he didn't wait to find out. He hurried back to where the group were still playing.

'Mick – Mick,' he said urgently, but kept his voice low. 'There're two folks coming—'

He'd hardly got the words out before there was a hurried scramble to pick up the coins, for everyone to stuff their winnings into their pockets and run. They ran in all directions, like rats down a drainpipe, Josh thought. He'd never seen anyone move so quickly. In seconds, there was no evidence of what had been going on, except perhaps for the circle of trampled grass and undergrowth. Mick gripped Josh's arm. 'You come with me,' he said, and hustled him down the slope on the opposite side to where the figures were walking up the path.

'Just act normal, like we're out for a walk. In fact, we'll stand here admiring the view and I'll be pointing out places of interest.' He glanced over his shoulder. 'Here they come,' he said, beneath his breath. He stuck out his arm, pointing towards the buildings. 'You see that big church, well, that's our cathedral. It only got cathedral status same year as the war started an' then over there—' He swung his arm round, still pointing over the city, just as two policemen – a sergeant and a constable – came up behind them. Mick glanced over his shoulder. 'Hello, officers. What brings you up here on this cold day?'

'You know very well, Mick Dugdale. You and your cronies, that's what.'

'And who's this, might I ask?' the constable asked, nodding towards Josh.

Mick put his arm around Josh's shoulders. 'You may indeed, officer. This is my friend, Josh Ryan. He's come to live next door to us.'

'And what do you do, lad?'

'I work at Waterfall's.'

'Oh aye, I know it,' the sergeant said. 'Good place to work. I've an uncle worked there for years, he has.' He paused and then nodded towards Mick. 'But you want to be careful of the company you keep, young feller.'

'Oh officer, you wound me.' With a dramatic gesture, Mick put his hand over his heart.

'Aye, an' I would an' all, if I had my way. Just watch your step, m'lad, because me and *my* lads have got you in our sights. Now –' he nodded down the slope where all the others had fled – 'I 'spect they've all scarpered by now and there's nowt for us to see. But think on, owd lad. You just think on.'

The two officers turned and went back down the path. When they were well out of earshot, Mick breathed a sigh of relief. 'By, that were a close 'un.' He slapped Josh on the back. 'Well done. You did a good job there, mate.'

But as they walked home, Josh wasn't so sure. He was still feeling a bit bemused by what had happened and more than a little uncomfortable. The only thing that cheered him was the rustle of pound notes in his pocket. He'd be able to give his mam some extra this week and, if necessary, he could explain it away by saying that Waterfall's had given him a Christmas bonus.

As they parted in the yard outside their homes, Mick gripped Josh's arm and said, 'Now, remember, keep your mouth shut about what's gone on today. You understand, don't you? Don't even tell your pretty Emily about this, orreight?' And, to underline his point, he squeezed even harder until his grip hurt.

'Of course not, Mick. I won't say a word.'

'Good.' Now Mick slapped him on the back. 'Good lad.'

Twenty-Eight

On New Year's Day, Emily waited in the park until it grew dusk. Everyone else had left now, hurrying home to the warmth of a fire as the evening grew even colder. She shivered and reluctantly walked slowly back to Garden Street. Where was Trip? Why hadn't he come to meet her as they had arranged? Had something happened to him?

'Where on earth have you been?' Martha snapped as Emily entered the house. 'I need help with your father. His breathing's bad. Get your coat off and give me a hand to get him to bed. I've put a heated brick in his bed. He'll be warmer there. You can take his tea up to him later and feed him.'

Emily pushed her own anxiety about Trip aside as she saw that her father's breathing was laboured and painful. His face was grey, his lips purple.

'He ought to see a doctor,' Emily muttered, but Martha waved her suggestion aside with a sharp, 'I can't be affording doctors. You still don't bring enough in,' she said nastily. 'Even though you fancy you're a businesswoman now.'

They struggled to get Walter up the stairs and they were both breathless by the time he was lying on his bed.

'Now,' Martha gasped, 'help me undress him.'

'I can't do that, Mam. Leave the poor man some dignity, for Heaven's sake.'

Martha waved aside her protests. 'He left his modesty in the trenches, Emily. You have to help me. He's a dead weight when he's like this.'

'Where's Josh? He could help you.'

'Out with Lizzie. He's been mooning about the place ever since before Christmas. They'll be getting engaged soon, I shouldn't wonder.'

Emily bit back the retort that her brother was already promised to Amy; it was not something her mother wanted to hear and Emily had no wish to aggravate Martha's present bad mood. Not for her own sake, but for her poor father's.

Josh stumbled in very late, long after Martha had gone to bed. Emily had sat up waiting for him; there was something that had to be said. He was a little worse for drink, but not so drunk that he couldn't understand what she was saying to him.

For the first time in her life, Emily lashed Josh with her tongue.

'Have you a thought for Dad? Mam says we can't afford a doctor for him and here you are, wasting money on beer and the like.' Her deep anxiety over Trip made her speak even more sharply to her brother than she would have done. But once started, there was no stopping her. 'Have you been out with Lizzie?'

'I might have been,' he mumbled, startled by Emily's anger. 'Wha's it got to do with you?'

'Plenty! Have you forgotten Amy?'

Josh blinked and stared at her for a moment, almost as if that was exactly what he had done. Then he laughed – the silly laughter of the inebriated. 'Amy? Who's Amy?'

'Your fiancée, Josh. The girl you left behind in Ashford and haven't bothered about since.'

'I have,' he muttered, suddenly morose once more.

'But she doesn't care about me any more. She's never written. Not once.'

'Don't you want to find out *why* she's not written to either of us? You asked her to marry you and I thought I was her best friend. We've both written – several times – so why have we heard nothing from her in return? And, if you are getting close to Lizzie –' Emily noticed at once that Josh now avoided meeting her gaze and looked a little sheepish – 'I think the least you can do is to go and see Amy first. See how *you* really feel. And be honest with her – with both of them, if it comes to that. Lizzie and her mother have been very helpful to us. I don't want you hurting her either. I've tried to warn her, but she doesn't listen to me.'

'Or me, if it comes to that,' Josh said ruefully. 'I . . .' he began and then hesitated.

'What?'

'I don't really know how I feel, Em, and that's the truth. I loved Amy – I know that.'

'Loved? Past tense?'

Josh sighed. 'I still do, I suppose. But she's not here and—'

'Lizzie is.' Emily finished the sentence for him.

Josh nodded, looking so woebegone that Emily felt sorry for him. He was such a kindly young fellow, he wouldn't hurt a fly and he certainly wouldn't want to hurt either of the girls.

Emily moved to him and put her arm through his, smiling up at him. 'Listen to your big sister for a moment. Go back to Ashford – just for a visit – to see Amy. It might help settle things in your own mind – one way or the other.'

'What if it doesn't?'

'We'll cross that bridge when we come to it. But,'

she added, lowering her voice, 'if you'll take my advice, don't tell Mam you're going. Get up early next Sunday morning and just go. Trip said he'd take you once he got a sidecar. But he wasn't at the park today.'

'Wasn't he?' Josh said mildly, but Emily could see that his mind was elsewhere.

'And for Heaven's sake, stop going out with Mick Dugdale and his mates and spending all your hard-earned money when Mam's saying we haven't enough for a doctor for Dad.'

Suddenly, Josh put his hand in the inside pocket of his jacket and pulled out a fistful of pound notes. He threw them on the table with an angry gesture. 'There, is that enough for you? That should pay for several visits from a doctor. Might even get him a bed in the hospital, if that's what you want.'

Emily stared open-mouthed at the money. 'Josh – where did you get all that?'

Suddenly, Josh realized what he had done. In his frustration at her nagging, he'd forgotten to guard his tongue. He tried using the same ploy he'd used to his mother.

'It's what I've got left from my Christmas bonus.'

But that wasn't going to work on Emily as it had on Martha. She was far too shrewd and knew a lot more about the cutlery industry than their mother did.

'Don't give me that. Waterfall's doesn't give bonuses. Come on, tell me.'

'You're to promise not to tell anyone.'

'Just tell me, Josh,' Emily said, her tone tight.

'I've been out with Mick – not Lizzie – and we go up to Sky Edge and play pitch and toss.'

Emily pulled in a startled breath. 'Gambling, you mean? But – but that's illegal, Josh. Oh my goodness! What if you'd been caught?'

'We nearly were,' he admitted. 'On Boxing Day. That was the first time Mick took me up there and these two coppers came up and—'

'And you haven't had the sense to keep out of it since? Oh Josh, what have you got yourself into?'

He shrugged. 'I can't see the harm in it, myself. It's like we used to play when we were kids, Em. You know, heads or tails. That's all.'

'Maybe, but we didn't *bet* on who was going to win, did we? It's the betting that's illegal, unless you've got a licence. And I don't think Mick Dugdale has one, do you?'

They stared at each other in the soft lighting. Neither of them could think of anything else to say but they were both fully aware now of the enormity of what Josh had got involved in.

At last, Emily said, 'You'd better get to bed. We've work in the morning, both of us.'

As he paused at the stairs, he murmured, 'I'm sorry, Em. I'll sort it out, I promise. And I'm sorry about Trip. But he'll be all right. Maybe he hasn't come back after Christmas yet. I expect his mother wanted to see a bit more of him.' He grinned suddenly. 'There must be some compensations for being the boss's son.'

He crept quietly up the stairs leaving Emily thinking, Not when Arthur Trippet's the boss, there aren't.

Now she had two worries and she didn't know which frightened her the most: Trip not turning up to meet her or Josh being involved in activities that were regarded as criminal.

Twenty-Nine

Trip wasn't in the park the following Sunday or the week after.

'Haven't you heard anything from him?' Josh asked her.

Emily bit her lower lip to try to stop the tears from starting in her eyes. But the lump in her throat prevented her from speaking. Sadly, she shook her head and turned away.

She felt Josh's hand on her shoulder and heard him say, 'If you don't hear something soon, I'll go to Trippets', if you like. Mr Bayes might know something.'

'Thank you, Josh,' Emily said huskily. 'What about you? How's – everything?' He'd been out again the previous weekend, but this time he'd persuaded Mick to let him take Lizzie out to the theatre. Anything, he thought, was better than getting in deeper and deeper with Mick Dugdale and his exploits. Even if it meant giving Lizzie the wrong idea. For the rest of the week, Josh had seemed distracted and he had made two serious mistakes at work, which had resulted in another warning from Mr Crossland.

'I don't reckon you listened to a word I said last time, did you, lad? You've been seen with Mick Dugdale. Well, it'll do you no good.' He stepped closer and lowered his voice. 'Look, Josh. You're a nice lad. I like you and – most of the time – you're a damned good worker. But this week your mind's been elsewhere and I can't have that when you're operating dangerous machinery. And if you're going to spend your free time with the likes of him, then I'd have to think seriously about keeping you on here. I'll give you a tip, lad, though I'd ask you to keep it to yourself. My nephew's a copper and they've got Mick Dugdale and his gang in their sights. I wouldn't like to see you caught up in that, 'specially if there are some arrests soon.'

Josh gaped at him and actually trembled inside.

Hoarsely, he said, 'Thanks, Mr Crossland. I'll mind what you say. Really, I will.'

As he walked home, Josh was deep in thought. He would keep that piece of knowledge to himself; he wouldn't even tell Emily and he certainly wouldn't say a word to Lizzie, though he did feel guilty. Whatever they said, Mick had been good to the Ryan family in all sorts of ways and it was Mick who'd been instrumental in helping the girls set up their 'little missuses' business. Josh sighed. Whatever was he going to do?

'Josh, you really ought to go to Ashford and sort things out.' Despite her own ever-growing worries about Trip, Emily was still anxious about her brother.

Josh turned away. 'Soon, Em. I'll go soon. Another week or so won't make a lot of difference now.'

'It might, where Lizzie's concerned. She does nothing at work but talk about you when the machines are off and even when they're on sometimes, but we've all stopped lip-reading her.'

Josh smiled thinly. 'You're right, of course. Things are getting a bit more – well, you know – between Lizzie and me. It would be better if I knew once and for all.'

'Then for Heaven's sake *go*, Josh. And the sooner, the better.'

Josh gave a lot of thought to what Emily had said. In fact, he thought of little else. She was right, of course, about Amy and Lizzie, but she didn't know the half of it. He'd give anything to be safely back in Ashford with Amy and well away from Mick Dugdale.

The following evening, when Josh arrived home, he was agitated and kept glancing anxiously at Emily. She could see that he was itching to tell her something. As soon as they could, they left the house and went outside. Emily pulled her coat tightly around; it was bitterly cold.

'Trip's gone,' Josh burst out.

'What do you mean?'

'I went to Trippets' for you, like I promised. Mr Bayes said there was a terrible row between Trip and his father just after Christmas. Trip stormed out of his office, roared off on his motorbike and no one's seen him since.'

'What was the row about? Did Mr Bayes know?'

'Not really . . .'

'He'll have gone home. That's where he'll be. Back in Ashford.'

'I don't think so. Mr Bayes said he did hear the final words. Mr Trippet told him to get out of the factory, that he was no longer a son of his and – and that he wasn't to go home.'

'Not go home!' Emily was shocked. 'But what about his mother? Mrs Trippet is a lovely lady. Look how much she's always done in the village. Surely she wouldn't stand by and see her son treated like that.'

'Huh! I bet old man Trippet rules the roost. She'll

have to do what he says or risk being thrown out too, I shouldn't wonder.'

'But Trip's his only son. His heir.'

Josh didn't answer.

'I must find out where he is, Josh. If you don't go to Ashford, then I will.'

'I'll go. I've got to be the one to go.'

'When?'

'Just as soon as I can.'

Two more weeks went by and it was the beginning of February. Josh still made excuses not to go to Ashford. With each day that passed, Emily became more and more frantic to find out something – anything – about Trip. She comforted herself with the thought that Trip would have gone home at least to *see* his mother, even if he couldn't stay at Riversdale House. He'll be all right, she told herself, but somehow she couldn't convince herself and she was irritated with Josh that he was still putting off going to Ashford both to see Amy and to find out about Trip. If Josh didn't go that weekend, she promised herself, then she would.

'Any letters, Mam?' she asked when she came home from work every night and, each time, Martha shook her head.

It was the second Saturday of February when Emily, tired and dispirited, sat helping her father to eat his evening meal. 'You look good tonight, Dad,' she said, trying to sound cheerful for his sake. The last person she wanted to worry was her beloved father. 'Are you feeling a bit better?'

She hadn't expected him to reply; Walter hardly ever responded to anything that was said to him. Most of the time, he just sat sunken in gloom, probably with horrific memories of the trenches going through his mind that would then bring on a bout of shaking. But tonight, he was sitting up straight, there was no shaking and he was staring at her, his eyes bright, and he looked as if he was trying to tell her something.

'What is it, Dad?' Emily said softly.

Walter glanced warily across the room to where Martha and Josh sat at the table eating their tea. Emily looked at them too and then her gaze came back to Walter's face. Slowly, he put his fingers to his lips. Emily nodded that she understood. There was something he wanted to communicate to her but not, it seemed, in front of either Martha or Josh, or maybe both of them. She nodded and whispered, 'Later, Dad, eh?'

There was the ghost of a smile on his mouth, something Emily hadn't seen for years.

After tea was finished and the washing-up done, Josh went out and Martha went upstairs to change the sheets on Walter's bed.

When they were both safely out of earshot, Emily said softly, 'What is it, Dad?'

Walter opened his mouth, trying hard to speak, but the words would not come. Then he spread his left hand and with his right forefinger he made a sign as if he were writing something.

'You want to write something?'

Walter shook his head and repeated his action. Then he acted out folding a piece of paper, putting it in an envelope, licking the edge and sealing it.

'You want to write a letter?' Again, Walter shook his head. Then he pointed to the clock on the mantelpiece above the range, behind which were one or two official-looking letters.

Emily pointed at them. 'Is there something in one of

those you want me to read? No? Then I wonder . . .'
Emily frowned. He was trying desperately to tell her
something.

'It's something about a letter, is it?'

Now Walter nodded.

'Letters we've written or ones written to us.' As he
nodded again, Emily asked, 'Both?'

Another nod.

Now Walter put his hands together and acted out
tearing paper and then tossing it into the range fire.

'Letters have been torn up and burned. Is – is that
what you're telling me?'

Again, his answer was 'yes'.

Now Emily stared at him, wide-eyed. 'But – who?
And – and why? And which letters?' And then she knew.
Without Walter having to make any more signs, she
knew. But she had to be sure.

'Who, Dad? Who destroyed the letters?'

Slowly, Walter glanced up towards the ceiling.

'Mam? Mam did that?' Emily whispered, shocked
now beyond belief.

Walter's eyes filled with tears as he nodded. Emily
took hold of his hands and held them tightly as she
asked, 'Amy's letters to us?'

Walter gave a sob, but nodded.

'What about ours to her, because we've both written
to her and left them on the table for Mam to post for
us?'

He put a shaking hand to his head as he nodded
again.

'And – and has there been one for me recently from
Trip?'

Another 'yes'.

Emily was horrified and yet there was a little comfort

in the thought that Trip had written to her since he'd gone missing.

Now, Walter's eyes were frightened as he pulled one hand away from her and put his finger to his lips.

'I must tell Josh,' she said urgently. 'He must know, but I promise we won't say a word to Mam.'

At once Walter relaxed and, as they heard Martha's footsteps coming down the stairs, he fell back in his chair and closed his eyes, exhausted by the supreme exertion of communicating with Emily. She stood up as Martha came in. 'Is his bed ready, Mam?' With a great effort Emily managed to make her voice sound normal. 'He seems very tired.'

'I'm not surprised. He's been on edge all day. I don't know what the matter is.'

I do, Emily wanted to shout. Maybe he watched you burn yet another letter, probably one for me from Trip, and he just couldn't bear the deceit any longer. But instead she pressed her lips together and said nothing. 'I'll help you,' she said, with surprising calmness. 'Have you got a brick heating in the oven?'

Martha nodded. 'I'll take it up and we'll get him into bed.'

Tenderly, she touched her father's hand. 'Come on, Dad. Let's get you upstairs and you can sleep.' As her mother left the room again, she whispered, 'Don't you worry about a thing.'

But what would Josh say and do when she told him?

Thirty

After her father was safely in bed and, to Emily's relief, asleep, she left the house and went in search of Josh.

'Hello, luv,' Bess Dugdale said as she answered Emily's knock. 'You lookin' for Lizzie?'

'No, actually, it's Josh I was looking for. Is he here?'

'Sorry, luv, no. He hasn't been round here of an evening for several days now.' She stepped close. 'Have they quarrelled, d'you know?'

'I . . . don't know, Mrs Dugdale.'

Bess was thoughtful for a moment, then she shrugged. 'Lizzie seems OK. If there'd been a row, she'd have been in a right teking, I can tell you.'

Emily tried to smile. The news she had to impart to Josh would change everything. 'If you do see Josh, please tell him to come home.'

'Is it your dad, luv?'

'No, no, he's fine, but – Josh is needed at home.'

'Well, he's gone out with Mick and his mates. I do know that, though our Lizzie's fuming about it. She wanted Josh to take her out, it being Saturday night.' Noticing Emily's worried frown, Bess said, 'But don't you worry about your Josh. Mick's a good lad. He'll look after him.'

If Emily had known exactly where Josh was at that moment, she would have been truly alarmed.

*　　*　　*

247

As Josh arrived home from work at lunchtime, Mick had been hovering in the courtyard. 'Orreight, Josh?'

Josh forced a grin. 'I will be, when I've had a good wash and called it the weekend.'

'Be ready at six tonight. Pete's picking up a car and taking us out of the city for a little drive.'

Josh felt a wave of relief; there couldn't be any harm in a drive in the countryside. It'd be good to get out of the smoke and dust of the narrow streets. Now Josh smiled genuinely. 'I might have to help Mam with me dad before—'

'Can't Emily help? Or they can call on my mam for help. Tha's gotta be ready at six, mate. Pete can't have the car for long. He's – er – borrowing it.'

'All right, I'll be ready.'

As soon as he got in, he said, 'Is Emily home?'

'Not yet. Working late – again. I think she makes a lot more of this little business of hers than it really is. Anyone would think she's angling to be Master Cutler one day.'

'Mick's asked me to go out with him tonight. We're going for a ride in the countryside. Is that all right, Mam? I mean, Emily will be home soon to help you with Dad.'

'Of course, it is. You go out and enjoy yourself. You've worked hard all week and you've been so good giving me extra money. You deserve a bit of fun. Your dad's a bit on edge today, but he's all right. We'll manage him.'

And so Josh, believing that all the evening held was a merry drive out into the countryside in Pete's borrowed car, had gone happily to meet up with Mick.

Pete arrived in an open-topped Model T Ford. Gary

was already sitting beside him as Mick and Josh paused to admire the motorcar.

'By heck, Pete, you've got a good 'un tonight. Shame to—'

'Look quick,' Pete shouted above the noisy engine. 'I don't want to hang about.'

When Mick and Josh had climbed into the back, they were off with a jerk as more and more folks on Garden Street came out of their houses to see what the commotion was. Mick waved grandly, just as if he were visiting royalty as the car reached the edge of the city and began to chug up the hill towards Baslow. Soon, they were out in the countryside and the cold wind was biting their faces and chilling them through. This wasn't quite the nice drive Josh'd thought it would be; his teeth were chattering.

'Is it much further, Pete?' Mick shouted. 'We're perished back here.'

'Not far. Just down this narrow lane . . .' He swung the car to the left and it bounced and jolted over rough ground. About half a mile down the lane, he turned left again into a grass field and drove across it towards a huge barn.

Josh was now beginning to feel apprehensive; this was no ordinary drive out into the country. Now he could see the moving shadows of several men – in fact, a lot more than several, there must be at least a hundred, he thought – all moving towards the barn. Pete drew the car to a halt alongside one or two other vehicles on the far side of the building, out of sight from the lane.

'Come on,' Mick said, climbing out. 'Josh, I want a word before we go in.' There was excitement in his tone. Pete and Gary moved away, following the other men into the barn.

'I want you to be me runner tonight, Josh.'

'What is this, Mick? Another pitch and toss game?'

'Nah! It's bare-knuckle boxing. A lot more money to be made here, mate. Now, you go around the crowd taking bets, orreight? And you write out a slip for each one, 'cos we'll never remember all this lot. Pete and Gary'll be doin' it an' all, so you don't have to get round every-body.'

Josh sighed inwardly. Why had he been so naïve? A ride into the countryside on a winter's evening? He must have been mad to have believed such an unlikely story. But, sadly, he only realized it now. And now was too late!

They stepped inside the barn, which was surprisingly warm. In the centre was a makeshift boxing ring, with bales of straw placed to form an empty square.

'The lads like to see the boxers before they place their bets,' Mick said, 'just to see who they like the look of. Now, here're some bits of paper and a couple of pencils. Don't forget to write 'names down of who places what, 'cos you can't trust no one in this game.'

That, Josh could well believe!

Two men, dressed only in their vests and long johns, climbed over the bales. They took up their positions in opposite corners, their backs to the ring as they held out their hands to their seconds, two more men at each corner who appeared to be binding their boxer's knuckles with straw. Josh shuddered as he imagined what was going to happen and for the first time he was grateful he had a job to do and could avoid watching the bloodbath.

He weaved in and out of the crowd as bets began

to be taken. Soon he had run out of all the pieces of paper that Mick had given him and broken the tip of one of the pencils, but his pockets were bulging with money. As the first bout of the evening began, he threaded his way through the crowd to Mick.

'You've done well, Josh. Lizzie would be right proud of you – if she knew, which she mustn't. You know that, don't you, Josh?' His tone was deadly serious now. Gone in an instant was any joviality. 'No one must know. Orreight?'

Josh nodded, but avoided meeting Mick's penetrating gaze. 'What do you want me to do now, Mick?'

'You can watch the match with the rest of 'em, if you want, or you can help us count the money and take our dibs. When it finishes, we'll have to pay out to those that have won.'

'I'll help you,' Josh said quickly.

Mick had set himself up in a corner of the barn with an upturned box as a table. Pete and Gary arrived with their takings and the four of them began to count the money. Josh had never seen so much money in one place. He noticed that Gary tried to secrete a pound note up his sleeve, but Mick's sharp eyes saw him. He gripped his friend's arm and hissed, 'Don't you try that on me, mate, else I'll break your knuckles for yer.'

'Sorry, Mick.' Gary was immediately contrite. 'It's just that I ain't ever seen so much money.'

'You'll get your share. I'm always fair with you, ain't I?'

Subdued, Gary nodded. 'Sorry, Mick. It won't happen again.'

'It better hadn't,' Mick said warningly but then he was all smiles again.

There were three bouts and to Josh each one seemed

bloodier than the previous one. He was glad to run around with the winnings and then busy himself taking the next lot of bets. He didn't want to see two men trying to knock each other senseless. It was a gruesome sight and Josh felt sick every time he caught a glimpse of the fighters. The very last bout seemed worse than the previous two. They battered each other, until straw bits from their bound hands were sticking to each other's facial wounds. Josh was glad – yet sorry at the same time for the chap on the floor – when it finally ended with a knockout.

When it was all over and the winners paid out, Mick gave Pete, Gary and Josh their earnings for the evening. As the crowd began to disperse, Mick said, 'Right, we've earned a few beers now, lads. There's a crate hidden under those bales over there. I brought 'em when I did a recce yesterday.'

Gary grinned and headed to the corner whilst Pete said, 'Mick always checks out a place first, just to make sure it's as safe as it can be. And we never go to the same place twice running. Mind you,' he added, glancing round. 'We've been here before. 'Bout six months ago, I reckon, but it were light nights then and a bit more risky. Folks don't come out so much when it's dark and cold. Not even coppers.'

They drank the beer sitting on the bales that had formed the ring, talking over the events of the evening.

'I fancied that big feller, the fair-haired one, in the first fight, to win, but he didn't last long. I thought it were a poor show, that fight,' Pete said. 'A lot of my punters weren't happy, Mick.'

But Mick only shrugged.

'The other two were good, though,' Gary put in. 'Everyone went away happy enough in the end.'

'Right,' Mick said standing up. 'We'd better get moving. Put the bales back where they belong, Gary, and take the crate and the bottles out to the car. It'll fit on the back seat between me an' Josh.'

As they were leaving, Mick paused at the doorway to take a last look around, then he extinguished all the lamps and set them near the door. Seeming satisfied that no trace of what had taken place that night remained, Mick gave a nod and led the way out of the barn. Outside, the wind seemed even more bitter and stung their cheeks.

'Are we doin' the usual with the car, Mick?' Pete asked.

'Yeah, but not here. We'll . . .'

Whatever he had been going to say stuck in his throat as half a dozen bulky shadows appeared out of the darkness.

'Evening, Micky lad.'

'Steve,' Mick said and Josh was certain his voice didn't sound so cocksure now. 'What you doin' here?'

'Keeping an eye on my territory, that's what.'

'*Your* territory?' Mick laughed, but it was obviously forced. 'I didn't know this was your patch.'

'Really?' Steve didn't sound as if he believed him.

'Yes, really, mate. I wouldn't tread on your toes. You should know that. We're mates, aren't we? You and me against the world, eh, Steve? Isn't that what we used to say?'

Steve gave a grunt, which could have been interpreted either way – yes or no. Then he stepped closer to Mick until their noses were almost touching and, in the moonlight, Josh was sure he saw the flash of a razor blade as Steve's hand moved up towards Mick's face.

'I ain't about to swing for you, Mick Dugdale. You

aren't worth that, but I'll slash you, if you're trying to take over my patch. See?'

Mick couldn't even nod acquiescence; the sharp blade was so close to his cheek. 'I'm not, Steve. I swear I'm not.'

Steve dropped his hand, stepped back and nodded. 'Glad to hear it. I don't mind you using Sky Edge as long as it doesn't clash with my nights, but this place is mine. See?'

'Orreight, Steve. We won't use it again.'

Steve's hand came up again swiftly and Mick flinched, but this time there was no knife as Steve patted Mick's cheek. 'That's a good boy.' He turned away and spoke to the other men ranged behind him. 'Orreight, lads, we're done here.'

'Aw, ain't we havin' a fisticuffs, Steve?' one of his henchmen said, sounding disappointed.

'Not now. It'll start to get light soon and farmers'll be about. I don't want to attract unwelcome attention.' As he walked away, he glanced at the car and called back over his shoulder, 'And I wouldn't go back into town in that. Word's already out. But don't do owt near here.'

'Right,' Mick said. 'Thanks.'

As they walked away, Mick muttered, 'Let's get going before he changes his mind. We'll get well away from here, as near home as is safe and then walk the rest.'

They drove a few miles from the field, back towards the city, but at the top of the last hill Pete halted the vehicle at the side of the road. 'This do, Mick?'

'Yes, fine. We'll leave you to it, Pete. Come on, you two.' The other three climbed out of the car and headed off down the road. The city lay below them, a few lights still twinkling through the darkness, though most law-

abiding citizens would still be in bed. Josh had no idea
of the time, but he guessed it was well into the early
hours.

'Mek haste. It'll be going up in a minute.'

'What will?' Josh's curiosity got the better of him at
last.

Gary groaned. 'We told you he was a barm pot,
Mick. He's still wet behind the ears.'

'He's orreight, ain't you, Josh? He knows how to
keep his mouth shut and he didn't try nicking off his
mates tonight like someone I could mention.'

At that moment there was a roar behind them and
they all turned to see the flames lighting up the night
sky.

'Oh God, it's the car. It's caught fire. What about
Pete?' Josh made as if to set off back towards the car,
but Mick grabbed his hand. 'He's set it on fire deliberately. Listen, that's him. Here he comes. Now, we'd all
better scarper.'

'Why's he done that?'

'I told you,' Gary muttered.

'Shut up, will yer, Gary? Leave this to me.'

As a breathless Pete caught up with them, the four
of them began to run at a steady pace down the road
until, about half a mile on, Mick suddenly said, 'Stop.
I can hear summat.'

They all stopped, standing very still and listening to
the sound of a motorbike's engine coming closer.

'Quick. Into the ditch.' As they scattered, Mick
grabbed Josh's arm and dragged him to the left. 'Not
that way. You'll roll down the hill. Here, stick close to
me and keep your head down.'

They slithered down the bank and splashed into icy
water in the bottom of a shallow ditch.

'Ugh! My feet—' Josh began and then found Mick's hand clamped firmly over his mouth as he pulled him down. They crouched in the ditch, below the level of the road, as two motorcycles roared past towards the burning car.

As the noise receded a little, Pete whispered, 'Were they coppers?'

'Dunno,' Mick said, 'but we're not waiting to find out.' He hauled Josh to his feet and they climbed up the bank and resumed their running, this time at a faster pace.

Thirty-One

It was almost dawn by the time Josh stumbled into the house. Though he'd drunk a lot of beer in the barn, the cold night air, together with the fear and the shock of realizing what he'd been involved in, had sobered him. As he crept into the bedroom, Emily woke up. She had only been able to doze on and off as she wanted to talk to Josh the moment he came in. No doubt he'd be a little worse for drink but, hopefully, not so drunk that he wouldn't be able to take in what she had to tell him. It was a good job it was a Saturday night, she thought, and he had no work the next day. As soon as she heard the creak of his bed and knew he had undressed and got into bed, she got out of her own bed and went round the curtain.

Sitting on the edge of his bed, she shook him by the shoulder. 'Josh, Josh, there's something I must tell you.'

'Won't it wait, Em? I'm tired.'

'Yes, I bet you are. Been spending all your wages again?'

'No, Mick was in the chair tonight – treating everyone. He'd had a bit of luck, he said. So no, I haven't been spending all my wages and I've plenty left for Mam.' This lie he'd worked out as he'd walked the last few yards home, when Mick had said it was safe to walk at an ordinary pace.

'Less suspicious now, we're amongst houses. You

only want one nosey old beggar to look out of his winder . . .'

As they'd parted in the court, Mick had pressed three pound notes into his hands. 'You did well tonight, Josh. You're one of us now.'

The intended compliment only brought dread to Josh's heart.

'Josh – don't fall asleep. I've got something to tell you. Josh . . .' Emily shook his shoulder again. 'Listen to me.'

With a groan, Josh pulled himself up in the bed and rubbed his eyes. 'Go on, then. Is it about Trip? Have you heard from him?'

'Not exactly. But Dad told me something tonight that explains everything.'

'Dad told you? How could he? He can't speak.'

'I know, but he made signs and I understood.'

Josh gaped at her as if he didn't believe her, but then he said, 'Go on.'

'Mam's been burning letters. Letters from Amy and, I think, ours to her as well.'

For a long moment in the dim light of the candle, Josh stared at her. 'You must have misunderstood. Mam wouldn't do that.' Then, after a long pause, there was doubt in his voice as he added, 'Would she?'

'Oh, I think so,' Emily said bitterly, a hard edge to her tone. 'To get what she wants, she'd do anything. She admitted to me a while back that she hadn't been truthful with us when she brought us to Sheffield. Mr Trippet never said he'd help you get a job, but she brought us anyway. I expect that's why you got the sack from there when he found out you were working there despite what he'd said.'

Josh ran his hand through his hair. 'My God! How could she do such a thing to us? We're her children.'

'She's ambitious for you. She wants you to be someone. An important someone and she'll stop at nothing to achieve it.'

'But to do that! I can't believe it. Are you sure you really understood Dad, Em?'

'I'm sorry, but yes, I am. But you must promise me something.'

'What?' Josh hardly seemed to be listening now, so Emily shook him gently. 'Listen, you mustn't say a word to Mam.'

He blinked and stared at her through the gloom. 'Why ever not?'

'Because you'll let Dad down if you do. She has the caring of him, don't forget.'

'You mean, you think she'd take it out on him?'

'I don't like to think so, Josh, but I never thought she'd destroy our letters.'

Josh sighed. 'That settles it. I'll go to Ashford. I'll set off first thing tomorrow morning.'

'You mean this morning,' Emily pointed out.

'Whatever, but I'm going. 'I'll get up as usual and get dressed in my best suit. Mam'll think I'm going to church, but I'll set off for Ashford. Wake me up, Em, won't you?'

As she got up from the bed to return to her own side of the curtain, Josh grasped her hand. 'I'll see what I can find out about Trip while I'm there.'

Emily smiled wanly, not trusting herself to speak as her eyes filled with tears. Oh Trip, whatever must you be thinking of me, if you've written and not heard from me in return?

As Josh closed his eyes, he felt a sense of relief flood

through him. Now, after what Emily had told him, he wanted to go to see Amy and find out the truth for himself more than anything else, but he was also honest enough to admit to himself that this could get him out of a very nasty situation that was developing. And if his journey there and back took him longer than one day – which it very well might – well, he wouldn't be missed on a 'Saint Monday'!

Until he was walking down the main street in Ashford, Josh hadn't realized just how much he'd missed the place. It felt good to be back and yet his stomach was churning with nerves. He didn't know what to expect when he met Amy. Even from a distance he could hear the clanging of Bob Clark's hammer on his anvil. Josh hesitated. He didn't know who he feared meeting the most: Amy or her father.

He'd been lucky that he'd managed to beg a lift with a carrier all the way to the village and now, in the afternoon sun, as he drew near the open door and his shadow fell across the floor of the smithy, the man paused in his work and glanced up, expecting to see a customer with a horse to be shod urgently or a fence to be mended. When he saw Josh he dropped his heavy hammer and straightened up slowly. It was as he did so that there was a movement near the back door of the smithy, open to let a draft through the workplace that was hot winter and summer alike from the heat of the roaring fire, and Josh saw a small child standing there. The child's face was in shadow, but Josh could see that it was a little boy about a year old. His hand resting on the door jamb, he was standing perfectly still as, no doubt, he had been taught by his mother . . .

Josh's heart leapt in his chest. Amy! Amy had a child.

She had found someone else and had a child. Perhaps – there was no perhaps about it; she must be married. Perhaps in one of the letters he had failed to receive, she'd told him. Josh felt a physical pain in his chest and he closed his eyes briefly. Amy was married. And to someone else. In that brief moment before anyone spoke, before explanations could begin, Josh knew what a fool he had been. He had lost her; the only girl he'd truly loved.

Still, Bob did not speak and the child remained motionless, staring at the stranger across the distance between them.

'Mr – Clark.' Josh's voice was husky. 'I'm sorry. I – I shouldn't have come.'

Now Bob moved towards him and stood in front of him, his face an expressionless mask. 'Why *have* you come back, Josh? Is it for Amy? Or have you come to tell her that you've met someone else? I must know.'

'But – I don't understand.' Josh gestured towards the infant. 'Obviously, *she*'s the one who's found someone else. Who is it?' His tone was growing belligerent. And yet, he knew he had only himself to blame. 'Is she married?'

'Answer my question.' Frowning, Bob barked the question.

And now, Josh could answer truthfully. Lizzie faded from his mind and there was only Amy. 'I've come back to see her because, if she did write to me, I never got her letters.' He stopped short of telling Bob Clark about his mother's mischief-making. 'Did she get mine?'

Bob's frown deepened. 'She got one shortly after you left, but after that – nothing.'

'I wrote to her the minute we got to Sheffield.' Josh ran his tongue around his lips that were suddenly dry.

Now he remembered that he had posted that one himself. 'And I've written several times since. And so has Emily. But, because I never heard, I stopped. I thought she must have met someone else. And now –' he nodded towards the small boy standing quietly at the back of the workshop – 'I see that she has. Did she tell me about him in one of the letters I never got?'

'Amy did write to you,' Bob said quietly, 'but she stopped when she didn't hear anything from you. She never got those letters either. They must all have – gone astray.' It was the kindest way Bob could have put it, but he had his suspicions as to what might have happened. Someone had intercepted all the letters; those from Amy to Josh, his to her and even Emily's to Amy. Someone who didn't want to see the couple together. Someone who was so ambitious for Josh that she didn't think Amy was good enough. Martha Ryan was the only person who would have had the opportunity to do such a thing. Bob Clark guessed the truth without anyone having to tell him. But he said nothing to Josh. Instead, he smiled. The young feller was here now and by the expression on his face it looked as if he was devastated by the thought that Amy was married to someone else. In that moment, Bob didn't blame Josh. He moved closer and put his hand on Josh's shoulder. His voice was husky as he said softly, 'Amy isn't with anyone else, Josh. That little lad –' he gestured with his head towards the little boy standing so quiet and still – 'is your son.'

Josh's mouth dropped open. For a moment, he was dumbstruck. Then, hoarsely, he whispered. 'Why ever didn't she tell me?' he began and then added swiftly, 'Oh, the letters . . .'

But Bob shook his head. 'No, she didn't tell you –

not even in her letters. She didn't want to put pressure on you to marry her if . . . Well, she thought – when she didn't hear from you – that you were the one who'd found someone else.'

Guilt flooded through Josh at the thought of Lizzie. However was he going to tell her this piece of news? For now, there was no doubt what he was going to do. His decision made, Josh straightened his shoulders and walked slowly towards the little boy. Squatting down in front of him, he said gently, 'Hello, little feller. What's your name?'

He didn't know if the child could talk yet, but he could certainly walk well. He looked sturdy and quite steady on his feet.

The boy stared solemnly at him with clear, hazel eyes that were so like Josh's own.

Bob had moved closer and said now, 'He doesn't say much yet. He's not quite one. His first birthday's in a couple of weeks' time. His name's Joshua Henry – after you – but we call him Harry.'

Josh felt the lump in his throat and, silently, he held out his arms. Harry glanced up at his grandfather briefly and then stepped forward. Tenderly, Josh picked him up and murmured, 'Let's go and find your mam, shall we?'

She was in the kitchen, stirring something in a large saucepan on the hob. She must have heard a noise at the door for, without turning round, she said, 'If that's you, Harry, stay there. This pan's very hot.'

Josh was silent for a moment watching her. She was just as he remembered. Perhaps her waist had thickened slightly, but then, he reminded himself, she had borne a child. His child. And she was still his lovely Amy.

How could he ever have even thought of being unfaithful to her?

'Amy,' he said softly so as not to startle her. 'It's – me.'

She stood perfectly still for a long moment before letting go of the wooden spoon, stepping away from the range and turning slowly to face him. At the sight of him standing there with their son in his arms, tears flooded down her cheeks. He held out his free arm to her and she flew to him, wrapping her arms around his waist and burying her face against him.

'Oh Josh, Josh!'

Thirty-Two

Later, over their evening meal, which Amy managed to stretch to include Josh, they talked over everything. But Josh's glance kept sliding towards the little boy sitting at the table with them in the high chair that Bob had lovingly crafted. He could hardly believe it. This was his son.

'We must get married,' he murmured, his gaze still on the boy, 'as soon as we can. My mother can't stop us now.'

Amy and her father exchanged a glance and then Amy burst out laughing. 'Well, isn't that the most romantic proposal a girl ever got and in front of her father too! Shouldn't you ask his permission first?'

Josh grinned. 'Sorry. I'll go down on one knee, if you want me to, Amy. Only—'

'What do you think, Dad? Ought I to marry this reprobate who leaves me for years without so much as a letter?'

Before Bob could even open his mouth, Josh burst out, 'I did write. I swear I did and your dad says you wrote to me, but I never received any of your letters. I wrote and Emily wrote too, but we never heard. They – they went astray.' Maybe one day he would tell her the truth, but now was not the time.

Amy blinked and stared at him across the table. 'Oh. I see.' But she didn't really understand. Amy's trusting nature would never believe anything bad about anyone, and especially not about Josh's mother. But Bob would. Oh yes, he could believe it. Anyway, he told himself, that was all water under the bridge, as the saying went. Josh was here now. That was all that mattered.

'I'll have to go back and collect my things,' he said and then he saw Amy's smile disappear and fear come into her eyes. 'I will come straight back, Amy. I promise you.'

Amy looked down at her plate as she nodded, but now she could not meet his eyes. Josh turned to her father. 'I mean it, Mr Clark. I'll work a week's notice and then I'll come back and find work round here. On a farm, maybe, or . . .'

'Your old house is still empty, lad. No one's taken it and no one else in the village has set up making candles either.'

Josh's eyes gleamed. 'Then maybe I could start up again.' He turned to look back at Amy, but she was still sitting with her head bowed. She'd believe all this when she saw it happening. She'd lived on promises before that had not come true. Though, she supposed, now they had, albeit a little late. Slowly she raised her head and smiled tentatively, wanting so much to believe him but not quite able to – yet. But her father seemed to trust Josh, saying, 'You could see the owner of the property. See if he'd grant you the tenancy.'

'Do you know who it is? I never knew. Father dealt with all that and then Mam took it on when he . . . when he . . .'

'How is your dad?' Bob asked softly.

Josh pulled a face. 'Not good – worse, if anything, than when he was here. We should never have gone there. But my mother . . .' He stopped, not wanting to sound disloyal and yet he was now seeing for himself what anguish she had caused all round. He sighed and came back to the topic of the cottage next door. 'If the owner's Mr Trippet, there's no chance he'll let me have it.' His tone was bitter and both Bob and Amy noticed it. They exchanged a glance, but said nothing for the moment. 'No – no, you're in luck. Mr Osborne at the corner shop opposite is the owner. He owns one or two houses in the village.' Bob chuckled. 'An enterprising man is our Mr Osborne, and he always liked your family. He was a good mate of your dad's – is, I should say. I'm sure there will be no problem there. In fact,' he added, getting up and walking to the mantelpiece above the range, then lifting down a mug, 'he entrusted me with a key so that I could keep an eye on the place for him, seeing as I'm right next door and attached to the property, and so that I could let him know if I saw or heard anything untoward.'

Josh jumped up and held out his hand for the key. 'I'll take a look right now. It'd be perfect for us to live next door, wouldn't it?'

'Aye,' Bob said, swallowing his disappointment that his daughter and adorable grandson would be moving out. But, he consoled himself, they'll only be the other side of the wall. For Heaven's sake, man, get a grip on yourself. Josh is going to marry Amy and make an honest woman of her. He watched as Josh took Amy in his arms, not caring who saw. He kissed her forehead. 'I'm so sorry,' he murmured, 'but I will make it up to you, I promise.'

Tears started in her eyes. She clung to him for a moment and then, releasing her hold, gave him a little push towards the door.

Ruffling his son's hair as he passed his chair, Josh

walked out of their home and opened the door of the cottage where he had lived for most of his life. He pushed it open and was met by a stale, unlived-in smell. The whole place was thick with dust even though he knew his mother had left it spotless. But it was a long time now since anyone had lived there. He walked through the empty rooms, remembering. In the front room there were still traces of his candle-making business there, though his tools were still in Bob Clark's safe-keeping. But soon, he vowed, they'd be back here and he'd be working once more at the bench in front of the window. And he'd be here with his wife and son. Josh smiled as he turned to leave.

It was as he was about to step out of the front door that he heard a noise from an upstairs room. He hadn't thought to check up there, assuming that all the rooms would be in the same state of neglect.

Rats, he thought. I must be sure to get rid of them before we bring little Harry here. At the thought of the boy, Josh's heart swelled with pride. He climbed the stairs to see how bad the infestation was. He'd get the local rat catcher in to clear it whilst he was away for the week. He reached the top of the stairs, confident that the only living creature he was about to encounter would be a four-legged animal with a long tail. He did not expect to see a person – a squatter – up there, but when he opened the door he saw the floor littered with the remains of some food, a rough mattress and blanket on the floor and a pile of clothes. He glanced round the room and saw, huddled in the corner, the shape of a man whom he presumed to be a tramp who had taken shelter in the deserted cottage. Josh paused for a moment, his heart constricting with sorrow that any human being should be in such dire straits.

'Hello, old feller. I'm so sorry—' he began and then gasped as the hunched figure unfolded himself from the corner and struggled to his feet.

'Oh my God!' Josh exclaimed. 'Trip!'

Thirty-Three

Trip was in a dreadful state. He was painfully thin, his clothes dirty and dishevelled and the anguish in his face was pitiful to see.

'Come with me. You need some food inside you, right now.' Josh took hold of his friend's arm and helped him across the room and down the stairs. Trip was frail, like an old man, and Josh was reminded poignantly of the many times he'd helped his father up and down these very stairs.

Next door, Amy's eyes widened as she saw the state of their friend and Bob helped Josh settle him in a chair by the range.

'Whatever's happened?' he asked, and when Trip didn't answer, Bob looked towards Josh. But, though his mouth was a grim line, for the moment, Josh said nothing. Amy bustled about the kitchen preparing a plate of food for Trip. Luckily, there was still a little stew left over from their meal, but Bob warned, 'If you've not eaten properly for some time, Trip, don't eat too much or too fast. Take it steady. Amy, love, get him a glass of milk – that'd be a good start.'

After drinking and eating a little, Trip looked up at them and said hoarsely, 'How can I thank you? I've nothing.'

'Don't even mention it,' Bob said. 'But whatever's happened?'

'My – father's thrown me out. Out of my work and – out of the house too. He – he's disowned me. He wouldn't even let me speak to my mother. What on earth she must be thinking, I don't know.' He glanced up at them. 'I'm sorry about breaking in next door. When I can find work, I'll pay for the window. I'm sorry . . .' He dropped his head into his hands and his shoulders began to shake.

Trip – strong, merry, hardworking Trip – was sobbing as if his heart would break.

'Look, Trip, don't worry. No harm done. We –' Josh glanced at Bob for approval and when the older man nodded, he went on – 'will replace the window. Tell us – but only if you want to, of course – what brought all this on?'

Slowly, Trip lifted his head. His eyes were red-rimmed, his cheeks hollowed, his whole face gaunt. Josh didn't think he'd ever seen the young man – any young man, for that matter – look so awful.

'I . . . don't know if I should tell you.'

'Then don't, Master Thomas,' Bob said swiftly, still unable to address him in any way other than how he always had. His father, Arthur Trippet, had always been the acknowledged squire of the district and his son had deserved due deference. 'Don't tell us anything you don't want to.'

But now Thomas smiled wryly. 'Please, Mr Clark, it's just Thomas – or even better, Trip. That's what all my friends call me. You've been my friend for years, I hope, and you're certainly being a good friend to me now.' He sighed and then looked up at Josh. 'You see, it's all to do with Emily.'

'Emily?' Josh was puzzled. 'I know she's been worried to death about you ever since you didn't turn up to

271

meet her in the park. When she knew I was coming back here to see Amy, she asked me to go to your home to see if you were there. But what can she possibly have done to have caused this trouble for you?'

Trip shook his head. 'Nothing. Absolutely nothing. It's what I've done that my father doesn't approve of.'

Mystified, Bob, Josh and Amy exchanged glances; Trip was talking in riddles.

'I've committed the cardinal sin of falling in love with your sister, Josh, and my father doesn't approve. We had an almighty row in his office at the factory and he said that unless I promised to break all ties with her, he would disown me. So, I walked out there and then and I haven't been back since. I came home, hoping to see my mother. Oh, not to get her to plead my case or anything like that – I wouldn't dream of putting her in such an awkward position – but I just wanted to tell her myself what had happened. But he arrived back home before me and I haven't been able to see her. He seems to have stayed at home a lot more recently – probably on purpose, to see if I turned up.' He glanced at Bob. 'I did think about asking you to take a message to her, but I didn't want to involve anyone else. My father can be ruthless, and if he thought that you were helping me . . .' He paused for a moment but his meaning was obvious. 'I daren't think what he's told her.' He sighed. 'I suppose I acted a bit hastily. I wrote to Emily and told her that I was coming back to the village and asked her to write back care of the post office here, but . . . but I haven't heard anything.'

Nor will you, Josh thought resentfully, if my mother's burned your letter too. Instead, he said gently, 'Emily never got your letter, Trip. I can vouch for that. She's half out of her mind with worry about you. She's been to the park every Sunday since New Year's Day and has been desperate to hear something from you. In the end, I went and talked to Mr Bayes. He told me about the quarrel with your father, but he didn't know it was about Emily.'

'Father had seen us at the Armistice Ball together and then he made some more enquiries and heard that we'd been meeting every Sunday.'

'How did he find that out? He's never in the city at the weekends.'

Trip seemed to hesitate for a moment and then, making up his mind, decided to confide in his friends completely. 'My father has a mistress in the city.'

Josh gaped at him and repeated stupidly, 'A mistress? Your father?'

'Oh, it's quite the done thing in middle-class society,' Trip said bitterly. 'They marry for money or influence and then take their pleasure where they can find it.' He looked up. 'I'm sorry, Amy.' For the moment he had forgotten she was there. 'I shouldn't be talking this way in front of you. But you see, I don't want to follow in my father's footsteps in that way. I want to marry for love. And I love Emily,' he finished simply. It was all so straightforward to the uncomplicated, truthful young man who, deep down, despised his father's way of life. He wondered if his mother knew about her husband's paramour.

As if reading his thoughts, Josh asked, 'Does your mother know about her, do you think?'

Trip shrugged. 'I shouldn't think so. I hope not.'

'But how does she – his mistress, I mean – fit into all this?'

'My father was so furious, he spilled it all out – how he'd asked Belle Beauman to find out if Emily and I were still meeting. Evidently she'd been going to the city's parks on a Sunday for months, until she saw us.'

'Oh my goodness, Mrs Beauman. That was the name of the woman we met in the park. She pretended to be ill and me and Lizzie took her home.' He had spoken Lizzie's name without intending to do so, but he was so wrapped up in Trip's tale that he forgot to guard his tongue. Out of the corner of his eye, he saw Amy look at him, a question in her eyes, but now was not the time to get involved in lengthy explanations.

'And then we met her with you, didn't we?' Trip went on.

'Did you know about her before that day?' Josh asked. 'Because I thought at the time you stared at her a bit funny.'

Trip laughed wryly. 'I didn't until I went to work at the factory. The other men took great delight in deliberately making snide remarks about my father's fondness for music-hall dancers. So, I guessed that he had a mistress somewhere. And then, one day, one of the young lads let her name slip. Mrs Belle Beauman. But it was a bit of a shock to meet her in the park that day, I have to admit. It's one thing to think that your father has a mistress, quite another to come face to face with her. But, of course, that was exactly what she was there for: to meet us – Emily and me – and report back to my father. Oh, how devious he's been. He played a waiting game. He knew several weeks before Christmas, before my birthday even. I think that's why he bought me an expensive motorcycle, just to make me even more – *grateful* to him. But it doesn't work like that, not with me. It only makes me despise him even more.'

'Where is your motorbike?'

Trip's mouth tightened. 'I used it to get here and then I sold it to buy food, but I didn't get much for it and the money soon ran out.'

'Oh Master – I mean, Trip – why ever didn't you come to us?' Bob was reproachful.

'I was too embarrassed, Mr Clark.'

'Does your mother know where you are?'

Trip shook his head. 'I just daren't show my face at the house. I don't know what he'd do if he caught me there.'

'Then I'll go and see her,' Josh said at once.

'No, Josh,' Trip said with more vigour in his voice. 'It's Sunday, isn't it?' He looked up at the others, as if he'd lost count of the days. 'He's always home at a weekend.'

'I must go back tomorrow. I can't risk not going into work on Tuesday morning. I don't want to get the sack for a second time.' Josh smiled wryly as he added, 'Though I suppose it wouldn't matter so much as I'm leaving anyway.'

'Leaving? Why?'

Now Josh's smile broadened into genuine pleasure. 'Because I'm coming back here to marry Amy.' He turned and beckoned to the little boy, who had been hiding behind his mother's skirts and whom Trip had not noticed. 'This little chap is my son.'

Trip stared at Harry, then rose unsteadily to his feet and held out his hand to Josh. His voice was husky as he said, 'You're a lucky fellow, Josh. And you, Amy, I'm delighted for you both.' He held out his arms to her and kissed her on both cheeks. 'I just wish . . .'

He said no more, but they all knew that he was longing to find the same happiness with Emily.

'I'll make up a bed for you, Trip, on the sofa in the parlour, if that'd be all right?'

'Oh Amy, I can't—'

'Yes, you can,' she said firmly. 'You'll stay with us until we get all this mess sorted out. And tomorrow, when your father's gone to the city, I'll go and see your mother, but you must tell me what you want me to say to her, though don't worry about that now. You look as if you could do with something else to eat in a little while and then bed.'

'What about Josh? Where's he to sleep?'

Josh looked embarrassed and Amy blushed, but it was Bob who came to the rescue. 'I'll see Grace Partridge. She'll find you a bed for the night, though she might give you a bit of a telling off for having deserted Amy. And be warned now, lad –' he wagged his finger in Josh's face, half in jest, half in seriousness – 'if you stay away again, I'll come and find you, armed with a shotgun.'

They all laughed a little awkwardly, but then Amy said, 'Josh, can you make a bed up on the sofa for Trip in the front room? Dad, will you look after Harry whilst I get Trip something else to eat? It's time you stopped working anyway. You don't reckon to work on a Sunday. It's disgraceful. What will the vicar think?'

'It was a rush job for a farmer. He needed a sturdy gate sharpish.'

'One more day won't hurt,' Amy said firmly. All three men gaped at her and then glanced at each other.

'My little Amy, all grown up,' Bob murmured. Then he added teasingly, 'Are you sure you still want to marry this bossy woman, Josh?'

Josh's answer was very serious as he said softly, 'I've never been more certain of anything in my life.' Though silently, he thought, How I'm to face my mother and Lizzie too, I don't know.

But if Amy has grown up, then so must he. He must become a man.

Thirty-Four

It was too late to talk to anyone when Josh finally got back to the city on the Monday night. He crept upstairs and into the attic, undressed quietly and got into bed. But sleep eluded him. He had so much to think about. First, he had to face tomorrow and all its difficulties but, at the end of the week, he would be hurrying back to Amy and his son. At the thought of the little boy, Josh smiled in the darkness and all his misgivings about telling his mother and explaining to Lizzie faded into insignificance. And there was an added bonus to all this; he would be escaping from Mick Dugdale's clutches.

Amy didn't sleep well either that Monday night. She was torn by an overwhelming happiness that Josh had come back to her and that he had never intended to hurt her. It had all been a dreadful misunderstanding because their letters hadn't reached each other. But disturbing Amy's sleep, too, was the thought of facing Mrs Trippet. Now, she regretted offering to see Trip's mother, of whom she'd always been in awe. Despite the childhood friendship of the four youngsters, invitations to Riversdale House had never been forthcoming. Amy had only seen Trip's parents at a distance. Even when they wanted work done at the smithy, or candles from Josh, the orders were always brought by one of their servants. However, she took heart in Mrs Trippet's kind gestures over news of Amy's pregnancy. Aunty Grace had told her that Constance Trippet had been the leading force behind the villagers' acceptance of the news.

'But for her,' Grace had said, 'it might have been very different.'

But at last, in the early hours, Amy fell asleep with a smile on her mouth as she remembered the date. Today was St Valentine's Day.

'I've found Trip,' were Josh's first whispered words to Emily early on Tuesday morning.

'Where? How is he? What happened?'

'Hey, hang on a minute,' Josh laughed, but then his expression sobered. 'He'll be all right, but he was in a bad way when I found him.'

Emily gasped and her eyes widened with terror. Now, there was no doubt in Josh's mind that the two people he loved dearly were meant to be together. Swiftly, he explained everything that had happened and reassured her that Trip was truly all right, ending, 'And Emily, I have a son. A dear little boy called Joshua Henry after me, but known as Harry.'

Emily stared open-mouthed at him for a moment before questions poured from her lips. 'Oh Josh, how wonderful. How old is he? Is he like you? My goodness – I'm an aunty!' She clasped her hands together in excitement and then, calming a little, asked seriously, 'What are you going to do?'

She could see that already there was a new-found determination in her brother. Gone was the indecision and the kowtowing to their mother and even his weakness over Lizzie. He was going to stand up to both of them.

'I'm going to give a week's notice and then I'm going back to Ashford. I shall start up the candle-making business again and – if I can get the tenancy – we'll live in The Candle House. We'll be married as soon as we can – when I'm of age, if Mam still withholds her consent before then.'

Emily was thoughtful for a moment before saying quietly, 'What if Mam decides to go back to Ashford? There's nothing for her here if you leave.'

'She'll stay with you, won't she? You're making a real success of your business now.'

Emily smiled ruefully and said quietly, 'No, Josh, she won't stay here for me and besides, I wouldn't want her to. Dad would be better back in the countryside.'

'Mm, well, they could come back home. Amy and me – and Harry –' there was such pride in his tone as he said his son's name – 'could live with Mr Clark. I'm sure he wouldn't mind that. In fact, I think he'd be pleased as punch. When we were talking about living next door, I saw his face. I don't think he wants them to leave his house, even to live next door!'

'That's all right, then. If Mam does want to go back, I'm sure she'd get the tenancy back if the house has been empty all this time. And now, I'd better get myself ready to go to Ashford.'

'What about your work?'

'Hang work! This is Trip we're talking about. Besides, the three of them can cope for a couple of days.' She grinned as she added, 'I'll take a "Saint Tuesday" and Wednesday, if I have to.'

At the reference to Lizzie, Josh's face sobered. He'd been so wrapped up in his plans for returning to Ashford and marrying Amy and – he could still hardly believe it – becoming a proper father, that he'd almost forgotten that he had a very unpleasant task to do first, to say nothing of telling his mother.

He was not sure which woman he dreaded facing the most.

When he woke, Trip seemed much better, but after breakfast, Amy – already up and busy dressing Harry – insisted that Trip should go back to the sofa.

'You need a lot of rest and some good food inside you. Then we'll see about you getting out in the fresh air. And let me have any washing you want doing. Washday should have been yesterday, but with so much going on, I've put it off until tomorrow now. With all the excitement, I was late up this morning to get the copper going.' She smiled, the happiness shining out of her. 'But no matter. One day's as good as the next, isn't it? Now, Dad's gone to his work and if you could keep an eye on Harry for me, I'll go and see your mother. What do you want me to tell her?'

'Whatever you like, Amy. I trust you.'

'What about your father's – er – mistress?'

Trip was thoughtful. 'I just don't know if she has any inkling.'

'I'll be tactful, I promise.'

Trip smiled weakly. 'I know you will. Good luck – and thank you.'

As she neared the big house at the end of the street, Amy's stomach was churning with nerves. She went round to the back of the house, to the tradesmen's entrance, and knocked. A housemaid in a black dress, with a pristine white apron and lace cap, opened the door.

'Hello, Amy,' Polly greeted her. 'Whatever brings you here?'

'I've come to see Mrs Trippet.'

The maid frowned. 'She doesn't normally see anyone without an appointment being made first.'

'This is important. It's about Trip – I mean Thomas.'

'He's in the city. He lives and works there now. He doesn't come home very often. Oh dear!' The girl clapped her hand to her mouth as a thought struck her. 'Is he all right? Has something happened to him?'

'Yes and no,' Amy said. 'He's all right, but something has happened. I really need to see your mistress, Polly.'

'Come in, then, and I'll see what I can do.'

Amy waited in the kitchen, chatting to the cook, Mrs Froggatt, but her mind was hardly on the words the woman was saying, so anxious was she about seeing Mrs Trippet.

It seemed an age before Polly returned. 'The mistress will see you, but she's puzzled as to why you wish to see her.'

Amy's stomach felt as if it turned over. This was going to be far more difficult than she'd imagined; and she'd imagined plenty through the long night!

She was shown into the morning room where Mrs Trippet was seated on the window seat. She was holding a book, but she laid it aside as Amy entered the room and, smiling, patted the seat beside her.

'Come, we can talk here and Polly will bring us some tea or coffee. Which do you prefer, Amy? You don't mind if I call you "Amy", do you?'

'Of course not, ma'am. And tea would be lovely, thank you, and I must thank you for all the kind gifts you've sent me over the past year.' She blushed. 'It meant a great deal to me to have your understanding and support.'

'No need for the "ma'am", my dear. "Mrs Trippet"

will do nicely. And it's been my pleasure to help you. Now, what can I do for you this morning? Is there something you need for your little boy?'

They were sitting on either end of the curved window seat so that they were facing each other.

'It's about Trip, ma'am – Mrs Trippet. I mean, Thomas.'

'Call him Trip if it's easier for you. I know that's his nickname amongst his friends.'

'He's here in the village and he's staying with us.'

Constance frowned. 'But – but why? Why doesn't he come home?'

This was harder than Amy had imagined. She'd believed the woman would know that her husband had dismissed Trip from his work and had disowned him. She had expected to see a distraught woman, anxious for any news of her son. Now Amy was obliged to tell her the whole sorry story. She took a deep breath and plunged in.

'Your husband and Trip had a big row just after Christmas and Mr Trippet dismissed him from his work and – and –' she ran her tongue around her lips that were suddenly dry – 'he told him not – not to come home any more. He's disowned him.'

'Disowned him?' Constance gave a disbelieving laugh. 'He can't do that.' But as she stared at Amy's solemn face, she realized that was exactly what her husband had done. Her amusement died instantly. 'Why?' she whispered.

'Trip was keeping company with Emily Ryan in the city. They used to meet every Sunday afternoon in the park. Mr Trippet found out about this and ordered him to stop seeing her. When Trip refused—'

'He threw him out,' Constance murmured, 'from home and his inheritance too.'

Amy nodded and for a long pause neither of them spoke. Whilst Constance was trying to take all this in and formulate some questions, Polly brought in the tray, set out cups and saucers and poured tea. When the maid had left the room, Constance asked, 'Is he in love with Emily?'

'Yes, he says so.'

'And does she love him?'

'Josh says so.' She smiled now at the memory of Josh's words. 'He says she's loved Trip since she was twelve.'

'Josh Ryan? You've seen him?'

'He came back on Saturday. He – we're going to be married.' Now the girl blushed a little as she added, 'He's the father of my baby, but he didn't know anything about him. But now he does.'

'And he's going to do the honourable thing,' Constance murmured again.

'It was Josh who found Trip. He'd been living rough – squatting, I suppose you'd call it – in The Candle House. It's been empty since the Ryans left. He's in rather a bad state, Mrs Trippet.'

Constance gasped and her hand fluttered to her mouth. 'Oh, is he ill?'

'Not exactly, but he soon might have been, if Josh hadn't found him. He was half starved and his clothes – well, they need a good wash. But I'll see to that.'

Constance now reached out a trembling hand towards Amy and tears started in her eyes. 'Oh please, tell him to come home. Today. Now!'

'I'll tell him, Mrs Trippet, but I don't know if he will. I don't think he would dare. He just wanted me to tell you what had happened and to let you know that he's all right. He thought you would have heard and be worried about him.'

'Oh, I most certainly would have been, had I known. But my dear husband,' she went on with bitter resentment in her tone, 'said not a word to me about any of this.' She was thoughtful for a moment before saying, 'How did he find out about Thomas and Emily?'

'I . . . perhaps Trip had better tell you that himself.'

Constance eyed the girl shrewdly. 'But you know, don't you?'

Always a truthful girl, Amy was obliged to nod.

'Then you tell me.'

Amy bit her lip before saying, 'He . . . he got someone he knows in the city to . . . to spy on them.'

Constance's eyes narrowed. 'I can see you are finding this very difficult, my dear, so I'll save you the embarrassment. Was it his mistress, by any chance, Belle Beauman?'

Amy gasped and stared at the woman, who smiled wryly and sighed. 'Oh yes, I know all about Belle Beauman. I've known for years.' Constance considered the girl for a moment. The older woman had few real friends, other than perhaps Grace Partridge, and none she dared confide in. Oh, she was well known and well respected in the village, but that was not quite the same as having a confidante. But she felt instinctively that Amy, young though she was, could be trusted not to gossip. The girl had been the subject of speculation herself recently and knew what it felt like – though, in fairness, the tales had not been malicious. If anything, taking their lead from Constance herself and from Grace Partridge, the villagers had rallied round and been very protective of one of their own. She wondered, though, what sort of reception young Josh would get now that he was back. Constance almost laughed aloud as she visualized Josh being attacked by a few umbrellas when the women of the village saw him again.

'I suppose it must sound strange to you that I have stayed with my husband, knowing that he was being unfaithful.' She paused a moment, but Amy sat quietly waiting for her to continue.

'Divorce is an ugly, messy business in any society and I stayed with him and turned a blind eye for several reasons, really. I suppose the main one was Thomas.' She was silent for a moment, thinking how to phrase her explanation, which might sound mercenary to the young girl who was so in love with Josh.

'My husband and I were not head over heels in love with each other when we married. We were good friends, we liked each other and we both wanted certain things out of a marriage. Being an only child and not particularly pretty, I wanted security and I wanted children. Arthur needed the money I could bring to the marriage from my father. A dowry, if you like. So, it was an arrangement that suited us both. And then there was Thomas.' She paused again and her voice shook a little as she added, 'I never wanted him to be an only child, but I had two miscarriages, after which the doctor told me I should have no more children. I was unlikely to survive if I tried again and I had no intention of leaving my Thomas motherless.'

'I'm sorry,' Amy whispered, and she was. She felt empathy with the woman. Even after all these years, Amy could still see the pain in Constance's eyes. Harry's birth had been surprisingly easy and Amy hoped to have more children now that Josh was coming back and they were to be married, whatever Martha Ryan said.

'So you see, in a way, I can't blame Arthur. Men have their needs and it wasn't as if I was hopelessly in love with him. My heart, Amy, is still intact, I can assure you.' She met Amy's gaze steadily. 'Are you disgusted at me?'

'Heavens, no,' Amy said swiftly. 'Your world is very different to ours, Mrs Trippet.' Knowing that the woman had paid her a huge compliment by confiding in her in this way, Amy felt bold enough to add, 'But I feel sorry for you.'

'Don't be, my dear,' Constance said briskly. 'I am quite content. I have everything I need and I have my wonderful son. At least . . .' She paused and now there was real fear in her eyes. 'Amy, he is going to be all right, isn't he? I mean, he's not seriously ill? You would tell me?'

Amy shook her head and smiled. 'He'll be fine. He just needs rest and good food.'

'Then he must come home where I can look after him.'

'But his father . . . ?'

Constance stood up, determination in her action. 'For once, his father will do as I say. Now, let us go down and see Cook. She will pack up a hamper and Kirkland –' Constance referred to their chauffeur-cum-handyman – 'can go back with you. I don't want Thomas to be a burden on you. Later today, after Mr Trippet gets home and I've spoken to him –' her tone hardened with determination – 'Kirkland can fetch Thomas home in the car.'

'That's very kind of you, about the hamper, I mean, but please, let us do this for Trip. He's our friend. Let him stay with us until he feels a little better and until you've spoken to his father. I'm sorry to have to say it, but Trip won't come home if his father is here.'

'Well, if you're sure.' Constance didn't want to insult the girl, but she was aware that an extra – very hungry – mouth to feed might be a strain on the smithy's resources.

'I am,' Amy said firmly. 'And if there are any . . . problems, he can stay longer with us.'

As they walked to the door of the morning room together, Constance patted her hand and said, 'Thank you for coming to see me, my dear. It can't have been easy for you.'

Amy looked up into the older woman's eyes and said candidly, 'You're a nice lady, Mrs Trippet. Everyone says so.'

Constance laughed. 'That's good to know. I take part in a lot of the village activities, but I often feel I haven't any real friends, except perhaps Grace Partridge. We get on very well, but –' she squeezed Amy's hand gently – 'I feel as if I've made one today.'

'Thank you,' Amy said huskily, touched by the woman's sincerity. 'And I feel the same.' She, too, felt as if she now had someone else she could turn to if she needed help or advice. Not for the first time in her life, she felt the lack of a mother's presence in her life. However close she was to her wonderful father, just now and then a girl needed a mother figure. She had felt it most keenly when giving birth to Harry, even though Mrs Partridge – the closest woman she had to a mother – had been beside her holding her hand.

When Amy arrived home, Harry was safely in his cot for a nap and Trip was still asleep, but later she told him, 'Your mother wants you to go home. She said

Kirkland would fetch you in the car this evening, but I've persuaded her to let you stay with us a little longer. Just until you're feeling stronger and until she's had time to talk to Mr Trippet.'

Trip shook his head. 'I can't go home. I don't want to cause trouble for her. My father can be nasty when he's in a temper and I've just witnessed the worst I've ever seen him.'

'Your mother seemed very strong to me. Very determined.'

Trip blinked. 'Really? I've never thought of her like that.'

'Oh, I think she is. She knew all about Belle Beauman. She said she'd known about her for years.'

The news obviously came as a surprise to Trip, who was thoughtful for some moments. 'You're right,' he said slowly. 'She's shown great courage. I presume she stayed because of me.'

Amy nodded. 'That was part of it, yes, a big part, I'd say, but also, just think, Trip, if she'd left your father, where would she have gone, how would she have lived? It wouldn't have been easy and – if your father had been vindictive—'

Trip laughed ironically. 'And he would have been, believe me.'

'Then he'd have seen her penniless and, no doubt, have prevented her from ever seeing you again.'

Trip sighed. 'She may have had some money of her own left to her by her father, but I've no idea about that and you're right about one thing: Father would definitely have had custody of me. Poor Mother.'

'She told me she was content enough. She has her interests and, above all else, she has you. I think the only real sadness in her life was the loss of her babies. She would have loved to have had more children.'

'And I would have liked to have had brothers and sisters. Still,' he added, smiling, 'I have you and Josh and – and Emily, if – if . . .'

'Oh there's no "if" about it. You wait and see, once Josh has told Emily he's found you and all about what happened, she'll be on this doorstep within hours. You mark my words.'

Thirty-Five

During the afternoon, there was a knock at the Clarks' back door. Amy opened it to find Constance Trippet standing there.

'I hope this is not an intrusion, but I would like to see Thomas.' She smiled apologetically. 'I couldn't keep away.'

'Of course, Mrs Trippet, please come in. He's in the parlour.' As she closed the door and led her visitor through to the best room, Amy said, 'He had quite a good breakfast and he's eaten a little dinner. His colour's better, but he's still very tired. Here we are.' She opened the door quietly and tiptoed in. Trip was lying on the sofa, his head on two cushions. He was sound asleep.

'Don't wake him, Amy. I'll just sit here with him, if you don't mind.'

'Of course. I'll bring you some tea.'

'Oh, I wouldn't want to trouble you. You must be busy. And your little boy . . .'

'Harry's fine. He's in his playpen in the kitchen. So no, it's no trouble. I could do with a cuppa myself.'

'Then, if you're sure, a cup of tea would be most welcome.'

They had been talking in whispers, but Trip stirred and, as Amy left the room, he rubbed his eyes and sat up.

'Mother! Whatever are you doing here?'

'I've come to see you, my dear, and to take you home.'

'I . . . can't go home. He—'

'I know all about what's happened and you're coming home with me. *I* will deal with your father.' There was more determination and spirit in her tone than Trip could ever remember hearing before.

'I don't want to cause trouble between you and Father.'

'You won't,' Constance said shortly.

'You mean – you mean, you agree with him.'

'I most certainly do *not*. I want you to marry for love and for no other reason, Thomas. If it is Emily Ryan you love – and you're really sure about that – then so be it.'

Trip sat up straight, startled by what his mother had said. 'You really mean it?'

Constance nodded. 'My sole purpose in life is your happiness. Now, my dear, will you please come home?'

Trip hesitated a moment longer before nodding and murmuring, 'I really shouldn't encroach on the Clarks' kindness any longer, but—'

At that moment there was a commotion outside the door of Amy's parlour and a loud voice saying, 'But I must see him, Amy.'

'That's Emily,' Trip said, making as if to rise, but his legs were still weak and he fell back against the cushions.

Instead, Constance went to the door and opened it. 'Emily, my dear, do come in.' And Emily rushed into the room and flung herself down on the sofa next to him.

'Oh, Trip, Trip, are you all right?'

He smiled and opened his arms to her. She leaned against him and wept.

'There, there,' he comforted. 'It's going to be all right. Mother's on our side.'

Emily raised her head and stared at him. 'She is?' Then she twisted round to look at Constance, who had resumed her seat. 'You are?'

'I just want Thomas to be happy, and if you're the one to make him happy, then—'

'Oh I will, I will. I promise I will. But his father has disowned him. I can't allow Trip – I mean, Thomas – to lose his inheritance. He might come to hate me for it.'

'Never,' Trip said, with more strength in his voice than any of them in the room had thought possible.

'I'll bring that tea I promised. And an extra cup.' Amy, who had followed Emily into the room, turned and left. She was no longer involved in the decisions to be made.

'Oh Trip,' Emily said. 'I love you so much. I couldn't let you give up everything for me.'

'And I love you enough to do just that. Besides,' he added, with a spark of his old humour, 'I'm expecting my clever wife, with her growing business empire, to keep *me*.'

Emily pulled a face. 'It's a long way from being an empire. My mother calls it a tin-pot business.'

Trip touched her face tenderly. 'Then she hasn't got the faith in you that I have.'

Constance cleared her throat, reminding them that she was still there. She was about to speak, but Amy came in carrying a tray with three cups of tea on it, 'You'll excuse me not joining you,' she said tactfully as she handed them out, 'but I must see to Harry.'

'I can't wait to meet my nephew, Amy,' Emily said, letting the girl know that she understood and accepted the situation.

Amy was about to leave the room, but she turned back briefly to ask hesitantly, 'Has – has Josh spoken to his mother yet?'

'I left early, so I don't know. It won't be easy, but he's determined to come back here, Amy. Don't worry. I'm on his side. I never thought we should have gone to the city in the first place; though,' she turned and gazed at Trip once more, 'if we hadn't, I might not have found Trip again.'

After Amy had left the room once more and the three had drunk their tea, Constance said, 'So, Thomas, you will come home, won't you?'

Trip sighed. 'Father will never allow it.'

'I've thrown him out.'

At the same time as Constance was sitting in Amy's comfortable parlour, Arthur was visiting Belle. For several weeks, Arthur had kept the news from her. He had fully expected his son to come crawling back, begging forgiveness and promising never to see Emily Ryan again. But it had not happened. Arthur was angry that he had misjudged Thomas and yet somewhere deep inside him – though he would never acknowledge it – there was a sliver of pride that his son was made of sterner stuff than Arthur had supposed. Having always dictated the progress of his son's life – boarding school, starting work in the lowest position in the factory – Arthur had not realized that his son had become a man; a man who was prepared to fight for what he wanted – for the woman he wanted.

At his words, Belle paled. 'What – what do you mean?'

'I've disowned him. No son of mine is going to ally

himself with a common slut like Emily Ryan – the daughter, I may say, of my former cleaning woman.'

'He refused to stop seeing her?' For the woman who had been brought up in the back streets of the city and who had lived on her wits and her looks, the thought that anyone could turn their back on a comfortable lifestyle and their future handed to them on a plate, was absurd.

'He did – so out he went.'

'You don't really mean it?'

'I most certainly do.'

'But he's your son and heir. What does your wife say?'

'She doesn't know yet. But there's nothing she can do about it. She'll do whatever I say.'

Belle was thoughtful. Arthur was so sure of his wife's compliance, but Belle wondered if his confidence was misplaced. Every mother will fight for her son, she thought. But for now, she said no more. Now, she must entertain her wealthy protector and sooth his anger, especially as perhaps now . . .

But she would think about that later.

'Lizzie, I must talk to you.'

Josh had decided that, of the two women, he preferred to face Lizzie first. So, on the Tuesday evening after work, he knocked on the door of the Dugdales' home.

'Then I'll leave you two lovebirds to it,' Bess Dugdale said, heaving herself out of her chair.

Oh dear, Josh thought. This is getting harder by the minute.

When the door had closed behind her, Josh took Lizzie's hands in his and looked her straight in the face. 'You've been a good friend to all of us since we got here. No one has helped us more than you and your mother – and Mick, if it comes to that – and I'm very fond of you, but I've never led you on, never let you think it was ever going to be more than that.'

Lizzie stared back at him, a faint blush appearing in her cheeks, her eyes bright with anger already as she realized what was coming.

'Oh yes, you have. You've kissed me, Josh Ryan. On the night of the ball. And you wanted more, if I'd let you. Don't deny it.'

Josh sighed. He couldn't deny it, not any of it. He was a virile young man and she was an attractive girl, who'd made no secret of the fact that she wanted there to be more between them. And there had been a point – a very dangerous point on the night of the most recent ball, when over a year had passed and he still hadn't heard anything from Amy – that he'd been tempted to let things take their course with Lizzie. But something had held him back. And now he knew why. Deep down, he'd always loved Amy.

There was no easy way to tell her, so he said bluntly, 'I'm going back to Ashford. I don't belong in the city. I only came because it was what my mother wanted.'

'Are you indeed? And what if I kick up a right stink? Your mother likes me. And Emily's my friend.'

'Emily tried to warn you from the start that I was promised to Amy, didn't she?' When Lizzie made no reply and avoided meeting his steady gaze, he insisted, 'Didn't she?'

'I didn't believe her. I thought it was because this slut, Amy, was her friend and she was being loyal to her.' Now her head snapped up again. 'But I've been her friend and she's not being loyal to me now, is she?'

'This has nothing to do with Emily. Nothing at all.'

Lizzie's eyes narrowed. 'I could ruin her, you know. Her and her precious business. The girls would all follow me – do what I said.'

'And you think that would win me over? That I'd give in to your threats? My sister is made of sterner stuff than that, Lizzie.' He forbore to tell her that Emily had gone to Ashford today for her own reasons. He was seeing Lizzie in her true colours now and he didn't like what he saw. He'd had a very lucky escape, because, if the truth were known, when he'd heard nothing from Amy for so long, he'd started to become dangerously fond of Lizzie. But thank goodness he'd paid a visit to Ashford when he did.

'Where is Emily, by the way? She hasn't been in work today.'

'She's gone to Ashford.'

'Oh, to see her *best* friend, has she?' Lizzie said bitterly.

Josh ran his hand distractedly through his hair, wondering whether or not to tell Lizzie exactly why Emily had rushed back to Ashford. He decided to say nothing; Lizzie was in a bad enough mood already.

Then, as if suddenly realizing she was alienating Josh rather than winning him over, Lizzie smiled coquettishly up at him and wound her arms around his neck. 'Oh Josh, don't you know I love you? I didn't mean what I said about Emily. I was angry and hurt. I thought – I thought you liked me.'

'I did – I do, Lizzie. I like you very much and if – if things were different, then perhaps . . .' He broke off.

'Then why? Why are you going back to Amy?'

'Because – because I love her. I've never stopped. And besides, she's had my baby.'

'What?' Lizzie gasped, her arms fell from his neck

and she stepped back. Then her eyes narrowed as she asked nastily, 'How can you be sure it's yours? You left there over a year ago.'

'Because the little chap's almost a year old,' Josh said quietly. 'I know he's mine.'

'Huh! I wouldn't be too sure, if I was you. But that's your pigeon.'

Lizzie knew she was beaten. There was no way she was going to prise Josh away from Amy and her child, who, he believed rightly or wrongly, was his.

And now her devious mind turned back to how she could reap her revenge, if not on Josh, then on his sister. But she decided she would think about the matter carefully. She would plan her tactics and she would say nothing to Josh. Once he was back in the countryside with his precious Amy, then Miss Emily Ryan had better watch out. Didn't they say that 'Revenge is a dish best served cold'? Then that was how it would be: cold and calculating.

Now she played the heartbroken, jilted girl. She allowed the tears to flow until Josh was moved to put his arms around her and say, brokenly, 'Lizzie, I am sorry. Truly I am. I wouldn't have hurt you for the world.'

She sobbed all the harder against his shoulder, but they were crocodile tears. Inside, she was seething with anger. No one, but no one, humiliated Lizzie Dugdale and got away with it. If she couldn't hurt Josh directly, then she would do so by ruining his beloved sister.

And she knew just the person to help her do it.

Thirty-Six

Josh had been unable to talk to his mother that morning before he'd been obliged to go to work. After he'd seen Lizzie, as his mother stood at the sink washing up after their meal, he put his arms about her waist and said, 'Mam, I have something I need to tell you. Please – leave that for now. Dry your hands and come and sit down.'

Martha had not missed Emily yet and knew nothing about her journey to Ashford. Emily was often as late as this coming home from work and so her mother had thought nothing of her daughter's absence from the tea table.

'Don't tell me you've lost your job again, Josh Ryan, because if you have—'

'Come and sit down with Dad and I'll tell you both.'

Martha snorted. 'Huh! He'll not know what's going on. All right.' She dried her hands on a rough towel and sat down on the opposite side of the range to where her husband spent his days.

'I think he understands a lot more than you think, Mam,' Josh murmured, thinking back to what Emily had told him about the letters and how Walter had managed to communicate the facts to her.

'Mebbe, mebbe not. Anyway, never mind about that now. Out with it. What have you been up to?'

Josh moved a chair closer and sat between them.

'I've been back to Ashford to see Amy and I've decided to give my notice in here and go back there permanently.'

'You'll do no such thing, Josh. You're getting on nicely here and—'

'Mam, just listen, please. Amy has a baby – a little boy – and it's mine.'

'Well, if you think that, you're more stupid than I thought you were.'

'He's nearly a year old, Mam. I know he's mine.'

There was a noise beside him and he turned to see his father holding out a shaking hand, his mouth working as if he were trying to ask a question, but no sound would come out.

Josh took his father's hand between his own. 'Yes, Dad, you have a grandson. A wonderful little boy called Harry.'

Walter nodded, and it might only have been his shaking that made it seem so, but Josh was sure that, for a brief moment, his father gripped his hand. He took it as a sign that Walter was pleased with the news and that he agreed with what Josh intended to do. Which was more than could be said for Martha. 'I'll not let you. You're still under age. You will do as you're told, Josh Ryan, and—'

'No, Mam, I'm sorry but I will not. My duty is back in Ashford. Our old house is still empty . . .' He paused and decided not to tell her about Trip at present. 'I'm sure you could get the tenancy back, if you asked.'

'I have no intention of asking anyone for anything. We're not going back. *You*'re not going back.'

'Yes, I am. I'm going to marry Amy.'

'Over my dead body.'

'Don't say things like that, Mam, please, because it's what I'm going to do.'

'You're not old enough to get married. I won't give my consent.'

'Then I shall wait until I am. The villagers have been very good towards Amy and I think they will be with me, once they know I'm back for good. And I'll make sure they know that it's *you* standing in the way of me doing the honourable thing.' He didn't like threatening his mother, but it was all he could think of to do.

'You can't get the tenancy of The Candle House.'

'No,' he said quietly, 'but Mr Clark can.'

Mother and son stared at each other in a battle of wills.

Walter made a noise in his throat and waved his hands.

'I think,' Josh said quietly, 'Dad agrees with me, don't you?'

This time Walter nodded vigorously; there was no mistaking his meaning.

'Where's Emily? Why isn't she home? She'll side with me,' Martha said. 'She'll not want to go back, not now she's got a nice little business going. Why you couldn't be more like your sister, I don't know.'

Josh laughed, but without any bitterness. 'Yes, you're right, Mam. Emily should have been the boy. She came first and got all the ambition and drive. I just want a quiet life with Amy and my son.' As he said the last words, there was the light of love in his eyes and a glow of pride. And Martha knew that, this time, she had a real battle on her hands. But she was not ready to capitulate yet.

She sighed and asked again, 'Where is Emily?'

'She's gone to Ashford.'

Martha stared at him for a few moments. 'Whatever for? This has nothing to do with her.'

301

'Well, no, not exactly, but you see, when I went back, I found poor old Trip sleeping rough in our old home. He was in a dreadful state.'

Now, Martha's mouth dropped open and she gaped at her son. 'Thomas Trippet? Why?'

'He'd had a huge row with his father and Mr Trippet threw him out of his work and his home too, by the sounds of it.'

'But – but he's Arthur Trippet's heir to his company. His *only* heir. Why on earth would he do a thing like that?'

'He found out that Trip had been meeting Emily every Sunday and when he forbade Trip to see her any more, he refused.'

'And he disowned him because of that?'

'Apparently.'

'Then Trip's the fool and Emily must tell him so. He can't lose his whole future because of her.'

'He's in love with her and she with him.'

'Stuff and nonsense. He should marry someone of his own class. Someone who will bring more to the marriage than she ever could.'

'Mam, this is your own daughter you're talking about. And we've just been saying how ambitious Emily is. She'd be a marvellous wife for him. In fact,' he grinned, 'I think she has more drive than he has.'

'You think her little tin-pot business, running a team of buffer girls, is a resounding success? It's hardly "big business", is it?'

'"Little acorns", Mam. You know what they say about "little acorns"?'

But her only reply was a snort of derision. And if Josh thought she was finished, then he was very much mistaken.

Thirty-Seven

When Emily arrived back in Sheffield on the Wednesday evening, it was to walk into a maelstrom of anger and recriminations. The quarrel between Martha and Josh had escalated but, strangely, amidst it all, Walter seemed unperturbed and able to ignore the shouting going on all around him.

'You're an ungrateful little brat, Josh Ryan,' Martha screeched. 'You'll live in poverty all your life. You'll never amount to anything.'

'Then Emily will do that for you. She'll amount to something.'

'Nonsense, she's a girl. What can a girl do? She'll get pregnant like that little slut, Amy, and bring more shame on this family.'

'There's no need to talk about me as if I'm not here,' Emily said, removing her hat and coat. 'Besides, I shall be marrying Trip and, yes, I might get pregnant then, but not before. Sorry, Josh.'

Josh shrugged. 'Don't apologize. I did wrong by Amy, but I mean to put it right.'

'I know you do and you'll be happy with her. But,' she went on, turning towards her mother, 'what are you going to do, Mam?'

'Oh, somebody's actually thinking about me, are they? That's very kind of you, I'm sure.'

Emily touched her mother's arm. 'Why don't you

take Dad back to Ashford – back home? He'd be so much better there.'

Suddenly, Martha's shoulders slumped as if all the fight had gone out of her. 'So, you don't want me to stay here with you?'

'There's no need, Mam. Dad – and you – would be better off back home. You'll be back amongst friends and there's your little grandson to get to know.'

Slowly Martha lifted her head. 'I suppose you're right,' she said slowly. 'You don't want me, do you?'

'I'll always want you, Mam, but I don't *need* you here to look after me.'

Martha glanced towards her husband. 'He would be better off back in the countryside. You're right about that. All right, then. Once Josh is settled, we'll go back, that is, if we can get the tenancy of our old home back.'

'I'm sure you will.'

'And I'll move in with Amy, her dad and – my son.' The pride with which Josh spoke the final two words was not lost on his family.

'If you're sure you're doing the right thing, Josh,' Martha said flatly, 'then I won't oppose your marriage to Amy any longer. I'll sign whatever papers you need.'

Josh moved to put his arms around her. 'Thank you, Mam,' he murmured against her hair. 'That means a lot to me.'

'I'll need to look for work of some sort. I can't expect you to keep us all, Josh, if you've a wife and child.'

'We'll work it out, Mam,' Josh said.

Emily stared at him. The change in her brother was amazing. He was the happiest she'd seen him since before they'd left Ashford. Now he was decisive and confident.

Emily gave a silent nod of approval and smiled. 'Right then, I'm off to bed. I've an early start in the morning.'

Alone in the bedroom they would not have to share for much longer, Emily asked, 'What did Lizzie say? I presume you've told her.'

Josh's face clouded. 'I told her first – before Mam. She's not best pleased, to put it mildly.'

'I bet she isn't.'

Josh bit his lip, wondering whether to tell his sister about the threats which Lizzie had made against her, but he decided to say nothing. He believed that the girl had said things in the heat of the moment and hadn't really meant them.

And so Emily was unprepared for the onslaught that faced her the next morning when she arrived at work.

Emily opened the door to the workshop and called out her usual cheery 'Morning, all.' But today there was no answering chorus. Instead, the girls were standing near their machines. Although they were dressed in their workaday clothes and covered with newspaper, they were not working. The machines were silent. Emily glanced around at the solemn faces; Nell's face was set with what looked like disappointment, Ida looked anxious and the youngest girl, Jane, whom they'd only set on the previous week as an errand girl, was actually weeping.

'What's happened? What's the matter?'

Lizzie stepped forward, her arms folded across her chest, her eyes glittering with anger. 'You, Miss Emily Ryan. You're the problem. At least your brother is.'

Unease began to seep through Emily as she began to understand, but Lizzie's next words left her in no doubt. 'Josh has jilted me and humiliated me. And Yorkshire lasses don't like that. And they stick together. They're loyal. And you're not one of us, so we want you out. We're taking over this business. And tha can mog off right now.'

Emily glanced round again at the faces. Nell was biting her lip, Ida was avoiding her gaze and Jane's sobbing grew louder. Emily felt sick in the pit of her stomach. She had started this business and, little though it was, she had felt it was hers.

'And you'll be able to manage all the business side of it, Lizzie, will you? Getting the orders? Paying the bills and the wages?'

'It can't be that difficult,' Lizzie sneered. 'You've always made the running of things so important just to make yourself sound the the big "I am". We'll manage.'

Emily said no more. She knew Lizzie was quick and intelligent, but Nell could hardly read and write. But, obviously, it was no longer her problem. She shrugged. 'So be it, then. If you come into my little office with me, Lizzie, I'll just make up what money I'm owed and I'll leave you to it.'

Nell's eyes widened. 'You're going? Just like that? Without a fight?'

Emily sighed. 'Josh has let Lizzie down in a way, but I wouldn't go as far as to say he's *jilted* her because he never meant her to think they were anything more than just friends.'

'I don't think friends kiss like he kissed me on the night of the ball,' Lizzie said nastily.

Emily faced her. 'I didn't know that, Lizzie. Then I'm sorry – sorry if he has led you on to believe he was becoming fond of you, but I did try to warn you at the start.'

'Did she?' Nell glared at Lizzie.

'She's friends with this Amy trollop that he's going back to in Ashford. And she is a trollop,' Lizzie added, 'because she's had his baby. At least, he *says* it's his. But what proof has he got? That's what I say. But if he's daft enough to believe her, then that's his loss.'

'Oh well, if he's going back to do the decent thing by a girl he got in the family way, then that's a bit different,' Nell said, seeming to soften a little, but Lizzie rounded on her.

'Don't you start to side with them, Nell Geddis, else I'll throw you out, an' all.'

'There's no need for that, Lizzie,' Emily said. 'I'll go.'

'Are you going back to Ashford too, then?' Nell asked.

'No. I'm staying in the city,' Emily said firmly, but she told them nothing about Trip losing his job too. What they would both do, she didn't know. She had thought that at least she had work to support them both for a start, but now that too was gone. But Emily was young and strong and a hard worker and now she had a skill literally at her fingertips. And so had Trip. There'd be plenty of work for them, even in these difficult times; they just had to find it.

'Lizzie, are you really sure about this?' Nell was obviously having second thoughts now. 'I mean, if Emily warned you . . .'

'Nell, if you side with her, then you're out an' all.'

Nell shrugged. 'Sorry, Emily. I can't afford to lose my job.'

'I don't want you to, Nell. Nor any of you. I'll just collect my things and what I'm owed and be gone.'

'He's what?'

Arthur Trippet, arriving home on the Friday afternoon,

was incensed when he heard the news that his son was at home and asleep in his own bedroom.

'Thomas is here and he is staying here until he is quite well,' Constance said calmly. 'He's been sleeping rough since you threw him out and has not been eating properly.'

'You get him out of this house this minute. Do you hear me?'

'I could hardly *not* hear you, Arthur. I expect half the village can hear you ranting, but I will do no such thing. He stays here until he is well enough to leave of his own accord.'

'"Own accord" be damned. I have disowned him. I went to my solicitor this morning and remade my will.'

'That is your prerogative,' Constance said calmly.

'I've disinherited him too,' he said, trying to needle his wife. Her serenity was infuriating him. 'From the business. He'll have no job, no money – nothing. And I want you to change your will so that he gets nothing from you either.'

'Do you now?' Constance seemed unperturbed.

He stepped closer, almost threateningly, but Constance stood her ground. 'I rather think,' she said, smiling smugly, 'that Thomas and Emily will do rather well together. They'll have no need of your little factory.'

'*Little*, is it?' Arthur bellowed. 'That *little* factory keeps you in the lifestyle you enjoy.'

'And it was my father's money that enabled you to keep the factory going when it hit a bad patch,' Constance said quietly, resisting the urge to shout back at him. 'And, legally, I am an equal partner. Don't forget that, Arthur.'

Arthur turned purple in the face and, for a moment,

looked as if he might explode. 'So, you intend to let him stay here, do you? Against my express wishes?'

'I do.'

'Then,' Arthur growled, 'I shall not be living here until I hear that he has left.'

If he had thought to rattle Constance's resolve, it didn't work, for she merely inclined her head and said, 'Very well.'

As he turned from her and flung open the door, Constance said, 'I will send word when he has left. I presume you will be staying with Mrs Beauman. Please give her my kind regards.'

Arthur stood very still for a moment, but he did not turn around and went out through the door without another word.

Once Martha had realized that any further argument was futile, events moved very quickly. Josh had written to Amy to tell her what was happening and this time his letter reached her:

I hope this will be all right with both you and your dad especially, but Mam and Dad are coming back too. If they can get the tenancy again, they want to move back into The Candle House. I would work there, of course, like I did before, but live with you, your dad and little Harry. I have to work a full week's notice until next Friday, but on Saturday, 25 February, Amy, we'll be back home . . .

Martha packed up all their belongings and, the day after Josh had worked his notice, they left Sheffield to go back to what, in their hearts, they all still called home. Emily went with them to help them settle in and to see Trip again. But she was determined to return to the city.

On hearing the news from Josh, Amy had cleaned the house next door from top to bottom. On the day the family were expected, she lit a fire in the range and cooked a hot meal that wouldn't spoil if they were later than she expected. Just before four o'clock the removal van drew up outside the house. Josh was first out and shouting, 'Amy, Amy, where are you? We're here.'

She came out of the smithy leading Harry by the hand.

Josh swept them both into his arms and Martha, climbing stiffly down from the cab of the van, saw the touching reunion. She turned to help Walter down as Emily got out of the back of the van where she and Josh had travelled. It had been an uncomfortable ride, but they were here at last and she went at once to help her mother.

Emily lowered Walter gently into the chair by the range where already a fire burned and an appetizing aroma came from the oven.

He looked up at her, a tremulous smile quivering on his mouth and his eyes filled with tears.

'What is it, Dad?'

His mouth worked. He was trying valiantly to speak. Emily waited patiently, knowing this was important to him. At last – at long last – for the first time since before he'd gone away to war, Walter whispered hoarsely just one word. 'Home!'

Now Emily's eyes filled with tears too and she

nodded. 'Yes, Dad,' she said, her voice husky. 'You're home again.'

He leaned back in his chair and closed his eyes with a contented sigh.

Thirty-Eight

Two hours later, having helped unload the van, Emily was free to visit Riversdale House and as she walked up the village street her heart fluttered with excitement at the thought of seeing Trip again. She met one or two villagers and was obliged to stop to speak to them and to answer their kind enquiries.

'Yes, we've come home. At least my parents and Josh have. I'm going back to Sheffield.'

She must have said the words half a dozen times before she arrived at the big house at the end of the street and walked up the driveway. She went round the house to the back door where she was greeted by Polly and shown into the morning room where Constance was sitting with her embroidery.

'My dear girl, come in. Polly, please lay an extra place at the dinner table—'

'No, please. I've already eaten with the family. Amy had cooked us a meal, but please don't let me delay you. I – I should have realized. I can come back later.'

'Nonsense,' Constance said firmly, laying aside her needlework. 'You can sit and talk to us while we eat.'

'Oh, but—'

'There's only the two of us. Mr Trippet isn't here. He has decided to stay in the city whilst Thomas is here, so we don't stand on ceremony when there are just the two of us.' She turned to the maid. 'Polly, please tell Master Thomas that Miss Emily is here. You don't mind me calling you Emily, do you?'

'No, of course not.' But Emily felt herself blushing. To be treated as an equal by Constance Trippet was unnerving.

After a few moments, during which time Constance made kind enquiries about their journey and her father's health, Trip came hurrying into the room. Without any embarrassment, he put his arms around Emily and kissed her. Emily leaned back and looked up into his face, 'You look much better.'

'I feel it.' He grinned. 'Mother's been wonderful about this whole sorry affair. She's on our side, but it's high time I went out and found work, so, I'm coming back to Sheffield with you.'

'You can stay with me. My family have come home, so I'm on my own in the house we rented.'

'Oh, but I couldn't do that, Emily. It would ruin your reputation.'

'Well—'

'It wouldn't if you were married,' Constance said quietly and the two young people turned to look at her in amazement. 'You're both of age now, or at least almost. Your twenty-first birthday is next month, isn't it, Emily? You won't need anyone's consent then. It could all be arranged quite quickly – unless, of course, you want a big, lavish wedding?' She glanced at Emily, who shook her head swiftly. 'No, I don't. But Amy and Josh will be getting married very soon. Why don't we ask them if they'd mind having a double wedding? Would you mind that, Trip?'

'Of course not. It's a lovely idea.'

'And we could hold the reception for both of you here on the lawn at the side of the house, if the weather is kind. And if it isn't, then there's plenty of room in the house.'

'Oh, but we couldn't . . .' Trip and Emily spoke together, but Constance held up her hand and said decidedly, 'I insist. Call it my wedding present to you, if you wish.'

'What about Father?' Trip asked hesitantly.

Constance shrugged and her expression hardened. 'Your father can do exactly what he likes. If he wishes to attend the wedding, then he can. If not . . .' She left the words hanging in the air, but it was obvious that she didn't care one way or the other.

After he'd eaten dinner with his mother, whilst Emily sat beside him feeling rather awkward but soon made to feel at ease by Constance, Trip and Emily walked down to The Candle House. Emily was encouraged to see that Trip was much stronger now. Hand in hand, they walked into the house to see Walter sitting in the chair by the range. In front of him, on the hearthrug, Amy was kneeling beside her son, already dressed in his nightshirt.

'This is your grandpa, darling,' she was saying. 'Say, "Hello, Grandpa."'

From the doorway Emily and Trip watched quietly as Harry regarded Walter solemnly for a few minutes. Then he smiled and said, ''Lo, Pap-pap.'

Emily stifled her chuckle. Harry had straightaway found his own name for the new grandfather in his life.

Walter's eyes filled with tears and a ghost of a smile spread across his mouth. Suddenly, Harry ran to a toy box in the corner of the room and picked out an ABC book. Coming back, he climbed up onto Walter's knee, settled himself and opened the book. Pointing at a picture on one of the pages, he looked up at his grandpa and said, quite clearly for one so young, 'Cat, Pap-pap.' And then he waited. Now, Walter's mouth worked as he tried to make a noise. 'C-ca . . .'

'Cat.' Harry repeated and waited again. After four attempts, Walter managed to say something that was recognizable as the word. Harry turned the page. 'Dog.' And the effort was repeated.

'The little chap's very advanced for his age, isn't he?' Trip whispered, watching the heart-warming sight of the little boy on his grandfather's knee.

'Yes,' Emily said proudly. 'But his mother and his other granddad spend a lot of time with him. And now he has another grandfather.' Emily pressed her face against Trip's shoulder to stem the tears of relief. Her father was going to be all right now that he was back home in Ashford and she was sure that Harry's bright chatter would bring Walter even further out of his world of silence.

And coming into the room together, Martha and Josh saw Emily with Trip's arm around her. For a moment, Martha looked uncertain and then she sighed and nodded. A slow smile spread across her face. 'It looks like we might have two weddings to organize, then.'

Emily lifted her head. 'That's what we've come to talk to you about, Mam. I'm going back. I never thought I'd hear myself say it – but I adore life in the city. I'll always love the countryside and my home – my roots – but there's something about Sheffield. The people are so friendly and it's exciting and – and –' she searched for the word – 'vibrant. And there are so many opportunities.' She glanced at Martha. 'You were right about that, Mam. It just wasn't for Josh, but it is for me. Oh, I know there's a dark side, but there is to every big city. Besides,' she added, as if it answered everything – and it did – 'Trip's going back and I want to be with him.

315

It's where he wants to be and, as the tenancy on the house in the court in Garden Street isn't up yet, it seems sensible for him to live with me.' As Martha opened her mouth to protest, Emily added swiftly, 'So his mother suggested that we should be married first.' Now she glanced at Amy and Josh. 'We wondered if you'd agree to a double wedding?'

Josh glanced down at Amy. 'What do you think, love? It's up to you.'

'Mrs Trippet has said she'll organize a wedding reception for all of us on the lawn at Riversdale House.'

Amy's eyes widened at Emily's words and she glanced uncertainly at Trip.

'Yes, it's true. Do say "yes". We'd have such a lovely day.'

So it was agreed and it would not take long to call the banns in Ashford's church and arrange two weddings.

Mick had been away from the city for over a week. After the run-in with Steve Henderson, he had decided to disappear for a few days, just to let things cool down. So, it wasn't until the Ryan family had packed up and gone that he came home to find Lizzie in tears.

'She's been like this for days,' Bess told him angrily. 'It's that young rascal next door who's to blame. I'd get you to sort him out good and proper, our Mick, if the wretch hadn't done a bunk already.'

'Eh?' Mick was suddenly afraid. Had Josh turned informer on him and his mates? He'd been a little unsure of Josh's real commitment to the gang, anyway. 'What's he done?'

'He's jilted your sister, that's what. Gone back to the village they came from to marry a girl he left pregnant there.'

For a brief moment, Mick felt a stab of admiration. So, old Josh wasn't the goody-goody he'd seemed, eh? But then, hearing his sister's sobs grow louder until they became like a banshee's wail, he changed his mind. He muttered an oath under his breath and went to sit beside Lizzie on the sofa. 'Want me to go after him, Sis, and give him a good hiding?'

Lizzie's tears stopped miraculously, as if a tap had been turned off. She lifted her head and her eyes narrowed as she said, 'No, let him go. I've thought of a much better way to hurt him. I'll get back at him and at her at the same time.'

'Who? This girl he's—' Mick began, but Lizzie was shaking her head. 'No, not her. Emily, of course. I thought she was my friend, but she's betrayed me too. And nobody betrays the Dugdales, now, do they?'

Mick hugged her to him, 'No, luv, they don't.' He'd help his sister get her revenge any way she wanted, but he couldn't help feeling glad that it was an affair of the heart that was causing all the trouble and not a betrayal of him and his cronies.

It had been agreed that Trip should stay with his mother until the weddings to regain his full strength, after which he would return to the city to look for work too.

But Emily returned to the court in Garden Street to sweep and dust the whole house that was now hers and soon would be Trip's too. She was lucky; the rent had been paid for the next month and with only herself to keep, the money she'd received on leaving the little business would be enough to last three weeks. After the wedding – for which Trip's mother was generously paying – they would both come back to the city to look for work. She ventured out only rarely in the weeks she was there; she didn't want to run into any member of the Dugdale family if she could help it and there was plenty of work in the house to keep her busy. She cleaned every room and papered the walls and painted the doors, skirting boards and picture rails. She scrubbed all the floors and black-leaded the range until it shone.

The morning after everything was finished to her satisfaction, Emily was about to pack her few things to leave when there was a knock at the door. She opened it to find Bess Dugdale standing there, her arms folded across her ample bosom, her foot tapping with ill-concealed anger.

'Oh, so it is you, is it? Rosa said she'd seen you, but I thought she must have been mistaken. I didn't think you'd have the cheek to show your face here again.'

'Mrs Dugdale, I'm very sorry for what has happened. I tried to warn Lizzie when we first came here that Josh had a fiancée back in Ashford, but she wouldn't listen. She set her cap at him and that was that. I didn't want her to get hurt. You and your family have been very good to us.'

'Oh aye, I know that. You wouldn't have had your little business, if it hadn't been for our Mick sorting everything out for you.'

'He helped us a lot, I'll not deny that.'

'Well, I don't know what you're going to do now, missy, but you'll get no more help from him. In fact, you'd better watch your back.' She wagged her forefinger in Emily's face. 'Mick's not taken kindly to the way your dear brother's treated our Lizzie.'

'Mrs Dugdale, I . . .' But Bess had turned on her heel and was marching back to her own house, outrage in every step.

Thirty-Nine

The morning of the weddings, Saturday 15 April – just over a week after Emily's twenty-first birthday – was blustery, but fine.

'If only the rain keeps off,' Emily said, as the two girls readied themselves in Amy's bedroom. 'Mrs Trippet has said the buffet reception will be in her dining room but that people can wander out into the garden if it's not raining. At least it's not too cold.'

Amy was wearing her mother's wedding dress; it was old-fashioned but still in good condition and Amy was proud to wear it. She knew it was what her father wanted. Emily's dress was a simple, but pretty, evening dress in cream that had belonged to Trip's mother and had hardly been worn. Mrs Trippet had had it altered to fit her new daughter-in-law and be suitable as a wedding gown.

Both girls carried small posies, generously donated by Mr Osborne from the corner shop, and Grace Partridge had supplied both girls with something blue. She'd chuckled as she presented them each with a blue garter. 'Now, have you got everything else to satisfy all the old superstitions?'

'I think so, Amy's dress is old and so's mine, in a way. We've both got new underwear and now we've got something blue –' she turned to Amy – 'but what have we got that's borrowed?'

Both girls frowned at each other, trying to think what they could borrow from someone.

'I know,' Grace said. 'Borrow a handkerchief from each other.'

'Oh, what a good idea.' Hastily they swapped white lace handkerchiefs and then they were ready.

It would be a proud moment for Bob Clark to walk his daughter up the aisle to stand beside Josh. Grace held Harry in her arms though they all doubted the little chap would remember much about the day.

'But he can't be left out,' Grace had declared. 'I'll look after him and I'll take him out if he's noisy.'

But Harry didn't make a sound. He knew Grace Partridge well and he knew his mam and his granddad would be coming soon and there, waiting for them, too, was the man he was learning to call 'Daddy'. The little boy gazed around the church as they waited for the brides to arrive. His child's eyes were wide with wonder at the huge space; the pretty stained-glass window above the altar, casting coloured light upon the floor, the curved arches and the shining pews and the organ music playing softly whilst they waited. His gaze wandered over the beautiful floral displays that adorned every windowsill – daffodils, tulips and wild spring flowers – arranged by the women of the village, who were all there now with their families to witness the marriage between the two young couples. It seemed as if the whole village were crammed into the church, all dressed in their Sunday best, whispering amongst themselves as they waited along with Harry. A double wedding was unusual in the small village and no one was going to miss it, nor were they going to forego a chance to visit Riversdale House and be royally entertained.

There was only one person absent: Arthur Trippet.

Stubbornly, he had stayed away from the celebrations, vowing to his wife that he would not return until 'all this silliness is over'.

There was a rustle amongst the congregation as the organ struck up 'Here Comes the Bride' and all heads turned to see the bridal parties enter the church.

Amy and her father came first and, behind them, Emily walked on her own followed by Martha pushing Walter in a wheelchair, which had been kindly loaned by one of the villagers so that Walter could be at his daughter's side on her special day. Martha had been very subdued since the family's return to Ashford. She could see for herself the happiness shining out of Josh's eyes, had witnessed him taking up candle making again and how the villagers flocked to him for their orders, all of them saying, 'How we've missed you, Josh.' As for her husband, in the few weeks that he'd been back in Ashford, Walter's condition had improved beyond all their hopes and today there was no shaking. His eyes were clear and bright and he seemed to know everything that was going on. When it came to Emily and Trip's part of the service and the moment for Walter to give her away, in answer to the vicar's question, 'Who giveth this woman . . . ?', Walter's voice rang loud and clear through the church: 'I do.' There was a ripple of surprise and pleasure amongst the congregation and Emily's eyes filled with tears. Her happiness was complete.

After the service, everyone walked the short distance to Riversdale House to be greeted by Constance Trippet and made welcome in her home. It could be said to be the happiest day of Constance's life too, for it was a great deal happier than her own wedding day had been.

When everyone had food and drink and were happily

chatting to one another, Constance drew Martha aside. 'Well, Martha, my dear, since we are related now, I think we should dispense with formality, don't you?'

Martha blinked. 'If you say so, ma'am – sorry, Constance – but I find it a little awkward, since I was going to ask you if you knew of any cleaning jobs in the area. Josh is doing well, but he has his own family to support now. We can't expect him to provide for me and Walter long term.'

'Oh, I'm sure we can help you there. I hear Mr Osborne is looking for some part-time help in his shop. That would be nice and handy for you, wouldn't it?' Constance glanced shrewdly at Martha. 'Your husband still needs a deal of help, I expect.'

Martha nodded. 'Yes, but he's much better since we came back and having a little grandson has cheered him up no end. Oh, Constance,' Martha added, with tears in her eyes, feeling suddenly able to confide in this kindly woman, 'I've made some dreadful mistakes. I'll never forgive myself for all I've put my family through. I was so ambitious for Josh that I was blind to everything else and everyone else.' She shuddered. 'To think what might have happened. I could have caused Walter's death and – and there was something else I did that I'm ashamed of now. I just hope Josh and Emily never find out. They – they'd disown me for sure.'

Constance formed her reply carefully, for she knew now about the missing letters and what had happened to them. With forced casualness in her tone, she said, 'Well, I'm sure whatever it is, they'd forgive you, but today is not the day for recriminations or looking back. Today is all about the future, Martha, so raise your glass of champagne and let's drink to that.'

They clinked glasses and Martha laughed as the

bubbles tickled her nose. 'I don't know how to thank you for giving them this wonderful day.'

Constance gazed across the room to where Trip was standing close to Emily, looking down at her. 'It's thanks enough to see my son so happy, Martha. May they always be as happy as they are today.'

The two women touched glasses again and Martha took another sip of champagne, feeling a little light-headed already.

'And now I think it's time they cut the cakes. Go and find Walter, Martha. He mustn't miss this.'

Constance had arranged for two cakes to be made. Mr Osborne's wife had made and iced them. 'You'll have different friends you want to give a piece to,' Constance explained. 'And besides, you've shared everything else; I thought you should each have your own cake.'

Walter was wheeled in front of the table where the cakes stood. Now, he had Harry on his knee and together they watched as the two couples, laughing and joking together, stood side by side to make the first cuts. The guests clapped and cheered and then Polly carried the cakes away for Mrs Froggatt, still wearing her best hat, to cut into slices.

It had been a wonderful day for both families. Trip and Emily were to spend the first night of their married life at Riversdale House. As Josh and Amy left to go home, Trip said, 'We must go back to Sheffield tomorrow afternoon, but how about a walk up to Monsal Head in the morning? Just for old times' sake, eh?'

His suggestion was greeted with a chorus of 'What a lovely idea!'

As Trip and Emily stood on the driveway to wave

them goodbye, Trip called, 'And be sure to bring Harry. It's high time he saw more of our lovely countryside.'

The following morning, Mrs Froggatt packed a picnic basket and Kirkland drove the two girls, Harry and the hamper to Monsal Head in Constance's car whilst Trip and Josh walked up. They sat on the top of the hill to eat, looking out over the dale and pointing out the passing trains to the little boy.

'We must do this again when the weather's warmer,' Josh said. 'We can take Harry down to the weir and let him run on the grass.' He glanced at Trip and Emily. 'You'll come back to Ashford as often as you can, won't you?'

'Of course, we will,' Trip said, getting up. 'But now we really must be going. Kirkland should be coming back for us in a few minutes. I told him two o'clock.'

Back at Riversdale House, Trip kissed his mother goodbye and said, 'We must look for work tomorrow morning.'

For a brief moment she clung to him, then, with a brave smile and a brief nod, she stood back and patted his shoulder. 'Good luck to both of you. Come, Emily, my dear, give me a kiss. I'm thrilled to have a daughter-in-law. You will write to me – both of you – won't you?'

'Of course,' they chorused. 'And we'll come and see you as often as we can,' Trip added. 'I've been lucky enough to be able to get my motorcycle back and even a sidecar with it. The local farmer I sold it to when I came back to Ashford bought it for his son, who took it out and promptly fell off and broke his arm. The lad doesn't want to see it again. So, I've bought it back from him for the same money he paid me. "Just take it out of my sight," he said. So, we'll be able to get here to see you easily. And now, Mrs Trippet Junior, let's see how you fit into my new sidecar.'

Laughing, he picked her up in his arms and settled her in the seat.

'Here, my dear, you'll need this,' Constance said and moved forward to place a broad-brimmed hat on Emily's head, tying it firmly in place with a silk scarf. 'Now, off you go.'

Constance stood at the end of the driveway, watching until they disappeared round the corner at the end of the street. Near The Candle House, all Emily's family had come out to wave and, as the motorbike roared up the slope of Greaves Lane, it seemed as if everyone in the street had come out to cheer them on their way.

After a day settling in together back in the court, Emily decided that they must look for work straightaway.

'We've the rent to find on the first of next month,' Emily said. Trip took her in his arms and nestled his face against her neck. 'Is that all the honeymoon we get then?'

She chuckled and pressed her face into his shoulder. ''Fraid so, but it's all going to be honeymoon from now on.'

They stood together, just holding each other for a long moment before reluctantly drawing apart.

'Then we'd better start today, Mrs Trippet.'

'I'll go and see the girls. See if they've had a change of heart.'

Trip pulled a face. 'I wouldn't get your hopes up.'

When they stepped out into the yard, there was a strange atmosphere. At the corner house, Mrs Nicholson was standing on her doorstep. She glared briefly at the pair and then turned her back on them, stepped back into her house and slammed the door. Across the yard, Mrs Jacklin hurried Rosa's two children away, almost pushing them along in front of her and averting her glance from Emily and Trip. Once, she would have called out a friendly greeting, but not today. From the workshop across the yard came the sound of Bess Dugdale tapping as she made another file. Then the noise stopped and the door opened.

'Oh, so you're back, are you? Well, don't expect a welcome in this court. You'd have done better to find somewhere else to live.'

'Mrs Dugdale, please . . .' Emily crossed the cobbles towards her. 'You know I tried to warn Lizzie from the start, but she wouldn't listen.'

'Then Josh shouldn't have led her on. Going for walks in the park every Sunday for all to see just as if they were a courting couple. Escorting her to the ball. He's not treated her fair, Emily, and that's a fact. And if you've come back to live here, then you'll get no help from any of us. Not this time.'

Trip touched her arm. 'Come on, Emily. Leave it.'

Sadly, Emily turned away. She was sorry to lose the goodwill of their neighbours and wondered just how long she and Trip would be able to live in such a cold and unwelcoming atmosphere. But they set off together, hopeful that by the end of the day both of them would have secured some kind of employment.

They separated with a kiss and went in opposite directions; Trip to seek work in the bigger factories, Emily to visit the small workshop she had helped to set up. It was worth a try, though she wasn't hopeful.

As she walked through the door, she was greeted by the noise of two buffing wheels, whilst two lay idle. Only

326

Ida and a girl she didn't recognize were working and there was no sign of the errand girl, Jane. She glanced around and saw Lizzie and Nell talking together in the far corner. Above the noise of the machinery, she couldn't hear what was being said – and she had never quite mastered the art of lip-reading – but by the look on both their faces, and the fact that Nell was standing with her hands on her hips, Emily knew they were arguing. Ida had spotted her standing uncertainly by the door and she went across to Nell and Lizzie to speak to them. Then all three girls looked in her direction.

Emily lifted her chin defiantly. She had a right to be here; hadn't she helped to start all this?

Lizzie said something she couldn't hear, but it was Nell who walked towards her.

'Come outside a minute, Emily. We can't talk properly in here.'

They stepped outside and turned to face each other. 'I'm sorry, Emily,' Nell said at once, 'but Lizzie is adamant you can't come back here, even though . . .' She paused and bit her lip.

'Even though . . . what, Nell?' Emily prompted.

Nell sighed. 'Since you left, the business has been going downhill. Even in that short time. We've lost two of our customers – our biggest – and haven't been able to replace them. Even Mr Hawke has removed his trade. Lizzie hasn't got your business head, nor has she the right attitude with the customers. Oh, she flirts with the men, flutters her long eyelashes at them, but that's not what businessmen want, is it?'

Emily shook her head. 'But she won't let me come back?'

Nell shook her head. 'Won't hear of it. That young lass we set on just before you left, Jane, she's gone and

327

we can't afford to pay an errand lass now. And she was shaping up to be a really good worker – she was almost ready to start training on a wheel – and although we've taken on another lass, Flo, her work's rubbish at the moment, to be honest. Lizzie won't condescend to work at the machines any more and me and Ida can't do it all. We'll lose more customers, if this goes on, just because we can't cope with the work we are still getting.'

'I'm sorry, Nell,' Emily said, and she meant it. 'But if Lizzie won't let me come back, there's nothing I can do.'

Nell eyed her for a moment before stepping closer and lowering her voice. 'If you decide to set up somewhere else – and I reckon you could – let me know, won't you?'

Emily stared at her. She'd thought that Nell and Lizzie were bosom pals. As if reading her mind, Nell smiled wryly. 'Oh, I can guess what you're thinking. I'm being disloyal to Lizzie, but to be honest, I don't agree with the way she's treating you. I know what she's like with men and I believe you when you say that you told her from the start that Josh was engaged to someone else. But if Lizzie gets a bee in her bonnet, she keeps it buzzing. She won't give in. I know I'm her friend, but when it comes to my livelihood, then I'm afraid that's where friendship ends. I – I don't tell many people this, Emily,' she glanced around to make sure no one was listening and then lowered her voice, 'but I've got a kiddie to support. I can't afford to be out of work.'

Emily knew Nell wasn't married, but she hadn't known she had a child. Nell went on to explain. 'I was a fool, taken in by a charmer who turned out to be a real bad 'un. Me mam was a brick. She looks after Lucy all day while I'm at work. That's why I never come out in the evening. It's not fair to expect Mam to do more than she does already. I do let Lucy's dad see her now and again, but there's no way I want a bloke like him in our lives permanently. He's a wrong 'un and he was a mate of Mick Dugdale's at one time, though I think there's been a bit of a falling out. Anyway, that should say it all. My dad was killed in the war, so you see I have to work to support the three of us.'

'Nell – I'm sorry and I wish I could help you, but I'm desperate to find work myself at the moment.'

Nell nodded. 'Keep in touch, though, won't you? Are you still living in that court off Garden Street?'

Emily nodded. 'At the moment, but no one is speaking to us.'

'Huh! Lizzie again, I expect.' She paused and then added, 'Us? I thought your family had all gone back to Ashford?'

Emily smiled. 'They have, but Trip and I are married and we've come back together to find work.'

Nell smiled and squeezed her arm. 'Well, that is a bit of good news. I'm right pleased for the pair of you. You and Trip will do well together. You've got each other.' There was a wistful tone in her voice and Emily was moved to give her a swift hug.

'Good luck, Emily.' And with that, Nell hurried back inside.

Forty

Emily tramped the streets for the rest of the day, but there was no work to be had and when they met again at home that evening, Trip had the same story.

'There's nothing – at least, nothing that anyone will give me. I really think my father has a hand in all this. Some of the foremen and managers I spoke to looked distinctly uncomfortable and avoided meeting my eyes. I reckon he must have put the word around amongst his cronies and they aren't willing to cross him. So, I went to see Mr Bayes just to see if he knew anything.'

Emily gasped. 'Weren't you worried you might run into your father?'

Trip shook his head. 'No, I know where he parks the car when he's at the works and it wasn't there, so I thought I was pretty safe.'

'And what did Mr Bayes have to say?'

Trip set down his knife and fork as he finished the meal that Emily had prepared. 'Not much. He seemed a bit agitated. Kept saying that he was so sorry about what had happened between Father and me and asking if my mother was all right.'

'Does he know your mother?'

Trip frowned. 'I suppose he must have met her a few times over the years. Not that she comes to the factory often, but I think she used to attend the annual ball in the early days.' Trip sighed. 'I suppose he thought that perhaps all the trouble had upset her, but I was able to put his mind at rest and tell him that she was on our side and how she'd helped us.'

'I expect your father's said nothing to him about – about us.'

'No – he didn't even know we'd got married, but then I must be persona non grata with my father.'

Emily laughed. 'What's that mean when it's at home?'

Trip grinned sheepishly. 'Sorry, I didn't mean to sound—'

Emily touched his hand. 'I know you didn't. But tell me what it means.'

'It's Latin and means "an unwelcome person".'

Emily was not in the least offended by his use of words she didn't understand; his education had been far superior to her own, but she was willing to learn. Now, she almost wished she hadn't asked. How sad, she thought, for him to feel like that.

Swiftly, she changed the subject, trying to erase the pensive look on his face. 'You know I went to see Lizzie and the others, well, there was nothing doing there. Not that I thought there would be, but Nell came outside to talk to me. The business is falling apart. Lizzie isn't running it very well and they've lost several customers. Nathan Hawke is one of them.'

Trip looked up. 'Did you go to see him?'

Emily bit her lip and shook her head. 'I didn't like to. He was so good to us and helped us so much when we first set up.'

'Then I think you should. It's worth a try, Emily. He must have had good reason to take his work away from them.'

'I don't know how he'll greet me,' Emily said

worriedly. 'He might blame me for the breakdown of the buffing business.'

By the end of the week, when there was still no job offer for either of them, Trip persuaded Emily to see Nathan Hawke. 'He can only send you off with a flea in your ear. I'll come with you, if you like. I really think he's our last hope.'

Emily's concerns were unfounded. Nathan Hawke greeted her, literally, with open arms. 'My dear girl, how glad I am to see you. And you've got young Thomas Trippet with you too,' he said, smiling and holding out his hand towards Trip.

'We're married now, Mr Hawke.'

The little man beamed. 'That's even better news. So, you've come back to your little business, I take it.'

Emily shook her head. 'I'm afraid Lizzie and I had a falling out over a personal matter and I was asked to leave. So it's no longer Dugdale and Ryan – just Dugdale.'

'Mm,' Nathan said thoughtfully. 'I thought something must have happened because it was Lizzie who came to collect and deliver the work.' He sighed. 'And I'm sorry to tell you that I've had to remove my patronage from there. The work was no longer up to standard and when I asked why Nell wasn't still doing all my work as we'd originally agreed – because I knew she wasn't – Lizzie was so off-hand and said that no customer could demand a particular buffer. I was getting complaints from *my* customers and I can't have that. I'm a one-man band and I can't afford to lose their good will. So, I had to take the bull by the horns and stand up to Mick Dugdale. I've been expecting reper- cussions, but nothing's happened yet. So, are you looking to work for someone else or are you going to set up again on your own?'

Emily stared at him. 'We've been tramping the streets – both of us – and no one will offer us anything. But I have to admit that I hadn't seriously thought about setting up again myself.' She turned to her new husband. 'What do you think, Trip? Could we do it?'

Trip chewed thoughtfully at his lip. 'I think you could, Emily, yes. But there wouldn't be anything for me. It was the making of the cutlery that I learned. Mind you, you need premises and then there'd be machinery to buy . . .'

'No problem about a workshop,' Nathan said. 'Upstairs is still empty and, as you know, I own it, so it can be yours if you want it. There's a wooden staircase to it outside as well as one inside, so you don't even have to come through my workshop all the time.' He chuckled. 'More's the pity! It would make my day to see a bevy of pretty buffer girls passing through my workshop every morning. But,' he went on, more serious now, 'you can have it rent free until you're up and running.' He held up his hand as Emily was about to protest. 'It needs a bit of work before you can use it, so if you do that, I'll waive the rent for at least six months. And there are still some old machines up there. I'll see about getting them repaired.'

'Oh Mr Hawke, I could hug you.'

With a wink at Trip, the older man said, 'Well, don't hold back, luv. T'ain't often I get the chance to hug a pretty lass. Now,' he went on briskly when Emily had given him a grateful bear hug, 'about you, young feller. I'm surprised you can't find work. George Bayes – he's a good friend of mine and we play bowls together – always said what a quick learner and an excellent worker you were. His words were, "He'll mek a fine master cutler one day and be a good boss to work for, an' all." I've heard rumours, but I don't really know what the truth is. So, tell me – what's gone wrong?'

The man had been so kind to them that Trip felt he could confide in him. 'My father threw me out. He's disowned me because I wanted to marry Emily. Father didn't marry my mother for love, he married her for her money. I expect he wanted me to do a similar thing. Marry someone who was "suitable" in his eyes. Well, I wasn't going to do that.' He put his arm around Emily's shoulders. 'Whatever happens, I know I've done the right thing even if – even if it means being estranged from my father.'

Nathan glanced at the young couple. He was sure that Trip meant every word he said, but the older man knew only too well what strains and pressures could be brought to bear. He hoped their love was strong enough and that one day Trip would not come to resent Emily because she had been the cause of the rift with his family.

'What about your mother?' he asked quietly.

'She paid for our wedding and held the reception for us at home. She's on our side, but I just hope my father doesn't take revenge on her in some way.'

'Oh, I wouldn't worry too much about that. From what I hear, your mother still has independent means of her own. Her own father was astute enough to leave her well provided for.'

'Was he? I didn't know that, though I had wondered. I'm relieved to hear it.' Trip paused a moment and then asked, 'How – how do you know all this?'

Nathan tapped the side of his nose. 'There's a cutlers' grapevine, my boy. I don't miss much of what goes on in this city. And besides, like I said, I'm good friends with George Bayes. He's worked for your family's firm a long time. What he doesn't know about the Trippets isn't worth knowing.'

The three of them laughed together and then Nathan said, 'I tell you what, Thomas. How about you come and help me a bit? I'm getting arthritis in my hands and they're quite painful at times. I can't promise you full-time work and I can't pay you much, but it'll keep the wolf from the door whilst Emily gets her business set up again and, of course, all my buffing work will go to you, lass.'

'Oh Mr Hawke,' Emily said, with tears of gratitude. 'I think that deserves another hug.'

Forty-One

So, Emily started over again, setting up a little buffing business just as she had before, but this time, she was completely on her own, so Nathan's work filled most of her time. For the moment, she didn't need to look for any more. Trip started working alongside Nathan, the older man teaching him the gaps in his education where the making of cutlery was concerned.

'It's all very well, you learning from the bottom up, and I suppose your father was right in that, but you only learn one process at a time in a factory. I'll show you everything I know.'

So Trip, quick and eager, learned far more from the little mester than he had in the years he had worked at Trippets'. And best of all, he was only downstairs from where Emily was working. They'd worked hard together to clean out and restore the little workshop and now she was installed and happily busy.

One morning, when she'd been up and running for about three weeks, she paused in her work at the wheel to wrap a batch of spoons she'd just finished polishing. She heard footsteps on the stairs outside and the door opened. She looked up to see Nell standing there. Emily went towards her. As she drew nearer and Nell's face was visible, she could see that there was a despairing, almost desperate, look in her eyes.

'Oh Nell, whatever's the matter? Is it – your little girl?'

Nell shook her head. 'No, no, she's fine. At least –' she stopped and gulped painfully – 'she would be, if only – if only . . .'

'Is it your mother, then? Has something happened to her?' Emily couldn't imagine what could have caused Nell to be in such a state. 'Come inside and sit down. I've only old wooden boxes for us to sit on, I'm afraid, but—'

'It's fine,' Nell said swiftly, 'but I shouldn't keep you from your work.' Even so she stepped into the workshop and sat down. Then she glanced around her. 'Are you working here on your own?'

'Yes. Mr Hawke gives me all his work, but I've no other customers so I can manage for the moment.'

'I see.' Nell's tone was flat and Emily felt it held disappointment. She couldn't think why. And then Nell burst out with the reason for her visit as if she couldn't hold back the words any longer. 'I'm out of work. I haven't worked for three weeks.'

Emily gasped. 'Oh no! It wasn't anything to do with my visit, was it? Did Lizzie see you talking to me and . . . ?'

But Nell was shaking her head. 'No, it wasn't that, but it did happen soon afterwards.'

'What did?'

'We – the business closed. We couldn't run it any more. For all her fine words, Lizzie was useless. Oh, she was a good buffer girl, I don't deny that, but after she got rid of you – and it *was* her, Emily, who wanted you gone, not the rest of us – she became the big "I Am", fancying herself as a businesswoman. But you

337

were the brains behind it all. We all knew that – all except Lizzie. Even Mick couldn't help her this time.'

'Oh Nell, I'm sorry, truly I am.'

'It's not your fault. None of us blame you.'

'So, are you all out of work now? Even Lizzie?'

Nell nodded.

'She's never said anything, even though she's living next door in the court. Mind you,' Emily gave a wry smile, 'none of the Dugdale family are speaking to us. In fact, no one is.'

'Well, she wouldn't, would she? Too proud to admit she was wrong.' There was a pause before Nell said tentatively, 'Emily, would you come back and start up the business again? We've still got the premises, because we've managed to scrape up the rent between us, just in case.' Nell grasped her hand. 'Oh Emily, please say you will.'

Emily bit her lip and frowned, thinking hard. 'I'll have to talk to Mr Hawke first. He's been very good to us and this is his workshop that he's rented to me. I don't want to let him down. But I don't think Lizzie would—'

'We don't want Lizzie involved any more – or her precious brother. Ida and Flo agree with me; we just want you to come back. And don't forget, our workshop belongs to Mr Hawke too, so he's going to lose one or the other anyway. And maybe you could keep this place on too. Just think about it, Emily, you could have two workshops running.'

'That's only if I can get back the work that Lizzie has lost.'

'You will and more besides. I'm sure of it.'

Emily laughed. 'You've more confidence in me than

338

I have in myself. But let me think about it and talk to Mr Hawke and Trip.'

'May I come back tomorrow?'

'Of course.'

Nell hugged her and, as she hurried away, Emily warned, 'Not a word to the other girls yet. Not before I've had time to . . .'

But Nell had gone and Emily was very doubtful that she would be able to keep the news and the glimmer of hope it represented to herself.

'I'm sorry for them, of course, I am,' Nathan said later that day when they'd finished work and Emily had told him and Trip about Nell's visit. 'But you can't take on more workers when you haven't got the work for them, Emily.'

'I know,' Emily said worriedly, 'and I haven't time to go out looking for more customers.'

'There you are, then,' Trip said triumphantly. 'Just take on one person – let's say Nell, if she's the best worker – whilst you go out and find the work.'

Emily glanced at Nathan, who was thoughtful. 'What do you think, Mr Hawke?'

Suddenly, he smiled, 'Since both premises are mine and I'm going to lose one of the rents anyway, let's keep both. Take Nell on to work upstairs here – to take your place – and set the other girls back on round there.' He nodded towards the adjacent street. 'We can give it a try. How many girls are there?'

'I think only Nell, Ida and the young girl, Flo, now Lizzie's gone. Nell said they'd all agreed they don't want Lizzie involved this time and besides, I don't expect she'd want to come back.'

'You're better off without her,' Trip said. 'She'd only cause you more trouble out of spite.'

'One note of caution, though,' Nathan said. 'Make sure all the girls know that this is a month's trial to see how it goes and that they'll maybe need to start on a reduced wage until you've more work.'

So when Nell returned early the following morning, she was overwhelmed to hear what had been proposed.

She flung her arms around Emily and hugged her. 'I don't know how to thank you.'

'It's Mr Hawke you have to thank. He's the one taking the risk, really.'

'Oh, the girls will be thrilled.'

'There's just one thing. We all agree with you about Lizzie, so it's only you, Ida and Flo.'

'You're right not to have her back – even if she'd come. She's a vindictive little madam and you want to watch out when her brother gets to hear about us setting up again. There's no knowing what he might do.'

Emily frowned. She was beginning to hear several hints about Mick Dugdale. Even Nathan had made a remark about him. She opened her mouth to ask Nell what she meant but the excited girl couldn't wait to tell the other two. 'We'll work really hard for you, Emily, I promise.'

'Oh Nell, I know you will. I want you to work here on your own – you were always the best worker – and Ida and Flo can work at the old place.'

'When can we start?'

Emily smiled. 'Tomorrow morning.'

And then Nell was off and running and it wasn't until she was halfway down the street that Emily realized she still hadn't asked her what she meant about Mick Dugdale.

The following morning the three girls, already dressed in their buff-brats – white caps now, since Emily thought they looked much nicer, even if it meant more washing, and red neck-rags – arrived and were introduced to their benefactor, Nathan Hawke. They shook his hand and thanked him prettily.

'Dear me, such lovely girls. Now, where did I put my spectacles? I must have a proper look at you. Ah, here they are.'

He perched the steel-rimmed spectacles on his nose and looked the newcomers up and down. Then he smiled and nodded. 'You'll do.'

'We'll all work really hard for you and Emily,' Nell said, as the acknowledged leader of the three of them.

'Right,' Emily said to Ida and Flo, 'you two go back to the Rockingham Street workshop. Nell's going to work upstairs. I shall take my turn at a wheel as much as I can, alongside Nell here, but I need to concentrate on finding more work for us. Ida, I shall call round often, but you're in charge of locking up the premises in Rockingham Street.'

'What about an errand lass?'

'Can't afford one at the moment, not for either place, but if work increases, then we'll see.'

'I'll do it for both workshops, if you like,' Flo said, readily. She was a small, thin girl, and rather pale faced, Emily thought, but Nell had told her that whilst Flo wasn't very good at buffing yet, she was always willing and eager to learn. And her offer showed that she was not afraid of hard work. 'I don't mind getting up early. Me mam's got a new babby and 'ee wakes the whole family up at six in the morning for his first feed. We only live a bit further down Rockingham Street. I can

341

nearly fall out of my bed straight into work. And then I can do a bit of roughing when I can.'

'We need you to learn more now than just removing the dents and marks from spoons and forks,' Emily said.

'She'll be orreight, Emily,' Ida said. 'She just needs a bit of encouragement, that's all. Lizzie was supposed to be teaching her, but she was very impatient.' She put her arm around the younger girl. 'I'll see you learn all the different processes, luv. And mebbe you can come round to Nell here sometimes and watch her.' She bent her head close to the girl's ear, but they all heard her deliberately loud whisper as she added, 'She's the best buffer I've ever seen, but don't tell her I said so.'

With the other three girls set to work, Emily went home and dressed in her best clothes and went out to seek more orders.

When the girls had gone, Trip, who had already begun working alongside Nathan, paused and said, 'I think they'll be all right, Mr Hawke.'

The older man chuckled. 'With your lovely wife in charge of them, my boy, they can't be anything else.'

Forty-Two

Lizzie knocked on the door of the apartment where she and Josh had taken Belle. She was a little nervous, not knowing what her reception would be. She was even more flustered when she saw the man sitting in Belle's front room, whom she recognized as Arthur Trippet, even though Belle made no attempt to introduce them to each other. She, too, seemed ill at ease now.

But then Lizzie smiled inwardly. Actually, she thought, this was perhaps working out better than she'd hoped. She knew all about Arthur disowning his son. And, of course, living in the same court – how had they dared to come back? – she knew, too, that Trip and Emily were now married and that Emily was trying to establish another business in the workshop above Mr Hawke. And, if the latest rumours were true, to reopen the business that Lizzie – and her brother Mick – had helped her to start in Rockingham Street.

'You want to go and see Mr Trippet,' Mick had suggested. 'They're all taking no notice of me just now. That bugger Hawke has taken a stand against me and the other little mesters are following his lead. But he'll regret it, you mark my words. They all will. I'm working on it, Sis, I promise, but you go and see old man Trippet. Word has it he's disowned his son. For a start, you can get back at the little bitch through her beloved husband.'

'I can't go to his factory. He'd send me off with a flea in my ear.'

Mick had frowned, his devious mind working quickly. 'What about that woman you met in the park when you were with Josh? Belle Beauman?'

At the mention of Josh's name, Lizzie's face hardened as she nodded. Now Mick grinned, ''Cos I've got a bit of news for you about her, that's if you don't already know. She's old man Trippet's whore.'

Lizzie's eyes widened. 'Really? Now that is interesting.'

'Why don't you go and see her?'

And so, on her brother's suggestion, Lizzie had come to see Belle. She was disconcerted for a moment, finding Mr Trippet there, but perhaps it was all meant to be, for it was really his help she wanted and to talk directly to him was far better than asking his mistress to intercede for her.

She took a deep breath. 'Mr Trippet . . .'

For a moment, the man looked startled and cast an angry glance at Belle for having invited the girl in. He didn't want all and sundry knowing his business, but as the girl began to speak, he realized that perhaps, after all, she could be useful to him.

'I have a very juicy bone to pick with your new daughter-in-law.'

'She's no daughter-in-law of mine,' Arthur snapped.

Lizzie now smiled openly and put her head on one side with a coquettish gesture. 'Then,' she said softly, 'you will have no objection to me trying to – er – throw a spanner in her works.'

Arthur's face brightened. 'None at all. But how do you intend to do that?'

'She's started up a little buffing business again and

got all Nathan Hawke's buffing work back and Trip – I mean, Thomas – is working for him. Nell and the other two girls, who were *my* employees, have gone to work for Emily. They are traitors, that's what they are, and I want to ruin the lot of 'em.'

'What happened between you and the Ryan girl?' he asked bluntly, still refusing to call her by her given name.

Lizzie glanced at Belle. 'I was walking out with her brother, Josh, but he jilted me to go back and marry the little slut he'd got pregnant in Ashford and I blame Emily for encouraging him. She knew how I felt about him. Besides,' she ran her tongue around dry lips. She could be pushing matters a little too far, but she plunged in, hoping that she recognized a ruthlessness in the man sitting in front of her that was in her own nature. 'Besides, if I hurt his precious sister, I hurt Josh too.'

Arthur smiled grimly and nodded slowly. 'I see. It's all about revenge, is it?'

'Absolutely.'

He was thoughtful for several moments, whilst both Lizzie, and Belle, too, grew increasingly anxious. They were both unsure exactly what his reaction was going to be. And then Arthur gave a low, rumbling chuckle. 'Then, I think, my dear girl, that we could be useful to each other. I can certainly speak to all my fellow cutlers to prevent them putting their business her way. That should stop the little madam.'

And now Belle relaxed too. Although she had never thought of herself as a vindictive woman – she had lived in the shadow of Arthur's marriage for so many years without a word of complaint – she now saw a way to bring about a plan of her own.

'There's not much I can do to prevent Thomas

working for Hawke, but I can certainly do something about *her*.'

'That'll do me. I have nothing specific against your son, to be honest.'

'Well, I certainly have and, like you say about her brother, if I hurt her, then I hurt my son too.' He balled his right hand into a fist. 'Not physical harm, you understand. I don't want that, but I'll ruin them both, if I can. If I have my way, they'll never work in this city again.'

As Lizzie took her leave, Arthur stood up and shook her hand. 'Keep in touch. You'd better not come to my factory, though.' He nodded towards Belle. 'You can always leave a message with Mrs Beauman.'

As the girl left, Belle wondered what the next day would bring, for she had a surprise of her own for Arthur Trippet.

The following morning was Sunday, and Arthur announced that he thought the coast would now be clear for him to return home to Ashford. 'If Thomas and his new wife –' he spat out the words – 'are back in the city, then it means that Constance is alone and my wife,' he said bitterly, 'has a lot of explaining to do.'

'Do stay for luncheon, Arthur, please.'

'Very well,' he agreed, not knowing that he was about to get a shock that would have repercussions for years to come.

Just before the meal was due to be served by Belle's one and only maid, whose services were paid for by Arthur, there was a knock at the front door. The maid glanced at Belle with wide eyes and a fearful glance towards Arthur, who was sitting, quite unperturbed, reading the previous day's *Times* newspaper. Calmly – although she was quaking inside – Belle nodded to her maid to open the door and admit the person, who came every week at this time, although he had been unable to visit whilst Arthur had been staying with her. After a few moments, the door to the sitting room opened and the maid ushered in a tall young man of about sixteen with dark hair and brown eyes. He hesitated for a moment and glanced at Belle, but at a nod from her he came slowly into the room.

Arthur looked up at him and then stared fixedly at him for a long moment. The young man met his scrutiny steadily as Belle rose slowly to her feet and went to stand beside the newcomer. She tucked her arm through his and hugged it to her. In a voice that was unsteady, she said, 'Arthur, this is my son, Richard.'

Arthur struggled to his feet, his face thunderous. 'Is it indeed? You kept that very quiet. I suppose my money has been keeping him too, has it?'

'Arthur,' Belle said quietly and now her voice was strangely calm, 'he is *your* son too.'

For a moment, Arthur stood very still and then he fell back into the chair with a groan. His hands shook and his face worked.

'Quick,' Belle said, rushing to his side, 'get a glass of water and send for a doctor. I think the shock has caused him to have a stroke.'

But Arthur was waving his hands frantically and shaking his head. 'No, no,' he gasped. 'No doctor.'

If the moment had not been so serious, Belle might have laughed as she realized the reason behind Arthur's refusal to send for medical aid; he didn't want to be caught at her house.

After a few moments, Arthur had recovered enough to glare at Belle and then at Richard. 'So, you didn't think fit to carry out my orders all those years ago. What is it? Fifteen, sixteen years? So why have you not told me of his existence before?' And then, before Belle could speak, he answered his own question. 'I expect you thought your meal ticket would disappear.'

He continued to stare at Richard, who met his gaze fearlessly, yet without belligerence or insolence. It never occurred to Arthur to question whether the boy was actually his; Richard's resemblance to his half-brother, Thomas, was unmistakeable. There was no doubt in Arthur's mind that the young man standing so calmly before him was indeed his son.

Quietly, Belle said, 'If you wish to end our friendship, then I shall quite understand.'

Arthur grunted. 'Oh, sit down, the pair of you. You make the place look untidy.'

Belle and her son glanced at each other and then did as he asked.

'So, I still have a son after all, have I?' Arthur mused, his gaze never leaving Richard's face.

'You have two,' Belle dared to say.

Arthur shook his head. 'No, not now. Thomas is lost to me. I won't have deliberate disobedience.'

Belle bit her lip. She wanted to defend Trip, to say that all the young man had done was to fall in love. Didn't that count for anything with Arthur? Evidently, she thought, it did not.

'So, how old are you? What school do you attend?'

'I'm sixteen, sir, and I'm at the King Edward the Seventh School.' The boy's voice was low and cultured.

Arthur's mouth was tight. 'And I presume I have

been supporting you all this time. Why have I not seen you before? Where do you live?'

'Richard was placed with foster parents just after his birth. He still lives with them, but comes to see me every Sunday. Normally, you are not here on that day.'

'And when did he learn about me?'

'He's always known that I am his mother. I told him about you when he was twelve and all about my – my past.' She glanced at her son with fond eyes. 'He is a mature young man for his age and he understood. I'm sorry that I have deceived you over Richard's existence. When I fell pregnant and told you, I was shocked to the core that you told me to get rid of the baby. I couldn't do it. And then when you stayed away for so long – I thought at that time you were never coming back – I decided to keep him.' It was as if they were talking about a puppy or a kitten, not a living, breathing human being. Richard was infuriated, but he had the sense to keep his face expressionless and to say nothing except to answer his father's questions politely. Although he'd known exactly who his father was for the past four years and had learned about – and understood – his mother's way of life, he had never expected to meet Arthur Trippet. At school he kept quiet about the relationship; his friends thought his foster parents were his natural parents. No one knew – or guessed – that his real mother was the mistress of the wealthy factory owner, who was well known in the city and who wielded power over the lives of all his employees, including his legitimate son, Thomas.

'Well, well, well,' Arthur murmured, stroking his moustache thoughtfully for some minutes, whilst Richard sat, outwardly placid, awaiting whatever decision Arthur Trippet was going to make. 'You know,

Belle,' Arthur said at last, 'I could be very angry with you that you disobeyed me and have deceived me all these years, but in the circumstances I now find myself, I am very pleased that he – exists.'

'He's doing very well at school,' Belle said proudly. 'He's very good at maths and his schoolmasters think he could go to university if—'

Arthur shook his head. 'No, he will leave school at the end of this term and take up a place in the offices at my factory. If he's as clever as you say, he can learn the administrative side of the business.' He was thoughtful for a moment and then his eyes narrowed as he said slowly, speaking directly to the boy, 'If you do well, I am prepared to acknowledge you as my son and perhaps, one day . . .'

He left the sentence unfinished, but there was no mistaking the meaning behind his words. If Richard did well, he would one day inherit the works.

'And now,' Arthur heaved himself to his feet, 'I will go back to Ashford. I shall have great pleasure in informing my wife that I still have a son.'

'Aren't you staying for luncheon, Arthur? It's all ready.'

'No. Next week, Belle. Next week I'll come on Sunday and we'll all have luncheon together.'

Driving his big car home, Arthur began to feel a little unwell, but it was to be expected, he told himself. He hadn't eaten since breakfast and his rotund stomach was beginning to rumble with hunger. And he had had a few shocks just lately. First, finding out that Thomas had disobeyed him and now this. Belle had deliberately deceived him and had kept their son's existence a secret all this time. And he was incensed that Constance had gone against all his wishes. But at least Thomas would no longer be at home; he was now married to the Ryan slut and living back in the city.

Arthur Trippet was not a forgiving man and whilst it suited him to acknowledge Richard as his son – and to use him to exact revenge on his legitimate son – he was deeply angry with Belle. He wondered how he could punish her without harming the boy. It would not be easy. And there was this other matter about which the girl – Lizzie Dugdale – had sought him out. She could be very useful to him too. He'd heard of that family name before. Mick Dugdale was fast becoming a notorious name in the area as the leader of a gang, and as a man who ran several illegal activities in and around the city, and who, at the moment, was cleverly avoiding the police. He had now set up as a rival to Steve Henderson's gang, according to Arthur's source of information. No doubt the rivalry would one day escalate into street warfare. Arthur had no intention of being on the wrong side of the law; he had his reputation to think of, but if, through an intermediary like Lizzie, he could engineer a few activities that, whilst not causing physical harm to anyone – he had no stomach for that – could cause hardship to those who had crossed him, then he would be satisfied.

As he drew into the driveway of Riversdale House he could see that Kirkland was still busy attending to the ravages which the wedding reception had left upon the lawn. He glowered at the man, but said nothing. It was not Kirkland's fault. He'd only been following Constance's orders. Ah yes, he thought, as he climbed out of his car, today has been a good day all round. And now, my dear wife, I have something to tell you. Something I am sure you will not want to hear.

Forty-Three

Arthur found Constance sitting in the morning room, with her embroidery on her lap.

'So,' she greeted him bluntly, 'are you here to stay, Arthur, or just to collect your things?'

He snorted with humourless laughter. 'If anyone's leaving this house, my dear, it won't be me. This is *my* house, Constance, and don't you forget it.'

'Bought with my father's money,' Constance said mildly. She was feeling surprisingly calm whilst Arthur grew red in the face.

'Money that was handed to me at our marriage. It was your "dowry", to coin an old-fashioned word.'

'Ah yes, our marriage. What a disappointment that has been. If it hadn't been for Thomas's birth, I would have said it has been a disaster for both of us. But I have to thank you for our son.'

'*Your* son, if you like.' Arthur was shouting now. 'He is no son of mine. Not now. And you had the gall to use this house for the fiasco of his wedding to that – that *slut*.'

'Oh, it was more than just that, Arthur. It was a double celebration. Emily's brother, Josh, married Amy Clark. They had a joint ceremony and a reception here. It was a lovely day. You should have been here.'

He was glaring at her. 'I could turn you out, you know. And then where would you be? Homeless, penniless and your reputation in ruins. Your fine friends in the Friendly Society wouldn't want to know you then. And I doubt Thomas and his new wife would be able to support you.' He tone became a sneer. 'They'll have enough difficulty finding work in the city, if I have anything to do with it.'

Constance raised her eyebrows. 'Oh, I should do very nicely, thank you, Arthur. I still have a small cottage in Over Haddon and an annuity, which my father was wise enough to set up for me at the time of our marriage. It seems he didn't trust you as much as you thought. Incidentally, none of the expense of the weddings has come out of your pocket. I paid for it out of my own income.'

'*Your* income!' Arthur exploded. 'Why did I know nothing of this? Anything you have belongs to me.'

'For a businessman, Arthur, you are strangely ignorant of the law. Thanks to the Married Women's Property Act, I have control over my own assets and, again, thanks to my father's foresight, I am well provided for.'

'Then you can leave, you can pack your bags and go.'

'I'll go as and when it suits me, Arthur, and not before.'

'You'll – you'll go when I say.' As Arthur prodded his finger at her, his speech suddenly sounded slurred. He swayed a little and reached towards a chair to steady himself. 'I am . . . still master in . . . this house.'

'If that is so, why did you not stay and throw your son out for the second time?'

'I – I thought I owed it to you as his mother to have a little time with him. I didn't realize you would be foolish enough to support his ridiculous marriage and – and make us the laughing stock of the village.'

'I can assure you that is not the case. The villagers enjoyed the weddings. They all came.' Arthur's face turned purple, but Constance pretended to ignore it. 'The Clarks are popular and Walter Ryan is a war hero in the eyes of his neighbours. And as for our son, it seems they all love him.'

Arthur clutched at the back of the chair. 'Thomas is no longer my son. Do you hear me? And I have a surprise for you, my *dear* wife. I have another son: Richard.'

'So you have, my dear. Richard Beauman. Let's see, he must be about fifteen or sixteen now. Is that right?'

Arthur gasped and lowered himself into the chair. He gaped at her. 'You – you know?'

'Oh yes, I know all about Belle Beauman and her son. I even know where she lives, though I have not, as yet, visited her. I presume that is where you have been living for the past few weeks.'

'But – but how did you know about the boy? Even I didn't know of his existence until this morning.'

Constance smiled grimly. 'I made it my business to know. Once Thomas had been born and you had your son and heir, you never came near me again after the miscarriages. I am not an ignoramus, Arthur. Men have their needs, I know that, and so I realized you must be seeking your pleasures elsewhere. You are not the sort of man to consort with street prostitutes and so I deduced that you must have set up a mistress some-where. It wasn't difficult to find out the details.'

'A private detective, I suppose.'

Constance bent her head. Though she had used no such method, she did not disillusion her husband. She had no wish for him to find out from whom she had obtained the information. That might well put the person concerned in a very dangerous position. Certainly she had no wish for harm to come to them.

'Well, you might as well know now. I intend to take Richard into the firm and train him in the administrative side of the business. One day, he will . . . he will . . .' Arthur made a strange gurgling sound and fell forward, crashing to the floor. Calmly, Constance laid aside her embroidery and rose. She stood over him, looking down at him for a few moments, before ringing the bell for assistance.

Arthur had had a stroke, but the doctor was sure that he would make a full recovery. His speech was slightly slurred, but that was improving with each day. Other than that, there were no lasting effects.

'Constance,' Arthur said, seeming to ignore the fact that only hours ago he had ordered her from the house. 'Please – go to the factory. See Mr Bayes. You know him, don't you?'

Constance nodded.

'Ask him to run things until I get back. He's an able man.'

'Of course I will, Arthur. We must keep the business going; after all, it's your son's inheritance.' With that, she left the room leaving Arthur unsure of the meaning behind her words. Was she just referring to Thomas? Had she meant son's, singular, or sons', plural? He couldn't tell.

Ernest Kirkland drove Constance to the works in Sheffield in Arthur's big car. Though Constance used her own little car around the local area, she was not used to driving into the city. Parking in the yard of the

355

factory in Creswick Street, Ernest held open the rear door for her to alight.

'I shall be here most of the day, Kirkland, so please feel free to go into the city. Mind you get something to eat. I will reimburse the cost, of course.'

'Thank you, ma'am.' The man bowed his head politely. He liked Constance – all the staff at Riversdale House did – but he hadn't a lot of time for Arthur.

Constance entered the factory and found her way to the offices where she hoped to find George Bayes. Arthur had a rather grand office at the end of a corridor, but, next door to it, George Bayes had his office and next to that was an even smaller office where two men worked at handwritten sales, purchasing and wages ledgers. Beyond that was a room where two women clattered on typewriters.

Constance tapped on the door to George Bayes's office. At the invitation to 'come in', she opened it and entered. George Bayes looked up from his paperwork and, for a moment, a startled look crossed his face. Then, as she closed the door behind her, he rose and came around the desk, holding out his hands to her.

'Constance, my dear,' he murmured.

'George,' she said a little unsteadily, allowing him to take both her hands into his. They gazed at each other for several moments before he murmured, 'How good it is to see you. It's been a long time.'

There was a deep friendship between them – unknown to either Arthur or George's wife, Muriel – that had existed for years. It was not a physical relationship but there was affection between them that had begun before either of them was married, for they had lived in the same village as youngsters. But life and circumstances – mainly Constance's dictatorial father – had quashed any hope of the blossoming of romance. But that young love had never died and whilst George in particular had been 'happy enough' with his wife and Constance was content with her son and her comfortable lifestyle, both of them often wondered 'what might have been'.

'Please sit down, my dear. I'll get one of the girls to rustle up some tea for us.'

'If it's not too much trouble,' Constance said and, removing her gloves, she sat down.

'Nothing's too much trouble for you,' he murmured, his eyes twinkling saucily, and Constance laughed. For a few moments, she felt like a young girl again.

George Bayes had been the son of the village wheelwright and blacksmith and he'd come to Robert Vincent's farm with his father when wagons needed repair, and Constance would often walk their horses down to the village smithy to be shod. The two youngsters were drawn to each other and for a while they'd enjoyed an idyllic childhood; roaming the countryside, fishing the streams and rivers, tobogganing down the Derbyshire hills on snowy winter's days. But as they grew older, both sets of parents thought the attachment unsuitable.

'He's not good enough for you, Constance,' Robert had declared when Constance was still only fifteen. After that time, one of his farm labourers always took the horses to the blacksmith. Strangely, to both the youngsters' minds, Alfie Bayes had also been against their friendship. 'Her old man,' he'd told the young George, 'will never let it come to anything, lad, and he'd likely do my business harm. He's only to put the word about and farmers will take their trade elsewhere.'

Now, as they both remembered the bond that had

been between them, they smiled, a little sadly, at each other.

'Oh, Constance,' George whispered, 'why didn't we run away together?'

'We couldn't, my dear, we really couldn't at fifteen. How could we? At that age, as the Bible tells us, I "honoured my father". I wouldn't have dreamt of disobeying him. And by the time we were older, things had moved along. Arthur had been "chosen".'

George nodded and his voice was husky as he said, 'I did love you, Constance. I watched you walk out of the church on his arm on your wedding day and I thought my heart would break.'

Constance rarely cried, but now tears filled her eyes. 'If only I had known.'

For several moments, there was silence between them as they gazed at one another. At last, George cleared his throat. 'So, my dear, what brings you here? Is it because his nibs is ill?'

Constance chuckled at the nickname George – and she guessed the whole of the factory's personnel – had given her husband. Then her expression sobered. 'He has had a lot to deal with just recently, which has resulted in a mild stroke. Nothing serious. The doctor thinks he will make a full recovery, but Arthur asked me to come to see you to ask you to "hold the fort" whilst he takes a few days off. I doubt he'll stay away long, even though he shouldn't drive for a while. No doubt he'll get Kirkland to bring him.'

'I'm sorry to hear that. I wouldn't wish him any harm. In most respects, he's a good employer, though a little swift in his sackings, if the truth be told, when something or someone doesn't suit him.'

There was another pause whilst they looked at each

other, drinking in the sight of each other after an absence of several years.

'He's found out about Richard Beauman,' Constance said quietly.

'Has he indeed? Is that what caused the stroke?'

'Partly, I suspect, but I think it was also about Thomas.'

'Ah. Of course, there's that too. How is Thomas?'

Constance smiled. 'Happily married to Emily Ryan and back in the city.'

'Yes, I did know. He came once when they first arrived back. He wanted to know if I could help him to find work, which sadly, I was unable to do. You can probably guess why.'

'Arthur has put the word out?'

George sighed. 'Mr Trippet has made it very difficult for any of his fellow cutlers to employ Thomas. Your husband wields a great deal of power in this city, Constance. And whilst they're not exactly afraid of him, they are reluctant to go against his wishes deliberately.'

'That I can believe,' Constance said wryly.

George nodded. 'But I've heard rumours since that Emily has set up in business again.'

'Yes, Thomas wrote and told me all about it. Oh George, you should have read his letter, so full of love and admiration for his lovely young wife.'

'I was very sorry to see Thomas go. One day, he would have been a credit to you both as head of this works. And I was sorry to lose Emily's brother, Josh, too. He was a good worker, though I have to say his progress was slow. He didn't really take to the work. I think his heart lay elsewhere.'

'Don't worry about Josh. He's back in Ashford at his candle making and happily married to his childhood sweetheart. They have a wonderful little boy. They had a double wedding with Thomas and Emily.' Her voice softened as she said with sadness, 'I was so sorry not to be able to ask you to join us that day, but I really wasn't sure whether Arthur would turn up at the last minute. He didn't, though. I expect he was with Belle. And coming back to Belle and her son—'

'I often wonder if I did the right thing in telling you all about her – and her son.'

'Certainly, you did. It helped me a lot.'

George was surprised. 'Really? How? I thought you would be devastated. I pondered what to do for a long time.'

'It relieved my feeling of guilt, George, that I no longer loved my husband. I doubt I ever did, really. Nor him, me. It was a marriage of convenience pushed forward by my father and Arthur's ambition.'

'If only . . .'

'Don't, George. Please don't.'

He smiled ruefully at her and sighed. Their chance – if there had ever really been one – was long gone.

'There's something else I think I should warn you about, George. Now that Arthur has disowned Thomas and found out that he has another son – albeit an illegitimate one – I think he will bring Richard Beauman here.'

'To the factory?'

Constance pursed her mouth and added, 'I think it's to punish both Thomas and me.'

'Punish you? Whatever for?'

'Because I defied him. I took Thomas back into our house and I held his wedding reception there too. Arthur is an unforgiving man.'

'You think he's going to have Richard start at the

bottom and work his way up? The way he was making Thomas do?'

Constance shook her head. 'No,' she said flatly. 'He intends to start him in the offices so that he can learn the administrative side of the business.'

George stared at her for a long moment before saying. 'Oh.'

'I think,' Constance said slowly, 'he now intends to make the boy his heir.'

Forty-Four

When Arthur was strong enough, he resumed his trips to the works, but only on two or three days a week. George Bayes was managing things quite well, though it was not like having the guiding hand of the owner on the helm. Because his 'secret' was now out, Arthur saw no reason to hide his visits to Belle any more and so he had Kirkland drive to her house and sit outside for several hours at a time.

On his first visit after his illness, Belle could not hide her surprise. 'I began to think you weren't coming any more. I thought you were too angry with me.'

'I've been ill,' he told her shortly, making little of what had happened to him. 'I was very angry with you, at first, but whilst I've been recuperating, I've had time to think. My son – my *legitimate* son – has sadly disappointed me by marrying beneath him. I want nothing more to do with him and I care not what happens to him.'

Belle gasped and stared at him. She could hardly believe the man's callousness. When he'd first told her that he'd 'thrown Thomas out', she hadn't really believed that it would be long lasting. She'd thought that when his temper cooled, he would make it up with Thomas. Though where that would have left Richard, she didn't dare think. Probably dismissed as having served a useful purpose for his callous father. If such action had been directed towards her own son, whom Arthur had not wanted and had made no secret of the fact that he hadn't, then she might – perhaps – have understood it. But to disown the son who had been born in wedlock, the one who had been brought up to believe himself heir to a thriving business, was beyond her understanding.

Whatever else she had done in her life, she loved her son devotedly and had done her best for him. She had placed him with loving foster parents, but never hid her identity from him. She had seen him every weekend throughout his childhood. She'd ensured that he had had a good education and now she was rewarded by the fact that he understood – and accepted – her situation without recriminations or censure.

And now, when Arthur seated himself and began to explain his plans for Richard, she could hardly believe that what she'd hoped and dreamed of was actually coming true.

'I wasn't sure you really meant it, Arthur, especially since you haven't visited me again since then – I didn't know you were ill – but I am so grateful that you're going to do something for our son.'

Arthur had the grace to nod and say, 'Well, I owe you something, Belle, after all these years of discreet devotion. You have never once caused me humiliation and, as far as I know, the only time you have disobeyed me has been over Richard's birth. But I am prepared to overlook that. It suits me now to do so.' He hadn't quite given up the notion of punishing her in some way for her deception, but he didn't want it to affect the boy. He had another use for him.

When Richard finished his schooling in the summer of 1922, Arthur took him to the works and presented him, without embarrassment, to his employees, particularly to George Bayes, who was to take the boy under his wing and see that he was taught the workings of the office. George hoped he looked suitably surprised when the introductions were made.

But the arrival of Arthur's illegitimate son by a former music-hall dancer was the talk of the factory for days and rippled out into the streets of the city. Trip heard about it from Nathan Hawke and when he told Emily, she was shocked.

'He's *sixteen*? Do you mean your father has known Belle Beauman all that time?'

'So it seems. And there's something else. He has let it be known that my half-brother is now his heir.'

'Do you think your mother knows about that?'

'I don't know.'

'It's put you in a bit of an awkward position, hasn't it?'

Trip nodded, chewing his lower lip. 'Do you think I should tell her?'

'How can you? You're barred from visiting her now that your father's living back at home.'

Constance had, of course, written to Trip to tell him of his father's illness, but there had been no invitation for him to visit, not from her and certainly not from Arthur.

'According to what Mr Bayes told Mr Hawke,' Trip went on, 'he's going to set Richard to work in the offices, so that he can learn the administrative side of the business.'

'You mean, he's going to make his illegitimate son his heir just because you married me? Oh Trip, I'm so sorry. You shouldn't have married me.'

'I'm not sorry and, yes, I should have. Come here.'

They both rose from the table and he took her in his arms, holding her close. 'I will never, for a moment, regret having married you, my darling. Don't ever think that.'

Emily clung to him. She believed he meant what he said, but she wasn't so sure.

Despite Nathan Hawke's goodness to them, Trip's future was not going to be what it might have been – what it should have been.

Though they had each other, the future looked very uncertain.

Constance sat in the morning room, debating with herself. It was now the last week in August and some three weeks earlier, shortly after he had introduced Richard into his family's firm, Arthur had had a second stroke, a much more serious one. Constance had at once engaged a professional nurse when, for several days, Arthur's life had hung in the balance. Slowly, he had recovered although he was now physically incapacitated and hardly able to talk. Nor could he write what instructions he wished to give. And Constance knew he still wished to give directions as to how his business should be run, but she chose to act as if she couldn't understand him.

She had asked him but one question, 'Do you want Thomas to come back?'

When his answer had been a violent shaking of his head, she had turned on her heel and left his bedroom. Since then, she had left his care to Nurse Adams and to Kirkland, who helped her when a man's strength was needed. The weather was unseasonably wet and cool, but Constance hardly noticed; she was too busy working out a scheme in her mind. And this morning she was ready to go into action. She rang the bell and when Polly appeared, she asked her to find Ernest Kirkland.

'Please ask him to come to the morning room.'

When the man entered the room a few moments later, a little nervously, Constance smiled at him. 'Please sit down, Kirkland.'

'Oh, I couldn't, ma'am, I'm in me gardening clothes.'

'Of course. I'm sorry.' Constance's smile broadened. 'Kirkland, I want to ask you if I can trust you?'

The man frowned. 'I should hope so, ma'am. I've worked for you for several years now and—'

'I'm sorry, I'm not making myself very clear. Of course I know you are as honest and trustworthy as the day is long.'

The man's features relaxed.

'What I mean is, can I trust you with my secrets? I wish to do certain things and I don't want my husband, or the rest of the staff, finding out.'

Now his expression cleared. This he could understand. Maybe the lady had a lover and he wouldn't blame her if she had and hadn't he kept the master's mistress secret for years? No one had ever found out about Belle Beauman from his lips.

'I can be discreet, ma'am.'

Constance chuckled, guessing what was in the man's mind. 'Oh, I'm not indulging in clandestine affairs, I promise you. It's to do with my husband's business and – and my son.'

'Ah – I see.' Now he thought he understood. He, and all the staff for that matter, knew about the trouble between father and son and in private they all sided with Master Thomas, but, of course, it wouldn't do to say so. But Ernest was shrewd enough to realize that, with Arthur's illness, the reins now lay in Constance's

366

slim, but capable, hands. 'Of course, ma'am, you have my word.'

'Good. Then tomorrow morning I want you take me in *my* car to Sheffield and so that no questions are asked, I will drive to your house on the far side of the village to pick you up. I wish I had the nerve to drive into the city myself, but I just haven't. Chesterfield is my limit and that is where I shall tell the rest of the staff I am going.'

Constance often drove into one of the nearest towns to shop, usually to Buxton, but just occasionally to Chesterfield.

'I understand. What time would you like me to be ready?'

'About nine thirty? Will Nurse Adams be able to manage him without you for a day, d'you think?'

He nodded. 'I'll ask her and I'll tell the rest of the staff that you have given me the day off as I have some personal business to attend to. Would that do, ma'am?'

'Certainly, Kirkland. Thank you.'

As the man turned to leave the room, Constance watched him go, a smile on her lips. She knew she had found an ally.

Constance set off at nine o'clock the following morning, having ascertained for herself from the nurse that her husband was no worse and that there was nothing the young woman needed for her patient. 'Mr Kirkland asked me last night when he helped put the master to bed, ma'am, but I said I could manage this morning. He's got some personal business to attend to, he said.'

Constance had nodded, satisfied that Kirkland had so far played his part.

Out of the gate, she drove straight ahead and then

turned left at the end of the street into Greaves Lane, past the smithy and The Candle House. She gave a cheery wave to Bob Clark, who had already been at his anvil for three hours. She also waved towards the front window of the Ryans' home. Even though she couldn't actually see Josh, she knew he would be at his bench and might just notice the noisy car going past. She must call and see Martha very soon, she reminded herself. The whole family – Bob Clark too – had been very kind when they had heard of Arthur's recent illness, enquiring about him each day and offering practical help if it was needed. In fact, all the villagers had been genuinely sympathetic towards Constance. She halted the vehicle outside Ernest Kirkland's cottage and by the time she was sitting in the passenger's seat, he had emerged from his cottage and climbed in behind the wheel.

'Which way do you want me to go, ma'am?'

'As long as we set off in the direction of Chesterfield to start with, that's fine.'

As they drove, Constance shouted above the noise of the engine, 'I want you to take me to see Trip and Emily first, please, Kirkland. Do you know where Mr Hawke's premises are?'

Ernest nodded. Conversation was difficult and they didn't speak again until Ernest was pulling up outside Nathan Hawke's workshop.

Constance climbed down and knocked on the door. Trip opened it and gaped at her. Then an anxious look came into his eyes. 'Is it Father?'

'No, he's no worse, but no better either since I last wrote to you.' She paused and then added, 'Aren't you going to invite me in?'

'Oh – yes – of course. Sorry. I was so surprised to

see you here. I thought something must be wrong.' As he held open the door for her, he glanced out and saw Ernest sitting behind the wheel. 'Ah,' he said, smiling now. 'I wondered how you'd got here.'

With the introductions made, Constance looked around. 'Emily works upstairs, does she?'

'Yes, but she's gone out to see customers. There's only Nell who actually works here and the other two girls are in Mr Hawke's other premises in Rockingham Street.'

'How's business?' Constance included Mr Hawke in her question.

'We're doing nicely, thank you, Mrs Trippet, considering the difficulties businesses in general are experiencing in these unsettled times. I think we might see a change of government at the next election in November. With unemployment rising to over a million early last year, I think the voters will be looking elsewhere for their leadership. Still, you haven't come here to talk politics with me.' His eyes twinkled at her over his spectacles perched on the end of his nose. 'I'm sure your visit's to do with these wonderful young people I have work-ing with me now.'

Constance smiled, for what she had in mind might well rob the man of at least one of his workers. However, for the moment she said nothing but perhaps the intui-tive Nathan saw something in her face for he said gently, 'I was sorry to hear of your husband's illness. I have told Trip that if he is needed at home – or even at his father's works – then he must go. He must not feel obligated to me if he is required elsewhere.' He paused and then added, 'How is his business fairing without Mr Trippet at the helm?'

Constance met his direct gaze. 'I will be perfectly

honest with you, Mr Hawke, since perhaps it will affect you. I don't know how much you know . . .' She glanced at Trip for guidance.

'Mr Hawke knows everything, Mother.'

Constance nodded and continued, 'It's very doubtful if my husband will ever be well enough to return to running the business. He has put his – um –' she hesitated for a moment, not quite knowing how to describe Richard Beauman, then said, 'Thomas's half-brother in charge. He is recently out of school and knows nothing about the business. Mr Bayes says the boy is doing his best, but it is too much to have such a burden placed on his young shoulders.'

'Can George Bayes not run it? He's been there a long time.'

'That would have been the best solution, yes, but George has been placed in an awkward situation. Arthur has acknowledged Richard as his son and made him his heir.'

'Mm, yes, I see,' Nathan said.

'But Arthur seems to have forgotten that legally I own half the business.'

'Really, Mother?' Trip was surprised. 'I didn't know that.'

'It was one of the provisions my own father insisted upon when we married and he gave Arthur a very generous dowry, as they liked to call it. As the years have gone by, I think Arthur has completely forgotten that my name is still on the deeds. I wondered if, by some means, he had had it removed, but I have checked with our solicitors and no, I am still an equal partner in Trippets'.'

Trip blinked and glanced from one to the other. 'I still don't know how that might affect me.'

Nathan chuckled. 'If I'm right, your mother has the power to reinstate you as heir to her half of the business. Is that correct, Mrs Trippet?'

Constance smiled and nodded, pleased that the shrewd man had understood at once and had saved her the uncomfortable task of explanation. 'It is, Mr Hawke, but before I put matters in motion, I had, of course, to find out if Thomas is willing for me to do that and also to give you fair warning that, if he does agree, you will be losing your assistant. You have been so good to both Thomas and Emily that I feel guilty—'

Nathan held up his hand. 'Please don't, Mrs Trippet, I beg you. Thomas has been a great help and it's been good to have his company, but, to be honest, there is not really enough work to keep us both going full time for very long. And besides, his rightful place is in his family's business.'

'Thank you, Mr Hawke,' Constance said and Nathan knew that her thanks were not only for employing her son, but also for all the help he had given Emily too. She turned back to Thomas. 'I had to be certain you are agreeable.' She pulled a wry face. 'I'm not going to force you into something you don't want to do.' And the unspoken words lay between them – 'like your father'.

'Well, I wouldn't have wanted to leave Mr Hawke in the lurch.' He glanced at Nathan. 'But since he seems to approve, then yes, if you can manage it, I'll gladly go back. But – but what about Richard?'

Constance laughed. 'I'm on my way to see his mother now.'

At this, both men stared at her, glanced at each other and then burst out laughing. 'Now I've heard everything,' Trip said.

Forty-Five

Kirkland parked outside the terraced house where Belle Beauman lived, where he'd parked the Rolls-Royce several times recently, but this time he had a different car, a different passenger.

'Will you be all right, ma'am? Do you want me to come with you?'

'No, I'll be fine. I'll try not to be too long.'

'No problem. I'll just sit here and read my newspaper.' He glanced around him. 'It's a nice little car, this. I've never driven it before.'

'It suits me,' Constance said as she climbed out and approached the front door.

'Good morning, Mrs Beauman,' she said, when a startled Belle opened the door. 'May I come in? There's something I would like to discuss with you.'

'Oh – er – yes. Please do.'

Belle was trembling. She feared that Constance had brought more bad news about Arthur. Of course, she knew about his recent serious illness; Richard had brought the news home from the factory. She had lived on tenterhooks ever since, daily expecting to hear the worst. And now his wife, of all people, was sitting in her front room, drinking tea and making polite conversation by admiring Belle's home. It was ironic, Belle thought, quelling the desire to laugh out loud, that everything had been paid for by the woman's husband.

Constance placed her cup and saucer back on the tray. 'You will have heard about Arthur's illness, I presume.'

Belle nodded, twisting her fingers anxiously.

'His life is not in danger, but this second stroke has left him paralysed and unable to speak. He will never be fit enough to run his business again.'

Or to come here any more, Belle thought. I shall never see him again. Tears prickled the back of her eyelids, but the actress in her came to the rescue. She lifted her head and met Constance's gaze with outward equanimity, as another thought came into her mind: She's come to turn me out of my home.

'Your son, Richard, has been placed in charge of the factory, I understand.'

Belle nodded, not trusting herself to speak and Constance went on, 'But he's not coping very well, is he?'

Belle shook her head and said huskily, 'It's hardly fair. He's only sixteen. Mr Bayes should be in charge.'

'I quite agree, but I have a suggestion to make and I hope you will agree.'

Constance then went on to explain that she would like her son, Thomas, to return to the works and that the two half-brothers should be made joint owners and run the factory together.

'I have discussed this at length with my solicitor and this is possible.'

'What will Arthur say?' Belle ventured hesitantly.

'My dear, Arthur can say nothing. I think he understands everything that's said to him, but he cannot voice his opinion.'

'But you can do it legally – without his permission? Won't he be required to sign things?'

'Our solicitor has said there is a way round all that

since he is now incapable. We need the doctor's agreement, of course, that he is no longer "of sound mind", but because I am already a partner, there should be no problem.'

'Do you think Arthur will – would – agree?'

'I really don't know. I shall tell him, of course, and I think I shall know if he understands.'

'I hope the shock won't bring on another stroke.' Belle bit her lip and now she could not stem the tears filling her eyes.

Constance was thoughtful for a moment. The woman sitting opposite her obviously cared about Arthur. 'Would you like to come and see him?'

Belle gaped at her. 'Are you serious?'

'Belle – may I call you Belle? – I've known about you for years and, in a way, I have reason to be grateful to you. Ours was not a love match, but a marriage of convenience.' She went on to tell Belle something of her life with Arthur. 'So you see he gave me what I wanted most – a son – and I lead a comfortable life. I have no bitterness or resentment against him – or you, which, had I been in love with him, no doubt I would have had. I will always care for him and do my best for him and I suppose that is a love of sorts, but it is not the kind that promotes jealousy.'

'I feel sorry for you.'

Constance shrugged. 'Don't be. I am content.' She put her head on one side as she observed the woman, who was still pretty even though she was now in her middle age. 'If anything, I should feel sorry for you. I have stood in the way of him marrying you.'

Now Belle laughed with genuine amusement. 'That would never have happened, Constance. Arthur would never have *married* the likes of me. I was a music-hall singer and dancer at the Hippodrome. He used to come every week on a Saturday night and I remember I was singing "The Boy in the Gallery". It's Marie Lloyd's signature tune. Do you know it?' Belle hummed the music and Constance nodded.

'Well, when it got to the bit about waving a handkerchief, there was a flurry of them in the audience, but it was Arthur I noticed because he stood up and waved vigorously. I couldn't fail to see him. And after that . . .' She needed to say no more. Constance could guess that Arthur had become an ardent 'stage-door Johnny' and had showered Belle with chocolates, champagne and flowers.

By the time Constance took her leave, the two women were surprised to find that they actually liked each other. Hesitantly, Belle said, 'If you can find out if Arthur would like me to visit him, I would love to see him, but—'

'I will,' Constance promised. 'If he does, then I will write to you and have Kirkland fetch you in the car.'

'You're very kind.' Belle was overwhelmed by Constance's attitude, but after meeting her and hearing about their married life, she understood why Arthur's wife had no animosity towards her.

'And now, I'm on my way to visit the factory and to meet your son. I hope he will be agreeable to my suggestion. I already have Thomas's approval.'

'Really!' It was another surprise for Belle as she added, 'I think Richard will feel very relieved. He's been having sleepless nights.'

'I don't wonder. It was very unfair to put him in such a position, but we'll sort it out.'

With a nod and a wave towards her unlikely new-found friend, Constance climbed back into the motorcar, leaving a bemused Belle watching the vehicle until it turned the corner out of sight.

'My dear, how are you?' was George Bayes's greeting as he took Constance's hands into his. 'I've been thinking of you and wondering how you've been coping. How is he?'

Again, Constance explained Arthur's condition, the reason for her visit and her proposal. When she had finished, George was beaming. 'That's a very sensible solution, Constance. I can't tell you how pleased I will be to have Master Thomas back here. Richard Beauman is a nice lad, willing and in many ways capable – or he will be, given time – but he's only sixteen. It's too much to expect of him.'

'You won't feel slighted because you're not to be made manager?'

'Heavens, no!' George said with asperity. 'I'm quite happy doing what I do. I've enough responsibility as it is, and Mr Trippet has always paid me generously. I have no complaints.'

'That's a relief to me,' Constance murmured. 'I wouldn't want you, of all people, to be unhappy. So,' she said after a slight pause, 'may I now meet Thomas's half-brother?'

Having been told who was waiting to see him, Richard came into the office a little hesitantly, a worried look in his brown eyes, but Constance held out her hand, smiled and said, without preamble, 'I have a suggestion to make, though I have to have your father's approval first – if, indeed, he is able to give it.'

She paused for a moment, drinking in the sight of the young man. He was so like Thomas, it was uncanny. There was no mistaking that he was Arthur's son. Then she explained to Richard everything that had happened that morning and as she did so, the anxiety seemed to fall away from him. When she had finished speaking, he was smiling.

'This is amazing – *you*'re amazing.' He glanced at George Bayes. 'Am I dreaming, Mr Bayes? Because if I am, please don't wake me up.'

The three of them laughed and Constance left the office well satisfied with her day's work.

'And now, Kirkland, you and I are going to find a nice little hotel where I will treat you to a late luncheon.'

'Oh ma'am, I don't think—' he began but she waved his protestations aside.

'Nonsense, Kirkland. It's the least I can do.'

'Nurse Adams, how is he this evening?'

'A little better, I think. He seems calmer.'

Constance grimaced. 'Oh dear, I rather think I could be about to alter that. Will you stay with me, please? I have something to tell him which may upset him.'

'Of course, if you wish me to.'

'I think it best.'

They entered Arthur's bedroom together and Constance sat down by the bed whilst Nurse Adams stood at a discreet distance, though she was able to keep watch on her patient.

As she looked at him, Constance was moved to feel real pity for the man who now lay inert with his face twisted to one side. Only his eyes showed any life and they were watching her now with a mixture of wariness and defiance.

'Arthur,' Constance began gently, 'you do understand, don't you, that you will never be able to run the works again?'

The man blinked and then slowly, he nodded. Thank goodness, Constance thought, he did understand what she was saying to him.

'Richard has been doing his best, but he really is too young and inexperienced to cope and business is falling off already. And so, I have come up with an idea to solve the problem.'

Arthur could not speak, but it was as if his eyes were saying, 'Go on.'

'But it concerns Thomas.' She hesitated, expecting an agitated reaction, but none came so she pressed on.

'You may recall that legally I still own half the business.' She paused, waiting for this to sink in, for him to remember. After a moment or two, he nodded.

'To save the business, I intend to have Thomas take up his place – his rightful place – and to work alongside his half-brother. Richard is a nice boy. I've met him today and I think they will get on very well together.'

She waited again and then, at last, said softly, 'Arthur, I don't *need* your approval to do this, but I do want it.'

Slowly, Arthur nodded and then reached out with the arm that he could still move. She took hold of his hand. 'What is it? Is it about Thomas?'

A nod.

'Do you agree to him going back?'

Another nod.

'So, what is it?' She couldn't guess and glanced up at the nurse, who came forward.

'I think perhaps, Mrs Trippet, he would like to see Thomas.'

Constance turned back to him. 'Is that it, Arthur? Do you want Thomas to come to see you?'

He nodded again.

'You – you want to make it up with him?' Her question was hesitant, but his answer was firm as he nodded quite vigorously.

'And Richard – would you like to see Richard too? And what about Belle? I am happy for Belle to come here, if you would like to see her.'

This time it was Arthur who hesitated, but Constance could see the pleading in his eyes.

It was all the answer she needed.

Forty-Six

'Oh Trip, it's such wonderful news.'

Trip put his arms around Emily. 'It's all working out for us now, isn't it? I'm back in the business. Richard and I are getting along very well together. I rather like having a brother, though it's a bit of a strange situation. And best of all, I've been accepted back home. *We*'ve been accepted back home.'

On the day that Trip had journeyed to Ashford to see his father, Emily had gone with him. She had thought she would stay with her own family whilst he went to Riversdale House but he wanted her at his side.

'Mother insisted you are to come too,' he told her.

When they entered Arthur's bedroom, the man in the bed bore no resemblance to the one who had brought them so much unhappiness. He was a shadow of the man he had been and Emily was moved to pity; Arthur Trippet looked in a much worse condition than did her own father now, for Walter was improving daily. He was talking, albeit slowly, the terrible shaking had all but stopped and there was a constant smile on his face whenever his grandson was around.

Though Arthur could not speak, father and son had settled their differences and, by holding out his good hand to her, Arthur had welcomed Emily too.

'But you look as if you don't quite agree,' Trip said to her now. 'What's wrong?'

'I just wish – oh I'm being silly, I know, but I don't like the neighbours not speaking to us.'

'Then we'll move. We'll look for somewhere else.'

'Can we afford to?'

'We can't afford *not* to, if you're unhappy.'

'It's just that they were once all so friendly. It's such a difference. Lizzie tosses her head in the air and walks away, Mrs Dugdale just glares at me and the rest of the neighbours do their best to avoid me. Even Billy, and he was always so friendly.'

'Well, he's pining for Lizzie, isn't he? Always has been. He's going to take her side, although, I'd've thought he'd have been pleased to see the back of Josh. It gives him more of a chance now.'

'And Mick gives me the creeps.' Emily shuddered. 'Every time he sees me, he's got this sort of smirk on his face as if he knows something I don't or as if he's planning something.'

'Then the sooner we move, the better. I'll start looking tomorrow.'

But they'd left it a day too late. When Emily arrived home the following evening, she found the door into their home had been forced open, the lock broken. For, despite Bess Dugdale's pronouncement when they'd first arrived, Emily had always locked their door. She glanced around the courtyard behind her. There was no one about, though she had the unpleasant feeling that she was being watched. The tapping still came from the workshop across the yard and no doubt Lizzie was out seeking employment, but it was Mick or one of his mates she was most afraid of finding inside. She hadn't forgotten the fear she'd felt the night some of his cronies had waylaid her in an alley. He wouldn't help her now, she thought. But she couldn't stand out here until Trip came home; she had no idea how late he would be. Tentatively, she pushed the door wider and then took in a sharp breath. Everything in the kitchen had been smashed. Broken crockery littered the floor, drawers had been wrenched open and their contents scattered. Curtains had been torn from the window and furniture upturned. The stew that she had left simmering gently on the hob for their evening meal had been tipped into the sink. The range – her pride and joy – had been daubed with white distemper and the fire doused. The peg rug on the hearth lay in shreds.

She was still wary that there could be someone in the house, so before stepping inside, she listened, but all was eerily quiet. Even the tapping from the workshop had paused. It was as if everyone was listening – and waiting. At last, taking a deep breath, she stepped inside and crossed the room to the staircase.

In the bedroom she now shared with Trip – the one that had been her parents' room – it was the same. Their clothes and all the bedding had been torn or cut to pieces, even Trip's best suit, and the mattress looked as if it had been hacked at with a knife. She was gazing round at the devastation when she heard a noise below. Not caring who it was, anger giving her courage, she hurried downstairs, flinging open the door to see Trip standing amidst the shambles. 'Oh Em, who's done this?'

'I don't know, but I've got a good idea, haven't you?'

Trip nodded and his face hardened. 'Then I'd better have a word with Master Dugdale.'

'No,' she said sharply. 'Leave it. He's got his so-called friends to back him up. We're no match for them. We'll leave. We'll just go. Now – tonight. I don't care where, we'll just go.'

'We should report this to the police, you know . . .'

'No. It'll just escalate, if we do that. Besides, it's probably over now. Lizzie will have had her revenge.'

'You think Lizzie did this?'

'Not personally, no, but I think her brother did, or he organized it.'

They salvaged what they could of their belongings, wrapped them in a blanket and then they left the court. It was dark by now.

'Where are we going?' Trip said.

'We'll go to one of the workshops just for tonight. The one in Broad Lane above Mr Hawke's would be the best.'

As they neared the building, Trip said, 'There's still a light on, on the ground floor. I'd better see if Mr Hawke is all right.'

He tried the door, but it was locked. 'That's strange,' he murmured. 'He never locks his door.'

'Maybe he does at night-time, if he's working late,' Emily said, trying to peer through the grimy window. 'He's there. I can see him sitting at his bench.'

Trip rattled the door and then knocked, calling out, 'Mr Hawke, it's Trip. Are you all right?'

'He's getting up and coming to the door,' Emily said, leaving the window and waiting beside Trip.

The door opened, but Nathan turned away and went back to his workbench. They stepped inside. 'Are you all right?' Trip repeated. 'You're working late.'

'Aye, I've a job I wanted to finish for Nell to start on tomorrow.' He sat down at his bench again. 'Nearly done. I'll be off home in a minute.' Then he became aware of the bundles they were carrying. 'What are you doing back here?'

Emily frowned. Something wasn't right. Nathan

wasn't his usual cheery self. He seemed on edge and she was sure his hands were shaking. Was he ill? She moved closer and then she saw the bruise around his eye. 'What happened, Mr Hawke? Has someone—?'

'No, no,' he said a little too quickly as he waved aside her question. 'I fell. I'd – misplaced my glasses and tripped over when I was looking for them.'

Trip and Emily glanced at each other and then around the workshop. Everything seemed in place. There was no sign that Nathan had had a visit from the vandals who'd wrecked their home.

'Well, if you're sure, we'll go and try to make ourselves as comfortable as we can upstairs for the night.'

Nathan's head shot up. 'What? What d'you mean, "upstairs"? Why? Have you been turned out?'

'Not exactly. Our home has been smashed up. Emily got home first, but thank God they'd gone before she got there.'

Nathan was silent for a moment and then he sighed. 'Sit down, the pair of you. I'd better tell you. Maybe I should have done before, but . . . sit down, sit down. It's time you knew.'

With a mystified glance at each other, Trip and Emily sat down on two upturned boxes and waited whilst the older man polished his glasses and turned on his chair to face them.

'Where shall I start, because I don't know how much you know?'

'I've no idea,' Trip said, 'because I don't understand what it is you want to tell us.'

'You know about the gangs in this city, don't you?'

Trip shook his head and Emily frowned. 'No,' they said together.

'Ah, well, I rather thought Emily didn't, but I thought you might have, Trip. After all, you've been living and working in the city for a little longer than Emily. But then,' he smiled a little, 'you don't move in that sort of company. I'm surprised you hadn't guessed though, Emily, living next door to one of the leaders of a gang.'

Emily gasped and her eyes widened. 'Next door? Oh, you don't mean . . . ?' She stopped and then went on, flatly, 'You do, don't you? Mick Dugdale.'

Solemnly, Nathan nodded.

'You remember when you first came to see me about starting a little missus business?'

Emily nodded, silent now and quaking inside. She didn't think she was going to like hearing what Nathan had to say.

'I would have been pleased to help you girls, anyway – I think I said so at the time.'

'You did.' Emily's voice was a croak, her mouth dry.

'But Mick had to be the heavy-handed big brother and threaten that if I didn't let you have my premises free of rent for at least the first few months, I'd soon find I hadn't any premises left to let out.'

'Isn't that what they call an "extortion racket"?' Trip said.

'Very similar, Trip, yes,' Nathan said drily. 'He also went to "talk nicely" to some colleagues of mine to persuade them to put their business your way.'

'Oh no!' Emily was horrified. 'Mr Hawke – please believe me, I knew nothing of this, I promise you. None of us did.'

'I believe you, lass, but can you be sure about his sister?'

'I . . .' Emily began and then she stopped, so many memories coming back to her. Lizzie's veiled threats

385

over Josh. 'I really don't know,' she ended lamely because, now, she didn't.

As if reading her mind, Nathan said, 'And I reckon it's a good job your brother has gone back to Derbyshire. He was getting reeled in good and proper by Mick and his gang. George Bayes was telling me that he'd heard it on good authority – that authority being Eddie Crossland, whose nephew's a copper – that Josh'd been seen up on Sky Edge with Mick. The police had thought there'd been a pitch and toss game going on, but by the time Eddie's nephew and his colleague got there, they'd all scarpered. They post lookouts, you know.'

Emily was shaking her head. 'I knew Josh had been playing this pitch and toss and that they'd been gambling, which I understand is illegal, but I didn't know that police were after them for it. I had no idea it was so serious.'

'Let me explain, my dear. Since the war, there have been these gangs springing up in the big cities and, sadly, Sheffield's no exception. And with the unemployment situation getting worse, they are becoming more powerful. The police force is taking steps, I know, but it's a formidable task.'

'But what do they do?'

'Run illegal betting . . .' He went on to tell her all he knew about the activities of the gangs in the city.

Emily was appalled and tears filled her eyes. 'Oh, how naïve and foolish I've been. I had no idea.'

'You mustn't blame yourself. You came from a peaceful little village where such things are unheard of. And you, too, Trip. You were protected because of who your father is. They're all cowards – they don't tackle anyone with a big enough name to put them in the courts. They target the little people, who can't stand up for themselves.'

'It's awful, and to think Josh . . .' Now it explained so much. Why he had lost his money one minute and then been flush the next, how he'd been preoccupied and how, too, he'd seemed so relieved to be going back to Amy. But he had, Emily thought, shown himself to be courageous. He'd come back and told Lizzie of his decision face to face. He hadn't just slunk away and stayed there. She shuddered to think what might have happened, what Mick might have done if he'd caught up with him, and now she sent up a silent prayer of thankfulness that Josh and the rest of her family were safely back in Ashford.

'You don't think,' she said in a small voice, 'that they'll follow Josh?'

Nathan shook his head. 'No, I don't. You can get lost in a big city – you can go to ground quickly and easily, but there's nowhere to hide in a small community who look out for each other. And, Emily, please don't blame my lovely city. Most Sheffielders are wonderful people. It's just a few crooks who've got the upper hand for the moment, but it will end. One day, someone will come along and sort them out.'

'In the meantime, though,' Trip said soberly, 'we've got to keep each other safe. Emily, you're not to walk home from work alone. I'll come and meet you.'

'What about Nell? She's no one to look after her.'

Nathan gave a low chuckle. 'Nell will be all right. No one will dare to touch Nell Geddis.'

Knowing Nell as she did, a big, strong lass, who could lash anyone with her tongue and use her fists if she needed to, Emily didn't question Nathan's words.

'And I'm sorry I wasn't truthful with you earlier. I

387

had a visit from Mick Dugdale this evening.' Gingerly, he touched the bruise over his eye. 'And it was anything but friendly.'

'Oh no!' Emily put her hand over her mouth and tears filled her eyes. Trip's face was thunderous as he muttered, 'He's got to be stopped.'

'Anyway,' Nathan said, 'it's high time we were finding you two young people somewhere to sleep. And you're not going to stay upstairs,' he declared in a tone that brooked no argument. 'You're coming home with me.'

Forty-Seven

Lizzie had heard about Arthur's serious illness and she'd heard, too, that he'd made peace with his son and even with Thomas's new wife, Emily. The rumours were rife about his two sons now running Trippets' together.

So, she thought, Arthur would no longer be seeking any kind of revenge against his daughter-in-law, but Lizzie was not prepared to be so forgiving and, daily, she pondered what she might do to bring about her former friend's downfall.

'You leave it with me,' Mick told her. 'I'll pay her a visit and her benefactor, Mr Nathan Hawke. I've a score to settle with him, an' all.'

'I don't want anyone getting hurt, Mick,' Lizzie said, suddenly afraid that involving her brother could lead to real trouble.

'I thought that's exactly what you wanted. I know Mr Hawke helped you at first, but then he did the dirty on you, removing his buffing work from you so that you had to close down. And I'm sure it was him influenced your other customers to do the same. He ruined you, Lizzie.'

'Probably, but . . .'

'But what? You're not going soft on me, Lizzie, are you?'

'No, but . . . it's just – if I'm honest—'

Mick guffawed. 'Honest? The Dugdales? Don't make

me laugh. Just leave it with me, eh? I know what needs to be done.'

'What are you going to do?'

'Best you don't know. That way you're not involved, are you?' He tweaked her nose playfully. 'You trust your little brother, don't you?'

Lizzie didn't answer. She was not sure that she did.

Emily glanced up as she heard footsteps – more than one pair – climbing the outside staircase up to the workshop above Nathan's. The two girls from the Rockingham Street workshop had already gone home, calling in on their way to report on their day's work and what they had ready to do the next day, but Emily and Nell had stayed working late to complete an order for Nathan. He'd already left his work to go home, shouting up the inside staircase, 'Goodnight' to Nell and, 'See you later' to Emily. Trip and Emily were still lodging with him and he seemed to be enjoying their company.

'Take your time to find somewhere nice, Thomas,' he'd said. 'You should be able to afford somewhere better now.'

And so, though Trip was looking, they hadn't yet moved into their own home and had been staying with Nathan for just over two weeks.

'Well, if it isn't pretty Emily and Nell too.'

Emily's smile faded as she saw Mick standing in the doorway. There was a wicked glint in his eyes; a look that Emily didn't like. And, even more worrying, two of his cronies were standing behind him. But she forced herself to say pleasantly, 'Hello, Mick. What brings you here?'

She saw him glance down to the back yard below

before stepping inside and closing the door behind him, leaving his two sidekicks outside.

'You do, pretty Emily.' His lascivious grin widened. 'Though I hadn't expected to kill two birds with one stone.'

Nell came to stand beside Emily, her hands on her hips. 'What do you want, Mick?'

His eyes narrowed.

'Revenge.'

Nell frowned, obviously puzzled. 'What on earth are you talking about?'

But Emily felt a quiver of fear; she knew exactly what he was talking about even before he said, 'For Lizzie. For my *sister*.'

Nell shrugged. 'It was Lizzie who threw Emily out of the business. If you're talking recriminations, it should be the other way about.'

Mick stepped closer and thrust his face close to Nell, but she stood her ground. He jabbed his finger towards Emily. 'Her precious brother jilted our Lizzie. You don't do that to my sister without having to answer to me.'

'So?' Still Nell was not prepared to cringe in front of him. Emily was shaking inside but she, too, was determined to show no outward fear. 'Your quarrel's with Josh, not with Emily.'

'He's not here, is he? He's scuttled off back to Ashford like the yellow coward he is. But his sister's here and I can hurt him by hurting her, 'cos Josh loves his sister, doesn't he?' His nose was almost touching Nell's as he grabbed her collar and said viciously, '*Just like I love mine.*'

Emily swallowed her fear. 'Let Nell go, Mick. She's nothing to do with this.'

He glanced scathingly at Emily. 'Are you stupid, or

what? She knows too much now, doesn't she? Besides, I've a score to settle with her precious boyfriend, an' all. He's trying to push me out of every scam going. He wants to rule the roost. Well, it's not going to happen.'

This was news to Emily, she hadn't realized that Nell had a boyfriend now. She never talked about him, although she had mentioned . . . Her wandering thoughts were pulled back to the present with a jerk as Mick walked towards her, menace in every step and every word.

But Nell was not about to give in. 'If you harm either one of us, Mick Dugdale, you'll start a gang war. Is that what you want?'

Mick didn't deign to answer her; he just dismissed her warning with a wave. 'Now then, pretty Emily. What to do with you, eh? What would hurt your dear brother the most?' He ran his finger down her cheek. 'A cut down here, d'you reckon? Spoil your pretty face for good an' all? Or what if me an' me mates have a good time with the both of you, eh?'

Still Emily managed to keep still and return his stare, though she shuddered inside to think what fate lay in store for her – and Nell.

'Please, Mick, let Nell go,' she whispered huskily.

'I don't give a damn about her. It's just her bad luck she's here. Besides, she was a traitor to my sister, an' all. She came running back to you for work – never even tried to stick by Lizzie. No, Nell's got a lot to answer for, to say nothing of her precious Steve.'

Steve? Emily frowned, trying to pull a memory into her mind. Nell had once spoken about someone called Steve being the father of her little girl. Steve, who was a bad 'un . . .

As if to stop questions being asked, Nell said bravely,

'Emily's husband'll be here in a minute. He's coming to meet her from work.'

Mick laughed. 'Oh, yes, the famous Thomas Trippet. And why do you suppose my two mates are outside keeping watch, eh? He'll not get in here. He'll not be able to save his lovely wife. But if he really is on his way here, then he'll be able to watch the fun, won't he?'

The two girls glanced at each other, the same thought in their minds. Could they rush Mick? Overpower him and escape? But outside were his henchmen, two of the biggest bruisers Emily could ever remember seeing. They were the same two who had accosted her that evening in the alley, but this time Mick was not here to save her; he was here to join in.

As if reading their minds, Mick raised his voice. 'Pete, Gary, get in here. These two aren't as helpless as they look.'

The door flew open, crashing against the wall and the two ugly looking men stepped inside. 'What d'you want us to do, Mick?'

'Tie 'em up. Hands behind their backs and their feet. And gag 'em too. I don't want anyone to hear 'em screaming.'

The biggest and ugliest of the two grinned, showing blackened and broken teeth. 'Are we going to have a bit of fun, then, boss? You stopped us before, remember? Besides, her precious brother left town owing me money.'

For a moment, Mick's eyes glinted and then, with obvious disappointment, he shook his head. 'No. Shame, but we'd be risking getting caught. Just get 'em tied up.'

The girls did not give in easily. They bit, they

393

scratched and kicked, but they were no match against three burly men who worked as a team to tie up first Nell and then Emily. Then they stood looking down at the girls writhing on the floor and struggling to free themselves. Emily's lip was bleeding. Nell had a bruise on the left side of her face and her eye was swelling where Pete had struck her across the face. Their ribs hurt and the ropes were cutting into their wrists and ankles; the gags were choking them.

'Seems a shame to pass up on a—'

'Let's get on with it,' Mick said testily. 'You got the petrol, Gary?'

Both girls tried to splutter, their eyes wide with fear as they realized what was going to happen. Emily shook her head wildly, but Mick only laughed.

'This'll teach your brother not to mess with the Dugdale family and when he's standing over your grave, pretty Emily, he'll think about what he's done.'

Already Gary was splashing petrol over the machines and on the floor. It trickled through the uneven boards to the floor below.

'Not on them,' Mick said, pointing to the two girls. 'I want 'em to suffer as the flames get nearer and nearer. Right, you go.'

Gary threw down the empty petrol can and lumbered towards the door, followed swiftly by Pete. Mick paused in the doorway and looked back at the two girls. For a fleeting moment, there was a look of regret on his face and Emily struggled to sit up, pleading with her eyes, but then his expression hardened and from his pocket he took out a box of matches, struck one and cast it on the floor.

There was a roar as the petrol caught light and then the door slammed and he was gone.

Forty-Eight

In Ashford, the two families had no idea of the trouble in the city. Josh worked hard and his candle-making business was growing steadily. Between him and Bob, their little family was well provided for and he helped his parents whenever he could, both financially and practically.

Martha had laid aside all her ambitions for her son when she could see how happy and contented he was. Walter was much better and she was besotted with her little grandson. She had found a part-time job with Mr Osborne in his shop and she cleaned at Riversdale House on two days every week.

'There's so much more washing to do with Arthur's illness,' Constance explained to her, 'and I'd much rather you did it than employ an extra maid.'

Constance was a frequent visitor to The Candle House and enjoyed playing with Harry. She was hopeful that one day soon she would have a grandchild of her own, but it was early days yet.

Belle visited Riversdale House often. The two women had confided in each other about their early lives. The contrast between their two upbringings was enormous and yet, they became friends. Arthur's condition changed little, but he was no worse and the nurse moved in permanently.

*   *   *

'Now, Martha Ryan,' Grace Partridge said one morning. Martha had become so much more likeable since her return to the village and Grace was big-hearted enough to offer an olive branch. 'Your old man can be left for an hour or two now, I'm sure, so why don't you join the Female Friendly Society? Mrs Trippet and I will certainly recommend you as a member. Do say you will?'

And so Martha found her place back in village society once more and, soon, it was as if they'd never been away. In fact, it was better than before. Only Emily was missing from their family circle.

'But she's happy in the city, isn't she?' Martha comforted herself and couldn't prevent a little prickle of pride that her daughter promised to be the one who would make something of herself one day.

So, not all Martha's dreams had been completely shattered. There was always Emily.

Smoke filled the workshop and the girls began to choke as the flames crept nearer. Emily wriggled closer to Nell and pushed at her, trying to tell her to roll onto her side. As she did so, Emily shuffled down to where Nell's hands were tied behind her back. She pushed her gagged mouth close to Nell's fingers. Understanding, Nell managed to pull the gag away from Emily's mouth and then Emily pulled at the ties binding Nell's hands with her teeth. It seemed to take an age for the ties to loosen – time they could not afford – but at least nearer the ground the smoke was not so intense. But the flames licked nearer and nearer. At last, Nell was able to pull her hands free. Immediately she rolled over and sat up, pulled the gag from her own mouth and untied her ankles. Then she released Emily from her bonds.

'Quick,' Emily gasped. 'Let's get out.'

They crawled to the top of the stairs leading down to Nathan's workshop and staggered down to the floor below. The air was clearer for the moment, but already the upstairs floor was burning furiously and igniting the ceiling of the ground-floor workshop.

Holding on to each other, they staggered towards the door leading into the street. Emily grasped the door handle, turned it and pulled.

'Oh no. It's locked.'

'Bastard!' Nell muttered and began to hammer on the door and shout as the ceiling gave way and burning boards crashed to the ground.

'The window,' Emily gasped.

'No good. Look.'

The window was barred.

Together, they banged on the door again, coughing from the smoke they'd inhaled. More burning debris from the upper floor fell around them.

'I reckon this'll soon be alight,' Nell gasped. 'We've got to get out.'

And then they heard the most wonderful sound in the world: a key turning in the lock. They stood back as the door was flung open and Nathan Hawke reached in to pull them out into the fresh air.

'I've sent for the fire brigade, but I didn't know anyone was in there until I heard you hammering on the door. Whatever happened? Though I reckon I can guess.'

At a safe distance from the fire, the two girls sank to their knees coughing and retching. Then they sat together on the ground, their arms wrapped around each other as the clanging sound of a fire engine came nearer.

Nathan bent over them and repeated his question, 'What happened?'

Before Emily could answer, Nell gasped, 'Mick Dugdale, that's what happened.'

Nathan straightened up, as if he needed no more explanation. 'I thought as much. Well, this time he's gone too far and it's all my fault,' he murmured, his gaze now on his burning property. The two girls staggered to their feet and moved to the other side of the street as the fire engine drew up and men began to unwind the hose.

'No,' Emily said shakily, trying to reassure the man, who had been so good to them. 'It was all about me – well, about Josh, really.'

Nathan shook his head. 'No, it's my fault. I refused to pay him extortion money any more. That's what had happened the night your house was trashed, Emily. That's why he gave me a black eye and that's why he's burned down my workshops.' Now that he knew both girls were shaken, yet not seriously harmed, Nathan moved away from them to watch the firemen trying to save what they could of his premises.

'Then he has killed two birds with one stone, as he put it,' Nell muttered. 'In fact, three, if you count me, an' all,' she added bitterly, wiping the grime away from her eyes with the back of her hand, but only succeeding in making her face even more streaked with black dust.

'Then it's everything,' Emily said. 'He wanted to hurt me because he says Josh jilted Lizzie.'

'And me because I deserted Lizzie's sinking ship and came back to you looking for work and he's got a beef with Steve. But he's met his match this time. We're not letting him get away with this. I'll tell Steve.'

Emily gasped and stared wide-eyed at her. 'So, are you still—?'

'Not like that, but I let him see Lucy now and then. He's the leader of one of the biggest gangs in the city. A rival of Mick's. He'll soon see off Mick Dugdale and his thugs.'

'Oh Nell, I don't think you should. It could start a street war. Let's tell the police.'

But Nell shook her head firmly. 'Our sort don't go to the police, Emily. That would escalate things and get us into more trouble.' She stared at Emily for a moment before adding, 'You know what I mean, don't you?'

'I understand that, but—'

'No "buts", Emily. Just leave it with me, eh?'

Emily sighed. She didn't like it. She'd always been brought up to be honest and truthful and to be letting Mick Dugdale get away with it was entirely wrong.

'Look, luv,' Nell went on, trying to explain how things were in her world. 'The gangs in this city rule the roost at the moment. One day someone will come along who's on the right side of the law and they'll sort it all out, but until that happens we've got to fend for ourselves and the best way to do that is to keep out of trouble.'

'But what you're suggesting is asking for more trouble.'

Nell shook her head. 'Steve'll deal with it. He'll put the frighteners on Mick and his boys. I'll make sure he understands that's all I want him to do.'

'And – and he'll do that for you, will he? I mean – as you're not still with him.'

Nell nodded grimly. 'He'd like to get back with me – more than anything – but I've told him that I won't have Lucy brought up in that sort of a life. And in a way, I think he sees my point.' For a moment, her eyes filled with tears. And this, more than anything that had happened, shocked Emily. She had never seen Nell cry. 'He's a bad 'un, Emily, I know that. But I loved him – still do, if I'm honest – but since Lucy came along, well, it seems my maternal love is a lot stronger than what I feel for him. But he idolizes his daughter. He wouldn't see any harm come to her – or me. And he'll protect my friends too. You and Trip will be quite safe, but if we go to the police – and yes, I know we should do that – but if we did, all hell would break loose.'

'Mr Hawke might. We've told him who's responsible.'

Nell shook her head. 'No, I don't think so. Nathan knows the score and if he thinks this is his fault—'

'But it isn't. Not altogether.'

Nell squeezed her arm and they both went to where Nathan was standing. Nell touched his arm. 'We're lucky you came along. What made you come back?'

Nathan, still watching the fireman trying to save what they could of the building, murmured, 'I'd forgotten my glasses.'

The two girls glanced at each other and then clung to each other laughing and crying. 'He – forgot – his – glasses!'

Forty-Nine

Trip was enraged about the attack and terrified to think how near he'd come to losing Emily. 'I don't care what any of you say, I'm going to the police. And I've found us somewhere else to live. It's not fair for us to stay at Mr Hawke's any longer. We could be bringing yet more trouble to his door.'

'Oh, Trip, Nell says it will just make things far worse if you go to the police.'

'Emily, it's the right thing to do. Mick Dugdale is a thug and, but for Mr Hawke and his wonderful, marvellous habit of losing his glasses, Mick could be a murderer.'

'Yes, you're right, of course, but –' Emily bit her lip – 'will you talk to Mr Hawke first? Please. It was his premises that were burned down.'

Trip took her in his arms and held her close, his voice shaky as he said, 'And it was my wife I nearly lost. But, yes, I'll do as you ask. I'll talk to Mr Hawke first.'

Nathan Hawke agreed wholeheartedly with Trip. 'These gangs are ruining our beautiful city,' he said. 'I'll come with you, Thomas.'

By the end of the week, Trip had not only reported the incident to the police with Mr Hawke backing up his story, but he'd also rented a house in a terraced street some distance away.

'And now,' he said, 'you must put all that behind you and get back to work at the workshop in Rockingham Street. At least you still have that. Nell and the other two girls depend on you. I'll talk to the missus at Trippets' and see if she can put any extra work your way.'

Emily nodded. She was still shaken after her ordeal, worried about Nell and fearful of reprisals from Mick and his gang after Trip's visit to the police. On the morning after they had moved into their new home, she called to see Nathan at his house.

'You're not to blame yourself, my dear,' he reassured her when she began apologizing. 'Mick Dugdale had reasons for revenge on all of us, or so he thought. But, no real harm done. As long as you and Nell are all right, that's all that really matters. The rest is replaceable.'

Nathan seemed philosophical about what had happened.

'What are you going to do now, with your work place gone too?'

'I've been giving it a lot of thought, Emily. I still have the workshop in Rockingham Street and . . .'

Emily pulled a face. 'It's your only workshop now.'

Nathan chuckled. 'Well, that's where you're wrong. I have some other properties. Not workshops, admittedly, but I have two small shops in the city that are rented out, so, if you intend to continue in business, then I think, if I'm careful, I can afford to retire. The premises that were burned down are well insured, so I shall get a payout, all being well. As you know, the arthritis in my hands is getting worse, but I could always be on hand if you needed any help,' he added, and there was an eagerness in his tone that told Emily he was not ready to put his feet up permanently quite yet.

Emily was relieved and, after giving Nathan a quick hug, she hurried to work in Rockingham Street. Nell was already there. She'd got one of the idle machines running and all three girls were working. She looked up as Emily entered but did not stop her work. Instead, she mouthed, 'You all right?'

Emily nodded and mouthed back the same question. Nell grinned and said something like, 'Takes more than that to get me down.'

Emily gestured towards a box of finished cutlery and then to the door to indicate that she was going out again to make a delivery. By evening, when the girls stopped their wheels and took off their dust-blackened clothes, she was back and able to talk properly to Nell and the other two girls.

'I've taken more orders today than I've taken in a full week before. Word's got around, it seems, and everyone is falling over themselves to support us. Isn't it wonderful?'

'You know what I always say,' Nell said. '"It's an ill wind that blows no one any good". Sheffielders – the real people of Sheffield – are like that. Salt of the earth, they are. It's a pity these gangs are spoiling our image, but I've heard say that we're not the only city with that sort of trouble.'

Emily sighed. 'No, I don't expect we are.' She bit her lip, uncertain whether to tell Nell about Trip and Nathan's visit to the police. Then she decided that she had to be truthful with the three girls. Their business had to be based on trust and honesty.

When she'd finished, there was a moment's silence and then, much to her surprise, Nell said, 'Well, I can't blame them for going. We've got to start and make a stand against them sometime. Maybe this is the time.'

'What about—?' Emily began, but then stopped. She didn't know how much Ida and Flo knew about Nell's own association with a gang member. Nell glanced at the other two girls and gave a slight shake of her head, indicating that no, they did not know, so now Emily remained silent, waiting until Ida and Flo had left before asking again. 'What about Steve?'

Nell shrugged. 'He knows everything and he was as mad as thunder, but I begged him not to start anything that could escalate into gang warfare.' She grimaced. 'Not that I think he will take any notice of me.'

'Oh dear,' Emily murmured.

Nell was right; Steve Henderson, leader of a rival gang to Mick Dugdale's and his cronies, did not listen to her and on the Saturday night following the fire at Nathan Hawke's premises, street fighting between the two gangs broke out.

News came the following morning that the Dugdales' house had been broken into, that Bess and Lizzie – the only ones at home at the time – had been unharmed, but terrified as the thugs had smashed their furniture and belongings in front of them, threatening before they left that they would hunt Mick down and kill him.

'Where are Lizzie and her mother?' Emily asked Trip, who brought the news to the workshop.

'They've moved into our old house. They must have had to clear it up, but I expect they felt a bit safer there. And there's a round-the-clock police presence in the court now, both to protect them and to wait for Mick to return home.'

Nell gave a derisory snort. 'They won't catch him.

He'll be long gone. He'll have gone to the Smoke.' She paused a moment and then asked quietly, 'Any more news?'

Emily guessed she was angling to hear anything about Steve.

'Rumour has it that Mick's face was slashed in the fight, but he's not gone to a hospital in the city.' Trip, who'd learned all about Nell's connection with a gang member from Emily, now feigned innocence. He was not going to break Emily's confidence and if he did hear anything about Steve, he could tell them about it as if it were just general news.

Gradually, things settled down; Mick was gone and was now the object of a nationwide police hunt. Steve and his gang went to ground and the city was peaceful for a while. The following weekend, Trip and Emily went to Ashford to see their families and to reassure them of their safety. But the news had not reached them and all Emily told them was about their change of address. She didn't even tell them about the fire or the threats against herself and Nell, though she understood that Trip had told his mother, but had asked her to keep the news to herself.

'Emily doesn't want to upset her father. It's all over now and we can move on with our lives. Mick Dugdale's gone and whilst Steve Henderson is still, shall we say, active, we're protected by our association with Nell. Oh Mother, Emily's doing so well. I'm very proud of her. It's ironic, really, because I think it's Emily, not Josh, who's going to make a name for herself in the city.'

Constance smiled. 'Martha seems content now. She's besotted with her little grandson – they all are – and I can see an almost daily improvement in Walter.'

'How about Father?'

'He's what the medical people call "stable". He won't get a lot better physically, I'm afraid, but he does seem more settled in his mind. Belle visits often. In fact, I've invited her to stay for a week at the beginning of November and I've also asked both her and Richard to spend Christmas with us. I hope you don't mind.'

Trip chuckled. 'I don't mind at all, but it is a comical situation.'

'Yes, it is rather unusual, I have to admit,' Constance said with a serene smile. 'How are you and Richard getting along?'

'Very well – surprisingly. But since you have no problem with either of them, Mother, then neither have I. He's a really nice lad, actually, and very willing to learn. Mr Bayes has told me he's training him up to take over all the administrative side when he retires.'

'George? Retiring? Surely not.'

If Trip noticed his mother's use of Mr Bayes's Christian name, he didn't remark upon it. Instead, he said, 'It's not commonly known, but his wife is terminally ill. I think he's planning to take more time off to care for her. I've told him he must do whatever he needs to do.'

'He's been a loyal employee over many years,' she murmured, her thoughts seeming to be a long way off. 'I'm truly sorry to hear that.' And she was; Constance didn't like to think of life bringing George Bayes any unhappiness. Then she shook herself and brought her wandering thoughts back to her son. 'So, everything's quieter in the city now, is it?'

'Yes, for the moment. Perhaps it's all over.'

Back home in the little terraced house that they had worked so hard to make comfortable, Trip said, 'I think it would be nice if we invited Richard to dinner one evening. Perhaps on a Sunday, when you've a little more time to cook.'

Emily enjoyed being mistress in her own kitchen and, when time allowed, enjoyed experimenting with new dishes.

'Oh, I'd like that,' she said, her eyes shining. 'D'you think he'd come?'

'I can only ask.'

Richard was delighted to be invited to his half-brother's home. They were getting on very well running the factory as equal partners, but that was not the same as socializing together and being accepted as part of the Trippet family. He arrived with a bunch of flowers for Emily.

'I hope you like them,' he said diffidently.

'They're lovely – thank you. Oh my,' she added, as she looked at him more closely. Strangely, this was the first time she had met him. Emily didn't visit Trippets'; she liked to keep their businesses absolutely separate. She glanced at Trip and then back again at Richard. 'You're so alike, it's uncanny.'

The two young men regarded each other solemnly for a moment and then grinned. 'Yes, we are.'

'You even smile in the same way – your eyes crinkling up.' Then as an idea struck her, Emily said, 'Do you like walking in the hills, Richard? Trip does.'

'I – haven't really had the chance.'

'Then we must all go into the countryside for days out in the summer.' She laughed. 'Then I'll *really* see if you're alike.'

It was a merry evening, and when Richard left, Emily kissed him on both cheeks and said, 'We must do this often.'

Richard hesitated for a moment, glancing between them both.

'What is it?' Trip asked. 'Is something wrong?'

'No, no, it's just that – you've been so extraordinarily kind. I – I can hardly believe it. I mean –' he paused and looked at Trip – 'your mother is just an amazing woman to be so – so understanding. She's welcomed my mother and me into your family.' He shook his head as if he couldn't believe it, and certainly he could not understand it.

Trip put his hands on Richard's shoulders. 'We've all taken our lead from her and, yes, you're right. She is remarkable. Not many women would have done what she's done, but,' he chuckled, 'from what she tells me, she and your mother have become real friends. And *that* is truly incredible.'

'I certainly wouldn't be so understanding if it was you who'd – well, you know.'

'One day I'll explain it all to you, Richard, old feller, but for now, let's just be glad that everything has been resolved happily for all of us.'

Fifty

Trip wasn't quite right; there was just one matter unsettled in their lives. Tired though she usually was by the end of the day, Emily lay awake at night sometimes, thinking about Lizzie. When the Ryan family had arrived in the city, her first instincts about the girl had been right: they would either be the best of friends or the worst of enemies. And they had been both, but Emily regretted the animosity Lizzie felt towards her now. She hoped that the girl and her mother were all right and wished she could go to see them, but Trip had advised her not to go anywhere near the court.

Emily's venture was doing well and already she was looking for another premises close by to set up another workshop. Whilst other places were hard pressed to find work, her buffer girls were fully occupied and often worked overtime to keep pace with the demand for their expertise. 'We're building up a good reputation for careful work,' Emily reported back to her workers, for the other three girls had accepted that this was now wholly Emily's business.

'I don't know owt about running a business,' Nell said firmly, 'as I told you before. I'm just happy you're employing me and paying me a very fair wage, Emily.'

Ida and Flo felt the same. For some time the youngest member of the small workforce had doubled as an errand girl whilst learning the trade of a buffer girl in her spare time.

Emily turned to Flo. 'You're coming along very nicely now, Flo, and I'm thinking of letting you become a buffer girl full time and we can look for another errand girl. Are you happy with that?' She glanced at Nell and Ida.

'We could do with another experienced buffer girl, Emily. You're bringing so much work in now, we can hardly cope. And it'll get worse.'

'Hopefully.'

'Eh?' Nell looked at her in amazement and then, when she realized what Emily meant, she laughed. 'The girl's got big ambitions. Well, just so long as you keep me in employment, Emily Trippet, that's fine by me.'

'I'll ask around. There have been a few buffer girls laid off recently, I'm sure there will be someone suitable.'

'Don't get just anyone. She'll have to be good.'

The next day the situation was made worse. Ida came running to the little office where Emily worked in the corner of the workshop. She flung open the door, hair cap awry, her eyes wide with fear. 'Flo's been collared.'

Emily frowned; she had no idea what the girl meant, but she could see from Ida's expression that something awful had happened. She jumped up and ran out into the workshop to see Nell step back from her spindle, fling down the handful of spoons she was working on with a clatter and rush over to Flo at her machine. The young girl was almost in a state of collapse at the sight of her own blood.

'She was learning dollying,' Ida's voice was shaky with tears. This Emily did understand; it was the final polish with a calico wheel before spoons and forks went to be plated. 'Her finger rags got caught in the spindle and it's cut her hand.'

Swiftly, Emily fetched the first-aid box that she'd had the foresight to equip, from a shelf above her desk and hurried across the room to Flo. She staunched the flow of blood to reveal a long gash down the edge of the girl's left palm that refused to stop bleeding, but, thankfully, it didn't look too deep.

'I'm not going to hospital,' Flo was crying. 'I'm frit of hospitals. I'll see 'doctor me mam goes to.'

'There, it's not as bad as we thought. I'll bandage it up and take you home to your mam. See what she says. Come along, and, whatever happens, you must have the rest of the week off. We can't have muck getting in it.'

As Emily steered Flo down the stairs of the workshop and through the grinders' workshop to take her home, Ida whispered to Nell, 'We can't manage all the work we've got, Nell, not even if Emily takes a turn at a wheel. We'll just have to get someone else now.'

'Have you heard of anyone?'

Ida shook her head.

For a moment, Nell was thoughtful then she gave a quick nod as if she'd come to a decision. 'Leave it with me, Ida. I'll have a think.'

The following morning, whilst Emily was busy in her little office, which had been partitioned off to keep out the flying dust, someone came tentatively up the stairs to their workshop above the grinders'. Emily heard the two machines slow down. She emerged from her office to see that both girls had stopped work. Ida was staring wide eyed, but Nell had crossed the floor to meet their visitor. Emily turned her head and saw the girl standing at the top of the stairs, ready to flee if she was unwelcome.

'Come on in, Lizzie,' Nell said, taking her by the arm and leading her forward.

'Oh Lizzie!' Emily went at once towards her, her arms outstretched in welcome. But as she neared the girl, she saw that Lizzie was much changed. Gone was the merry look in her eyes, her lovely hair was dull and lifeless. She was thin and her skin had a sallow complexion.

Emily took hold of her hands. 'Whatever's happened to you?'

Lizzie made a strangulated noise in her throat and then burst into tears. Emily put her arms around her and led her further into the workshop, making her sit down on an upturned box. 'Ida, love, make Lizzie some tea, will you?'

'I went to see Lizzie and her mam last night,' Nell said, meeting Emily's gaze boldly. 'And told her to come and see you this morning. Emily, the pair of them are in a terrible state.' Nell's face was a mixture of emotions. She had once been close friends with Lizzie, but at the moment she was not sure how she felt. She needed to know just how much Lizzie had been involved in – or had known about – her brother's activities. Had she really been so wicked that she'd encouraged Mick to set fire to Nathan Hawke's workshops with Emily inside it? Nell and Emily sat down beside her, whilst Ida, having brought tea for the three of them, started up her wheel again and carried on with her work.

'Here, dry your eyes,' Emily said, fishing out a clean handkerchief from her pocket. 'Drink your tea and tell us how we can help you.'

'Oh Emily, I don't deserve it. After all I've done to you, how – how can you be so kind?'

'Because she's a kind person,' Nell put in. 'Much kinder than I'd be in her shoes, I reckon, but we want to know the truth. So come on, Lizzie, tell us.'

'I've come to beg your forgiveness, both of you, and to tell you that I never meant for you to be – to be attacked like that. Oh yes, I wanted some sort of revenge for what I thought Josh had done to me, but only to ruin your business, to get it closed down, but never – ever – to harm anyone.' She looked so pitiful, looking up at them with eyes brimming with tears and pleading for them to believe her.

'But is the reason you're so apologetic now because you want your job back?' Nell asked bluntly. ''Cos I could see last night that you and your mam are on the breadline.'

Lizzie nodded. 'Yes, we're – we've nothing. Steve Henderson's gang broke into our house and took anything of any value and smashed everything else. We've nothing – and with Mick gone . . .' She hesitated to mention his name, but it was the truth. He'd seen his mother and his sister never went short, but now he was lost to them. She was shaking her head sadly. 'We never knew what he was mixed up in.'

'You must have known,' Nell said tartly. Although she'd been the one to invite Lizzie here, she was determined to get at the truth – the whole truth – and she was not so forgiving as Emily. 'Where did you think he was getting his money from?'

'We – we just thought he was wheeling and dealing, maybe just a little bit on the wrong side of the law. We knew he ran pitch and toss games, that sort of thing, but we didn't know he was running a *gang*.'

413

'He was leader of one of the worst in the city,' Nell said bluntly. 'He and his thugs used to meet folk outside their place of work on payday and just take their wages off them for no reason at all. He ran an extortion racket and poor Mr Hawke fell foul of that.'

Emily frowned and turned to Nell. 'What – exactly – is this extortion racket everyone keeps talking about? I heard Trip mention it.'

Nell laughed wryly. 'Where they target businessmen – usually small ones – and promise they will not smash up their premises if they're paid money every week.'

Shocked, Emily stared at her, her mind working furiously. 'But – but we never got threatened.'

'Of course we didn't.' Nell nodded towards Lizzie. 'Because, then, she was one of us, but after she fell out with you – both of us, really – we became a prime target for Mick's revenge.'

'Did you know about this, Lizzie? About what he was doing?'

'No, I swear I didn't and neither did my mam. You can ask her, if you like. She's heartbroken. She was so proud of him, thinking he was clever and shrewd when all the time . . .'

'He was nothing but a nasty thug,' Nell said.

'Do you know where he is now?' Emily asked.

Lizzie shook her head. 'No, and that's the truth, because me mam says if he ever dares to show his face around here again, she'll drag him to the coppers herself. She's so ashamed and so am I.' Her voice faded away to a hoarse whisper.

Emily was thinking hard. She believed Lizzie, but maybe she was still being a bit gullible. She must consult Nell first before she said any more. She had grown closer than ever to Nell since their shared horrifying experience and she wouldn't go against anything the other girl said.

'Sit there a minute, Lizzie. I want to speak to Nell.'

The two girls went downstairs and out into the street so that they could talk privately and not be overheard.

'What do you think, Nell?'

'Employ her, you mean?'

'Yes.'

'Do you believe what she's saying?'

'I don't know – that's why I'm asking you. You've known her a lot longer than I have. Do *you* believe her when she says her and her mam knew nothing about what Mick was really doing?'

'That's the bit that worries me. Surely, they must have wondered why he always had so much money to splash around, but then,' she smiled wryly, 'mothers and sons, eh? They can be very blind to their faults and see only the best in them. And I was every bit as stupid over Steve when I first met him. For a long time I buried me head in the sand and refused to believe that he could have anything to do with gangs. How wrong I was,' she added bitterly.

'And Lizzie?'

'I don't think she's a bad person, just a bit silly and – and spiteful. She got a bee in her bonnet about your brother – that's the root of it all.' Nell sighed. 'Oh, aren't we girls silly over fellers sometimes?' She was thoughtful for a moment, but then she nodded. 'We'd been friends for a long time before she got besotted with your brother. Is she over him, do you think, or is she trying to get close to you again to carry out some sort of vendetta of her own?'

'I'll ask her straight out.'

'All right, and if she seems to be telling the truth,

then, yes, we'll give her another chance. Everyone deserves a second chance,' she added wistfully and Emily believed Nell was thinking of Steve. But the father of Nell's child was not prepared to give up his nefarious life just yet. Maybe in the years to come, if he did mend his ways, perhaps Nell would be prepared to give him another chance too. Emily hoped so. She would like to see her friend happy, but for the moment her concern was Lizzie and her mother.

They went back inside and Emily took hold of Lizzie's hand. 'Listen to me, if you're telling us the truth, Lizzie, and you promise you've no more quarrel with either me or Nell, then yes, you can come back and work for us.'

'But it's Emily's business now,' Nell put in. 'Not yours or mine. She's the missus. You understand? It's called "Ryan's" and we all work for her.' Nell prodded her finger towards Emily. 'And I'll tell tha summat fer nowt, Lizzie –' Nell's strong Sheffield accent seemed more pronounced whenever she was pressing home her point – 'this lass is going places and I, fer one, am hanging on to her coat tails.'

Lizzie's tears flowed afresh. 'Oh thank you, thank you. You – you don't know what this means to me.' She stood up and flung herself against Emily, weeping tears of gratitude against her shoulder.

'It's all right, Lizzie. It's all going to be all right. I'll call round to see you and your mam after work and bring you some food, just like she used to do for us.'

'Right, then, that's settled and I'd better get back to me work, since we're short-handed today,' Nell said briskly but, as she turned away, she added, 'But just remember, Lizzie Dugdale, one false step and tha'll have me to deal with. Understood?'

Lizzie wiped her eyes and nodded. 'Yes, Nell,' she said meekly.

'Tell you what,' Emily said, 'get yer hat on and I'll take you shopping right now.'

The two girls looked at each other, both of them remembering the words Lizzie had said to Emily when she'd first arrived as a stranger in the city. It reminded them of the friendship they'd once shared.

'Oh Lizzie, I've missed you so much.' Emily hugged her tightly as they laughed and cried together.

Only now was it all really over.

The Clippie Girls
Margaret Dickinson

Sisters in love. A family at war. A city in peril.

Rose and Myrtle Sylvester look up to their older sister, Peggy. She is the sensible, reliable one in the household of women headed by their grandmother, Grace Booth, and their mother, Mary Sylvester. When war is declared in 1939 they must face the hardships together and huge changes in their lives are inevitable. For Rose, there is the chance to fulfil her dream of becoming a clippie on Sheffield's trams like Peggy. But for Myrtle, the studious, clever one in the family, war may shatter her ambitions.

When the tram on which Peggy is a conductress is caught in a bomb blast, she bravely helps to rescue her passengers. One of them is a young soldier, Terry Price, and he and Peggy begin courting. They meet every time he can get leave, but eventually Terry is posted abroad and she hears nothing from him. Worse still, Peggy must break the devastating news to her family that she is pregnant.

The shock waves that ripple through the family will affect each and every one of them and life will never be the same again.

Fairfield Hall
Margaret Dickinson

A matter of honour. A sense of duty. A time for courage.

Ruthlessly ambitious Ambrose Constantine is determined that his daughter, Annabel, shall marry into the nobility. A self-made trawler owner and fish merchant, he has only his wealth to buy his way into Society.

When Annabel's secret meetings with a young man employed at her father's offices stop suddenly, she finds that Gilbert has mysteriously disappeared. Heartbroken, she finds solace with her grandparents on their Lincolnshire farm, but her father will not allow her to bury herself in the countryside and enlists the help of a business connection to launch his daughter into Society.

During the London Season, Annabel is courted by James Lyndon, the Earl of Fairfield, whose country estate is only a few miles from her grandfather's farm. Believing herself truly loved at last, Annabel accepts his offer of marriage. It is only when she arrives at Fairfield Hall that she realizes the true reason behind James's proposal and the part her scheming father has played.

Through the years that follow, Annabel will know both heartache and joy, but the birth of her son should secure the future of the Fairfield Estate. Yet there are others who lay claim to the inheritance in a feud that will not be resolved until the trenches of a bitter world war.

Welcome Home
Margaret Dickinson

There are some things that even the closest friendship cannot survive . . .

Neighbours Edie Kelsey and Lil Horton have been friends for over twenty years, sharing the joys and sorrows of their tough lives as the wives of fishermen in Grimsby. So it came as no surprise that their children were close and that Edie's son, Frank, and Lil's daughter, Irene, fell in love and married at a young age.

But the declaration of war in 1939 changes everything. Frank goes off to fight and Irene and baby Tommy, along with Edie's youngest son, are sent to the countryside for safety. With Edie's husband Archie fishing the dangerous waters in the North Sea and daughter Beth in London doing 'important war work', Edie's family is torn apart.

Friendship sustains Edie and Lil, but when tragedy strikes – and then Beth disappears – their relationship is tested to the limit. But it is Irene's return, during the VE day celebrations, that sends shock waves through the family and threatens to destroy Edie and Lil's friendship forever.